# PHOENIX'S REFRAIN

## LEGION OF ANGELS: BOOK 10

ELLA SUMMERS

**PHOENIX'S REFRAIN**

Legion of Angels: Book 10

www.ellasummers.com

ISBN 978-1-83655-096-9
Copyright © 2021 by Ella Summers
All rights reserved.

# BOOKS BY ELLA SUMMERS

**Legion of Angels**

Vampire's Kiss

Witch's Cauldron

Siren's Song

Dragon's Storm

Shifter's Shadow

Psychic's Spell

Fairy's Touch

Angel's Flight

Ghost's Whisper

Phoenix's Refrain

Demon's Mark

Gods' Battleground

Leda's Log

Wicked Witchcraft

**Immortal Legacy**

Angel Fire

Angel Fury

Angel Fever

**Phoenix Dynasty**

Firestone Fantasy

Silver Sorceress

**Paragons**

The Knights of Gaia

The Tree of Spirits

The Tribes of Magic

**Dragon Born**

Mercenary Magic

Magic Edge

Magic Games

Magic Nights

Blood Magic

Magic Kingdom

Fairy Magic

Rival Magic

Shadow World

Spirit Magic

Magic Immortal

Shadow Magic

Role-Playing Magic

**Sorcery & Science**

Sorcery & Science

Vampires & Vigilantes

Divination & Deceit

Bombshells & Battlemages

# CHAPTERS

CHAPTER ONE

Return to the Lost City / 1

CHAPTER TWO

A Clash of Heaven and Hell / 15

CHAPTER THREE

Deities, Danger, and Drama / 25

CHAPTER FOUR

The Rogue Guardian / 32

CHAPTER FIVE

New Orders / 48

CHAPTER SIX

Flirting with Danger / 57

CHAPTER SEVEN

Angel Lessons / 70

CHAPTER EIGHT

The Great Scheme / 85

CHAPTER NINE

Reunion / 96

CHAPTER TEN

The Magic Parchment / 112

CHAPTER ELEVEN

The Attack / 125

CHAPTER TWELVE

Surprise / 134

CHAPTER THIRTEEN

Apocalypse in the Plural / 142

CHAPTER FOURTEEN

The Garden Library / 160

CHAPTER FIFTEEN

Angels' Court / 179

CHAPTER SIXTEEN

Out of Pandora's Box / 190

CHAPTER SEVENTEEN

The Woman in the Drawing / 199

CHAPTER EIGHTEEN

Angelblood / 205

CHAPTER NINETEEN

Miracle / 216

CHAPTER TWENTY

Champions of the Immortals / 225

CHAPTER TWENTY-ONE

The Road of Time / 238

CHAPTER TWENTY-TWO

Leda / 281

CHAPTER TWENTY-THREE

Terrible Futures / 287

CHAPTER TWENTY-FOUR

Locked Out / 293

CHAPTER TWENTY-FIVE

A Moment of Magic / 300

CHAPTER TWENTY-SIX

Gaius Knight / 312

CHAPTER TWENTY-SEVEN

Calamity / 316

CHAPTER TWENTY-EIGHT

The Door in the Floor / 325

CHAPTER TWENTY-NINE

Eight / 338

CHAPTER THIRTY

The Pegasus Knight / 346

CHAPTER THIRTY-ONE

Phoenix's Refrain / 349

CHAPTER THIRTY-TWO

Countdown to the End / 359

CHAPTER THIRTY-THREE

Memory Stream / 367

CHAPTER THIRTY-FOUR

The Best Laid Plans / 401

CHAPTER THIRTY-FIVE

Sierra / 407

CHAPTER THIRTY-SIX

The Love Child of Order and Chaos / 423

LEGION OF ANGELS

# Phoenix's Refrain

## ELLA SUMMERS

# CHAPTER 1

## RETURN TO THE LOST CITY

*I* walked across the broken highway, which cut right to the middle of the Lost City. There, at the epicenter of desolation, the highway ended abruptly in a massive crater. I passed the rotting husks of buildings, relics of an ancient era. The city was a forgotten piece of the past, a throwback to a lost world that we'd never return to again, a world ravaged by the immortal war the gods and demons had brought to Earth.

The Lost City had lain mostly dormant for over two centuries. Treasure hunters sometimes braved the ruins in search of great fortune, but that very rarely happened. There might have been treasures hidden within the decaying buildings, but there were monsters hidden there too.

Sounds rang in my ears. The clash of swords. The rapid beat of gunfire. Magic, ancient and unyielding. Powerful and arrogant. So beautiful. And so terrible that it had consumed the city.

The Lost City lay on the Black Plains, the wide,

beast-infested expanses on Earth that humans shunned and where monsters reigned supreme. I sure wasn't here for the fun times. I'd come back here because this was where it had all begun…where the visions had first appeared to me.

The first time I'd seen the visions—these memories of the past—had been on a mission just a few months after joining the Legion of Angels, the gods' Earthly army. I'd had a few more flashes here and there in the two years since, but lately these visions flowed like the floodgates of the past had opened up and unloaded everything it had onto me.

That might have had something to do with my newly-gained telepathic powers. Or maybe the visions were another 'present' my demon mother Grace had left with me. Whatever the case, there was something about these visions from the past, something I was sure held the key to the future. I just had to figure out what they were trying to tell me.

And so I'd traveled to the Lost City against orders… hell, without even telling the First Angel where I was at all. But now, being here, I knew I'd made the right decision. The visions were strong here, in the Lost City, just as I'd known they would be. I could hear those memories all again in perfect clarity.

I saw Sierra, the angel with the red hair and the silver wings. She walked down the highway of the Lost City, the very same highway I was now standing on. And yet not the same. The highway of Sierra's era was intact. Mine had fallen into ruin. The tall buildings on either side of her shone brightly, the light of a pleasant sun bouncing off the pristine windows.

Nowadays, the buildings on either side of me could

hardly be called buildings at all. Their windows were shattered, their insides gobbled up by enemy fire and the slow, inevitable passage of time.

Sierra's city was not the Lost City. Back then, it had been called the Golden City. I'd seen that in the visions. I saw—no, I *felt* the ground beneath Sierra's feet shake. The Golden City was under siege. I recognized these visions. They were of the city's final golden moments.

The heavens roared. An angel landed beside Sierra.

"Sierra," he said, dropping to one knee.

"Why do you bow before me, Calin?" she asked him.

"Because you are the Keeper," he said. "You are our savior."

I knew Sierra didn't feel like a savior. She felt so…so lost. So trapped by her destiny, a destiny which had been forced upon her without her ever having any say in the matter. She felt like she'd been thrown into this whole war, a war she didn't understand, a war that had been raging since long before she'd been born.

"Sierra, we must hurry." Calin took her arm and led her to the gateway of the Treasury. "They are coming. You need to don the armor and wield the weapons of heaven and hell. You need to save us all."

The weapons of heaven and hell. I had encountered them before. Worn them before. I guessed I was Sierra's successor, a version of her in the present era.

The weapons of heaven and hell were immortal artifacts of great power, the power to kill a deity. They were unique among the immortal artifacts in that they could only be worn by someone with balanced light and dark magic. Whereas most immortal artifacts could be used by anyone with enough magical might to control them.

The memory faded away. Back in my time, I'd

reached the end of the broken highway. I looked down into the crater. Beside me, my sister Gin released a deep, uneasy breath.

"Leda, are you sure we have to go down there?" she asked, gaping into the crater. "I can't even see the bottom."

My sister Tessa giggled. "What's the matter, Gin? Where's your sense of adventure?"

"I left it back in my bed. Where I wish I had remained instead of setting out on Leda's crazy quest," said Gin.

Gin's words didn't fool me. She might have been a little scared right now, but she was even more excited. She was an avid reader of adventure books and had always dreamed of being part of a great adventure of her own.

"You love it, and you know it," Tessa told Gin. She wasn't fooled either.

Gin and Tessa weren't my sisters by blood, but they were my sisters in all the ways it truly mattered. We had grown up together under the guidance of our amazing foster mother Calli. It had been a good home, full of love and understanding and guidance. All those things that I didn't get from my blood parents: Faris, the God of Heaven's Army, and Grace, the Demon of the Faith.

I looked all around. Most of the Lost City had been consumed by the final battle for Earth and had deteriorated even further in the time that had passed since then. The streets had split open, and the buildings were slowly crumbling to pieces. Some of the underground structures were still intact, though.

"Don't worry," I told Gin. "I won't let you fall."

I wrapped one arm around her and the other around

Tessa. Then I spread my angel wings, beating them gently as I slowly lowered us into the crater, all the way down to the ground. Angel, my feline companion, hopped in after us.

We landed in what seemed to be an ancient airport. This was a time capsule of how things had used to be, a taste of the Earth before the gods and demons, before magic and monsters.

"This way," I told my sisters, my white cat Angel strutting by my side.

We walked down the long airport corridor.

A flash from the past hit me, and I saw Sierra walking down this very same corridor. She was wearing the weapons of heaven and hell, marching into battle. Her armor was silver, just like her wings. In her hand, she held a burning sword. Blue flames licked the blade.

Magic fire rained down from above. Sierra jumped aside to avoid the blast.

I blinked, my mind returning to my own time.

I sidestepped several holes in the otherwise-smooth ground. Time was a funny thing, though. The holes weren't where they were supposed to be, not where the magic had impacted the ground in Sierra's time. Who knew what had happened in the centuries since then.

Yeah, memories were weird, especially visions from the past. I'd once spoken to Nero about the memories that kept coming to me. He thought someone had buried those memories inside of me—and that the more my magic grew, the more of these buried memories I'd unearth.

But why was *I* seeing those memories? What was special about me?

Nero had an answer to that too. He thought that, like

the ancient angel Sierra, I was a keeper of the weapons of heaven and hell, powerful immortal artifacts. He thought I had a great destiny, as evidenced by my 'perfect' balance of light and dark magic.

Yeah, I was balanced—or at least my magic was. That's what I got for being the offspring of a god and a demon.

Or maybe that's why I was unbalanced, torn between two worlds, destined never to fit in either.

I reached out and traced my finger along the edge of the very large hole in the wall in front of me. Something had blown that hole in the wall. I wondered what spell had done it.

I led the way through the hole, up the many, many stairs that ended in another hole, this time in the ceiling. I climbed out, then reached down to help Gin and Tessa up. Angel crouched down, wiggled her butt a few times, then leapt through the hole. She landed soundlessly beside me.

"Good kitty." I scratched her under her chin, then rose from my knees.

We were standing on what had once served as an airport runway. The asphalt surface had cracked and fractured since those days. There were holes larger than my foot in it.

We walked a few minutes, then the broken runway ended abruptly with the skeletal corpse of a plane. We climbed through the plane, its shell eaten away by the winds of time.

As we made our way through the ruins, I caught more flashes out of the past. Of this city. Of Sierra.

Why was I seeing Sierra's memories? What was so special about her? Were we somehow linked through time because she had once worn the weapons of heaven and hell, just as I had?

My sisters and I jumped out of the wrecked plane. We followed the old train line. Angel led the way, balancing effortlessly atop the slim profile of the broken tracks.

It was this way. I knew it. I could feel it. The visions were drawing me in closer. Something important lay at the end of the line.

The visions were coming from there. But what were the visions trying to show me? And who had given me these memories?

A broken train blocked the tracks. I had to jump inside and crawl through it.

Another flash. The train rattled. Another piece of the past hit me. Sierra, the red-haired angel, jumped across the train car's roof. Her blade met a monster's body. There were more monsters below on the ground, lured there by the sounds of battle. A beast's jaws snapped at her. She cut across its body, severing it, splitting it in two.

But that was not the true enemy. Sierra pressed on. The real enemy had invaded her city. They were coming for her.

Sierra's memories weren't the only ones that lived on in this city. I saw a pale-haired angel too, wearing the weapons of heaven and hell, fighting unseen enemies in the city. She ran at them. She was outnumbered. There was no hope of victory or even survival, even with all her magic and the aid of these powerful artifacts. But she did not shy away from her duty. She charged into battle, nonetheless, to defend her city and meet her end. If she was going to die here, she would take as many of them with her as she could.

Sierra and the unnamed pale-haired warrior: they were two different angels. The pale-haired angel had lived long before Sierra. I just knew it. Centuries before. Maybe one of the angels had fought in the Final Battle for Earth all those years ago, but then what of the other angel? I knew of no other battles in the Lost City. I would need to ask Bella. She always knew everything about history, and if she didn't know, she knew just which book to consult for answers.

I brushed my hand across the graffiti painted on the inside walls of the train car. Rough depictions of two angels: one with pale hair and one with red hair. What did it mean?

The front of the train car ended in a building, like the train had crashed full-speed into the train station. We hopped out of the missing door on the side. There, on the walls of the station, painted all over, were lots of funny symbols. I recognized those alien symbols. I'd seen them before, way back.

They were from an old demon language. The signs seemed to point to my demon mother Grace. Maybe she'd been the one to give me these memories.

"You're awfully quiet, Leda," Tessa commented.

I'd passed most of our journey through the ancient airport and broken train line in silence, lost in the memories, in those flashes of the past.

"The memories are stronger here," I told her.

"Good," Tessa said. "Nice to know you're not going crazy or anything."

I flashed her a smile. "Well, I've always been crazy. Nothing new there."

When I slept, the dreams came to me. Memories, jumbled and juxtaposed. Out of time. Drifting on the satin sashes of time. Out of place. Whispering against my consciousness.

These dreams and visions had grown so frequent, they were distracting. They were trying to tell me something. Ever since my recent battle of the minds against the telepath Faith, I'd been having these dreams, or maybe since I'd been pregnant. Hard to say which one since they'd both happened around the same time.

I tried to work through all these scenes that seemed disconnected. They were from different eras, but something connected it all together. Something linked them. I could feel it. I just couldn't put my finger on it. Perhaps it was the weapons of heaven and hell? The two angels had wielded them, and so had I.

My gut told me that all of this was connected to what was happening with the Guardians. I couldn't say why. I just felt it. And I'd learned to trust my gut.

I hoped my confidence didn't come from somewhere deeper, like Grace's scheme for me. I hoped that I wasn't falling into her trap. Or Faris's trap either. Or the Guardians' trap for that matter.

Maybe Grace really was behind all of this. I could have gone to her and demanded answers, but demons, like gods, never gave you a straight answer to anything. That wouldn't have fit into their whole plan of universal domination and manipulating us lesser beings.

The ruins were quiet, except for the soft steps of our shoes against the shifting rubble. A shrill ring punctuated that stillness, a dramatic, orchestral ringtone from a movie of old.

I ignored it and kept moving.

"Are you going to answer that?" Gin asked me.

I shrugged. "No. Not really."

We kept going, and another minute later, my phone rang again, once more breaking the silence.

"Are you going to answer *that*?" Gin asked.

I pulled out my phone and glanced at the screen. "No," I declared and pressed on, deeper into the building.

Sure enough, a few minutes later, my phone rang again.

"Ok, Leda. What the hell is going on with you?" Tessa asked. "Who keeps calling you?"

"Various people," I said cryptically.

"Spill it."

Tessa gave me a look far too commanding for her young years. She must have learned it from Calli. Calli, with a single, silent stare, could squeeze secrets out of someone better than the Legion's Interrogators could with all of the tools and magic at their disposal.

"It's just Alec calling," I said as my phone rang once more. "He can wait."

The next time my phone rang, Tessa grabbed it from my hand. "You're ignoring people, aren't you? People from the Legion."

"Maybe."

Gin glanced down at my phone screen. "You're ignoring Harker too?"

"Wow, Harker's calling now," I commented. "That escalated fast."

"What is going on, Leda?" Tessa demanded. "Why is the whole Legion of Angels calling you?"

"Well, not the *whole* Legion of Angels," I said. "But this is certainly working its way up the hierarchy." I sighed. "Truth be told, I'm not exactly supposed to be on this mission. Or on any mission, for that matter. Nyx has grounded me. She told me I'm not to go on missions because of my *condition*."

"That makes sense," said Gin.

"That makes sense?" I repeated, exasperated. "How does it make sense? I'm pregnant, not an invalid. I'm just as powerful as I've ever been. Maybe even more powerful. No, scratch that. I'm *definitely* more powerful."

"Yeah, well, I guess the Legion wants to keep your baby safe," Gin said. "It's not every day that a child of two angels is conceived."

She was right about that. The child of an angel was a precious miracle indeed. And the child of two angels… well, there had only ever been one of those before, and he was the father of my baby. Even so, Nyx needed to chill out. But I supposed chilling out wasn't part of the First Angel's job description.

"I hope we don't get in trouble with the Legion for going off with a rogue angel," Tessa chuckled, looking at Gin.

"You know, you're right." Gin grinned. "Think we should call the Legion and turn her in?"

"Na. We'll give her a little time." Tessa turned toward me. "But we're keeping our eyes on you, angel."

I snorted. "I think we're finally here actually."

Gin stepped forward. This was why I'd asked her to come along with me to the Lost City. A broken door lay before us. I remembered it from my last mission through the city. It had seemed insignificant at the time, but now, yeah, my visions kept snapping to this spot. This place wasn't part of the memories, but I kept seeing flashes of this door. It was the key to the memories.

Gin was good at fixing things. *Really* good. And her lock-picking skills were second to no one.

Gin knelt down in front of the broken door and started looking it over. "There is a barrier of some sort here. Magic. It's weak right now because of the full moon."

The full moon was tied to the monsters and their shifting tempers. Right now, when the moon was full, the monsters' magic was erratic. And that erratic magic here in the Lost City had weakened the barrier of this broken door, eating away at it, making it hard for the barrier to hold its seal. Just as Bella had speculated. That's why I'd come here now when the moon was full.

The problem was the beasts always got a bit moody around the time of the full moon. Luckily, I was somewhat of an expert monster slayer.

My phone rang again. It was a number I didn't recognize. But the name 'Heaven' was displayed prominently on the screen. Must have been someone's idea of a good joke.

"Heaven is calling," I told my sisters.

Yeah, Heaven. As though *that* would make me answer the phone.

I looked up at the sky and said, "Nice try, Nyx."

I could hear the rumbling of beasts.

"What's that?" Gin asked, unsettled. She nearly dropped her tools.

"Don't worry about it," I told her. "I'm on it."

I was already up and swinging my sword through the overgrown centipedes. Damn, their armor was tough. I blasted one with a fire spell. It worked better than my sword.

"How are you coming with that door, Gin?" I called back.

"Just a little bit longer," she replied.

Tessa was helping her, holding her tools and keeping an eye out in case any of the beasts got past me. The centipedes were gone, but now I had some rather large silver wolves to contend with.

And by silver, I meant made of actual metal. They weren't covered in fur like normal wolves. They were made of some kind of strong metal, stronger than anything I'd ever encountered. My sword bounced right off them. Even my magic didn't put a dent in them. Nothing was hurting them. I managed to force them back with some well-placed telekinetic blasts, but they just kept rushing forward. We were being overrun.

"Now would be a good time to get that door open," I told Gin, trying to keep the panic out of my voice.

I didn't know what was on the other side. Hopefully, it wasn't more monsters. All I knew was things weren't looking good here. The monsters came at me from either side—and from above.

Magic flashed, and then the beasts were gone. A combined blast of fire and lightning had split them into little bits of metal. That blast had also knocked me on my ass.

I looked up and saw Faris. So he'd been the one to blast the monsters to bits. And save my life. Damn it. I really didn't want to owe Faris anything.

He pulled me to my feet. "You really must be more careful. You are carrying priceless cargo." He looked down at my belly.

Faris saw me as a moderately useful weapon, but he saw my unborn child as the weapon to end all wars.

"You didn't answer my call." Disapproval flashed in his eyes.

"Heaven. That was you," I realized.

"Naturally," he said smugly.

I shook my head in disbelief. "I should have guessed."

The God of Heaven's Army. Heaven. Made sense.

"All right then," Faris said, dusting leftover magic off his hands. "Let's do what we came here to do."

# CHAPTER 2

## A CLASH OF HEAVEN AND HELL

I gawked at Faris. "Do what we came here to do?" I repeated his words.

"Learn who is sending you these visions, of course."

I cast a suspicious look on him. "Why do you care?"

"I care very much that someone is trying to manipulate you. That someone has control over you. That someone can make you see things. I will free you of this invasive force."

It didn't require much thought to read between the lines.

"You wouldn't want someone else's finger on the trigger of your weapon," I said.

"Don't be so melodramatic, Leda," he replied coolly.

I snorted. "Says the right person."

"I took time out of my very busy schedule to be here."

His busy schedule of admiring his reflection in the mirror and getting his hair done. And—as the small droplets of blood on his outfit told me—torturing people. And planning his complete and total dominion over the known universe and everyone in it, at least if the hard, upward lift of his mouth was any hint to his motives.

"I am here to help you," Faris continued. "Now do you want to get to the bottom of these visions or not?"

I didn't trust the God of Heaven's Army for a second, but I *did* want to figure out these visions. And much as I hated to admit it, I could really use Faris's help. This place was teeming with monsters, and I didn't have a Legion support team with me because I wasn't supposed to be out here in the first place.

"These visions…could it be Faith again?" Tessa asked.

"The telepath's powers still have not returned," Faris said bitterly. "And I don't expect them to. Thanks to Grace." Then he glowered at me like it was all my fault.

"You called?" Grace said pleasantly, suddenly here beside us.

Faris glared at her. "What are *you* doing here?"

Grace met his hard scowl with an easy smile. "The same thing as you: looking out for our dear daughter."

"You expect me to believe that you came here out of feelings of motherly love and concern?" Derision dripped from every word that Faris spoke.

Nodding, Grace folded her hands together. "Of course."

"You aren't capable of love, Grace."

"I am capable of a great deal more than you, Faris," the demon shot back.

"A great deal more evil," Faris said. "Leda sees right through you. You must know that."

"Leda knows I have only ever looked out for her best interests."

"You poisoned her with Venom," he said, obviously

more for my benefit than for hers. "And you manipulated a crazed telepath into attacking her mind in order to fulfill your purpose of Leda's child absorbing that telepath's power."

"And you threatened to destroy her mind if she didn't completely surrender her free will to you." Grace's smirk was pure venom. "But who's keeping count?"

They locked gazes like two stags locking horns. Each of them was keeping a careful tally of the other's evil deeds. And each of them was trying to manipulate me, to control me, to get me to side with them and become their own personal weapon.

No way. That just wasn't going to happen.

"If you two are just going to fight, how did you ever agree on anything for long enough to create me anyway?" I quipped.

Faris and Grace said nothing, but their expressions told all.

"I see. You each believed you could gain the upper hand and steal me for your exclusive use. So how'd that work out for you? Not at all. You fought over your precious toy, and in the end, no one got me."

"I will admit that I underestimated Faris," said Grace. "Or perhaps I overestimated my soldiers' martial prowess. I never imagined Faris could make it past my defenses and steal you from me."

"I did not steal her." Faris's voice had frozen over.

"Ah, 'claiming what is rightfully yours' then?" Grace snapped. "That's how you see it, right? Calling it by another name doesn't change the essence of what you did, Faris. Stealing is stealing."

"We had a deal, Grace. The child was to be shared."

"A deal you had every intention of breaking."

He kept his face carefully blank. "I suppose we'll never know now, will we?"

"I suppose not."

They were glaring at each other so hard that the walls were covered in frost. Literally. Gin was still busily working to open the door, so she hadn't noticed, but Tessa looked at me as if to say 'your parents are so messed up'.

Yeah, didn't I know it.

It was Faris who broke the steely silence. "I didn't make it past your defenses, Grace."

She blinked in confusion. "What?"

"I didn't steal Leda. Or reclaim her."

Grace laughed. "You expect me to believe that?"

"At this point, I expect very little of you, Grace."

"I know what happened, Faris, and I know you were behind it. Leda was only a few weeks old when you came for her. I was staying in a secluded fortress, guarded by my most loyal soldiers. I thought Leda was safe, that no one could penetrate our defenses."

"I didn't—"

"You did," Grace cut him off shortly. "One day, I was tired, worn out from all the rituals I'd performed on Leda during my long pregnancy. I'd spent those weeks since birth recovering, trying to regain my strength, to grow strong enough for the final ritual on Leda. To make Leda strong. I went to get a drink of Venom from the next room. When I returned, Leda was gone. She'd disappeared without a trace. Vanished into thin air. Like magic."

"You believe I did this." His halo flashed briefly red before it returned to its usual golden hue.

"I *know* you did this," Grace growled. "For centuries,

you have been collecting magical beings with unique powers, Faris. A djinn could have teleported in and taken Leda and been gone the next instant, before I returned. That's how you got past my guards."

"I don't have any djinn." Faris cast a speculative look on Tessa.

"Don't even think about it," I warned him.

"Very few would dare speak to me in such a manner." He shot me a look laden with threat.

I allowed a smile to stretch my mouth, but my eyes remained locked on to him. "Well, I guess I'm just special."

"Yes, you are. One of a kind, in fact." His tone was icy. "Fortunately for you."

"Ah, Pops, stop it. I'm tearing up here."

"You are a very peculiar…"

"Weapon?" I filled in the blank for him.

"He was going to say *person*, but he just couldn't bring himself to do it," Grace laughed. "To refer to you as a person would be an admission that you're actually a living being with a will of her own."

"You might want to remember that too, the next time you devise ways to manipulate me," I told her.

Faris's maniacal laughter rang in my ears. "I told you Grace is a master manipulator."

I turned sharply toward him. "Don't celebrate too soon. I don't trust either of you as far as I can throw you —blindfolded. And with both my hands tied behind my back."

"As usual, your attempt to 'lighten the mood' with humor falls flat," he said in a bored voice, cutting out with his sword as a newly arrived monster jumped at us.

Grace shot a spell at another monster—and she shot

snark at Faris. "As does your attempt to turn Leda against me."

"Don't you two ever stop bickering?" I demanded of both my insane parents, joining them in attacking the winged rat-like monsters trying to swarm us.

"No," Grace said.

"Such a task is impossible as long as she continues talking," Faris added.

Grace rolled her eyes; it was such a human gesture. "You know, if I didn't have my hands full killing monsters, I'd kill *you* right here and now."

Faris's sword burst into flames. "You and what army?"

"I don't need an army to take you down, Faris. I don't even need any magic. I could do it with nothing but this knife." She held up a short knife in front of his face.

Faris gave the knife a cold, derisive look. "Pretty trinket. Try not to hurt yourself with it."

Grace and Faris rushed toward each other, murder screaming in their eyes. I should have let them do it. Their deaths would have saved me a lot of aggravation. But two deities engaged in a fight to the death was not a pretty sight. They didn't look out for anyone, and collateral damage wasn't even a problem in their book. Well, it was a problem in my book. A big problem. My little sisters were here, and I was going to keep them safe.

So I planted myself between my fighting parents. "Behave yourselves, or I'll kick both your asses. Seriously, two deities should be able to behave with better manners than a pair of lovestruck teenagers."

"What did you say?" Anger boomed in Faris's voice.

Grace stiffened. She puffed out her chest and rolled back her shoulders. "I beg your pardon?"

"You heard me," I said. "And, yes, you should be

begging my pardon. And my sisters' pardon too. Get your shit together or get a room."

Grace was stunned to silence. Faris looked like he was going to smite me. I forced myself to keep my eyes on him and not look up at the foreboding sky, even though I could hear it swirling up a storm past the big hole in the ceiling.

Tessa snickered, but the sound was so soft, I could barely hear it over the clinking of Gin's tools. My crazy parents and I didn't say anything for the next few minutes while Gin worked, Tessa helped her, and the rest of us fought off the flying rat monsters.

But at a lull in the wave of charging beasts, Grace turned to Faris. "So you are really going to continue this pretense that you didn't take Leda from me?"

"I did not take her. If I had, she would have grown up by my side, not on the streets of Earth's Frontier like a dirty urchin." When Faris looked at me, his nose scrunched up like he'd smelled something particularly foul.

Grace's eyes narrowed to slits. "So I suppose a newborn baby just got up and walked away all by herself?"

"Don't be ridiculous," he said impatiently. "Isn't it obvious who took her? It was your sister Sonja."

Grace laughed at him. "If Sonja had taken Leda, she'd have grown up by my sister's side. Or under her boot."

"Yes, but Sonja has never been very good at holding on to her toys." His brows arched. "Or at keeping them in one piece, especially the toys she steals from others."

"Thea," Grace said.

Faris nodded curtly. "To name just one of many examples. Instead of making a nuisance of yourself here,

Grace, what you really should be doing is talking to Sonja."

Grace seemed to be considering the idea, but then she shot him an incredulous look. "You're trying to get rid of me."

"Yes, of course I wish to be rid of you. You're getting on my nerves. But that doesn't mean I'm wrong about Sonja."

Grace's eyebrows furrowed. "I will deal with Sonja later. I'm not leaving."

"In that case, I hope you at least came armed with more than your charming wit and that adorable knife. More beasts are closing in on us."

Grace's lip twitched at the word 'adorable', but she unhooked a weapon from her back. It was an enormous trident glowing with purple magic, sizzling with telekinetic energy. "You should know by now, Faris. I always come prepared to fight."

An odd look crossed Faris's face, one I had never seen there before. One that I hardly recognized hidden beneath the smug mask of divine arrogance. Humor? Yes, humor. Something Grace had said amused him.

"I'm glad that you two have made up," I said, allowing my sarcasm to seep through. "So now we can deal with the actual problem."

A second army of flying rats had arrived, and they were even bigger and uglier than the previous ones. Their fur was bright green, like acid, and their eyes were as black as tar. I fought off the monsters, my god father and demon mother by my side.

But even working together, we weren't making a dent in their numbers. In fact, there were more of them here than ever before. And the monsters just kept coming.

I had to hand it to Faris and Grace. They were lousy parents but excellent warriors. They cut the beasts down like they were nothing at all.

A flash from Sierra's past hit me. I saw her fighting monsters. Monsters just like these. The vision froze me for a moment. I blinked, trying to pull myself back to the present.

The first thing I saw back in my own time was a monster jumping at me. Faster than I could think, Grace had thrown herself between me and the winged rat. She extended her hand toward the beast. I could feel a buildup of combined telepathic and telekinetic energy all around us.

The monster froze in place. It was just stuck there, mid-air, its body frozen by telekinetic magic, its mind crippled by her telepathic attack. Then Grace cut her trident, burning with magic, across the immobile beast, slaying it.

Her attack brought an old question to the forefront of my mind. "Why don't gods and demons have the magic of telepathy naturally? Why did you have to breed it into yourselves?"

"Because the Immortals were power-hungry fools," Faris replied.

I didn't even try to hide my smirk. "That assessment means a lot coming from you, Faris."

Grace was more serious. "The Immortals didn't want to give us the power to read their minds," she explained.

"Why not?"

"Isn't it obvious?" said Faris. "The Immortals were hiding something from us. And from them." He pointed at Grace.

"Both gods and demons have spent centuries trying

to figure out what it is the Immortals were hiding," she said.

"And have you learned anything?"

"No. But I will." Faris's voice was determined—and dangerous.

"I've managed to open the lock on this door," Gin announced.

I patted her on the back. "Great job."

I gripped the handle. The others stepped back to make room for me to open the door. Once open, I could see a curtain of glowing magic in the doorway. I poked the curtain with my finger. It felt like touching liquid caramel.

There was a growl and a scream from behind. I spun around to watch a final flying rat burst onto the scene out of nowhere. The monster jumped on Gin, throwing her to the ground.

Grace hit the winged rat with a spell, shattering it to pieces. Tessa rushed over to Gin. She set her hand on Gin's bloody throat.

Tessa looked up from our sister's motionless body. "She's dead," she declared, her eyes wide. "Gin is dead."

# CHAPTER 3

DEITIES, DANGER, AND DRAMA

I rushed over to my sister. Tessa was gripping tightly to Gin's lifeless body. She couldn't let go. I waved my hand over Gin, trying to heal her with Fairy's Touch, but she was already dead.

"Stop fussing over her," Faris scolded me. "We need to get going before the passage closes."

I turned on him, growling, "My sister is dead, and all you're worried about is your stupid passage."

"She is a phoenix. She will rise again. But we don't have time to wait."

"You really are a callous son of a bitch, Faris."

"And you're an emotional wreck. Pull yourself together, Pandora. We have work to do and no time to waste on useless tears."

"Faris is an insensitive ass, but he is right, Leda." Grace pointed at the glowing curtain of magic. "Look, the passage is already closing."

I saw it. The light curtain was flickering and buzzing like it was about to go out.

And right now I didn't care. Sure, Gin would live.

She would rise again, and it would hurt like hell. But that wasn't the point. Just because someone was basically indestructible, that didn't mean you stopped caring about them. Because once you started doing that, you were well on your way to treating all people as disposable. That was the gods' whole problem. And the demons' problem too. They didn't care about anyone. They didn't understand love, compassion, or anything that connected people to other people.

"If we don't do this now, we won't get another chance for a while," Grace said to me. "Not until the moon is full again. Don't you want to know who is sending you those visions? Don't you want to know why?"

Yes, I wanted that. Of course I wanted it.

"It isn't you?" I had to ask.

"No, Leda. It wasn't me."

And for some reason, I actually believed her.

"They're right, Leda. You need to go," Tessa said to me. "There's a reason everything happened this way, a reason we all came to be here on Earth and ended up with Calli. It's all linked, Leda, and you need to figure out why. Go find your answers. I'll teleport with Gin. I'll bring her back home."

I hesitated.

"Gin would want you to go and figure this out," Tessa said.

I rose to my feet. "All right."

I joined Faris and Grace at the glowing magic curtain.

"What is it?" I wondered. "A magic mirror, a passage to another world?"

"Not quite," said Grace. "It's certainly similar,

though. I don't think it leads to another world but rather to a secret place here on this one."

"Wherever it leads, it won't work for long," Faris said impatiently.

As we passed through the glowing curtain, I glanced over my shoulder. A winged rat had taken flight; it was trying to follow us through. But it stopped just before it reached the curtain. It whimpered like it wanted to go through but couldn't. More monsters had arrived. They looked agitated that they couldn't follow us. Tessa, holding Gin, vanished from sight.

"They got away," I said happily under my breath.

The ruined city faded away. We popped out the other end of the glowing curtain, suspended up in the air, nothing else but empty space all around us. Then a tornado shot up out of nowhere and swallowed us. Even beating my wings at full power, navigating the wild winds was tough. I grabbed my cat Angel before she got sucked in. The moment I wrapped my arms around her, wings sprouted out of her back.

"You really are a little angel now," I said fondly.

She opened her mouth to meow, but I couldn't hear her over the roar of the raging tornado.

That tornado was pulling us down. Down to the ground. Very, very slowly, it was drawing us toward a floating platform in the sky. My feet set down on hard rock.

The floating island was about the size of a football field and covered in asphalt, or some similar substance. I didn't see anything obvious to explain how it was floating like this. Must have been magic. Or Magitech.

The floating island didn't seem to be affected by the tornado. In fact, down here, standing on the flat pancake surface, that tornado felt like nothing more than a bracing wind. I could see it spinning around us, trapping us inside, on this peculiar island. It had zipped itself up around the island, so I couldn't see past it. My new reality ended in a tornado.

This wasn't a natural tornado either, the kind that rolled over land. This tornado had been spun together with magic. Just like the floating asphalt island.

Grace and Faris were looking around too. Faris threw a few spells at the tornado, obviously trying to break through it, but his spells just bounced back at him.

Grace laughed at his failed efforts. "Such a man's idea, to think he can overpower everything with brute force."

Faris's dark brows drew together. "I have a lot of brute force."

Grace laughed again. "Not enough, apparently."

"And I suppose you have a better idea?" Faris demanded.

"Naturally. We are going to wait this out."

Faris looked at the tornado, which was showing no signs of slowing down or fizzling out any time soon. "That is unacceptable."

"You always were so impatient, Faris."

"I have things to do. That's what it means to actually be important."

The look he gave her brought a frown to Grace's lips.

"I know what you're trying to do," she said.

"Good for you."

"And it won't work. I'm not impressed by your ego, nor cowered by your shameless arrogance. And neither is Leda." Grace looked at me.

"Keep me out of your lovers' spat," I said, not taking

my eyes off the tornado. The spell had to have a weakness. If only I could find it.

"It's a little late for you to be left out of anything, dear," Grace said breezily. "You are, after all, our daughter, and therefore very much at the center of our lives."

She smiled at me. The look on the demon's face was positively doting. Honestly, it really freaked me out.

But it made Faris laugh. "She isn't fooled by the motherly act, Grace."

"You aren't helping," she snapped at him.

"I have no intention of helping you carry out your nefarious scheme."

"Nefarious scheme?" She planted her hands on her hips. "What exactly do you imagine I'm scheming to do?"

"I don't know." Faris frowned as if the admission grated on him. "Or at least I haven't figured it out yet. But I will find out what you're planning. And I will stop you."

Her eyes twinkled with delight. "Well, aren't you a regular storm cloud on a sunny day."

Lightning flashed across the sky, visible above the swirling tornado.

"Very funny," Faris said drily to Grace.

"That wasn't my doing."

"Someone is coming," I told my unhinged parents.

The tornado wall parted slightly, like curtains being drawn apart, then two figures stepped through the opening. The tornado zipped closed behind them.

At first, I couldn't see much of the two people, besides their silhouettes. But as they came closer, my breath caught in my throat. I gasped. One of them was Zane, my brother, the very reason I'd joined the Legion of Angels and set off on this mad, mad path of deities, danger, and drama.

The other person was someone I didn't recognize, a woman with long black hair braided along the left side of her face. She was dressed in a leather suit that perfectly fitted her tall and slender body. She carried a long sword on her back.

My brother Zane wore a fitted t-shirt and a pair of thick pants made of a durable fabric, the kind you'd put on when you had to trek long distances across the wilderness. He'd cut his light brown hair since I'd last seen him. It was cropped short—and a little spiky. And he'd been working out. His chest was broader, his shoulders wider. It looked like I hadn't been the only one to step up my physical exercise these past two years.

I rushed forward to hug my brother. "You've gotten bigger," I teased him, pinching his biceps.

"So have you." Zane set his hand on my belly.

I looked down, blushing. "There really isn't anything to see yet."

"There is for me," he told me.

Zane was a telepath and a powerful one at that. He could see things that others could not, things that were there but hidden to the naked eye.

"In any case, congratulations, Leda," he said with a bright smile. "I know this isn't how you ever envisioned bringing a child into the world, but we will make it right. We will make it safe for her. I promise."

I set my hand over his, my eyes tearing up. "I know I can always count on you to have my back, Zane."

"And I can always count on you to have mine," he replied. "Joining the Legion of Angels to gain the magic to find me…" He whistled, clearly impressed. "You are the truest, bravest, craziest sister that I could ever ask for."

"But I didn't have to find you. You found me. However did you escape the Guardians?" I asked him.

"River got me out." He glanced at the woman at his side.

I looked at her. Something was…well, weird. Something was very off about all of this. I could feel it. Right now, my gut was warning me that this woman was a liar. It was warning me not to trust her.

But it was Grace who voiced my concerns. "That woman is a Guardian."

# CHAPTER 4

### THE ROGUE GUARDIAN

I looked at Zane. "She's a Guardian?"

"You can trust River," he said quickly. "She's different from the others. She helped me. She got me out of the Guardians' Sanctuary."

Faris gave River a cool, assessing look. "She is a Guardian. All Guardians want to destroy every god, demon, supernatural, and human in the universe."

"And all gods want complete dominion over the known universe and to subject everyone in it to their will," River countered.

"Of course," Faris said, unabashed.

Daddy Dearest sure wasn't helping matters.

I stepped forward and looked at River. "What makes you different from the other Guardians?"

"For one, I'm not trying to kill any of you," she said lightly.

"Why not?" I asked her.

River shrugged. "It's counterproductive."

"Counterproductive to your objective?" I guessed.

"Yes."

"And what is your objective?"

She spread her arms and smiled. "I can't say."

Typical. Just typical. One of these days, I'd love to have a normal conversation with someone.

"You know something about the visions I started having in the city two years ago—and am having again now, don't you?" I asked the rogue Guardian.

"Yes."

I waited for her to elaborate, but she didn't.

So I continued with my questions. "This place is connected to the visions."

"Yes."

"And you've been here before."

"Yes."

"Did you send me the visions?" I asked.

"No."

Well, she clearly wasn't going to tell me more about that. So I moved on.

I looked around at the swirling tornado that surrounded us. "What is this place?"

"An echo chamber."

"An echo chamber?" I asked, then felt a bit like an echo chamber myself.

"Memories are stored here. Think of this place like a vault for memories. The Vault can tune in to someone's mind and send them memories."

"That's some very complicated magic." Faris's tone was casual, but his eyes were very sharp.

"It is," River agreed.

"But the Guardians cannot use magic," I said. "They neutralize it."

River's smile didn't fade. In fact, it grew wider. "Like I said, I am not like other Guardians."

She didn't elaborate, and it was clear she wasn't going to.

"So you used this repository to send me visions?" I asked.

"Not I."

Of course not. Not that she was going to tell me who had sent me the visions.

"Ok, so *someone* used this repository to send me visions?"

"Some very specific visions," River told me.

"Why? Why connect to me? Why show me *those* visions?"

She smiled.

"You don't know?" I asked.

"I know, but I can't say," she said, for what felt like the one-millionth time since I'd met her five minutes ago.

This was starting to get really annoying.

"Ok, why free Zane from the Guardians' Sanctuary then?" I asked her.

"He was in danger there. He could not stay. If he were to die, everything would go wrong. You need him."

"I need his help, you mean? Does he play a part in your plans for me?" I asked.

"He plays a part in your life, Leda Pandora. In the journey to come, you will need his help. And you will need him. He's your brother. If he were to die, you would be distraught."

"And I'm supposed to believe that you care about my feelings?"

I'd meant it to be a snide, sarcastic remark. I hadn't expected a response.

River surprised me when she actually answered. "You are driven by your feelings. They make you who you are.

They motivate everything you do. Were your brother dead, you would act most unfortunately."

I wasn't sure how to take that, but it sounded like River was manipulating me every bit as much as Faris and Grace were. And she was definitely hiding something from me. Ok, *a lot* of things.

I looked around at this floating island. "Are there more places like this?"

"Yes. And no."

I thought she wasn't going to elaborate, but she surprised me again by continuing.

"There are secret stashes all over the world. Each one holds different treasures, different powers, different secrets. Some of the vaults are smaller than this one. And some are quite a bit larger."

"But they all share something in common, don't they? None of these stashes have monsters. There is no Magitech wall to keep them out, but the monsters do not cross the threshold."

Surprise briefly flashed across her eyes, like she hadn't expected me to make this conclusion, but she quickly recovered her cool composure.

"Indeed. The magic used to create the stashes repels the monsters."

"Like here." I thought back to my recent adventure in the Black Forest. "And at the Silver Shore."

"Correct. The Silver Shore is also a secret stash."

"And what lies inside the Silver Shore's stash?"

Her aloof smile was back. "I cannot say."

It had to be something important. Something big. The Silver Shore was enormous.

We'd found our way inside this Vault by essentially picking the lock. I wondered if the same could be done with the world's other secret stashes. But could it truly be that easy? The visions I'd been sent basically told me how to get inside the Vault. I didn't have any visions that revolved around the other stashes. Finding my way into those places would be like searching for a needle in a haystack.

"What is the purpose of the stashes?" I asked River.

"Isn't it obvious? It's the same purpose of any stash: to hide things safely until they are needed."

"Needed? For what?"

"I can't say."

Getting answers out of River was definitely a hit-or-miss endeavor.

"Did you make the stashes?" I asked her.

"No. I am merely using this one and a few others."

"Who made them then?"

"I can't say."

"Can't you say anything?" I demanded.

"I have said a lot."

She had. I really had learned a lot of things from her, but they all felt like partial answers, truths with the good, juicy bits withheld, teasers meant to draw me in and make me want more. There was that manipulation again. I truly was growing tired of having everyone pull my strings.

"So you've brought me my brother." I folded my arms over my chest. "Now what?"

"Now you will all leave this place. After that, it's up to you."

River made it sound like I had free will. I liked to think that I did. So why did it feel like I was dancing to someone else's drum?

"Goodbye," River said to Zane. Then she looked at

me—or, more specifically, at my belly. "Protect the child."

What kind of statement was that? Of course I'd protect my child. I'd protect her with everything I had.

"What do you know of my child?" I asked her.

She spoke with inhuman calmness. "I know that the universe will go to war over her."

Just like in the vision Grace had sent to Nero.

"Even now, forces plot to exploit her." She glanced at Faris and Grace.

*Yeah, tell me something I don't know.*

"A lot of people want to use her as a weapon," I said.

River nodded.

"Someone with the powers of the gods, demons, and Immortals isn't easy to come by," I said.

"That is so, though it's not the full reason they wish to control her," she told me.

"There's something else? What?"

"Ask your mother." She looked at Grace.

So did I. "What does she mean?"

"She is referring to the magic that the child absorbed from the telepath Faith," Grace sighed, like she wasn't happy to go into this. "Faith's powers were extraordinary, far beyond that of any other telepath I have ever encountered. She possessed the ability of future sight, a powerful kind of magic."

"You have it too," I remembered.

"Not like Faith did," said Grace. "I sometimes catch fleeting glimpses of the future, but Faith could see so much more. And she had some control over what she saw."

"Apparently, not enough control, or she never would have been defeated," I said. "She would have foreseen what was going to happen to her and avoided it."

"There are, of course, limitations to magic, Leda. And Faith was only mortal. Your daughter is not. She is, in fact, very, very powerful. Those limitations will hinder her less."

"Or not at all?"

"Perhaps. We shall see."

So my daughter was going to be even more powerful than I'd thought. That only meant even more people would be after her.

"There is something else," Grace said. "Your daughter would have absorbed Faith's powers of past sight as well."

The past…and now I was having more visions.

"I believe your unborn child's abilities of sight allowed someone to use this place to send you very vivid, very frequent visions over great distances," Grace told me.

I looked at River for confirmation, but her face was perfectly neutral, not giving anything away.

"Well?" I demanded.

"Your daughter did indeed absorb all of Faith's telepathic powers, but there is something else Grace has not told you," River said. "A power Grace is hoping the child possesses."

I looked at Grace.

The demon shot River a withering look, then quickly composed her face as she gazed upon me. "Visions of past events can be quite sporadic and incomplete, as you yourself have witnessed, Leda. It is a problem that was well-recognized by the Immortals. Long ago, in their studies of magic, they tried to remedy that."

"How?"

"The Immortals analyzed magic by separating their

'complete magic' into individual strands," Grace explained. "That's how they made vampires, witches, fairies, and all of the other original supernaturals. It is also how gods and demons came to be. We were a result of their experiments on light and dark magic."

Faris frowned, like he didn't like the idea of being the result of an experiment. Well, join the club, Pops.

"The Immortals were unhappy with the vagueness and imprecision of their past-gazing powers, particularly their historians who desired a complete picture of their entire history," Grace continued. "So they created two supernatural classes. Firstly, the ghosts, those people with the power of telepathy. And secondly, the unicorns, people with the power of magic-tracking, but also the power to read into a soul, into the fabric of their magic, the history of their magic, the events that created them and their magic. That too was a window into the past. Then, after studying both powers in isolation, after learning how to boost them, the Immortals worked toward combining those boosted powers into a single being."

"What happened?" I asked.

"Nothing, as far as I can tell," said Grace. "The Immortals were so focused on what had already happened that they didn't see what was coming: the end of their civilization."

"Because of the Guardians."

"Because of the Guardians," Grace confirmed. "They destroyed the Immortals before those past-gazing experiments could bear any fruit."

"You're trying to continue those experiments," I realized. "That's why you really performed those rituals on me when you were pregnant with me. And that's why you wanted me to absorb Faith's magic."

"I wanted your daughter to absorb it, yes," she said. "Magic gained before birth is so much more potent. It mixes with the child as it develops. I'm sure that's the key to channeling the kind of power to truly master the gift of past vision. That's the idea the Immortals were missing in their experiments. That's why I arranged for your unborn child to absorb all of Faith's powers. And that's why I performed rituals on you before you were born. There is a chance your child will have the power to tap into the complete memories of anyone she meets. The unicorn's power to see all that came before to create someone—magnified, focused, and extended by the power of telepathy."

My demon mother certainly didn't dream small. She was trying to accomplish something that had eluded even the original Immortals.

"Why are you telling me all of this?" I asked Grace. "Why reveal your secrets?"

"River knows it all already. She would tell you everything if I did not."

My gaze flickered briefly to Faris, then back to Grace. "Aren't you worried about revealing your secrets to Faris?"

"It cannot be helped." Grace frowned. "He knows most of this already. And as for what he doesn't know… well, Faris can't do much with it anyway."

"That's what you think," Faris said with a smug upward tilt of his nose.

"Going to proposition Ava or…" Grace laughed. "…Sonja to help you create another living weapon? Good luck with that. My sisters despise you even more than I do. And there isn't another demon who possesses as powerful telepathic magic as I do. Truth is, honey, you needed me far more than I needed you."

Faris scowled at her.

"Good," River said.

Good? What did that mean? Was she just trying to get us all fighting? If she really was still with the Guardians, that would certainly be their way: to make us fight each other so we're less of a threat.

River started walking away.

Faris stepped into her path, blocking her. "You may not pass."

River looked at him, totally unconcerned. "You can't stop me."

Amusement flashed in his eyes. "Of course I can."

River kept walking. Faris made a move to grab her, but the tornado swooped in and pushed him aside with such force that he flew across the platform. He immediately jumped up and launched a barrage of spells at River.

But the tornado surged forward and swallowed his magic. None of his spells ever hit River. Faris tried more spells, but none of them worked either. His wings burst out of his back, and he flew at her. The tornado reached out to swallow him, pinning him in place. He couldn't move a muscle. The mysterious swirling magic tornado had completely immobilized the King of the Gods.

"How are you controlling the tornado?" I asked River.

"I'm not. I merely understand it," she told me. "I know the rules of the Vault, something the god would do well to remember." She slid a reproachful glance at Faris. "No magic can be used to attack another within these peaceful walls, else the Vault will be angered."

A piece of the tornado swirled out and reshaped itself to form a platform beneath her feet. The platform boosted her up slowly, like an elevator, high into the sky.

It was so weird. The Guardians didn't have magic; they neutralized it. So even if River knew the Vault's secret ways, how was magic working with her in here too? Why did the tornado seem to be acting at her command rather than recoiling from her touch?

Before I could even begin to make a guess at those mysteries, she was gone. At that same moment, the tornado released Faris.

He glowered at the spot where River had disappeared. "I'm not done with you," he said, making his voice boom and echo off the tornado walls.

Then he ranted at her for a good minute. Honestly, I was pretty impressed by his eloquent curses. He swore pretty well—for a god, anyway.

"Watch your mouth in front of the baby," I scolded him. I couldn't help myself. The idea of telling Faris how to behave was just too funny to pass up.

"The child will need to endure far more than unfriendly language," he replied coolly.

Yeah, my daughter would have to endure much from him. I didn't like the speculative look in his eyes. Likely, he was already dreaming up ways to torture my child with new and inhuman training methods. And she wasn't even born yet.

I looked at Faris's feathers, which were black with gold highlights. "Nice wings."

His nose inched a little higher in the air. "I know."

I rolled my eyes.

"Don't feed his ego," Grace told me. "It's too big already."

"I was being sarcastic," I said, even though Faris's wings were beautiful, unlike his dark soul.

"Don't even bother. Sarcasm goes right over Faris's head," said Grace. "Trust me. I've tried."

"Trust her at your own risk," Faris warned me.

Then he turned around to blast the tornado. It blasted back.

He cursed River's name again.

"She's long gone. I don't think she can hear you," I told him.

Ignoring me, he tried hitting the tornado with more magic. It hit him back even harder. Grace pulled out her phone and used it to gleefully capture videos of Faris's battle with the tornado.

"To show the other demons later," she whispered to me with a wink.

"Stop throwing a temper tantrum," I told Faris, then I turned to Grace. "And, as for you, stop egging him on. You're both acting like children, not immortal deities. And to be honest, I am downright embarrassed to call myself your daughter." I brushed the concrete dust off my shirt, a souvenir from our earlier battle with the rats. "Besides, if you two hadn't been goofing off, you would have realized that the tornado is just using your own magic against you. It can only spit back at you what you give it."

"Of course we noticed," Grace said, looking offended.

"We aren't imbeciles," Faris added.

"Then why do you keep blasting the tornado?" I demanded.

"Because I am annoyed."

"When you have as much magic as we do, if you

don't release it regularly, it tends to explode rather horribly," Grace explained.

"Especially, when we're aggravated," Faris said.

"Or otherwise worked up or incensed."

"Honestly, the nerve of that girl River."

"Popping in and out."

"Uninvited."

"Unannounced."

"Unwanted."

"Like she owns the place."

"It's intolerable."

I wondered if they realized how ironic their words were, coming from people who popped in and out all the time, uninvited, unannounced, and unwanted.

"It's bitter, isn't it?" I said.

"What is?" Faris asked.

I smirked. "The taste of your own medicine."

He scowled at me. He looked like he was seriously considering smiting me.

Grace slanted a warning glance at him. "Do not smite our daughter."

So I hadn't imagined that look in Faris's eyes.

"Why should I not punish her for her disobedience?" If he'd pumped any more scorn into his words, he might have exploded.

"You know why," Grace said.

"The child she carries is immortal. It will survive. And surviving a good smiting now and again builds character."

"Your parents smote you all the time, Faris," said Grace. "So if it were true that a good smiting builds character, your character would be the universe's gold standard."

A smile lifted his lips. "It is."

Grace rolled her eyes.

Faris looked at me expectantly, as though I was supposed to speak up for him and declare his character to be beyond reproach.

"You're the perfect god," I told him.

He began to nod, then stopped. His eyes narrowed. "You are being insincere."

"Of course I wasn't sincere. Sorry, Pops, you're a grade A ass." I flashed him a grin. "Even River thought so, and she'd only just met you."

"River, the impudent wretch," he said in a low snarl. "How dare she lay a finger on the Lord of Heaven's Army and King of the Gods."

"Actually, she didn't lay a finger on you. A cute little funnel of wind did," Grace pointed out. "Apparently, you aren't as powerful as you think you are."

Chuckling, Grace showed me a picture of Faris that she'd snapped while he'd been stuck to the tornado. The photo was indeed funny, but I didn't laugh. I didn't want her to think things were ok between us. She'd manipulated me and Nero. Things were definitely *not* ok between us.

"Just wait until I share this little gem at the next meeting of the demons' council," Grace said lightly. "I trust you'll hear the laughter all the way back at that distant, barren, miserable rock of a world you call home, Faris."

"I am in no mood for your snark, Grace," Faris said coolly.

She tucked her hair behind her ears. "You're never in the mood for anything but world domination."

"If only you could set your sights so high," he shot back.

Grace took a forceful step forward. "What is *that* supposed to mean?"

"But instead, you let your sisters do all the fighting and scheming and ruling." A sardonic smile curled his lips. "While you hide behind their skirts."

Grace drew her trident, and red flames shot across the black metal. She swung her very large, very long weapon at him. He dodged.

"Now who's hiding?" she mocked him.

He blasted her with magic. She swung her trident, knocking away Faris's spell like a bat hitting a baseball. He had to duck again, which made her laugh and taunt him some more. He unleashed more magic on her. One spell burnt her hand, and she dropped her trident. Now it was Faris's turn to taunt her.

"So those are your parents," Zane commented as we watched Grace and Faris fight.

I sighed. "Unfortunately."

Zane patted my arm to reassure me. It helped—at least a little.

He glanced down at my cat. "Nice cat. It's big."

"Thank you." I stroked Angel under her chin. "She's aspiring to be at least as large as a tiger."

"She'll need to get big to handle your big magic." His eyes twinkled. "And your big attitude."

"You know what Angel is?" I said in surprise. "You know that she can channel my magic?"

"I know a lot of things."

I linked my arm with his. "I'd love to hear them."

"And I'd love to tell you. We have a lot of catching up to do, Leda."

"Absolutely." I glanced at Faris and Grace, who were still firing off their magic as much as they were firing off their mouths, doing their best to kill each other. "Any chance you know the secret, express way out of here?"

"Yeah, River told me how to get in and out of the Vault—without waiting for a full moon and picking the lock."

"Good. Now let's sneak out quietly while they're busy fighting. It might be my only chance to ditch Pops and Mommy Dearest. And, you know, my life would be far less complicated without them in it."

# CHAPTER 5

NEW ORDERS

Unfortunately, Faris and Grace noticed that Zane and I were riding one of those tornado elevator things off the flying asphalt island, and my annoying parents followed us out of River-the-rogue-Guardian's secret Vault.

We passed through the glowing curtain but did not return to the Lost City. The spell dropped us off inside my office in Purgatory's main Legion building.

I looked around. "Strange that it brought us here. The passages between portals are usually set, locked on both ends."

"Usually but not always," replied Zane. "According to River, the tornado elevator can take someone anywhere on Earth. It reads your thoughts to decide where to go. You must have been thinking of this place."

I glanced at the rather substantial pile of paperwork on my desk. "I was thinking of all the work I still have to do."

Zane looked at the stack. "When's the last time you filled out a mission report?"

"Uh…never."

I was kidding. Mostly.

"I'm not good at writing things down," I said. "My assistant Lucy usually does it for me. But she's on vacation right now. The last apocalypse was a tad too much excitement for her, so I told her to take a few weeks off."

Angel pounced on one of the piles of paperwork, sending loose sheets flying everywhere. I caught the wayward pieces of paper with my telekinetic magic and reformed the stack. On the plus side, thanks to my chronic case of disorganization, it wasn't any more chaotic than it had already been.

"You might not be good at filling out your paperwork, but your spells are topnotch, Leda," Zane said, grinning.

I returned the grin. "Thanks. I've been practicing. I can even fold the pages into little magic origami birds and make them fly. Wanna see? We could send a flock of them down the main corridor and watch everyone duck for cover."

"You might be an angel now, but you're still the same old Leda," Zane laughed.

"Of course. I'm incorrigible. Calli always told me that."

"You're not just incorrigible; you're incurable. What am I going to do with you?" Faris said, making himself comfortable behind my desk.

"Err, perhaps *not* try to turn me into a weapon," I suggested, flashing him my teeth. "I might misfire. And hit you instead."

Faris leaned back in my chair. It was sturdy, but I was still worried it might snap under the weight of his ego.

"Insolence is not an endearing trait in a daughter," he told me.

"I'm sorry you think so. I was hoping we could share a big hug later." I spread my arms wide.

Faris looked at me like he thought my kind of madness was contagious. "You're not as funny as you think you are."

"Sure she is," Grace laughed, opening up her arms to me.

I just stared at her. She'd called my bluff. Damn it. Grace chuckled.

"If you two are quite finished being ridiculous, I will be taking my leave of you now." Faris rose smoothly to his feet and grabbed Zane's arm.

"What do you think you're doing?" I demanded.

"Taking the Ghost, of course."

I knocked his hand away from my brother. "I don't think so."

"Indeed," Grace said stiffly. "*I* will be taking him."

Faris glowered at her. "If you think I will allow you to take him—"

"I didn't say I was giving you a choice, Faris."

"If either of you want to take Zane, you will have to get through me first," I declared. "He is under my protection."

"Don't be foolish, child. The Guardians likely let Zane go for a reason," Faris pointed out. "I intend to find out what that reason is."

"I do not believe for a second that Zane is working with the Guardians. I know my brother."

"He's not your brother," Faris said with strained patience.

"He is more my brother than you are my father."

"You're being very unreasonable. And quite emotional." He said it with distaste, like emotion was a sin.

"Zane was with the Guardians for a long time, Leda. Two years. Who knows what they did to him. Or how they've worked over his mind," Grace said gently—or at least she *pretended* to be gentle.

I had to say, I got really worried when my parents stopped bickering for a moment and actually agreed on something.

But still I insisted, "My gut tells me that this is the same Zane he's always been."

"Your 'gut' is irrelevant here," Faris said with obvious disdain.

"Leda, are you sure you're not just believing what you want to believe?" Grace asked.

Neither Faris nor Grace seemed impressed by my confidence in Zane.

"You're the Demon of Faith, Grace. So how about having a little faith?" I told her.

"Clever, Leda."

I took a bow. "Thank you."

"But you know things don't work that way," she said.

"Like I said, I know my brother. And I know you two too. That's why I'm not letting either of you take him. You're both itching for an excuse to nab a telepath, especially Faris."

Grace looked at Faris. "She's not wrong about you."

"Oh, do shut up." The expression on his face was positively searing.

My office door creaked open. I spun around to find Nyx stepping through the doorway. The First Angel was wearing her black hair short and straight today. It framed her face, following her jawline. Nyx possessed some pretty spectacular shifting magic. But she didn't seem to be in the mood for pretty things right now, not like when her hair was long and flowed weightlessly in the air, as though it were floating underwater. No, her hair was stern today. Just like her face. And her no-nonsense black uniform.

"Pandora." Her voice was somber, but also a tad exasperated. "I've been trying to contact you for hours."

"I hope it wasn't important."

Her eyes narrowed. "Don't play games with me. Nero tried to cover for you, but his excuses, creative as they might be, didn't fool me for a second. Where were you?"

"Out," I said vaguely.

"Obviously you were *out*. Because you certainly weren't *in*."

"I was just having some quality family time."

Nyx's face told me she didn't buy my story one bit.

"You have been fighting." She picked debris off my jacket. "Extensively." She pointed out the monster blood on my boots.

"That's normal with my family."

"You're pregnant."

"I know."

"Well, apparently, it just slipped your mind. Just like my orders for you to remain here."

"I was with Faris and Grace. Surely, a god's order supersedes your order?"

I glanced back at Faris, but he was gone. So was Grace. They'd both vanished. I'd thought the room had grown suddenly very quiet and peaceful.

Nyx gave me a hard look.

Typical. When I didn't want Faris and Grace around, I couldn't get rid of them. But when I actually needed them, they were nowhere to be found.

"They were right here just a minute ago," I told Nyx.

Nyx sighed, a rare show of emotion. "I believe you."

"You do?"

"No one is crazy enough to lie about going on an outing with a god and a demon."

"I might be crazy enough." Then I added quickly, "But I'm not lying."

Nyx shook her head. "So was this dangerous, monster-fighting excursion at least fruitful?"

"I guess. Kind of. We were in the Lost City."

"Didn't get enough of it your first time around?"

"Well, no. That's why I went back there. I've been having these visions again, like I had back then, and…" I stopped when I saw the look on her face. "You think I've lost my mind."

"No. I've had visions of my own."

"Oh, right. Of me at the head of a demon army."

Her dark brows drew together. "How do you know about that?"

Oops.

I smiled and shrugged.

"If you're going to eavesdrop on people's private conversations, Pandora, you should take care not to admit your guilt later."

"I'll try to remember that," I said quickly.

I didn't want her to remember what had happened after that conversation I'd overheard between her and Ronan. I didn't want her to know what else I'd seen that I shouldn't have. Because then I might have been in actual trouble.

"So the visions," I said. "They're coming from this secret place. The Vault, she called it."

"She who?"

"River. She claims to be a rogue Guardian."

"Be careful, Leda."

"I *am* being careful. I'm not even sure I trust River. She could be trying to manipulate us."

"So this River is the one who sent you the visions?"

"She said she didn't send me the visions. All she said is they came from the Vault. Like those memories were the treasures held in that vault. But like I said, I'm not sure I can trust her. If she's telling the truth, and she really is a rogue Guardian, she might be able to help us take down the Guardians. And if she's lying to me, well, we might be able to use her to take down the Guardians anyway. *If* we can find her again." I looked at my brother. "Do you know how to find her?"

But before he could speak, Nyx said, "That is your brother Zane."

"Yes," I said cautiously.

"Your brother who was abducted by the Guardians two years ago."

"Yes. He says River helped him escape the Sanctuary."

"Be careful," Nyx told me again, like I was never careful or something. "The Guardians might have let him go; maybe they want him out here for some reason." Nyx turned an assessing stare on him. "Or maybe he is willingly helping them."

Déjà vu. Faris and Grace had said the same thing.

"No, he's not helping them," I defended my brother.

"Just to be sure, I want the Legion's doctors to check him out," Nyx said.

"What do you think they will find?"

"I don't know. That's why I want him checked out."

"Nyx—"

"I'll go," Zane said, stepping forward. "I have nothing to hide." He smiled at me. "And the sooner they realize that, the sooner we can have a long-overdue reunion."

"And return home to see the rest of our family," I said.

Zane reached out to squeeze my hand. "Absolutely."

Two Legion soldiers stepped into my office. Man, Nyx worked fast. I hadn't even seen her call them in. She must have done it telepathically. And the soldiers must have been waiting just outside my office.

Nyx watched them lead Zane away. When they were gone, she turned to me and said, "Obviously, you're bored, Pandora. You have too much time on your hands. It seems relieving you of your duties wasn't a good idea after all. It gives you too much time to think up ways to put yourself in danger."

"I didn't go to the Lost City to be dangerous. I did it because this investigation is important," I insisted. "These visions mean something. Something with global—maybe even galactic—ramifications. It's important."

"So is my next assignment for you."

Apparently, my protests had fallen on deaf ears.

"What is the assignment?" I said cautiously.

"Some good, long hours in the classroom for lessons on angel decorum and etiquette. It's long overdue, and now that you're pregnant, you have all the time in the world."

"Angel school?" I groaned. "I would rather kill monsters."

"I know you would. But, much as you like to forget

it, the Legion of Angels is not a democracy, Leda. It's an army. So when I give you an order, you don't have a choice in the matter. And that means bright and early tomorrow morning, you will report to Classroom 169 in Building One for some long-overdue lessons in angel manners."

# CHAPTER 6

FLIRTING WITH DANGER

*E*arly the next morning, I sat in the Legion's canteen. Though the sun had barely risen a few minutes ago, the place was packed full for the breakfast rush.

Nero walked over to my table and sat down next to me, carrying two breakfast trays. He slid one across the tabletop to me.

"Thanks, honey," I said. "But what are *you* going to eat?"

He caught my hand as I tried to steal his tray too.

I smirked at him.

Under the table, Angel arched her back and rubbed against his legs.

He gave the cat a flat look.

She looked up at him and blinked. Then she let out a soft meow.

Nero tossed her a breakfast sausage.

My cat started tearing into it, purring.

"You're such a softy, Windstriker," I laughed.

"I don't believe anyone has ever referred to me as soft."

I allowed my gaze to pan up his hard, muscular physique. "No, I'd imagine not." I wet my lips. "Any chance I could ogle—er, observe you on the salmon ladder later?"

"I've already performed my morning exercises."

Shame.

"When did that happen?" I asked.

"While you were still asleep in bed." His mouth twitched. "Snoring."

"Angels don't snore," I protested.

"You aren't a typical angel, Pandora."

His eyes drank me in. The look in them…it made me want to jump across the table and pin him under me. I sent him the mental image.

"Careful, Pandora," he said, so quietly I could hardly hear him. "Or I'll have to reprimand you."

"Reprimand me?" I asked my husband. "For what?"

"For projecting inappropriate thoughts to a superior officer while on duty."

I braided my fingers together, smiling. "Oh, so that's not allowed?"

His gaze didn't waver from mine, not for a second. "No. It is not."

"Well, then, I guess you're just going to have to reprimand me." Under the table, I slid my leg against his.

He reached out to touch me, then stopped himself. "Leda, what are you doing?" he said, low and rough.

"Misbehaving." I slid my foot higher up his leg.

"This is most inappropriate. Anyone in the canteen could see what you're doing."

"Oh, right." I slid my foot all the way down his leg,

but I did it very, very slowly. "Remind me to order tablecloths for all the tables." I allowed my eyes to pulse silver, once. "Long tablecloths." I licked my lips slowly, then finally withdrew my leg.

For once, Nero was speechless.

I leaned forward on my elbows. "So what will it be? Pushups?"

"What?" Nero said, as though coming out of a trance.

I smiled. "Was your mind someplace else, General?"

"Yes. Several places."

His gaze dipped to my chest. My breasts suddenly felt very heavy.

I unzipped my jacket. "It's gotten hot in here, hasn't it?"

Nero didn't blink. "Yes." He looked like he was going to move forward and touch me, but he sat back in his chair and watched me instead. "You mentioned pushups. No, I don't believe that would be wise in your condition."

"Running laps?" I asked, feeling a little breathless.

"No. That is not a good idea either."

"It would be if you chased me," I said.

"Chased you?"

I felt the soft caress of his magic slip down my neck.

"You're not fast enough," he said. "I'd catch you."

That soft whisper of barely-there wind magic traced my collarbone.

His brows arched. "And when I did catch you, you'd throw water bottles at me so you could get away."

I laughed, which sent the stroke of whispered wind plunging between my breasts. My laughter roughened into a choked gasp.

Nero's finger sprang to my lips, silencing me. He leaned in and whispered, "We have company, Leda."

"Then you shouldn't have provoked me, Nero," I hissed under my breath.

His finger traced my lower lip. "I do believe you started it."

"Did I? I can't remember. I don't know who started it, but we both need to finish this now." I arched forward.

"What are you doing?"

I glanced at him through thick, lowered lashes. "Taking what's mine."

"Leda, we can't have sex in the middle of the canteen," he said sensibly.

Gods, he made even sensible seem sexy.

"Why not?" I asked, sliding my finger slowly across my lower lip.

"Because there are people here."

"Oh, right." I tried to picture a solution to this problem, but my brain was kind of distracted at the moment. I just kept picturing Nero naked instead. Finally, I said, "There aren't any people in my office."

He looked like he was considering it. Seriously considering it. I unwound my telekinetic magic, sliding it up his leg to help him decide.

His eyes smoldered. "You're flirting with danger, Pandora."

"Always." My self control was slipping. All I had to do was reach out and…

"Could you two lovebirds stop mentally undressing each other long enough to make some space?"

Nero's knee jerked up and bumped the underside of the table.

I looked up at our uninvited guest. "Harker, so nice of you to visit. Now goodbye."

Harker chuckled and sat down next to Nero, who had backed away from me to an appropriate distance. How boring.

"Leda, your top's undone," Harker said casually.

I looked down at my top, which I'd zipped lower to show off an impressive amount of cleavage. Not that it helped me anymore. Now that Harker was here, Nero was on his best behavior.

I tried to zip up my top, but it got stuck. I cursed.

"Problems?" Harker said lightly, clearly amused.

"Yeah, my boobs got bigger, so none of my tops fit anymore."

Harker chuckled. "Yep, you've got problems."

"Well, you try being pregnant."

"I don't believe that's anatomically possible, Leda. But if you're having trouble with your boobs, then I'm sure Nero would gladly lend you a hand."

"If only," I muttered bitterly, slouching back in my chair.

"Is this seat taken?"

My gloomy mood brightened as soon as I looked up to find Ivy standing beside our table.

"Of course not!" I told her. "Sit down, stranger."

Ivy sat down with her apple cinnamon muffin.

"How's Leila treating you back at Storm Castle?" I asked her.

"Great. It's all great there."

"You know, it's even better here," I told her.

"You know I love you, Leda."

I snickered. "But you love Drake more."

Ivy grinned, totally lovestruck. "Is that bad?"

"No, it's about time you two realized how you feel about each other. Everyone else knew ages ago."

"Surely not everyone."

I looked at Harker. "Everyone at the Legion's New York office knew, right?"

Harker nodded. "Naturally."

Ivy's face blushed as red as her hair. "Well, I guess Drake and I just needed time. But it was worth the wait."

"I'm glad you and Drake are happy, Ivy, but you two could have been happy here." I brushed away an imaginary tear.

"Drake is now a Dragon of Storm Castle. That job cannot be done from anywhere else on Earth," Nero pointed out.

"Yes, thank you, Mr. Sensible," I replied.

Nero's brows lifted. He must have known that I was annoyed with him because he hadn't taken me up on my offer of a steamy rendezvous in my office.

"Hey, Alec," Ivy said.

Alec Morrows, my new head of security, had stopped beside our table. "General Windstriker. Colonel Sunstorm." He nodded to Nero and Harker in turn. Then he bowed to me. "Boss." He winked at Ivy. "Doctor Happy."

Doctor Happy. That was the perfect nickname for Ivy.

"I must say I am very disappointed, Ivy, to hear you're now off the market. And dating my buddy Drake no less." Alec grinned at her.

Ivy grinned back.

"So, Alec, I guess you want to make a report or something," I said casually.

Nero's eyes widened, clearly horrified by my very

fancy, very soldierly words. They were words *totally* befitting of an angel.

"No wonder Nyx is sending you to remedial angel academy," Harker laughed.

I stuck my hand over his mouth and hissed between my teeth, "Do you think you could shout it out any louder, Harker? Honestly! I have a reputation to maintain."

Harker swatted my hand away. "I'm confused, Leda. I thought your special angel training is all about building up a new reputation." His eyes twinkled.

I rolled my eyes at him. "Haha. Very funny."

Alec sat down next to me. "Should I proceed with my report?"

I waved for him to continue.

"While you were, *ahem*, away on business last night, Nyx arrived here," Alec said. "General Windstriker met with her in your office and attempted to convince her that you were not indeed off on a fool's errand."

Alec spoke with a perfectly straight face, so unlike his usual, jovial manner. He must have been particularly amused right now.

"Out of curiosity, what did you tell Nyx?" Harker asked Nero.

"I told her Leda was visiting her family."

"Which is true," I said. "I was with Gin and Tessa."

Thankfully, Gin was recovering well from being, well, dead. Thank goodness she was a phoenix. I shouldn't have put her and Tessa in such danger in the first place. Calli thought so too. She'd called me up and told me off for at least an hour after my sisters had returned home. I'd felt like I was twelve years old again, not a powerful angel. Funnily enough, Calli hadn't seemed irked that I'd brought Gin and Tessa with me to the Lost City; she'd been more upset that I hadn't brought her along to look out for all of us. Like Nyx, Calli seemed to think I was made of glass now that I was pregnant.

"But then Faris and Grace showed up in the Lost City too," I said. "Uninvited, of course."

"Well, at least in the end, you got Zane back," said Harker.

"You've been talking to Bella."

After telling me off for an hour for putting myself and my sisters in danger, Calli had spent the next hour praising me for finding my brother. Then she'd called Bella and told her the good news.

"Yes. Bella told me last night." Harker couldn't hide his smile, the smitten kitten.

Oh, yes. The two of them had been spending a lot of time together lately.

"I have my eye on you, Sunstorm. You treat my sister right, or you'll have to deal with the Angel of Chaos." I pointed at myself.

Harker folded his hands together serenely. "I've been a perfect angel, I assure you."

"That's what I'm worried about."

Contrary to our reputation, we angels were hardly 'angelic' in the human sense of the word.

"Bella is very eager to see Zane again," Harker told me.

"I want to bring him home, but Nyx has insisted on running some tests. Nerissa checked him out physically last night. And Ivy is checking him out mentally today."

That's why Nyx had called Ivy away from Storm Castle.

Ivy rose from her seat. "Right, I'll be talking to your

brother starting in ten minutes. I just stopped by the canteen for a quick muffin and a chat with my favorite angel." She winked at me.

Then she left. Alec left with her.

I watched Ivy walk away. "I wish Leila hadn't poached Ivy and Drake from me," I said to Nero. "They're really good at what they do."

"Poaching soldiers. Sounds familiar," Harker commented.

I'd stolen some of his soldiers when I'd started the Purgatory office.

He winked at me. "How do you like the bitter taste of your own medicine?"

*How do you like the bitter taste of your own medicine?* I'd said something just like that to Faris last night. I hoped that didn't mean I was just like my hypocritical father. That was one of my greatest fears, actually: to be just like my parents. I sure was living up to that standard nicely. If I continued on like this, by the end of the year, I'd be trying my hand at playing the game of world domination.

Nero and Harker were staring at me strangely, so I pulled my mind away from those foreboding thoughts.

"It's only fun if I'm the one doing the poaching of soldiers," I quipped.

Harker snorted.

"I guess we'd better get going," I said with a heavy sigh.

The three of us stood up and walked out of the canteen. Angel trotted along after us.

"So, what are you boys up to today?" I asked them as we walked down the hall. Anything to get my mind off of my new assignment.

"It's classified," Harker told me.

I knew Harker was in town to work with Nero, but I didn't know the nature of that work.

"Classified? By the Legion?" I asked.

"By me," he replied.

*We are going after a diary,* Nero told me in my mind.

*Thea's diary?* I asked. *Bella told me it might hold answers about her past.*

*Yes. Bella seems to think her mother's diary is some kind of grimoire. And that it's hidden somewhere in Purgatory.*

"I see. Well, good luck with that," I told Nero and Harker aloud.

Harker frowned at Nero. "You told her."

"Of course. She's my wife. The mother of my child. We have no secrets." Nero took my hand and kissed it.

Harker rolled his eyes. "Love has made you foolish, Nero."

"I'm not the one dropping everything to go on a treasure hunt just to spend more time with a certain witch." Nero's green eyes twinkled with amusement.

"You *are* dropping everything to go on a treasure hunt."

"To spend more time with my best friend, you goon."

Harker's smirk faded, replaced by a genuine grin. He thumped Nero heartily on the back.

"You're a good friend," I told Nero.

Nero nodded smugly. "I know."

"And so modest," Harker added.

"There are qualities in an angel that are more important than modesty," Nero declared.

"Hold on a moment there, Nero. Don't give Leda all the answers before she goes to her remedial angel course."

"Shh," I growled. "Not so loudly, or everyone will find out about it."

"Nyx sent you to angel manners school." The expression on Harker's face was pure merriment. "I think it's safe to say *everyone* at the Legion already knows about that, Leda."

I sighed.

Nero set his hand on my back and began to massage it.

I forced a smile to show him I appreciated his sign of support. "Any chance that you'll ditch Harker and hang out with me today instead? We can play footsie under the desks."

"Tempting as that is, Pandora, I think that would distract you from the mission at hand," Nero chuckled. "Nyx might be trying to keep you busy, but she isn't wrong that you could use some lessons in dealing with angels."

"You're an angel, and I deal with you just fine."

"Pandora, if you dealt with all angels as you do with me, I would have no choice but to kill every last one of them," Nero said, his eyes smoldering with barely-contained volcanic fire.

The sharp jealousy, the fierce devotion in his words... I had to admit it sent tingles up and down my spine.

"Do you two need a few minutes? Or a room," Harker added in a mutter.

Nero and I stared into each other's eyes.

He stroked his hand down my face. "No, we're fine," he said quietly to Harker.

Then he leaned in and kissed me. His kiss was light and soft, but it left a hot brand on my lips. He stepped back. I touched my lips. They still buzzed from his kiss.

*You know, we might still have time for a little fun in my office,* I communicated telepathically.

Nero's face was blank, but his chuckles echoed in my mind.

*We just have to find a way to ditch Harker,* I added.

"These lessons are important, Leda," Nero said aloud. "You must take them seriously. Angel politics are not for the faint of heart. Or for the inexperienced."

"Or the unarmed," Harker added.

"You've survived earlier encounters with other angels because they were under carefully controlled circumstances," Nero told me. "The gods' challenges, various Legion assignments. But you have ruffled quite a few angels' feathers, Leda. Your pregnancy protects you from their retribution. But only for now."

"Pregnant angels are off limits," Harker explained. "Other angels aren't free to do to them what they usually could."

"Which is?" I asked.

Nero grew very still. "You know what Xerxes Fireswift's father did to my parents."

I nodded.

"That is not uncommon," Nero said. "And some of the other angels would jump at the opportunity to make a move against you, Leda. And against our daughter."

I felt a deep, penetrating chill inside of me, like a cold fist had clenched my heart. "What do we do?"

"Kill them if we must, but I'd prefer not to," said Nero. "Every angel has angel allies, so killing one angel tends to escalate quickly and spiral out of control. It's very messy, and we can't be sure we'll all survive a full-on angel blood war."

I couldn't stand to lose Nero or our daughter. Or any of my friends, for that matter.

"The better strategy is to head this off before it starts," Nero told me. "You need to learn to act appropriately with the other angels, or at least act appropriately with the angels who don't appreciate your natural state. Nyx's training course will help you with that."

"I will study hard," I promised him.

For the sake of our family. For the sake of our daughter.

We'd reached Classroom 169.

"Then I will wish you luck." Nero kissed my hand once, lightly, then he and Harker walked off.

I glanced down at my cat. "Well, Angel, it's just you and me now."

Angel looked at the classroom door, then at me. She turned sharply and strutted down the hall toward the nearest exit, her tail high in the air.

"Traitor!" I called out to her.

Now I was truly alone. I took a deep breath, then grabbed the knob, turning it to swing open the door. I entered the room.

I'd expected that Nyx would be the one teaching me to be a proper angel. After all, no one knew more about that than the First Angel herself. But I didn't find Nyx waiting for me in that classroom. I found someone far, far worse.

"Don't just stand there. Close the door."

Colonel Fireswift's cold, smug face stared back at me, watching me like a predator who had his unwilling lunch exactly where he wanted it.

## CHAPTER 7

ANGEL LESSONS

The new classroom had been renovated for the purpose of educating Legion initiates. Purgatory would start getting them soon, once all of our facilities were ready. And assuming there were still people who wanted to join the Legion.

After a recent string of rather spectacular disasters on Earth, it was safe to say the people's confidence in the Legion—and in the gods themselves—had been shaken. What stood out most in everyone's mind seemed to be the night the goddess Meda had stood on a rooftop in Purgatory and publicly declared that she was going to punish the Earth by purging it of most of its people.

Never mind that Meda had been controlled by one of the Guardians' magic collars. People didn't know that. And those who did know it were right now asking themselves how powerful the gods really were if they could be controlled like that. The truth was no one was truly all-powerful, much as the gods and demons hated to hear it.

I weaved through the rows of plain desks. The room's decor was sparse, utilitarian. The furnishings consisted of a perfect grid of twenty-five desks, all facing a whiteboard on the wall, and a metal trash can by the door. That was all. It reminded me of my old high school's unimaginative, uninspired classrooms.

I was going to have a chat with the folks handling our renovation. Classrooms needed a little more spunk, a little more fun, to keep people's spirits up. And keeping people's spirits up would make them work harder, which would increase their chances of surviving the Nectar.

That's how I preferred things. I wanted to help my initiates survive. Unlike most angels, I didn't see the Nectar as a way to weed out the weak. No, that was more like Colonel Fireswift's philosophy.

Speaking of Colonel Fireswift, he was watching me right now like I was a target he had in his sights.

"Take a seat, Colonel Pandora," Colonel Fireswift ordered me.

"You haven't been promoted yet, *Colonel*," I told him. "You aren't a general, an archangel. Which makes us the same rank. So you can't order me around like I'm one of your subordinates."

"That's where you're wrong," he replied smoothly. "You don't understand your situation perfectly. You don't understand the subtlety of the Legion's hierarchy, or of the angels themselves. Not that I'm surprised. You never were very good at subtlety."

I folded my arms across my chest. "Do you have a point?"

"The point is, Colonel, that I can give you orders because I am in charge of your current training. Which makes you very much my lessor."

Oh, he liked that. He liked it very much. I could see it in the sinister sparkle in his eyes.

A comeback was burning on my lips, but I had promised Nero that I'd behave. So I kept my mouth shut and sat down.

"Good," Colonel Fireswift said, but his sharp tone indicated he considered me anything other than good.

He set a tall stack of books on my desk. The tower cast a foreboding shadow over me.

I looked away from them. "So, Colonel, how have you been?"

His eyes narrowed to slits. "What are you doing?"

"Making smalltalk," I replied pleasantly.

"Then let this be your first lesson in angel etiquette: we don't make smalltalk."

"Why not?"

"Because angels do not talk about nothing. We speak only if we have something important to say."

"Ok, let's say you encounter another angel and you don't have anything to say to them." I did my best to look confused. "So you say nothing at all?"

"If you can't think of anything to say, there are books full of appropriate angel greetings. I will provide them to you."

"Oh, I don't need any books to fill awkward silences, Colonel," I said with an easy smile. "I always have something to say."

"I have noticed." He scowled at me. "In fact, it seems quite impossible to shut you up."

"You enjoyed our time together in the gods' trials." I allowed a smirk to shine through. "Admit it."

Colonel Fireswift rolled back his shoulders in indignation. "I will do no such thing."

"Come on. You know you want to."

His mouth tightened. "Why do you enjoy provoking me so much?"

I shrugged. "I guess because you react so well."

"You see, this is the problem with you, Leda Pandora. This is why the First Angel has sent you to me."

"Because Nyx thinks you need a little humor in your life?" I said with a smile.

His mouth fell open in outrage. "You wouldn't risk such insubordination if you knew I could actually punish you. But Nyx was clear. No beatings. No poisoning you. And no setting you on fire, no matter how much you might tempt me to do it."

Those sounded like direct quotes from the First Angel.

"So you're not allowed to maim me. How awful for you," I said, sarcastic.

"Yes. Yes, it is," Colonel Fireswift said, perfectly serious. "But I shall endeavor to make do as best I can within these inefficient perimeters. And you shall endeavor not to shoot off your mouth." He set down another book on my desk.

I read the title. "Angels in Conversation: Volume 1?"

"Yes. I prefer the conversations in volume four, personally. They are far subtler. But when one is training to be a proper angel, one must start at the beginning."

I opened the book at random and quickly skimmed a page. "Colonel, you do realize that these greetings are nothing else than smalltalk, right?"

"No," he snapped. "They are conversation starters."

"They are things to say when there's nothing to say. In other words, smalltalk. Talking about nothing."

"You are missing the point."

I looked up from the book—and into his sour face. "Then enlighten me." I smiled.

"The phrases in this book are deeper than they appear. They are rife with hidden meaning."

"Innuendo?"

"I prefer the word allusion."

"How very literary of you," I said. "But just so we're clear, these books will teach me to lace perfectly civilized remarks with nuanced threats, boasts, and otherwise subtly establish my dominance?"

He bristled at my statement. "To put it crudely, yes."

"Cool."

"*If* you devote yourself to mastery and reflection, rather than shooting off the first thought that flashes through your head," he amended.

"I can do that."

"Can you?" Colonel Fireswift snatched the book out of my hands. "We shall see. We'll now have a practice conversation and find out. You will begin."

I stood up. "Ok."

I returned to the door, then turned around. I walked back to him, as though I'd just come into the room.

I nodded crisply in greeting, as I'd seen Nero do. "Colonel Fireswift."

His nod was even crisper, so crisp I could have bounced bullets off of it. Not that I was tempted to try. No, that would have been too much fun.

"Colonel Pandora," he said.

*Your shoelaces are coming undone.*

No, I couldn't say that. That's why straight-laced angels like Colonel Fireswift didn't like me. Because I just said the first thing that popped into my head.

I had to pick something stately. Like work. Angels liked to talk about work.

"Nyx says you are to be promoted to general," I said.

"Yes," he replied, standing tall.

"But it hasn't happened yet."

A subtle dig that he was not currently a higher rank than I was.

Or maybe not so subtle. Colonel Fireswift gave me a sharp look.

"The world has been unsettled," he said. "There hasn't been time for my Archangel Trials."

The Archangel Trials. That reminded me of something that I'd been meaning to say—and made me totally forget what I was supposed to be doing.

"I can't believe the gods still want to go through with the Trials. After all that has happened, they—"

"Silence," Colonel Fireswift cut me off. "You will speak no further about the Trials."

"But I was there with Nero during his. You have to know—"

"I don't have to know anything," he said brusquely. "Speaking of the Trials is forbidden. You are going to get me into trouble." He looked up, almost nervously, as though the gods were listening to us at this very moment.

"I'm just trying to help," I told him, and I actually meant it.

But he threw my concern right back in my face. "I don't need your help."

"Actually, Colonel, you really do," I said. "And you *really* want to listen to what I have to say."

"No, I do not."

Gods, it was like shouting at one of the Legion's vending machines after it had eaten my money, except I at least *sometimes* got what I wanted out of those vending machines, if I only kicked them hard enough. This conversation, on the other hand, was going nowhere.

"It's important," I told Colonel Fireswift.

"Silence," he hissed with cold menace.

Damn him, he was so stubborn. And that stubbornness would be the death of the person he loved most in this world: his wife. That's what the Archangel Trials were all about. Sacrifice. If you wanted to be an archangel, the gods demanded you make this sacrifice. For Nero, that had meant sacrificing me, but we'd managed to wangle our way out of that no-win situation. The gods hadn't been happy about it, however, and the next prospective archangel wouldn't be so lucky.

But Colonel Fireswift didn't know about that, and he outright refused to let me warn him that the Trials would cost his wife her life. And that wouldn't just hurt Colonel Fireswift; it would hurt his son Jace too. Jace, my friend. I didn't want him to lose his mother.

And, also, much as I didn't like Colonel Fireswift, I was worried the Trials would hurt him too. No one deserved to feel such pain. I'd seen his face when he'd lost his daughter. Though he tried hard to hide it, he actually did have feelings.

The Legion really didn't want to do this to Colonel Fireswift either, not if they'd just stop and think about it. An angel in pain did not make a very effective soldier. And right now, we needed all the angels we had in order to fight the Guardians. Plus, I still thought it might come down to fighting the gods and demons too. We angels had to be united and strong.

United and strong. The thought renewed my motivation to truly understand angels. I had to win over the other angels. After all, we were all in this together. I just had to convince all of the other angels of that. It was the only way we'd survive what was coming, the only way we could make the Earth safe. And the only way I could keep my daughter safe.

"You started the conversation—ok, I won't say 'well', but it was adequate," Colonel Fireswift said. "But then you forgot what you were supposed to be doing."

"I know." I exhaled. "And I'll do better next time."

"Let's find out then." His face was carefully, conscientiously blank. "Again, from the beginning."

---

Colonel Fireswift and I played through angel conversations the whole morning. Then, in the afternoon, we moved on to the angels' political structure. Colonel Fireswift quizzed me. He had me list all the other angels and their territories.

"Nyx, the First Angel of the Legion with headquarters in Los Angeles. General Nero Windstriker, the Second Angel—"

"That is not Windstriker's official title," Colonel Fireswift scolded me.

Oh, right. That was just my nickname for Nero.

"General Nero Windstriker, Chief Marshal and Executive Officer of the Legion of Angels."

I still thought my title for him was way better.

"Colonel Leila Starborn, the Fire Dragon and Angel of Storm Castle; her territory is the Elemental Expanse with its headquarters at Storm Castle. Colonel Xerxes Fireswift, Master Interrogator, Angel of the Central Territory of North America with its headquarters in Chicago.

Lieutenant Colonel Jace Angelblood, Angel of the South Territory of North America with its headquarters in New Orleans. Colonel Harker Sunstorm, Angel of the East Coast of North America with its headquarters in New York City."

"The European territories next," Colonel Fireswift prompted me.

"General Rhydian Silverstar, Angel of North Europe with headquarters in Berlin," I said. "Colonel Dragonblood..." Oh, crap. What was Dragonblood's first name? "Colonel Vanir Dragonblood." I'd just remembered it from my Crystal Falls training invitation. Not that Colonel Dragonblood had actually made it to that training. "Angel of South Europe with its headquarters in Florence."

"Now the Australian territories," Colonel Fireswift said.

He was jumping all over the map. He probably thought that would confuse me into making a mistake.

"General Kiros Spellsmiter, Head of the Vanguard and Angel of West Australia with its headquarters in..." Shit, if only I'd ever been to Australia. "...Perth," I guessed. It was the only city in western Australia that I could remember. I knew I should have paid better attention in geography class back in high school.

Colonel Fireswift didn't correct me, so I must have guessed right.

"Colonel Desiree Silvertongue, Angel of East Australia with its headquarters in Sydney," I said, finishing up the continent.

Colonel Fireswift frowned.

"My answers were correct," I told him.

"Yes." His frown deepened. "They were."

"Shall I move on to another continent? I hear Antarctica is particularly chilly this time of year." I folded my hands together on my desk and smiled up at him.

"There is no Angel of Antarctica," he said humorlessly.

"It was a joke."

He just stared at me like I'd grown a second head.

"Never mind," I sighed. "I can tell you about the angels of South America. There's Lieutenant Colonel Oberon Stormbearer, Angel of Patagonia with its headquarters at Angel's Steppe."

Angel's Steppe was a new city, created after the monsters had come to Earth.

"And then Colonel Ariadne Ravenfall, Angel of Amazonia with its headquarters in São Paulo."

"Pandora—"

"And Colonel Brutus Heavensworn, Angel of the Andes with its headquarters in—"

"Oh, do shut up and stop showing off!" Colonel Fireswift snapped grumpily.

"You do not wish for me to continue with the exercise?" I asked serenely.

"No, it is clearly too easy. Any human could recite the Earth's angels."

Maybe that was true of the humans who subscribed to angel fan magazines or happened to be avid players of the Legion card game, but most humans didn't spend their time memorizing the Earth's angels and their territories. They were too busy struggling just to get by. Colonel Fireswift was such a sourpuss. He was just annoyed that I'd gotten his questions right, and now he didn't have an excuse to punish me.

"Anyone can memorize a few names and titles,"

Colonel Fireswift continued. "But do you truly understand what those names and titles mean? Do you know how an angel is named?"

"Of course. When a Legion soldier becomes an angel, the First Angel bestows an angelic name on him or her. Windstriker. Fireswift. Sunstorm."

"Yes, you have already listed angel names, but you have not answered the question. How does the First Angel decide on a name to give a new angel?"

"Uh…" I thought about it—and honestly had no clue. "I guess she picks something that sounds impressive and has something to do with the angel's powers or something important that they've done."

"Obviously," he replied impatiently. "But how are angel names constructed?"

"With great care and consideration?" I smiled.

He shook his head like talking to me hurt. "An angel name is a construction of two elements, typically references to martial or magical prowess, or sometimes acts worthy of holy recognition. In my case, 'fire' and 'swift'. For General Windstriker, 'wind' and 'striker'. And for Colonel Sunstorm, 'sun' and 'storm'."

"So you're saying that an angel name is always a combination of two words?"

"Yes."

"What about Pandora?" I pointed out.

An agitated crinkle formed between his eyes. "As usual, you're the exception, the one who broke the rules." He looked at me like it was all my fault.

"Nyx chose my angel name," I reminded him.

"She took it from Windstriker's silly nickname for you. I have never understood why the First Angel picked him to be her favorite."

"Well, Nero does kick ass pretty effectively," I said helpfully.

Colonel Fireswift dropped another stack of books onto my desk. "To gain a deeper understanding of angel history, here is some light reading."

I gaped at the tower of books. "*Light* reading?"

"Merely an overview. These books are a quick introduction to angel genealogy."

"So, angel family trees and stuff?"

I took the book off the top of the stack and started flipping through it. To my chagrin, there was more text than there were pictures. If all the books were like this one, I'd still be working through the stack when I went into labor—about eight months from now.

"Yes," he said. "Now I suggest you get started. There will be no need to talk. In fact, I insist that you keep your mouth shut."

And with that said, Colonel Fireswift sat down at the instructor's desk and flipped open his computer. As I started reading through the first book, I heard him muttering complaints that Nyx had forbidden him from setting me on fire.

---

While looking over the Legion's angel genealogy charts, I noticed something odd. Really odd.

"Hey, Colonel, I found something."

"You have managed to remain silent for only fifty-six minutes." His expression when he looked at me was so searing, it nearly burnt my eyebrows off. "I expected better, even from you."

"Never mind that now. This is important," I said

breezily. "Twenty-four years ago, there were a lot of angels' offspring born. Like Jace." I pointed to his family tree.

"I know when my son was born," he said coolly.

"And all those Legion brats in my initiation group two years ago. There were eight of them, including Jace," I remembered. "All of those Legion brats were born within a month of each other. Now, that's just not normal. Angels are notoriously infertile, but then, suddenly, eight of them all had a kid at roughly the same time?" I looked at him. "How many Legion brats are in a typical initiation group? One?"

"If there are even that many. Most Legion initiation groups have no angel offspring in them," Colonel Fireswift said.

"But then, two years ago, there were eight at once. You have to admit that's weird."

For a moment, he looked like he was considering my statement, but then he brushed it aside. "It was a fluke of magic, a one time thing."

"I was born during that fluke," I pointed out. "And so was Jace."

"Irrelevant."

"Irrelevant?" I picked up the book and showed him his own family tree. "There has to be something to this."

"Return to reading. *Silently*," he added, his words frosty.

"Don't you ever question things?" I demanded. "Don't you ever try to figure out why things are the way they are?"

"That there is your problem," he told me. "Questioning things." He sneered. "Sticking your nose in things that aren't your concern. Digging around in other people's business."

Someone was still sour that I'd tried to do him a gigantic favor by telling him about the Archangel Trials.

"It's exactly that sort of wayward behavior, Leda Pandora, that landed you in this classroom to begin with. That is the reason Nyx insisted you take remedial angel studies."

"On the other hand, it was because of my *meddling* and *digging* that I moved up the Legion's ranks so fast and became an angel," I retorted. "So there is merit in my methods."

"There is no merit in your…*madness*." He bit out the last word. "You are the child of two deities. You would have become an angel nonetheless, no matter how stupidly you acted. Because it's in your magic. In your blood." He shoved the book back at me. "But now that you're here, now that you're an angel, it's your duty to learn how to behave in a manner befitting of your station. And it's my heavy burden to ensure that you do."

With that said, he reached behind his desk. For a moment, I thought he might be reaching for a weapon, but instead he pulled out a thick bundle of papers.

"What is that?" I asked.

"A test to see how well you've been paying attention today," he said with savage delight.

Awesome.

"Sit down."

I returned to my desk and sat down. Colonel Fireswift set the test booklet on the desktop. It was as thick as a dictionary.

"You may begin."

Grumbling under my breath, I set out to answer the

first question, a word problem. It was a complex, convoluted situation of angel dominance that I had to suss out. I quickly skimmed through the test. The next five pages were dedicated to several almost-identical questions. I had to determine the pecking order of angels in (slightly) varying scenarios. Oh, joy.

Some time later, a quick glance at the clock—the only wall ornament in the entire room—told me that I'd been working through the test for over an hour, and I'd hardly made any progress. It didn't seem to end. The booklet was novel-length. I might very well be sitting here all night.

It seemed Colonel Fireswift had found a way to punish me that hurt more than being set on fire.

CHAPTER 8

THE GREAT SCHEME

By some miracle, I did make it through Colonel Fireswift's test in time for dinner, but that said nothing for how well I'd performed on it. My only consolation was that the evil angel had to spend the next several hours grading the boring thing.

"He's a sadist, I tell you," I complained to Nero over a private dinner in my apartment. "You should have seen the test. It was full of completely convoluted situations that would never ever happen in real life. They were totally unrealistic. And for each of these convoluted, unrealistic scenarios, I had to sort out who was dominant and what was the right protocol. Ahhh!" I pulled on my hair. "I'd rather have spent the day with that damn metal door you had us punch over and over again back when I was an initiate."

"I'll bet." Nero's bright green eyes twinkled. Apparently, he'd had a better day out with Harker than I'd had stuck in a stuffy closed room with Colonel Fireswift. "But you're not supposed to be maiming yourself by punching metal doors. Or overexerting yourself in general."

"There is no greater exertion than holding myself back from jumping across the desk and strangling Colonel Fireswift while he's prattling on about obscure protocols that haven't been used in two centuries."

"To be fair, some of those protocols have *never* been used," Nero replied.

"Then why learn them?" I demanded, exasperated.

He shrugged. "Because they could conceivably be used."

"You're not helping," I pouted.

"I'm sorry, Leda." He took my hand in his and gave it a squeeze. "This is just one battle you'll have to face without me."

"If you loved me, you'd order me to punch Colonel Fireswift in the face," I told him solemnly.

He chuckled. "If you incapacitate Fireswift, Nyx will only send you another instructor."

"I know," I sighed. "And from the profiles of the Legion's past and present angels, there are, shockingly, a fair number of angels who are even worse than Colonel Fireswift."

The thought depressed me, so I shoveled more food onto my plate. I knew I was eating to make myself feel better, that I was trying to lose myself in the euphoria of delicious food, but I didn't care. Comfort eating was healthier than running out and punching Colonel Fireswift because he'd annoyed me.

Nero watched me eat. "Your appetite sure has increased."

Right, and there was that too. Being pregnant meant no tasty food within reach was safe from me.

"I know," I said. "And I thought I was hungry when I had the Fever. I never knew what hunger was until now."

Nero glanced sidelong at my belly.

"You can rub it for luck if you want," I teased him.

Nero extended his hand and set it on my flat belly. He looked so happy it almost brought tears to my eyes. That was the other thing about pregnancy: the crazy, unstable hormones.

"Have you felt any movement?" he asked me.

"Not yet. I think she's still too small. Right now, she's just busying herself being a blackhole for energy." I looked around and found some cake on the table. I took that too.

"Maybe you should try some vegetables," Nero suggested.

I frowned at the bowl of peas he'd offered me. "Nah, healthy stuff makes me queasy. What I need is cake. Lots and lots of cake." So I took more cake.

"Leda?"

"Mmm?" I asked between mouthfuls of red velvet cake.

"Have you been taking your vitamins?"

I swallowed, then said, "They make me queasy too."

"Perhaps, we should get you some of those gummy bear vitamins," said Nero. "The ones targeted to kids who refuse to take their vitamins."

"Funny." I took more cake. "Very funny."

"I'm not kidding, Pandora." His hand flashed out and stole my plate—and my cake. "A baby cannot survive on cake alone. And neither can you."

"Excuse me, your holiness, but have you ever been pregnant?" I tried to retrieve my stolen property.

Nero lifted the plate out of my reach. "No."

"Precisely." I abandoned my efforts to reclaim my slice of cake; there wasn't much left of it anyway. "Then you really don't know what you're talking about, do you?" I grinned at him as I licked the icing off my knife.

The corner of his mouth twitched. "You're incorrigible."

"Actually, I've been very corrigible today. I didn't punch Colonel Fireswift, not even once," I said proudly. "Despite all of his carefully-crafted digs at my character."

"Good." Nero ate a slice of carrot off the end of his fork.

I had to admit it, the man could make even healthy eating look sexy.

"Good? Oh, you like when I behave myself?" I winked at him.

He met my eyes, giving me a look that incited a very different kind of hunger deep inside of me.

I glanced down to make sure my top was zipped down far enough.

"You're trying to seduce me," he chuckled.

"Is it working?" I asked hopefully.

His eyes dropped to my chest, lingering there for a moment. "Yes." His gaze lifted to my eyes. "But I promise to be a gentleman."

"I wish you wouldn't be," I complained.

"You're not supposed to engage in anything dangerous," he reminded me.

"When Nyx made that mandate, she meant killing monsters. Not sex, Nero."

"Angels are far more dangerous than beasts, Pandora." His voice was a soft caress. "And I couldn't restrain myself. You are more beautiful than ever before."

I blushed. "Ah, stop."

He set his hands on my cheeks and leaned in, meeting my eyes. "I'm serious. You're positively glowing.

And your magic…" He drew in a deep breath, his eyes closing. His tongue slid across his lips very, very slowly.

"Like catnip for angels?" I asked.

"Better. It's like the Fever."

His hand was suddenly on my thigh. Temptation tickled his lips. His eyes were undressing me.

I decided I liked that. I liked it a lot. I moved off my seat and sat on his lap, straddling my legs around him. I kissed him, long and slow and deep.

Nero moaned against my lips. His hands locked onto my hips. He lifted me up, then repositioned me on his lap. He now held me in an embrace, no longer a sexy straddle.

"No, it was better before," I complained.

"Behave, Pandora," Nero whispered against my lips.

"I've been behaving all day," I told him. "Now I want to play."

Nero caught my misbehaving hands. He trapped them in his, preventing me from roaming, from exploring his body.

"Behaving myself is no fun at all," I complained.

"I know." A slight smile twisted his lips. "But you need to keep it up."

I stuck out my tongue at him. "Spoilsport."

Then I withdrew my hands, keeping them to myself, like the good girl I totally was not.

"I am confident in your ability to behave yourself," Nero said.

I laughed. "Who, me?"

"Yes, you, Angel of Chaos. You are far more sensible than you pretend to be."

"Sensible." I pouted out my lips. "How sexy."

"I'm serious, Leda." And his face told me he meant it.

"If you punch Fireswift, I'm not entirely confident he would remember he's not allowed to punch back."

Nero set his hand on my belly. He held it there, like he was trying to protect our daughter from harm. I smiled at him, then rested my head on his shoulder. He continued to stroke his hand across my belly. His other arm was wrapped around me, his hand massaging my back. Nero was obviously very worried. Worried about me. Worried about our daughter.

"All right. I'll be boring and sensible," I promised him.

I couldn't stand to see him like this. So…so vulnerable.

Nero kissed the top of my head. "Thank you."

"Tell me about your day with Harker," I said. "I hope it was better than my day."

"We searched Purgatory, where Bella believes Thea's grimoire to be, but we didn't manage to find it."

"Need some help?"

His chuckle was dark—and deliciously decadent. "You're trying to get out of another day of angel class with Colonel Fireswift."

"Yep," I said shamelessly. "But that doesn't mean I wouldn't be an asset in the search for the grimoire. I'm quite familiar with all of Purgatory's nooks and crannies. Remember, I grew up in this town."

"So did Bella. And she was with us the whole time."

"Yeah, well, Bella is more of an indoor kind of lady," I said. "Remember, I lived on the streets for a few years before Calli took me in. When your very survival is dependent on hiding from gangsters and other street urchins, you get really well acquainted with all the best hiding spots in town. You need my expertise."

"You make a compelling argument."

I looked at him and smiled. "I do, don't I?"

"But Nyx isn't going to let you skip your angel lessons to rummage through trash bins and navigate the town's underground sewage systems."

"That's because the First Angel has no sense of fun." I gave Nero a hopeful look. "But *you* do."

His thumb traced slow, soothing circles into my palm. "Leda, why do I get the feeling you're trying to get me into trouble?"

"I have no clue what would give you that idea, General," I replied. "Because you know how I'm always so well-behaved." I winked at him. "Especially with you."

His laugh was a purr, pure and simple. And it sent tingly sensations cascading through my body.

"You know." I cleared my throat. I'd promised I would behave, and so had he. I was already regretting that promise. "So this grimoire sounds pretty important. It could give us answers about Bella's past. What happened to her mother? How is it her parents don't realize she was born? And why did Ava manipulate events so that Bella was born? Why did Ava want Bella to be my protector? What is Grace's plan? What is Ava's plan?"

Bella had told me Ava said both she and Grace had a plan.

"All of this matters to Bella," I said. "It matters to me too. And, you know what, it matters to the Legion as well. Gods and demons are scheming, and all this scheming seems to revolve around me and Bella—around this Earth, this place in the universe. Why did I end up here? Why did my sisters, my brother, and I all end up with Calli? It all means something. Something big."

"I agree with you, Leda," said Nero. "I truly do. This

is big. Bella believes Thea's lost grimoire is the key to decoding the mysteries of Thea's wand."

Bella had been trying to get Thea's wand to perform magic, but so far she couldn't get it to do anything at all, including even turn on again. Ava must have given the wand to Bella for a reason, though none of us had come up with a reasonable guess as to why.

"Yes, finding Thea's grimoire is important," Nero said. "But what you're doing in that classroom is also important, Leda. As you said, you are at the center of this all. Whatever is coming, you are going to lead the charge—or defend against the charge. And to do that, you need powerful allies. Angels."

"I know."

"We angels aren't easily swayed. You are the Angel of the People, Leda, but you aren't an angel of angels. The other angels have known each other for years, decades, even centuries. You're an outsider. You need to learn how to persuade angels, how to charm them and inspire them. How to lead them. Because it's so very clear to me that this is all about you. You will fight the coming threat, but only with a powerful army at your back will you succeed."

"You know all of the other angels," I said. "You're part of the angel in-crowd. Won't they listen to you?"

"They might—when faced with a common threat. But *you* need to convince them, not I. Because it will be you leading them. Only you can convince them to follow you."

"That won't be easy."

"No, it won't," he agreed. "That's why you need to be in that classroom, learning strategy, etiquette, and anything else that will help you deal with the other angels. The day will come when you will need angel allies, and it will come soon."

"Finding Thea's grimoire is also important," I insisted.

"It is, and that's why Harker, Bella, and I are all looking for it." Nero gave me a crooked smile. "Don't micromanage, Pandora. You're not the only one who knows how to hunt for treasure. And the rest of us can tie our shoelaces without your help."

I chuckled at the image of angels tripping over loose shoelaces. "Ok. So what are you three fearless shoelace-tying heroes up to tomorrow?"

"We'll start again on the streets of Purgatory early tomorrow morning. Bella and Harker are back at Calli's house, planning our search."

I latched on to the most important part of what he'd just said. "Ooh, so Calli had Harker stay for dinner."

"For dinner. And to grill him," he said. "Calli had that look in her eyes, the same one she gave me the first time I was over for dinner at your house."

I laughed.

There was a knock on my front door. I rose from the table and walked across the living room. When I opened the door, I found Ivy and Nerissa on the other side. And Zane was with them.

"So, what's the scoop, ladies?" I asked.

"Nerissa and I have both cleared your brother, physically and mentally," Ivy told me.

"His magic is quite odd, a mixture of light and dark," Nerissa added. "But that's to be expected after spending two years with the Guardians. Zane said they'd given him their Life potion several times."

"His mind is sound," Ivy said. "No sign of manipulation."

Zane walked past them. "Thank you, ladies." He turned and bowed to each of them in turn.

Nerissa blushed. Even Ivy looked like she was receptive to my brother's charms.

"You both have boyfriends," I told my friends. "And, as for *you*..." I snatched Zane by the hand and pulled him into the apartment. "... you know you're only supposed to use your gifts for good, not evil."

"Sorry, Leda, it's been two years since I've had a chance to flirt with anyone who's not evil or brainwashed," Zane replied.

His sheepish shrug was so convincing that even I nearly bought his boyish charm act. Half of the sixteen-to-twenty-year-old ladies in Purgatory had had their hearts broken thanks to my brother, and the other half of them were lining up to be his next big mistake.

"I will forgive you," I told Zane. "This time. But you really must learn to behave yourself. Learn from my stellar example."

Nerissa snorted, and Ivy choked on her own laughter. They'd followed us into my apartment.

I spun around and gave them a good angel glower. "Excuse me, I will have you know that I am an angel."

"That's hardly news, Leda." Ivy coughed.

I stood up taller. "I'm very dignified." I turned to Nero so he could back me up.

"You're the most dignified Angel of Chaos I've ever met," he said silkily.

Ivy was laughing so hard, she started choking again. Nerissa slapped her on the back, her expression amused. But that good mood soured the moment her eyes fell upon the many half-eaten cakes on the table.

"Leda, I do hope you're eating more than cake," Nerissa said, her face stern.

"I sure am. I'm eating lots of ice cream too."

"Have you at least been taking the vitamins I gave you?" Her voice was strained.

"They make me queasy."

Nerissa sighed, then shot me a long-suffering look.

"Dr. Harding, you need to order her some gummy bear vitamins," Nero told her.

Her forehead crinkled in confusion. "Gummy bear vitamins?"

"Don't listen to him," I said quickly.

Nerissa didn't say anything more on the matter, but I could tell the wheels of her mind were turning as she tried to figure out how to get more of those unappetizing prenatal vitamins into my body.

"So, you're free, Zane," I said after Ivy and Nerissa left my suite. "What do you want to do now?"

"I'd really like to go home," he said solemnly.

"Great idea. Nero and I will join you. Bella is home from New York. And Gin and Tessa are there, of course. We can all be together again. Can you imagine how epic that will be, after all this time? Calli has been nagging me to visit for dinner, and tonight I will." I wrapped my arm around my brother. "And I'll come with the best present ever: our beloved Zane is back."

# CHAPTER 9

### REUNION

All of my sisters were so excited to see Zane again that they all tried to hug him at the same time.

"Come on in," Calli said from the kitchen doorway. She was wearing her favorite cooking apron, one with a bright flower-and-bee motif. "I've made all of your favorite dishes. Dinner will be served shortly."

"So I didn't miss dinner?" I said as Nero and I sat down in the living room next to Harker. "Awesome. I'm famished."

Zane's eyes twinkled. "Didn't you just eat?"

"No, that was ages ago," I told him.

He snorted. "Yeah, about ten minutes ago."

The dinner bell rang. I glanced across the room to find Tessa standing there, the bell in her hand.

"Dinner is served," she said.

"That was quick." I stood up eagerly. "You could even say the timing of our arrival here was *divine*."

Tessa rolled her eyes at my lame joke, then we all followed her into the dining room.

"I've been thinking about the past a lot lately," I said

after we'd all sat down to dinner. "Those memories that led me back to the Lost City mean something. It *all* means something. We need to decipher the past in order to understand the present—and maybe have a chance to predict the future." I glanced at Nero, who was seated beside me.

He was very quiet.

"What is it?" Calli asked. "You know what's going to happen?"

"Something of it," I said. "Maybe."

"I have had visions of Leda," Nero told my family. "And of our daughter."

"You can tell the future?" Tessa's eyes went wide. She looked impressed—and a little scared.

"No." Nero shook his head. "I cannot."

"Grace sent him the visions," I said. "The night before Nero and I met."

"Be careful, Leda."

I knew Calli wasn't just warning me about the hot basket of rolls she'd just passed to me.

"I know," I said. "Grace is a demon and demons cannot be trusted. Nor can the gods, for that matter."

"Grace sent me those visions so that I would take notice of Leda when she stepped into my territory two years ago," Nero said.

"She wanted to bring us together," I added.

"Yes," Nero agreed. "But that doesn't mean the visions are false."

I sighed. We'd been over this again and again, so many times before. We'd gone in circles, trying to figure out the truth, but we just couldn't. Since facing Faith, since gaining new magic, I had tried to see into the future myself, but to no avail. I didn't seem to have the power to look into the future like my mother did. Maybe my daughter possessed that power, between Grace's rituals on me and her ensuring my unborn daughter absorbed Faith's powers. Though we wouldn't know that for sure until she was born.

"I'm definitely being cautious where Grace is concerned," I told Calli.

"What do the visions of your daughter show?" Calli asked.

Nero's eyes were as hard as granite. "The universe at war over her."

"I don't need any powers of future sight to know that's going to happen," I said. "Our daughter has the powers of the gods, demons, and the original Immortals. And she might have the power to tap into the collective memories of the whole universe, the knowledge and secrets of all the great and powerful civilizations like the Immortals. That is, if Grace's plan worked."

"There are many things the gods and demons—or the Guardians, for that matter—do not know of the Immortals' magic and research," Nero said. "Things like how to make immortal artifacts and how to create all combinations of supernaturals."

"With that knowledge, someone could also give themselves new powers, even passive magic," I said. "So whether or not Grace is trying to manipulate us, it's no secret that our daughter is in danger from those who would seek to exploit her."

Calli nodded. "You have a point."

"See, that's why I need to figure out what happened." I cut open the roll on my plate, releasing a tiny cloud of steam. "What happened in the past holds the key to the future, to my daughter's future. And to all our futures, for that matter. I need to know everything so I can protect her."

"We will, of course, help you in any way that we can, Leda," Calli promised.

I spread a generous layer of Calli's delicious garlic butter over each half of my roll. "Tell me more about your friend, the one who led you to all of us. The man named Gaius Knight."

"Gaius definitely led me to each of you. I just don't know why." Calli frowned.

"He sent you to the orphanage where you found me," Bella said.

"He once warned you against taking a job, which is why you were home when my mother brought me here," Zane added.

"He got you the treasure-hunting job that brought you to the Sea of Sin." Tessa looked at Gin.

"Where you met us," Gin said.

"And one of his jobs led you to me on the streets of Purgatory," I finished.

"Yes, Gaius led me to all of you." Calli's eyes panned across us, the five once-children that she'd taken in. "And once you were with us, Leda, I didn't see him ever again."

"He used you," I said. "He put you into position, so you could raise us."

Calli frowned. "So it would seem. But why?"

"You must be important. For some reason, it had to be you that raised us, Calli. And we had to grow up together. " I took another roll from the basket, turning it over in my hand. "River told me that Zane was important to me. She said the bond we shared was important. And Ava told Bella that she made sure Bella ended up with me, so she could be my protector."

"Perhaps Gaius Knight was one of Ava's soldiers, working undercover on Earth," Bella suggested. "Ava is the Demon of Hell's Army, and she is quite close with her sister Grace. They could have planned this together."

"I'm not sure, Bella." I frowned at the roll in my head. "Grace said I was stolen from her. She blames Faris for it."

"Grace might be lying," Calli pointed out.

"True. It sure wouldn't be the first time. It's just… well, Grace wanted to perform even more magic rituals on me as a baby, but then I was taken away from her before she could. I don't trust Grace, but I do think she'd have wanted to keep her weapon—me—close to her all those years. If nothing else, then to better manipulate me. Something else is going on here. This is bigger than just Grace's plans for me."

"I'm sure it is, but right now it's dinnertime, and no demon, god, or other kind of troublemaker has a place at my table." Calli winked at me.

"Even this troublemaker?" I pointed at myself.

"You don't make trouble, Leda. Trouble just follows you around like a lost puppy."

I frowned at her. "Thanks for the pep talk."

Calli patted me on the back. "You're adept at catching trouble by the tail. Just as I know you will this time. I have faith in you, Leda. You will find a way to keep your daughter safe. But the best way you can take care of your daughter right now is by taking care of yourself. You're eating for two now." She shoveled some carrots onto my plate.

"She's certainly been eating enough cake for ten," Zane commented, grinning at me.

"What's that?" Calli asked him.

"Never mind him." I poked the carrots with my fork. "His mind is still addled from a whole day of nonstop flirting with Nerissa and Ivy."

Zane stuck his tongue out at me.

"Leda, have you been eating dessert before dinner?" Calli asked with a stern look.

"No. Not technically."

"Because she hasn't been eating the dinner, only the dessert," Zane said helpfully.

I resisted the urge to flick my carrots at him. "I should have asked Ivy and Nerissa to put you through another few days of tests."

Zane smiled at me.

"Come on, Calli, are you really surprised?" Gin said.

"Leda has the biggest sweet tooth of any of us," Tessa added.

"Perhaps a bigger sweet tooth than all of us combined," Bella said.

Harker nodded. "She did once stick a fork through my hand because she thought I might steal her slice of cake," he said solemnly.

"You *did* try to steal my slice of cake," I told him. "I was only defending my property."

"But would you have defended a lima bean so violently?" he asked with a slight, sideways tilt of his head.

"Of course not. Lima beans are disgusting." I smirked at him. "And since when did you become such a wimp, Harker? A fork through the hand is nothing compared to what an angel must endure on a daily basis."

"There's a fine line between a badass and a masochist," Harker said pleasantly.

I rolled my eyes. "For the millionth time, the fork

incident occurred when I was under the influence of the Fever. I'm sorry."

"Why is she apologizing to me?" Harker said to Nero. "I don't think Fireswift is doing a very good job of teaching her to be a proper angel."

"I think making him Leda's instructor is more of a punishment for him than it is for her," Nero replied.

"Congratulations. You're both hilarious," I told them.

They nodded solemnly. Apparently, they hadn't picked up on the sarcasm in my voice.

"Fireswift has never been able to handle Leda," Nero said seriously. "I should speak to Nyx and insist that I instruct her instead."

"Nero, you know Nyx will never allow that," Harker said. "You are even less able to handle Leda than Fireswift can, at least when it comes to having her under you."

The pun was clearly intentional. Zane chuckled, Tessa and Gin started whispering amongst themselves, and Bella blushed.

Harker managed to keep his face blank, of course. Not as blank as Nero, though. He just stared at his best friend like he'd lost his mind.

*Love has made you bold, my friend,* Nero projected telepathically, to only Harker and me.

*Maybe Nyx should send him to angel charm school too,* I suggested.

I was only half kidding. We were all angels and were expected to maintain a certain level of dignity at all times. We angels weren't supposed to let things ever get personal, not even with our spouse or children. And definitely not with our family from before we joined the Legion. We were angels now. We had to be detached and above all earthly matters.

Ok, so that was one rule I was definitely not going to follow. I loved my family too much to pretend I didn't care about them.

*You're right, Nero, of course,* Harker said in our minds. *I forgot myself.*

*I do that all the time,* I told him.

*But Harker is not you, Leda. The Angel of Chaos does have a little more leeway, given your title. Though not as much leeway as you take,* Nero added.

*I know,* I replied. *I'm trying to behave like an angel. Just not around my family, ok? And that family includes you too, Harker. You're like a brother to me.*

Harker looked at me, his eyes wide. *Leda, I don't know what to say.*

*Just say you'll be my brother.*

*As long as I don't have to be Bella's brother too.*

I allowed my laughter to echo in their heads. *Deal.*

I was drawn out of the telepathic conversation by the clinking of silverware and dishes.

"Does anyone feel like we just missed a whole conversation?" Tessa asked openly. "I wonder what they said."

"This pasta is quite delicious, Ms. Pierce," Nero said to Calli.

Tessa frowned, obviously annoyed that no one else wanted to speculate with her about what Nero, Harker, and I had discussed.

"Thank you, General Windstriker," Calli replied to Nero.

The two of them had their professional relationship all figured out, even though I knew they secretly adored each other.

Calli handed me a bowl of tortellini. "Leda, have some more pasta."

And so I did. Calli's cooking really was delicious, so good that my mind wasn't even fantasizing about dessert the whole time I was eating dinner.

I took another bite of pasta, then said to my sister, "Bella, did you change your hair again?"

Her hair had changed when she'd taken possession of Thea's wand, turning platinum. But it seemed to be darkening again.

Bella took a strand of her hair between her fingers. "It's slowly changing back on its own, growing darker and more golden each day."

Indeed. It seemed to be almost back to her natural strawberry-blonde now.

"I think when I first grasped the wand, its magic did something to me, something more than just change my hair," Bella said.

"Like what?" I asked her.

"I don't know. I have been unable to perform any magic with the wand since that first time. That might be why my hair has gone back to the way that it was."

"So you believe the color of your hair is linked to accessing the wand's magic?"

"I think so, in some way, yes," Bella replied.

"Maybe it's like how my hair changes with the magic I use," I suggested.

"I tried using my own magic, but none of that changed my hair. I think it's all linked to the wand's magic, not to my magic."

I nodded. "Well, the wand was your mother's."

"Ava told me it was." Bella's forehead crinkled, like it always did when she was deep in thought. "And Ava told me the wand would lead me to Thea."

"Do you think Thea left a message for you to find?" I asked her.

"I don't think so. Thea doesn't even know I exist."

"How does that work exactly? Because I am very aware of my child inside of me."

"You can feel her?" Bella said, her expression suddenly hopeful and bright.

"Not like that. She's not moving. She's too small. But I can sense her. It's hard to explain. I can just feel her there. Her presence." I drummed my fingers against the tabletop. "Thea was a demigod, a born angel, so I bet she could have felt you too."

"I really don't understand it. Ava told me I need to stop thinking like a mortal. She said I need to open my mind, to redefine what's possible and impossible."

"That's pretty cryptic."

"It is," Bella agreed. "How can I possibly know what I don't know?"

I dipped one of the carrots in the pasta sauce, which improved its taste considerably. So I grabbed the pot and poured sauce over all my carrots.

"I suppose this is where your search for Thea's grimoire comes in?" I asked Bella.

"Yes. Well, I hope so, anyway." She watched me drown the carrots with a strange sense of fascination.

"How did you learn that Thea even had a grimoire?"

"Actually, it came to me in a dream."

I perked up. "A dream?" I wondered if Bella's dream was connected to my dreams. "What kind of dream?"

"It was fractured, like a few fragments of memories. Flashes of the grimoire, of Thea with it. None of it was very focused or concrete. Mostly it's a feeling, actually. A feeling that the grimoire is important."

"Ava could be manipulating you."

"Oh, I'm sure she is. She could have asked Grace to send me the memory of my mother just as Grace sent Nero a vision of you and your daughter. But that doesn't mean I shouldn't try to find the grimoire. Like you said, the past is the key to our future."

"Yeah. And all of this is related."

"I think so too," said Bella.

"Is there anything specific you can tell me about Thea's grimoire?"

"Only that it has something to do with me. I saw that it came to town, here to Purgatory, right when I came here."

"So that you could later find it?" I wondered.

"Likely."

"Maybe it's Thea's game plan. Or Ava's." It was certainly food for thought. "Nero said you didn't find the grimoire today. Where in town did you look?"

Bella talked me through the places they'd searched in Purgatory.

"You certainly were thorough," I finally said when she was done talking me through her day, several minutes later. "I'm surprised you thought of Shadow Alley. I was sure I was the only one of us who knew that place existed."

During my days living on the streets, I'd hidden there often.

"I've gone to Shadow Alley a few times to heal the sick," Bella said.

"And the Sunset Tower?" I shook my head. "I've actually never heard of that place."

"It's not actually a tower," she told me. "The name is a trick. I healed a guy there once too."

And here I'd thought I knew Purgatory better than anyone. Apparently not.

"I actually found something at the Sunset Tower," Bella said.

"A clue to Thea's grimoire?"

"I'm not sure."

Bella reached behind her and took a folder off the side table. She opened it to reveal an old piece of parchment.

I picked it up, turning it over in my hands. "It's blank."

"That's why I'm not sure if it's a clue to Thea's grimoire. I know this kind of parchment. It's magic paper. There's some kind of shifting spell on it. And it's incomplete." She pointed at the parchment. "You need to layer multiple pages on top of one another to reveal the message. Until then, we cannot know if this is a clue to Thea's grimoire, or just a recipe for chocolate-chip cookies."

"That would be an awful lot of effort to go through to hide a cookie recipe," I pointed out.

I tried not to think too much about the cookies. It would only make me hungry.

"And yet it's still possible that this has nothing at all to do with Thea," Bella said.

"Yes." I slid my fingertips across the parchment. "It is." I'd met a few bakers who'd gone to great lengths to keep their recipes secret. "But I'm going to be an optimist and say it's a clue to Thea's grimoire."

Bella smiled at me. "I think so too." She glanced at Harker and Nero. "The angels do not agree."

"Why not?" I asked them.

"We never said it wasn't a clue," Nero said.

"We simply pointed out that it would be quite a convenient coincidence if it were," Harker added.

"Someone sent Bella memories of the grimoire," I told them. "Someone wants her to find Thea, or at least get answers about her past. That doesn't make it a coincidence; it makes it a well-laid plan."

"She has a point," Harker told Nero.

Nero watched me. "She often does."

I flashed him a little fang—and blew him a kiss. Then I looked some more at the parchment with Bella.

"If someone wants you to find the grimoire, Bella, the other pages might be in town too," Gin said.

"Yeah, but where?" I wondered.

"We will have to search the town again tomorrow." Bella's eyes shone with determination.

"Try the Junkyard," Gin suggested.

"And the Bazaar," Tessa added.

"There are some dilapidated old buildings by the old pond that would make an excellent hiding spot," Zane said.

Then he grabbed the cherry pie and planted it in front of himself. And he'd accused me of having a sweet tooth.

"People say those old buildings are haunted," Gin said in a hushed whisper.

Zane laughed. "People say a lot of things. I've been there. There's nothing haunted about them."

"How do you know?" Gin asked, her eyes still wide.

"Because he liked to bring his dates there to give them a good thrill," Tessa told her. "Made them want to snuggle up to you, didn't it, Zane?"

Zane shrugged, looking totally unashamed. "Naturally."

"Do you have any more snuggling spots in town, Zane?" I asked him.

I figured they'd be pretty out of the way. Pretty secluded.

Zane listed a few of his secret spots, then dug into the pie.

"Ok, well, thanks to Zane's dalliances, you have a few places to check tomorrow," I said to Bella.

Calli pulled out another pie, which distracted me so much that I nearly missed her next words.

"I think you're going about this the wrong way."

"What do you mean?" Bella asked her.

Calli cut a piece of pie and slid it onto Bella's plate. "You found your first clue, the parchment, at the Sunset Tower."

"Yes."

"Where exactly?"

"In a box buried to the right of the old sculpture of Valora, the former Queen Goddess. Harker sensed magic there, and we dug up the box."

"The Sunset Tower used to house the town's orphanage. It's where I found you, Bella," Calli said. "And you were standing to the right of that sculpture when I met you. Right there where you found the page." She glanced at the parchment on the table. "How many pages do you figure you need to put together to make that whole?"

"Four. This one plus three more," Bella said instantly. She'd always been good at math.

"Four clues. And four of you." Calli's gaze panned across Gin, Tessa, and finally came to Zane.

"Four? How about five? What am I, the family dog?" I grumbled.

"What you are is at the center of this all, Leda," Bella said.

"Oh. Ok. Good. I always said I wanted to be the center of the universe when I grew up," I said brightly.

"Ava told me I was to be your protector," Bella said. "What if Zane, Tessa, and Gin were meant to be your other three protectors?"

"You're assuming Thea's grimoire has to do with me," I told her.

"Well, this is all related, right?" Bella slid her plate of pie to me.

I gladly took it off her hands. "Right."

"My mother brought me here. To this house," Zane said quietly. "This is where we met, Calli."

"Wait, so one of the clues is here, at this house?" I asked.

"Zane was standing outside when I first met him." Calli was already on her feet.

We all got up from the table and followed her outside.

Calli looked around for a few moments, then pointed to the small flower bed next to the garbage can. "There. Zane was right there, in the flower bed."

"*In* the flower bed?" I said curiously.

"He was very young," Calli replied. "He thought it was an excellent idea to dig up my tulips."

Harker closed his eyes. "I can feel magic here; it's similar to the other page. It's very faint. I have to really concentrate to notice it."

Nero waved his hand, using his magic to scoop up the earth. A wooden box rose from the new hole in the ground and floated into the air. Nero directed our treasure into the house. We all followed the floating box inside. Bella pulled a piece of parchment out of the box. It looked exactly like the first.

"Incredible," Zane gasped. "I wonder how long the page has been hidden in there."

Bella began pulling potion vials out of the drawers. "I did a test on the first page. I'm not sure I believe the results." She squeezed a drop of potion onto Zane's page. "And yet here it is again."

Harker looked at the blue-green color of the dating-spell potion before it faded from the page. "The clues were hidden long ago, before any of you were even born. Someone knew Zane would be at that exact spot when you met him."

Calli frowned. "That's certainly unsettling."

I agreed. I didn't like to think that everything was preordained, that we had no free will or choice in anything that happened to us. But worrying about it wouldn't change anything.

"There are still two pages of parchment missing before we'll be able to reveal this document's secrets," Bella said.

"The final two clues." I looked at my little sisters. "Calli, those two pages must be where you were standing when you met Gin and Tessa."

Her eyes lit up. "The Sea of Sin."

"So, then, what are we waiting for?" Gin asked, her voice positively chipper. "Who's up for a little field trip?"

## CHAPTER 10

THE MAGIC PARCHMENT

"Are you sure you're up for this?" I asked Gin.

"Of course. Why wouldn't I be?"

"Well, you did die the last time I took you on an excursion," I reminded her.

"Leda, I'm a phoenix. I was born to be reborn."

"Still." Thinking about Gin dying made me antsy, so I was trying not to think about it. "Maybe Nero, Harker, and I should retrieve the pages."

"No way, those are *our* pages." Tessa put her arm around Gin. "Gin's and mine."

"That's right. You three might be some badass angels in the Legion's army, but we are *all* a part of this. Tessa and I. Bella and Zane too. And Calli. Someone brought all of us to her for a reason. We have to figure out why." Gin looked at our foster mother. "Right?"

Calli nodded. "Right."

"It's not safe," I said.

What had happened in the Lost City last night had made me cautious. It had reminded me how very real, how very dangerous this whole endeavor was. After all, we were digging around in some pretty powerful people's plans, and they might not like it.

"Our lives will never be safe, Leda," Zane said. "Not until we figure out what's going on."

"Remember how annoyed you were when the First Angel took you out of the field and grounded you behind a desk for your own protection?" Bella reminded me. "You knew you had to figure out the past to secure your daughter's future, but Nyx wouldn't let you leave. You felt powerless. Just as we do now."

"Point taken." I looked at my family. "But if we do this, I'm not sure I can protect all of you."

"You see, Leda, that's where you have this all wrong," Bella told me. "I believe we were meant to protect you, not the other way around."

"That's what Ava meant for you to do," I said.

"It doesn't matter whether it was Ava's idea or our own." Bella set her hand on my shoulder. "We will protect you."

"From Ava," Gin said.

"And all the other demons," Tessa said.

"Guardians," Zane added.

"And gods," said Bella.

"We're in this together, Leda," Calli told me. "Let them come, whoever those foolish souls who seek to use us all might be. We will show them what family truly means."

"I love you all." I drew them into a hug.

"Of course you do. We're awesome." Tessa waved her hand, opening up a passageway that transported all of us to the Sea of Sin.

The Sea of Sin was a vast savannah on the plains of monsters. It was home to beasts and warlords alike, the world's most horrible and vicious varieties of both. The dull, brown grass stretched across the flat expanse, as far in front of me as I could see. At my back lay a dense wall of jungle.

Treasures of the past were still hidden here at the Sea of Sin, just waiting for anyone bold enough to claim them. That 'anyone' was usually a warlord, though sometimes others braved the wild plains in search of brighter fortunes. They usually met monsters instead.

Calli stepped into the jungle. "I found Tessa and Gin in here."

Fifteen years ago, Calli had been one of those brave souls to seek treasure here. She'd found it too—and she'd found the monsters and warlord bands too. She'd also found two young girls, only four years old: Gin and Tessa.

We'd been walking for a while when Calli stopped. "Here." She pointed at the base of a very large, very old gum tree. "That's where I found Tessa and Gin."

"We'd escaped the warlord Hellfire's camp," Tessa remembered.

"We were so scared," Gin said, shivering though it was very warm here.

It must have been so horrible to live through that and at such a young age too. That's why Calli had asked Zane back then, when he'd been so young, to use his magic to make them forget. I hadn't liked it when Calli had admitted this to me and Bella, but after hearing more about what had happened to them, I got it. And, looking at my sisters here now, seeing their very real fear, I almost wished those memories had stayed buried.

"I can feel it. The parchments," Harker said quietly.

And I could feel something else. "Monsters."

Roars rumbled from deeper inside the jungle.

Nero turned in the direction of the beastly noises. "The monsters are close."

I waved my hand, using my magic to quickly dig up a box just like the last one. Then I set it into Bella's hands.

Tessa whisked us away with her magic. One moment, we were there in the jungle, surrounded on all sides by the beasts who'd broken through the trees. And the next, we were back inside our living room.

"Your magic is useful," I told her in appreciation.

Tessa winked at me. "Told you."

I could finally exhale. "That was close."

"Too close," Nero said. "Those were razor-backed wolves."

"I saw that," I replied. "The razors were very prominent on their backs."

"I will not put you at risk like that again." Nero looked worried. Very worried.

I smiled to show him I was all right. "There was no risk. I can control monsters, remember?"

"I remember that your control over beasts is not absolute. And right now your magic is both very powerful and very erratic. You cannot depend on it."

I took his hand. "But I can depend on you."

"Yes," he said fiercely.

"The legendary archangel General Windstriker."

He leveled a commanding stare on me. "Don't kiss my ass, Pandora."

"But, General, if you truly are to be my new angel etiquette teacher, I simply must." I reached behind me, into the fruit basket on the side table, and grabbed an apple out of it. I handed it to him. "I'm hoping to be the teacher's pet."

"You're trying to use humor to distract me from my point. It won't work. Your life is too important to me." He set his hand on my belly. "Both of your lives are."

I leaned in and kissed him slowly. "I know," I said against his lips. "It's important to me too. Both of you are."

His eyes met mine. Feather-soft, his hand traced my jawline.

Harker cleared his throat. "Do you two need a moment alone?"

"Yes, please," I said. "But make it more than a moment. Make it at least an hour."

Nero kissed me softly, then stepped away. "That won't be necessary."

*Easy for you to say,* I told him. *You don't have the libido of a pregnant angel.*

The hint of a smile touched Nero's lips.

"Leda, I'm sure you didn't mean to project that thought to everyone in the house," Harker said, amused.

I frowned. "Did I?"

"I heard it," Zane said.

Gin raised her hand. "Me too."

Calli nodded. "Yes."

"So did I," Tessa said happily.

Bella cleared her throat uncomfortably. So I guess she'd heard it too.

My cheeks warmed. "Well, shit."

Nero was right. My magic was all off. It was just too powerful right now. I'd tried to project my thoughts to only Nero but I'd overshot and sent it to everyone instead. This was worse than the Fever. It was no wonder since I had a baby magic powerhouse growing inside of me.

"So, what's the verdict?" I asked Bella, who'd meanwhile performed the dating test on the two new pages we'd collected from the Sea of Sin.

"They are as old as the other two," Bella reported.

Like there had ever been any doubt. This whole thing —my siblings' past—had been meticulously planned.

"Which makes all four parchments older than the four of you," I commented.

"Yes," said Bella.

"Those pages were buried for a long time, since before any of us were born." I voiced all my thoughts aloud. There was no point in trying to think to myself anyway, since I was apparently broadcasting to everyone. "Like someone knew exactly where Calli would find Bella, Zane, Gin, and Tessa."

"Or someone buried the pages, then made sure Calli would meet each of the four children at those exact spots," Nero said.

I nodded. "Someone like Gaius Knight. But Calli hasn't heard anything from him for so long, not since the mission that led Calli to me, the last of her children she found. After that, Gaius just vanished without a trace." I looked to Calli for confirmation.

"Yes. I thought he'd been killed on a job, but given what we've seen, now I'm not so sure anymore. More likely, after I'd taken you five in, I'd served my purpose and he had no reason to see me again."

"It seems Thea's grimoire is related in some way to not only Bella, but to Zane, Tessa, and Gin too," I said. "But why? Why did Ava lead Bella down this path? And what does the demon have planned for all of you?"

"Let's find out." Bella stacked the pages together. There was a flash of magic, then the four pages were one.

"Cool spell, but..." I stared at the still-blank page in her hand. "Wasn't something *more* supposed to happen?"

"The pages were supposed to combine to reveal the parchment's secret," said Bella. "I'd hoped it was a map that would lead us to Thea's grimoire."

"Maybe it is and we still need to decipher it," Harker suggested. "Look there."

Bella took a closer look at the page. "The parchment isn't entirely blank."

"It looks pretty blank to me," I told her.

"There's a...shadow. I can't read it." She shook the parchment. "The pages combined together into one, so there's magic at play here. There has to be info in there, secrets hidden inside the parchment. I will need to decipher the page in order for us to use it."

"So, a recipe for some really good cookies?" I asked hopefully.

Bella was already grabbing a few books. "There must be some way to expose the secrets of the paper. I must consult my books."

But Calli closed Bella's books and pushed them aside. "There will be plenty of time for that later. Right now, we have more pressing matters. This is the first time in two years that we've all been together, the first time in too long that Zane is with us. We must savor moments like these, for who knows when they will come again." With that said, Calli set a cheesecake on the table.

Some time later, after a lot of cheesecake—and a lot of familial banter—dessert was over. Calli had been right. It was about time we were all together again.

I helped Calli clear the table. I even did it without magic, just in case I accidentally overshot the sink and shattered Calli's favorite cake plates against the kitchen wall.

Zane had gone outside with Gin and Tessa. From my place in front of the sink, I could see them throwing small balls at the cans they'd lined up on the fence, just like we'd done back when we'd been kids.

Bella stood beside me, drying the dishes that I washed. It all felt so normal, so completely unlike everything else going on in our lives. It was nice to be normal for a spell.

I had just finished telling Bella about my misadventure with Faris and Grace.

"Grace claims you were taken from her," Bella said.

"Yes, but she doesn't know who did it. She did accuse Faris of doing it, though." I handed over the plate I'd just washed.

She grabbed a new, dry towel. "Ava claims Grace sent you to Earth."

"Then one of them is lying. Or both of them are."

"The question is why."

"I don't know. And trying to think like a deity gives me a headache." I winked at her. "And a god complex."

Bella laughed at my joke. She had such a pretty, proper laugh. It was not at all like the wild chortles that came out of me.

"All I know is Ava has a plan for me," she said. "And that this plan seems to involve finding Thea. Maybe my efforts to locate Thea's grimoire will help me find her. But that really makes me wonder if I should be looking for it."

"Ignorance is not bliss when it concerns gods and demons," I told her. "Our best weapon against their machinations is to arm ourselves with enough knowledge to realize when they're trying to manipulate us, so that maybe we can even outfox them."

Bella said quietly, "Knowledge truly is power."

"Yep."

"Still, I feel conflicted, you know? I don't want to do as Ava wants, but I *do* want to find my mother. I want to understand how I came to be without either of my parents knowing I even exist," she said. "And I want to know how Thea, who doesn't know her own daughter exists, could have created a grimoire made up of four pieces, each one hidden where Tessa, Gin, Zane, and I met Calli."

Tessa popped into the kitchen—literally—and grabbed Bella by the hand, dragging her away from the sink. "Stop worrying, Mistress Witch, or you'll give yourself worry wrinkles. Come out and play." Tessa turned a reproaching glance on me. "I would invite you too, Leda, but your overbearing archangel considers throwing balls at aluminum cans to be too dangerous for you in your *delicate* condition. You might want to have a chat with him about that. I think all that overdosing on Nectar has made him paranoid and kind of crazy. Sexy too, of course. But so crazy."

Then Tessa pulled Bella outside, chuckling all the way. I joined Nero in the living room. Calli was there too, grilling Harker.

"You and Bella have been spending a lot of time together lately," Calli said calmly.

Uh-oh. It was that exact kind of calm she exuded when she was preparing to shoot someone.

"So we have." Harker was leaning casually against the wall, doing a superb job of looking unperturbed despite Calli's sniper stare.

Calli pursed her lips. "Dare I ask what your intentions are?"

"You may dare, but you might not appreciate the answer," he said smoothly.

"Now, see here, young man—"

"I am over two hundred years old," Harker said.

She frowned. "What's your point?"

"I am not a young man. In fact, I am older than you."

"In matters of love, all men are boys, no matter how old they are," Calli said.

"Or how angelic they are?" He gave one of his brows an enigmatic lift.

"All angels are trouble," Calli declared.

"Even Leda?" Harker posed.

"Especially Leda."

"Hey!" I protested.

"But Leda is family," Calli continued. "She would do anything to protect us, just as we would do anything to protect her. We love her."

I hiccuped.

Everyone looked at me.

"Sorry." I hiccuped again. "Calli's words have made me a little emotional."

Nero wrapped his arm around me and I nestled up closer to him.

Calli's level stare snapped back to Harker. "But *you* aren't family, Colonel. How do I know you aren't going to drag Bella into all your angel drama?"

"To be fair, Calli, Bella is the one who's dragged Harker into all her drama," I pointed out. "And, from the looks of it, he has loved every moment of it because it meant spending time with her."

"You are hardly impartial, Leda. He is your friend."

"Which means I know him well enough to vouch for his character," I told her. "And you trust Nero, right? Nero can vouch for him too. They've known each other forever."

"Sure I can vouch for Harker. He only kills people who actually deserve it," Nero told Calli seriously.

Harker shook his head. "You call that helping?"

Nero shrugged.

"I know you care for Bella, but I also know exactly how the Legion of Angels works," Calli said to Harker. "If the Legion discovers that you are magically compatible with one of their female soldiers, they will order you to marry her. And where will that leave Bella?"

With a broken heart. I'd been so excited to see Bella and Harker together that I hadn't thought about that. But Calli had. And one quick look at Nero told me he'd considered the possibility too.

Harker was silent. He looked like he didn't know what to say.

"Nyx is in no hurry to find Harker a wife," Nero told Calli. "It often takes years to find a soldier compatible with an angel. We're not a very fertile bunch."

"Whether it takes years or centuries, it doesn't matter," replied Calli. "It will happen eventually. In fact, the longer it takes, the more Bella will grow attached to him. And the harder the end will be for her."

"It's pointless to worry about things that are mere speculation," Nero said. "Perhaps the Legion will never find Harker a wife. Some angels never marry. Nyx had all but given up on finding someone magically compatible with me." He looked at me with love in his eyes.

"I'm happy things worked out for you and Leda,"

Calli said, her tone softening a tad. "But most Legion soldiers are not so lucky. And it's certainly not pointless for me to be concerned about Bella's future."

"This is a matter between Harker and Bella," Nero said. "In the end, it's not up to you or me."

"That's my point. In the end, it will be up to the Legion."

"They both know what they're getting into. Would you deny them happiness now because it might not work out later?" Nero asked her. "If no one ever took a chance on love, then no one would ever experience love."

Calli was quiet for a moment before she spoke again. "Angels aren't known for taking a chance on love. You've changed, General. For the better. If more angels allowed themselves to feel emotion, the world would be a brighter, kinder place."

"Does that mean you aren't going to stand in the way of Bella and Harker?" I asked her.

"I couldn't stand in their way if I wanted to. Bella is as stubborn as you, Leda. She's just better at hiding it." Calli shook her head, and her gaze shifted back to Harker. "Take a chance on love then."

Harker dipped his chin to her in acknowledgment.

"All right. Who's up for a cup of tea?" Calli said brightly, as though she hadn't just interrogated Harker.

She soon returned from the kitchen, holding a tray loaded with a steaming kettle and four cups.

For a few minutes, we all sat there in silence, sipping our tea. I could hear the ding of balls hitting aluminum cans—and the crash of those cans hitting the ground outside. And laughter. Lots of laughter, mixed with joyous shouting and cheering. It was good to have the whole family together again.

But then the shouts soured. Followed by screams. And gunfire.

I jumped to my feet and ran for the front door. Nero, Calli, and Harker were right behind me. I threw open the door and rushed outside.

That's when I saw her. Bella was lying on the ground, bleeding out everywhere.

# CHAPTER 11

## THE ATTACK

*I* spotted two assailants, dressed like ninjas from head to toe in black, with only a small slit for their eyes. I ran toward them, but Harker was faster. He moved like a tornado, rushing forward as magic exploded out of him, tearing through the air toward the assailants like a ribbon of telekinetic lightning. Trash cans exploded, clotheslines ripped apart, and the heavy wooden fence split down the middle—but when the smoke cleared, the assailants were gone.

"Did Harker disintegrate the two ninjas?" I asked Nero quietly.

"No. He didn't use that kind of magic. They're not dead. They got away."

"How?" I asked.

"I don't know. They're just gone."

I watched, wide-eyed as Harker took a quick loop around the yard to make sure the assailants weren't somewhere nearby, lying in wait. When that was done, he rushed over to Bella and began healing her wounds. I'd never seen Harker like this. So out of control. So explosive.

"What happened?" I asked Gin.

"Those guys in black just appeared out of nowhere," she replied. "We didn't see them coming."

"They fired at us," Tessa added. "Bella was hit and went down."

"Who were they?" I wondered.

Zane's face was pale. "It all happened so fast. They were suddenly shooting at us. I didn't think to read their thoughts. And then they were gone. I'm sorry, Leda."

"It's ok." I patted him on the back. "It's not your fault."

I glanced around the empty, partially-demolished yard and sighed. If only Harker's spells had knocked out the assailants, then we could have interrogated them.

I joined the others, who were gathered around Harker. He sat on the ground, one arm around Bella. The other arm, glowing with magic, waved across her body. From the looks of it, he'd managed to heal her injuries, but she'd lost a lot of blood. Her clothes were stained with it, and her skin was very, very pale. Her eyelids kept dropping. She was only partially conscious. Harker lifted her into his arms, carefully and gently, and carried her into the house.

"This attack can't be a coincidence," Nero told me. "Just an hour after we assembled the four pages that will lead us to Thea's grimoire, even before Bella can try to decipher the page, she was attacked."

"You think someone doesn't like that we're digging into our past. And they're trying to stop us from getting answers."

"Yes."

"They targeted Bella." Anger hit me, hard and merciless.

"She is the person best able to decipher the page."

"I'll put a team on the house, to protect Bella." I reached for my phone.

Nero's hand caught mine. "Harker has made himself her protector. I doubt he will be leaving her side anytime soon."

"Nero, I just spent the whole day roleplaying endless angel scenarios of dominance." And my head still hurt from the memories in that classroom. "This is my territory. And Bella is my sister. I have to protect her."

"But she's Harker's mate."

I blinked. "Bella didn't say anything…"

"She doesn't need to say anything. You saw the way Harker attacked the assailants without a thought: quickly, so they couldn't hurt her anymore, and so that he could heal her. Harker isn't acting rationally at the moment. If you don't let him take charge of Bella's protection, he will attack you. And then I'll have to attack him. That would be…" Nero frowned. "…messy."

I'd seen Nero and Harker fight each other, shortly after I'd joined the Legion. Memories of that fight flashed through my head. *Messy* was right. And both of them had grown more powerful since then.

"Escalation," I muttered.

"Precisely," Nero said. "I'd rather avoid a fight with Harker. We're all on the same side here."

"All right. I don't think I could assign a better bodyguard to protect Bella than Harker. But I have to officially name him her bodyguard. Since this is my territory and Bella is my sister, I need to willingly delegate to him the task of her protection."

"Harker still gets what he needs and you don't lose face." Nero smiled proudly at me. "I'm impressed that you figured it out."

"I guess Colonel Fireswift is a better teacher than you thought," I said with a smirk.

Nero's smile faded.

I punched him lightly in the arm. "I'm just kidding. I learned everything I know about being a proper angel from you, of course."

Nero appeared mollified. Somewhat.

We walked into the house. Calli was waiting in the living room with Zane, Tessa, and Gin.

"How's Bella?" I asked.

"Sleeping in her bed," Calli replied. "Harker says she should be completely healed by morning. He insisted on keeping watch by her bedside until she recovers. You were right, Leda. He is a good man."

"He really is," I agreed.

"But why would anyone attack Bella?" Calli looked uncharacteristically shaken. She really loved Bella.

"Nero and I suspect someone doesn't want us to find the answers we seek, and so they tried to take Bella out of the equation," I told her.

"No one will be taking my Bella out of the equation, not under my watch." And shaken Calli was gone, replaced by eagle-eyed, kick-ass Calli.

"Leda and I will set up magical defenses around the outside of the house," Nero said.

I followed him to the door. "Be right back."

We left the house together.

"Shall I cast the defensive spells, or do you want to do it?" I asked Nero.

"I will do it. You should watch what I do."

"So I can learn how proper defenses are made?" I chuckled. My spirits had lifted the moment I'd heard Bella would be ok.

Nero gave me a flat look. "Paint-filled balloons are hardly effective, Leda."

"Hey, I only did that once, and it was pretty effective, if I do say so myself. You were very colorful for a whole week." I grew more serious. "But I see what you mean. There's a difference between pranking someone and protecting someone. I want my sister to be protected by the very best defenses magic can create, and you're the most qualified to do that, Nero."

Nero started casting spells, while I committed to memory everything that he did.

"I've been making a list," he said as we moved on to the back of the house.

"And checking it twice?" I flashed him a grin. "Was I naughty or nice?"

Nero watched me for a long, reflective moment, then declared, "You'd be at the top of both lists, of course." He started weaving more spells. "But I wasn't talking about that kind of list. I've created a list of baby names."

"That's very domestic of you."

"I collected the names of great warriors out of the Legion's history and sorted them by the highest rank and honors achieved by each soldier."

"And that's very angel-like of you."

"Would you like to see the list?" he asked seriously.

"Sure. If I can show you my list."

"I would be pleased to review our lists together," he told me, like he was giving a mission report. "From where did you gain inspiration when creating your list?"

"Well, I haven't made it yet, but I'm thinking of drawing heavily from angel literature."

"Historical records?" he asked.

"No, literature. As in fiction. There are a lot of novels with angels in them."

"Most of which are completely preposterous," he said stiffly.

"Of course they're preposterous. That's what makes them fun to read."

Nero stopped casting spells long enough to give me a hard look. "You read novels about angels?"

"Yep. All the time. I especially like angel romance books. They're so educational. Did you know angels can have sex while levitating? Why haven't we ever tried that?"

"Because it's impractical."

"Do you think our wings would get in the way?"

"For instance," he said drily.

"Even so. You should read these books, Nero. You could learn a lot about yourself from them."

He watched me, his face a marble mask. "You have never actually read an angel romance novel, have you?"

"No, I have not." I snorted. "But it was *really* funny when you thought that I had."

He expelled a long-suffering sigh. "Leda, our daughter must bear a dignified name, one worthy of an angel."

"And she will. I promise. I know it's important to you."

"Yes. It is."

"We'll take a look at your list," I promised, feeling a little guilty for teasing him earlier.

"And you will listen to the historical background of the soldier who bore each name on the list?"

"Of course."

He looked at me like he thought I might make another joke. When I didn't, he nodded in satisfaction. "Good. You will need to remain focused. There are two-hundred-and-sixty-one names on my list."

My eyes grew wide. "It will take months to go through all of those names and their stories."

"That is precisely why I started the list now. It gives me time to add more names."

"How many names are you planning on adding?" I asked him, trying not to panic.

"No more than a few hundred," he assured me.

"A…few…hundred."

"The Legion has a long and rich history, Leda."

"Few hundred," I muttered.

"One can never be too prepared for battle."

"We're choosing a name for our daughter, Nero, not marching into battle."

"Both tasks require a serious, disciplined mind."

I watched him closely. Something wasn't right here.

"You haven't made a list of two-hundred-and-sixty-one historical baby names, have you?"

"No, I have not." He snorted. "But it was *really* funny when you thought that I had."

"This is payback for my joking about angel fiction baby names," I sighed.

He wrapped his arm around me and pulled me closer. "Yes, it is."

"Gods, I love you, Nero," I laughed.

"And I love you, Leda."

"Just out of curiosity, do you even have a baby name list?" I asked him.

"I do. But it is considerably shorter. And carefully curated."

"Curated, of course. I should have known you wouldn't make a list that included the name of every female soldier the Legion has ever had."

"No." He looked around the yard. "I've finished setting up the defenses."

"We're lucky Bella wasn't more seriously hurt earlier," I said as we headed back to the house. "With your defenses up, that should keep those assailants out, no matter how ninja-like they might be."

"Indeed. No one will get past my spells," Nero declared.

---

We decided to stay the night to keep watch over the house, just in case the ninjas were crazy enough to try to break through Nero's defenses. We were taking the night watch, so the rest of my family could get some sleep. They'd need to look after Bella tomorrow, when Nero and I had to return to work.

I laughed as I spread the blanket over us on the sofa.

"What's so funny?" Nero asked me.

"I'm just thinking about how much this totally goes against all those angel rules I learned about. For us to sleep on the sofa rather than be given the place of honor in the house…oh, how Colonel Fireswift would cringe if he could see us now!" I rubbed my hands together in delight.

"You extract enjoyment from the most curious things, Pandora."

"That's what makes life fun." I frowned. "Of course, if Colonel Fireswift does find out about this, he will probably use it to fail me in my remedial angel studies. Though I already took the written exam. Gods, could he be planning a practical exam too?"

I shuddered to think of what *that* might include.

"Worrying about what Fireswift might or might not do is a complete waste of time and sanity," Nero said. "I would know."

I looked fondly at him. "Yeah, you would, wouldn't you?"

As Nero told it, he and Xerxes Fireswift had been arch enemies since the day they'd met as boys.

"I will take the first watch," Nero said. "You try to get some rest. Being well-rested and calm in the face of Fireswift's tyranny is the best way you can annoy him. And unlike your usual antics, Pandora, he can't even fail you for that."

I draped my arms over his shoulders and moved in, kissing him lightly. "I like the way your wicked mind works, Windstriker."

# CHAPTER 12

SURPRISE

*I* awoke early in the morning, as the first rays of the sun hit the house.

I sat up on the sofa and looked at Nero. "You were supposed to take the first watch, not stay up the whole night while I slept."

"I like watching you sleep." He leaned over me and tucked a wayward strand of hair away from my face. "You snore so contently."

"Angels don't snore, remember?" I kissed his hand. "I even read it in one of my textbooks."

Nero pulled me up and drew me in close to him. He kissed the top of my head.

I glanced behind us and saw Calli's bedroom door was open. So were Zane's, Tessa's, and Gin's.

"The four of them left early to go shopping for a potion Bella said would help her heal and calm her nerves," Nero told me.

Purgatory's potions market opened early.

"So it's only Harker and Bella here in the house with us?" I asked him.

"Yes."

"How are they doing?"

"Bella has been asleep all night. And an hour ago, I ordered Harker to take a nap because he looked like shit."

I laughed.

"Harker tried to argue with me, but he backed down when I told him he won't be able to protect Bella properly in that sorry state. He fell asleep immediately."

"Yeah, I can hear him snoring," I chuckled.

Nero's brows arched. "I thought angels don't snore."

"You tell me. You've read every book in the Legion's extensive library."

"Perhaps not *every* book."

"But most of them."

"Yes," he said, a bit smugly. "I had considerably more time on my hands before you came around."

I winked at him. "But considerably less fun too."

"True."

"We're effectively alone in the house." I gave him my best rendition of bedroom eyes.

"I know that look."

"What look?"

"The look on your face, Leda. It means trouble."

I fluttered my eyelashes at him. "Me? Trouble? Never."

"It runs in your whole family," Nero told me. "Your sister Tessa blew me a kiss as they all headed out of the house this morning."

"Oh, was my sister flirting with you?" Butterfly laughter fluttered in my stomach—or maybe that was just last night's dinner.

"Your sister *always* flirts with me, except when she can flirt with Damiel."

"Then I'll make sure to invite your father the next time we come over here. And your mother too. It wouldn't be a real family dinner without some drama."

"Leda, you enjoy stoking the fire far too much," Nero said, wrapping his arms around me.

"Was that an invitation to stoke your fire, General?"

He snorted. "I hope your jokes improve as the day progresses."

"I doubt it. I wasted all my weekly snark on Colonel Fireswift yesterday. And he didn't even flinch. Ok, maybe he did flinch once or twice. In horror."

"Fireswift will survive. And suffering builds character."

"More words of wisdom from your father?" I teased.

"Damiel isn't wrong about everything."

That was high praise among angels.

"Nice to hear you two are getting along better," I said.

"We haven't tried to kill each other yet this month."

"Oh, come now. Don't be so melodramatic." I leaned in and kissed him. "Even though I know melodrama is very befitting of an angel. Especially the male angels. You're such drama queens. That's why Tessa loves you all so much."

Nero's face was as hard as granite. "You don't say."

"But I think my sister is just messing with you and Damiel to get a reaction out of you."

"I wonder where she could have learned that," Nero said drily.

My smile was pure innocence. "I have no idea what you're talking about."

"The first time we met, you propositioned me."

"I did no such thing!" I protested.

"You did," he replied with a smooth smile. "When I asked why you wanted to join the Legion, you said, and I quote, 'I hear angels are great in the sack'."

"That was not a proposition. It was my aggravation shining through at being asked that question twenty million times."

Nero pressed on, undaunted. "And then you offered to tell me your bra size."

"That was a joke!"

"Later you made mention to me of a 'second date'."

I narrowed my eyes at him. "You know, for someone with such a picture-perfect memory, you sure have a talent for rearranging reality to suit your purpose."

"Those are hardly mutually-exclusive skills. In fact, they are quite complementary. As I've told you many times, Pandora, you have to know the rules inside-out in order to bend them to your needs."

"Or outright break them."

He nodded. "If necessary."

"Necessary." I chuckled. "While we're on the topic of the sins of our first encounter, my love, was it truly *necessary* for you to interview me by sending me after three vampires? What do the Legion's regulations say about that?"

"An angel is given great leeway when it comes to commanding his territory and everyone in it." His words were possessive, his eyes glowing with magic.

"I wasn't yours yet," I told him.

"Oh, that's where you're wrong, Pandora." He tucked my hair behind my ears, his touch featherlight. "You were mine from the moment we met."

He was so close, only a sliver of space separated our bodies. If I drew in a deep breath, I'd brush against him.

"And I was yours from the moment I saw you in my dreams, the night before we met." His voice was melodic, drawing me in. "Something reached out to me across time and space and drew me to you."

"Grace."

"No, not Grace. She only sent me the dreams. There are forces greater than gods or demons at work here, Leda."

"Don't allow the gods and demons to hear you say that."

"We were always meant to be, Leda. The song-and-dance between us that started the moment we met was only a formality."

I wet my lips. "A very fun formality."

"Yes."

I finally dared to breathe—and brushed against the hard wall of his chest. His hands were on my hips, gripping me to him. My fingers scraped down his back. His tongue ravaged my mouth.

"Nero, I want you so much," I muttered.

I hadn't had him inside of me since we'd found out I was pregnant. And I couldn't take it anymore.

I climbed onto his lap. "Every moment without you is agony." I ground myself against him in desperate anticipation.

"Stop it, Leda," he whispered.

But he wasn't stopping. His kisses had grown fiercer, his hands savage.

"Yes," I moaned. "Like that."

"We can't," he said, his voice rough. "You know that."

"I don't care about the rules, Nero. And neither do you."

"No, right now I don't care about any rules." He kissed me. "But I do care about you. I love you." He slid lower to kiss my belly. "And I love you," he said, speaking directly to our daughter.

He slid up and kissed me once more on my lips. Then he pulled me into an embrace.

"I knew I should have thrown my panties at you," I grumbled.

Magic flashed in Nero's eyes. "Don't make me handcuff you to the desk, Pandora."

Then we both had a good laugh over that particular memory.

"How scandalous of you to make out in Callista's living room," a voice echoed off the walls.

I knew that voice. I glanced over the back of the sofa and met Damiel's amused eyes. Cadence stood beside him, her hands folded in front of her, looking very serene.

"What do you want, Damiel?" Nero demanded.

"You don't look very happy to see me," Damiel said.

"How observant of you."

Damiel wasn't fazed. His smile persisted. "Being observant goes with the job," he said lightly. "I was the Legion's first Master Interrogator, after all. And, honestly, I'm surprised Nyx hasn't offered me the job again."

"The position is already filled," I told him.

Damiel gave his hand a dismissive wave. "By a brute. Xerxes Fireswift has all the subtlety of a bloody spiked mace."

I couldn't argue with that.

"The fact that Nyx hasn't offered you the job has

nothing to do with Fireswift—and everything to do with you," Nero told his father.

Damiel laughed softly. "Indeed. I'm not very popular with the other angels. Perhaps I should join Leda in taking remedial angel lessons." His eyes twinkled. He looked very amused—at my expense.

"Yes, you *should* join me," I shot back. "I'm sure Colonel Fireswift would enjoy telling you how a proper angel must behave."

Damiel laughed out loud. I thought the walls might tumble down from his amusement.

"Shush," I chided him. "You're going to wake up the sleeping angel."

"Sunstorm could sleep through an earthquake." But Damiel gave me a graceful bow; the walls stopped trembling.

"What are you doing here anyway?" Nero's eyes hardened. "And how did you make it past the defenses I set up?"

"The magic defenses guarding this house are very impressive, but you need to rethink your strategy, Nero," Damiel replied. "The alarms go off when someone or something physically crosses the perimeter. Your mother and I never crossed the perimeter because we teleported right inside of it."

Nero seemed to be mulling that over. He was likely already trying to think up a workaround to the inconvenience caused by teleportation magic.

"As to your other question," Cadence said. "We're here because we need to tell you something important."

Nero looked concerned, like he was expecting another disaster. Honestly, at this point, I wouldn't have been the least bit surprised.

"What's happened?" Nero said it like he was asking who'd died.

"Oh, it's nothing like that, Nero. Nothing tragic. It's good news actually." Cadence's gaze flickered to Damiel. She took his hand. Then she looked at Nero again. "I'm pregnant."

## CHAPTER 13

### APOCALYPSE IN THE PLURAL

Nero just sat there and said nothing. I could understand his surprise. Not long ago, he'd thought both of his parents were dead, and now they were not only alive, they were going to have another child. A sibling for Nero, right when he was about to become a father.

Nero's gaze shifted from Cadence, to Damiel, then back to Cadence. "How did this happen?"

"I trust I don't need to explain how babies are made." Damiel's gaze dropped to my belly, then his eyes met Nero's and he winked.

Cadence was more serious. "As you know, after your wedding, Damiel and I went on a quest to retrieve several immortal artifacts. During that quest, I had the Fever. And now we're going to have a baby."

I stood up, grasping her hands in mine. I gave them a squeeze. "That's great."

Cadence looked so happy she could hardly contain herself. "After Eva and Jiro learned of my pregnancy, they asked us to come back to them and train as Keepers. An

Immortal child has not been born in so long. This truly marks the rebirth of a dying race—or, as some people thought, a completely dead race. We had plans to find others of Immortal blood, those who escaped the hunters."

"But those plans can wait," Damiel said. "The fight will come here soon, and Earth will be ground zero for the war between the Guardians, gods, and demons."

"Damiel and I aren't going to sit this one out. This is my home first and it will always be," Cadence declared.

A sudden shrill, ear-splitting noise tortured my eardrums.

I covered my ears. "What the hell is that?"

"My alarms," Nero told me. "Someone has tried to penetrate my defenses. Let me wake up Harker to guard the house, then we'll check it out."

"No need." Harker came out of Bella's room, rubbing his eyes. "That racket is loud enough to wake the dead. Go. I'll keep watch here."

We all ran outside, our magic primed. We found the intruder at the front fence. It was Nyx. The First Angel was battling the barrage of spells Nero had cast to trap any and all intruders who crossed the property line.

"Windstriker, this is your magic," Nyx growled. "I can smell it."

Nero waved his hand, and his spells stopped attacking Nyx. The clotheslines disengaged from her wrists and ankles, snapping back into place. The trees grew still again.

The First Angel approached us. She brushed a broken string from the clotheslines off of her uniform, then said to me, "This is your bad influence, Pandora."

I glanced sidelong at Nero. "So this is more dignified than paintballs?" I said, snickering.

"More effective anyway," he replied.

I grinned at him. "Nyx is right. I have influenced you."

"It wasn't a compliment," Nyx told me. "My angels used to know how to behave themselves."

Her tone was stern, but her eyes were amused. That was the whole duality of Nyx. She was the most dignified of all angels—and yet she had a better sense of humor than she cared to admit.

We all walked back to Calli's house and went inside. Harker was waiting there, on the sofa. He rose to his feet as soon as he spotted Nyx.

Nyx looked around the house, perhaps remembering the only other time she'd been inside, after Nero and I had returned here from the Lost City. I'd been sporting a fresh wound from an immortal weapon at the time. I still had the scar.

After she looked around, Nyx's eyes fell on Nero and me. "Well, you're still here." She sounded a bit annoyed.

"My sister was attacked last night," I said, defensively. "We think whoever is behind the attack might try again."

"Don't be so feisty, Pandora. Of course you can't let your sister die."

I thought maybe Nyx was allowing herself to show sympathy, that she understood the importance of family.

Until she spoke again. "If the Angel of Purgatory can't even protect her own family in her own territory, then she would appear very weak to our enemies. And those enemies would grow bold."

Yeah, angel mind games. I should have known. So that's where this sudden burst of supposed sympathy had come from. It wasn't sympathy at all; it was strategy. Nyx wasn't letting out her softer side today after all.

The front door flung open. Tessa and Gin rushed inside, holding Zane between them. He was bleeding. Calli brought up the rear. She closed the door after her, then holstered her guns.

Tessa and Gin set Zane down on the sofa, and I immediately started healing him.

"What happened?" I asked them.

"We were attacked outside of the potions shop. Zane was shot," Calli told me.

"More ninjas?" I asked.

"Two people, dressed in black, yes."

I poured more healing magic into Zane. "I did not just get back my brother only to lose him again."

"The bullet only grazed me. I'm fine, Leda."

"But the people who did this to you won't be." I'd finished healing his wound. I rose to my feet. "What happened to the ninjas?" I asked Calli.

She frowned. "They got away."

"Leda, I don't think this is about Bella and the grimoire we're looking for," Tessa said.

"What do you mean?"

"Zane was there with us last night, right next to Bella when the shot went off. She pushed him out of harm's way. I think the ninjas were aiming for Zane, not Bella."

"Someone *is* after Zane." I clenched my fists. "The Guardians are after him. She was telling the truth."

"Who was telling the truth?" Harker asked.

"The rogue Guardian. River. She said Zane was important to helping me, that he was important to my success in defeating them. Now that he's out of the Sanctuary, the Guardians are trying to kill him."

"You may bring your family with you," Nyx told me.

"Am I going somewhere?" I asked.

Nyx didn't answer my question. Instead, she looked at Cadence and Damiel. "You didn't tell them?"

"We were leading up to it," Damiel said.

"What could telling us that Cadence is pregnant possibly be a lead up to?" I smirked at him. "Unless you're going to tell me that you're moving in with us, so we can all be one big, happy family."

"There's been an incident." Nyx's voice was hard and sharp, like a crack of lightning. "Two angels were killed."

My smirk faded. My chest tightened. "Who?"

"General Spellsmiter and Colonel Silvertongue."

The angels General Kiros Spellsmiter and Colonel Desiree Silvertongue were brother and sister. They commanded the territories of West Australia and East Australia respectively, dividing up all of the continent between them. General Spellsmiter was also the Head of the Vanguard, an elite squad of Legion warriors.

"How were Spellsmiter and Silvertongue killed?" Nero asked Nyx.

"I sent them to the Sienna Sea."

I'd never been to the Sienna Sea, but I knew of its reputation. Located in Australia, it was a vast expanse of red rock and no trees. And monsters. Lots of monsters. Some of the most ferocious ones in the world, in fact.

Nyx continued, "It all started when a Legion team found something unsettling during a mission on the Sienna Sea: the ruins of Darkstorm's fortress had disappeared."

"Who is Darkstorm?" I asked.

"Darkstorm was a rogue dark angel, turned Pirate Lord of the Sienna Sea," Cadence explained.

"I've never heard of him."

"That's no surprise. He died centuries ago, long before you were born." Damiel looked at Nero and added, "Before either of you were born."

"It happened during my first mission with Damiel," Cadence said. "I'd just become an angel. Damiel and I set off across the Sienna Sea to search for Darkstorm—and for the immortal weapon he'd stolen, the Diamond Tear. Darkstorm was killed during the mission."

"What do you mean 'was killed'?" Nero asked. "You weren't the ones to kill him?"

"No," Cadence said. "It was Eva."

Eva the Immortal was Cadence's aunt, her mother's sister.

"Darkstorm had a failsafe. His life force was linked to his fortress. When Eva killed him, the fortress was destroyed," Cadence said.

"But if this fortress was destroyed centuries ago, isn't it kind of to be expected that it's finally gone?" I pointed out. "Reclaimed by the expanse, eaten by the sands, and all that."

"The ruins were still there a few months ago." Damiel glanced at Cadence. "They looked almost exactly as we'd left them."

"What were you doing back there, Damiel?" Cadence asked him.

"Retracing our steps—every step we took together before you disappeared. I thought doing that would give me some idea of how to find you."

Cadence took his hand. "And you did find me. Or, rather, I found you."

They looked at each other with so much love burning

in their eyes, love that hadn't faded after two centuries apart.

Nyx cleared her throat. "Yes, the ruins of Darkstorm's fortress were right where you'd left them—until they weren't. Last month, a Legion team found the ruins had disappeared."

"Did the soldiers try digging a little deeper?" I asked.

"An extensive excavation of the area unveiled nothing of consequence. Every bit of rock, metal, and glass that had once made up Darkstorm's fortress had vanished, leaving no hint behind that it had ever even existed at all."

I frowned. "Ok, that's...creepy."

"Indeed. That's why I sent Spellsmiter and Silvertongue to investigate. When they did not return, I sent in another team of soldiers. That team found the bodies of Spellsmiter and Silvertongue. And this is even stranger yet: the angels' bodies were laid out at the center of Darkstorm's ruins."

"The ruins had returned?" Nero asked.

"As though they'd never been gone," Nyx confirmed.

"That is really weird," I declared.

Everyone was silent—in total agreement with me, I guessed.

"Wait, this happened last month?" I asked.

"Yes," Nyx said. "Last month, we discovered the ruins were gone. I sent Spellsmiter and Silvertongue out immediately. The Legion team found their bodies a few days later."

"So they've been dead for a month."

"Approximately."

"Two angels have been dead for a whole month."

"I said that already, Pandora," Nyx replied impatiently.

"Two angels have been dead for a whole month, and we haven't heard a thing. Now, I'm admittedly a newbie angel, but I'm pretty sure my remedial angel training books were pretty clear that angels' deaths were a rather public affair. A grand funeral with many odes to their excellence and achievements, and so on."

Nyx's lips drew together, very thin. "Generally, yes."

"You covered it up," I realized. "You covered up their deaths."

Nero and Harker looked at Nyx in surprise—and with a fair share of annoyance. Maybe even a little hostility. None of us here had been big fans of Spellsmiter or Silvertongue, but they'd been angels. And angels' deaths weren't simply swept under the rug like this. It was disrespectful.

Nyx gritted her teeth. "It was necessary. Humanity is agitated right now. The Legion is agitated. Between the threat of the Guardians, goddesses going mad, supernaturals killing one another, monsters breaching the gates, and all other sorts of hellish apocalypses happening right now. We can't afford for humans to lose even more faith in the Legion. If we can't protect ourselves, our own angels, then how can we protect the people of Earth?"

Nyx was right. Humanity's faith in the Legion was dangling by a thread.

And when the First Angel of the Legion of Angels started referring to the apocalypse in the plural, you knew you were in really deep shit.

"Their deaths must be acknowledged," I said.

"They will be," Nyx assured me. "But first we have other problems on our hands. Spellsmiter and Silvertongue weren't the only ones killed. They had a team of twenty highly-trained Vanguard soldiers with them."

This was just getting better and better.

"Those twenty soldiers' bodies were found at the reappeared ruins too, weren't they?" I said.

"Not just found. Displayed. I told you the bodies of Spellsmiter and Silvertongue were at the center of the ruins. And the twenty dead Vanguard soldiers were positioned in a ring around them, like the rays of some kind of perverse black sun."

I shuddered at the image.

"There's more," Nyx said.

I wasn't sure I wanted to hear any more of this.

"At around the same time, we found similar scenes like this all over the world. Dead witches. Dead vampires. Dead elementals. Dead shifters and fairies, dead psychics and sirens. And a group of dead ghosts we hadn't even known existed."

"How did you ever keep this all secret from the public?" Nero clenched his jaw. "And from the rest of us?"

"With a lot of difficulty and even more magic," Nyx said.

I closed my eyes and shook my head. So much death.

"There's more," said Damiel.

My arms were folded across my chest; my hands gripped my upper arms, like they were holding on for dear life. I didn't want to hear more. I really didn't want to know.

"These multiple massacres happened on many worlds, all around the same time," Damiel said.

"The massacres were coordinated?" Nero's voice was

so level, so cold, just like it was whenever he shut off his emotions.

"It appears so," Nyx said.

I dared to open my eyes. My heart was racing, pounding. "How many people died?"

Nyx shook her head. "We don't have an exact number, but it was in the thousands."

"Who did this?" I could hardly speak, could barely say the words.

"We don't know," Nyx told me.

I sighed. The weight of the universe, of all those deaths, seemed to press me down into the ground.

"But we do have a lead," she added.

I looked at her.

"One of Ronan's soldiers was on another world at the time," Nyx said. "He survived a massacre. He got a reading on the assailants' magic. We're going to use that magical reading to track them down."

I stepped forward.

"No. Not you, Pandora." She cut me off. "You're not going."

"But after what they did—"

"After what they did, you're going to stay far, far away from them. For the safety of your unborn child."

"I can take care of myself." I set my hand on my belly. "And I can take care of her."

"Whoever these people are, they killed two angels and twenty elite Vanguard soldiers. They killed thousands of powerful magical beings. They killed gods. And I'm not going to risk that they kill you too." Nyx looked at Cadence. "Or you, Lightbringer. Right now, there is nothing more important for the two of you to do than safeguard the future of the Legion: those children of angels."

One quick glance at Cadence was all it took to tell me she was itching to go too, to do something. To protect the Legion, the Earth, her home, and all of those things she'd said just a few minutes ago.

"Don't argue," Nyx said. "Yes, I'm talking to you, Leda Pandora. For once, just obey my commands. You will be staying behind, but you won't be idle. I have a very special assignment for you both."

I narrowed my eyes with suspicion. "What special assignment?"

"Stay alive."

"You can't whisk me away to safety, separated from everything and everyone," I complained.

"You're always in the thick of things," Nyx commented. "It's time to take a break from all that. Stop being the center of attention."

"I'm not trying to be the center of attention. Trouble just finds me," I told her. "And now someone is trying to kill my family. I can't stand by and let that happen."

"Which is why you're bringing your family to stay with you. Honestly, Pandora, weren't you paying attention when I said that?"

"Nyx, that was a whole ten minutes ago. You can't expect me to remember everything you say—or hang on your every word."

I had to tease her, especially since everyone was expected to hang on the First Angel's every word.

Nyx shook her head. "You're supposed to be studying to be a better angel, not making jokes."

"So I'm still going to be stuck with Colonel Fireswift

in that classroom, rather than actually making a difference? Great."

"You will make all the difference in the world. And Fireswift isn't going with you. He's coming with me."

I perked up at her statement, my optimism returning. "So I don't have Colonel Fireswift as an instructor anymore? Awesome. Maybe I'll get someone better."

"Like Damiel," Cadence teased.

I turned to Damiel. "It's not you, is it?"

"Well, the First Angel did consider me for the job."

"I considered it for a very brief moment, Dragonsire. But then I quickly decided that putting you in charge over another angel's training would ruffle quite a few feathers at the Legion. They'd all worry that they might be the next one I'd put under your black thumb."

"The other angels don't approve of Damiel's sordid past," Cadence said.

"His past as the Master Interrogator or as a demon collaborator?" I asked.

"Both," replied Damiel. "Never mind that I never collaborated with the demons. But, nonetheless, clearly the First Angel doesn't think putting me in charge would send the right signal." He frowned, as if he didn't agree with her decision. "In fact, it would be sending exactly the right signal—to our enemies. It would tell them that I don't pull any punches. With me at the helm of our army—"

"With you at the helm of our army, the Legion would collapse into civil war," Nyx cut off his grand speech. "You're not a very unifying force, Damiel."

Damiel seemed to be thinking that over, but clearly he wasn't completely sold on her argument.

"Nyx needs the cleverest angels on her mission to

take down the angel slayers," Cadence told him with a smile.

Damiel looked appeased by her words. His chest might have puffed out proudly too. "And take them down, I shall," he vowed solemnly.

Nyx shot Cadence a look that might have actually been awe. It certainly was amazing how Cadence could so masterfully influence the hardheaded angel Damiel Dragonsire.

"Ok, come on. Tell me who is taking over for Colonel Fireswift in training me," I asked Nyx.

"You'll have to wait and see."

That was foreboding. It must have been someone really nasty. Otherwise, Nyx would have just come out and said it.

"Windstriker, Dragonsire, time to go," Nyx told them. "We have some angel slayers to hunt down."

Damiel kissed Cadence goodbye. "Take care of yourself, my love."

Nero set his hands on my shoulders and met my eyes. "I'll be back soon."

I kissed him. "You'd better be."

He looked agitated. "I don't like leaving you here, especially now."

While I was pregnant, he meant.

"Nyx has probably put a boatload of security on me and Cadence," I told him.

"She has," Damiel announced. "Vanguard soldiers."

Wow, Nyx was really going all out. The Vanguard was usually reserved for all-out assaults. They were offense, not defense.

"Even so, I should be here, by your side." Nero touched my face.

I draped my arms over his shoulders and leaned in closer. "Haven't you often told me that angels should delegate, not micromanage?"

"Funny."

I kissed him again. "Don't be so cranky, Nero. I'm sure the Legion's best and brightest soldiers can hold the line here for a few days. And your mom and I do know a thing or two about battling the forces of evil."

"Don't take any unnecessary risks, Pandora."

"What makes you think that I will?"

"Because you are rather reckless at times."

"Not anymore. I'm a changed woman. One day of classroom training with Colonel Fireswift on angel decorum has cured me of any and all wickedness." To prove my point, I shot him a wicked wink.

"Cured of wickedness?" He gave me a crooked smile. "I can see that."

"Seriously, Nero, I'll be careful. I'll keep her safe." I set a hand on my belly. "And I'll keep Cadence and your little brother or sister safe too."

His mouth came down on mine.

But our kiss was cut short by Nyx's loud clearing of her throat. It was accompanied by the rumble of an airship floating overhead.

I sighed and stepped away from Nero. Nyx was sometimes such a spoilsport.

There was a puff of magic and feathers from the airship above, then a winged soldier flew down and landed before us. I looked at him, a muscular man with chin-length hair and a two-day beard.

"Hello, sweetness."

"Stash?" I grinned at him. "What are you doing here?"

Stash was both my friend and my cousin. He was also a demigod.

"I'm here for you, Leda."

"For me? Wait a minute. You're the one who's replacing Fireswift? You're the one Nyx got to teach me?" I tried not to sound too excited, but Stash was great fun. Much more fun than the glass-is-all-empty Colonel Fireswift.

"No," Stash replied. "Nyx didn't send me here. Faris did."

Nyx gritted her teeth. Uh-oh. I sensed tension.

"To protect you," Stash finished.

"The Legion of Angels is perfectly capable of protecting itself without the interference of Heaven's Army," Nyx told him.

Stash sighed. "I know you're annoyed with Faris for stepping on your toes, Nyx, but you have to admit that things aren't safe right now. Two angels are dead. And thousands more are dead on many worlds. This isn't just an Earth problem. It's bigger than that. The more people protecting the Legion's future unborn angels, the better. You do want to keep them safe, don't you?"

Nyx folded her arms over her chest. "You know I do."

Stash flashed her an easy smile. "Then relax and let us do our thing."

"Us?" I asked.

"I brought along a team of soldiers from Heaven's Army. You might remember some of those misfits." Stash winked at me.

I smiled. "It will be good to see the gang again."

"They're excited because being around you means being at the epicenter of action," Stash told me.

My smile faded. "Apparently not this time."

"I wouldn't be so sure. Faris wouldn't have sent us if he didn't expect trouble."

Nero gave him a cool look. He didn't like the idea of trouble finding me, especially while he was away.

I squeezed Nero's hand. "Why did Faris send you all—specifically?" I asked Stash.

"Would you believe me if I told you that Faris is worried about you and didn't think you'd accept his protection if he didn't send people to guard you that you actually like?"

I considered the idea, but rejected it immediately. "No." I thought about it some more. "Did Faris actually say that?"

Stash chuckled. "No, of course not. He just ordered us to go. Didn't explain himself at all."

Just as I'd come to expect of Faris. The King of the Gods didn't ever justify his actions to anyone, friend or foe, equal or underling. Not that he considered anyone to be equal to him.

As Nyx, Nero, and Damiel spread their wings, readying to leave, I wondered who would be teaching me to be a perfect angel during my seclusion.

"Ok, seriously, Nyx, any hints on who will be training me?" I asked her.

"You won't have a trainer," she told me. "Your angel training is over."

"Wow, I've never failed out of something this fast before," I commented.

Nyx actually looked amused. "You didn't fail. Colonel Fireswift has graded your test and was forced to pass you."

"I passed? Me? The Angel of Chaos? And Colonel Fireswift was the one to pass me?"

I bet he'd hated that. He'd probably wanted an excuse to torture me longer with all the long lists.

"But wait. If I'm not doing remedial angel studies, then what will I be doing?"

"It's been brought to my attention that the humans think of us angels as rather unapproachable and not to be trusted," Nyx said. "I'm not particularly worried about the first, but I am concerned about the second. Right now, we need the humans and supernaturals to side with us. There are a lot more of them than there are of us. We need them to sign up, to help us grow the Legion."

So apparently Nyx had come to realize the Legion didn't have the best relations with humans and supernaturals. Yeah, I could have told her that.

"It's critical that we improve our relationship with humanity now, as we will need everyone united in the fight against the Guardians," she said.

I folded my hands together. "So the Legion's fear and the Pilgrims' propaganda aren't enough."

"No." Nyx frowned at her admission. "We need to make people trust us, to work with us. Just as we need to work with the gods and the demons."

The gods and demons had formed an alliance against the Guardians, but no one knew how that would play out in the end. Gods and demons had spent many millennia at war, many millennia of mistrust. It wasn't so easy to put that all aside.

"Pandora, you are an angel who lived among humans for a long time," Nyx said. "That makes you the perfect ambassador, the perfect bridge between worlds. And that is the task I have set for you: to gain the support of Earth's people, so more of them join the Legion's ranks.

You are to unite the supernaturals to work with us, not fight amongst themselves."

"You don't ask for much, do you?" I laughed weakly. "The supernaturals have been fighting forever. And the Legion has spent its entire history making people afraid of them. Humans fear both angels and supernaturals. Now you want me to convince them to unite and all work together? That's a big step, Nyx. A step I'm not sure they'll be willing to take. The task you've set me might very well be impossible."

"Then it's the perfect undertaking for you, Pandora. We all know firsthand that the Angel of Chaos defies the impossible."

"As often and as thoroughly as I can," I declared proudly. "All right then. Let's do this."

## CHAPTER 14

### THE GARDEN LIBRARY

"We have a stop to make before we set off on the hunt," Nyx told Nero and Damiel. "We're meeting up with two additional angels: Colonel Fireswift and Colonel Dragonblood. Fireswift and Dragonblood will join us on the hunt."

I didn't know Colonel Dragonblood. He was the angel who was supposed to have run my Crystal Falls training, but at that exact moment, his wife had gotten the Fever, so Nyx had sent Nero instead.

I did know Colonel Fireswift, however. And as fun as it sometimes was to annoy him with my crazy ways, I wasn't sad to see him leave. I could only spend so much time with Fireswift before his personality really started to grate on me. And then I got edgy.

Nyx, Nero, and Damiel spread their angel wings and flew off, leaving me and Cadence with Stash—and a really big Legion airship.

"One sec," I told them. "I just need to gather up my family."

Bella and Zane were all healed up. The problem was

with the rest of my family. Calli, Gin, and Tessa didn't go willingly into the airship, at least not without protest. So I told them that my worrying about them, my concern that someone was going to kill them, was causing me distress and that was hurting the baby. After that, they all caved and came with me, even Calli.

Yeah, it was a dirty move, but I'd do what I must to keep my family safe.

We all boarded the heavily guarded and armored airship. On the way in, I spotted my friends from Heaven's Army.

Octavian and Arabelle were waiting at the door.

Arabelle was the team's only female soldier, but I'd never gotten the impression that this bothered her. She was good at what she did, though occasionally irreverent. That was one of the things I really liked about her, that she was a god but she didn't take that fact very seriously.

Octavian, the tall and slender soldier next to Arabelle, was as reckless as the gods came. He wore black armor that resembled a suit—and he wore his fire-red hair in a long, skinny ponytail. His words were usually seasoned with a healthy dose of sarcasm.

He winked at me as I stepped aboard. "Hey, Pandora. Looks like we're on angel babysitting duty again."

"We promise to keep you out of trouble," Arabelle said.

Octavian tapped the hilt of his knife. "If that's even possible."

The other godly soldiers were waiting in the hall. Devlin, the team's straight-laced leader. Theon, the quiet and reflective god, who enjoyed soap operas and caramel-flavored ice cream. The big and bulky twins Punch and

Patch, identical right down to the tattoos inked into their dark skin.

Devlin gave me a professional nod. Punch and Patch flashed me two sets of bright, shiny teeth. And Theon...well, Theon looked at me like I might explode—and take him with me. I could understand his caution. I did kind of blow him up the last time we'd worked together, but in my defense, it was a total accident.

The gods I'd met in Heaven's Army were so unlike the seven gods who sat on the ruling council. They were so down-to-earth, so normal, so fun.

I liked Stash best of all, of course. He was my cousin, after all, and I'd known him back when we'd all thought he was just another werewolf, Stash included. I'd been little more than a fresh Legion recruit when we'd met at a fairy bar, where he'd earned his money armwrestling for dollars and tending bar. Now he was a demigod in Heaven's Army, and I was an angel. My, how much things had changed in only two years.

I glanced back as Harker stepped aboard, Bella by his side. The rest of my family followed. As Harker showed them to their cabins, I continued down the corridor. I'd spotted another old acquaintance.

"Nice to see you again, Dominic."

The airship pilot was an old friend of Nero's. I wondered how he'd come to be here.

"Pleased to see you again too, Leda Pandora," Dominic said pleasantly. "A lot's changed since we last met. Heard about the bun in your oven. Good to hear it was Nero who put it there."

Dominic was hardly subtle, but what could you expect from a man who slicked back his hair with grease and wore a leather jacket made of orange monster hide—and had the matching boots to go along with it?

I tried really hard not to laugh. Because that would have been totally inappropriate. "How did you come to be here, Dominic?"

"I've been doing contract work for the Legion, flying your airships. Nero set me up with the gig. Pay's good. Get to meet all kinds of interesting people and angels. And…" He glanced at Devlin and his team. "…gods too. Well, just came down to greet you, Leda. I'd better get back to piloting. This ship won't fly itself, but it'll crash itself into a building real quick if I'm not at the helm." Then he dashed up a staircase.

And I kept walking with Cadence, following Stash.

Nerissa was the next familiar face I spotted. "Leda, good, you're here."

"Nyx ordered me to come aboard. So where else would I be?"

"Where else indeed! Just two days ago, you disappeared to run off to some monster-infested city. And you ignored my calls. And everyone else's calls. The First Angel was quite agitated."

"How could you tell Nyx was agitated?" I wondered. "She's always so calm and collected."

"And she was. Mostly. But her hair was doing that underwater flowing thing that it does, and it was floating in a distinctly agitated manner."

"So Nyx's hair follows her moods just like mine does," I noted for future reference.

"Her hair is a tad more subtle than your hair, Leda."

"That isn't hard." My hair changed colors quicker than a mood ring.

"So these gentlemen…" Nerissa cast a furtive glance

down the hall, where Patch and Punch were standing. "…have helped me set up medical facilities on board. So I will be able to monitor the progress of your pregnancy." She looked at Cadence. "The progress of both your pregnancies. Congratulations, Colonel Lightbringer."

Cadence nodded in appreciation of Nerissa's words.

"Wait a minute," I said. "You've set up medical facilities on board? Just how long does Nyx intend to keep me on this ship?"

"I didn't ask, but I figure it's not as long as forever."

"Very funny," I told Nerissa sourly. But I didn't dwell on that. I'd just had an idea. "Nerissa, how complete are these medical facilities?"

"Very complete. Don't worry. I have everything I could possibly need to ensure you have a safe pregnancy and birth."

"Are the facilities sufficient for you to conduct research?"

"Of course." A suspicious crinkle formed between her eyes. "Why?"

"Oh, don't worry. It's nothing crazy. I just want you to do some research on finding a way to increase the survival rate of the Legion's initiates."

Nerissa let out a weak laugh. "You don't ask for much, do you? The Legion has been around for centuries, Leda. Don't you think that our doctors would have found some way to improve the survival rate of our initiates if that were even remotely possible?"

"No, I don't think so," I told her. "Because I'm willing to bet the Legion never looked into it. Being part of the Legion was always thought of as something holy, like you were chosen by the gods or something. So all those initiates' deaths were just dismissed as people who were unworthy."

Nerissa frowned. "You might have a point."

"Of course I do. And my point is I think the Legion needs to stop being so full of itself. I think lots of people could contribute, lots of people could thrive with just a little extra help. It's time to dispense with the whole level-up-or-die mentality that has always defined the Legion. The angels think it makes us all strong, but in fact, it makes us weak. Our numbers are falling. Roughly half of our initiates die before they can even become a soldier. Many more soldiers die along the way. There are people out there, wanting to help us, wanting to protect their world. But many of them never get to serve. They die before they've even held a sword. We must find a way to give them their best chance. We have failed them for far too long."

"So, basically, you are going for a complete and total upheaval of the Legion," Nerissa said.

"Basically, yes."

"The other angels won't like it," she warned me.

"Let me worry about the other angels. You worry about saving lives."

Nerissa nodded. She set her hand on my shoulder and gave it a squeeze. "You're a good person, Leda."

I waved her away, smiling. "All right now. Don't go getting sappy on me."

Nerissa snorted, then she turned and walked away.

"Leda, this way." Stash extended his arm, showing me the way. "We're almost there."

We passed more armed Legion soldiers in each and every hall. The other godly soldiers had repositioned themselves to cover more of the ship too. I caught a glimpse of Devlin patrolling the corridor Nerissa had taken. And I saw Theon standing guard outside a dining cabin. Cadence and I kept walking. Stash stayed by our side.

He ushered us into a large room. If I could have picked one thing it most resembled, I'd have said a library. There were bookcases on every wall that wasn't a window. But there were also plants growing everywhere. And birds chirping. Ok, it was a garden library.

"It's beautiful," I commented to Cadence.

"Yes," she agreed. "It truly is."

There were lounge chairs and sofas positioned throughout the room, intermixed with the plants. Cadence took one long look out of the large window that covered one side of the room, then she sat down on a cozy sofa.

"Hey, Angel!"

My very large cat was resting on another sofa. She came out of her catnap just long enough to glance at me, then she closed her eyes and went back to sleep.

"Nyx made sure my cat came along," I said. "She really does love me."

"The First Angel *loves* that Angel is a powerful accessory to your magic," Cadence said.

Angel helped me channel more magic than I could otherwise handle. The cat was very useful—and very cuddly.

"Cadence, have you and Damiel discussed baby names yet?"

"Not yet. It's quite early." Cadence poured herself a cup of tea from the steaming kettle on the coffee table.

"Nero brought up the topic of names," I said.

"Did he?" Cadence smiled. "I'm glad he's so excited."

"He truly is. He once told me that he wants lots of children."

"Then it's a good thing you're both immortal. The Fever doesn't come around every month, you know."

"Good thing too. If mine did, Nyx would keep me safe in this fortress forever." I looked around the garden library. It was very nice, but it was still a cage.

"Try to think of it as a vacation, Leda."

Cadence picked up the newspaper on the coffee table and opened it. The front cover had a big story about the Angel of Chaos and General Windstriker, the First Angel's right hand angel, expecting a child. There was an accompanying picture from our wedding.

"You know what, being a prisoner makes me hungry," I commented.

But before I could raid the snack bar, two Legion soldiers stepped into the room.

Both were female, one tall with golden hair and one short with dark, nearly black, hair.

The tall soldier was a lieutenant. I knew that from the metallic emblem of a paw print pinned to her uniform. She had rosy cheeks and a long, blonde braid. Every strand of the braid was picture-perfect, braided with machine-like accuracy. My braids never looked that good. I wondered how long it had taken her to perfect her braiding technique. Despite the precision of her braid—and the crispness of her uniform—there was a warmth in the woman's eyes, a warmth that her time serving the Legion hadn't managed to cool.

The shorter soldier's psychic hand insignia told me she was a captain, a Legion soldier of the sixth level. She was also a dead ringer for another soldier I'd once met: Selena Singh. Except, Selena Singh had been a major in the Legion. And she was dead now. She'd died in the battle at the Magitech barrier at Memphis, victim to a particularly nasty Venom bullet.

"Who are you?" I asked the two soldiers.

"Lieutenant Alice Jones," the taller woman said.

"You look familiar, Lieutenant." I hadn't met her before, of that I was sure. But there was something distinctly familiar about her face.

She smiled. "You know my son. He looks a lot like me."

"Your son?"

"Jace Angelblood."

So this was Jace's mother. But that meant she was also…

"You're Colonel Fireswift's wife."

"I am."

I looked her over. She had a friendly smile and a kind face.

"You don't look evil," I declared honestly.

Alice Jones laughed again. Alice Jones, such a normal, homely name for the wife of an angel like Fireswift.

"Believe it or not, I get that reaction a lot," she told me.

Wow, Colonel Fireswift's wife was a nice person. Who would have thought?

I turned to the shorter woman. "You look even more familiar, Captain."

"You met my big sister Selena," she told me.

Ah, that explained it.

"I'm Captain Andromeda Singh."

Fancy name. And yet, it was all wrong. Major Singh's name was wrong, for that matter.

"You and your sister are Legion brats, right?" I asked her.

"We were."

"But you don't have an angel name," I pointed out.

"Our angel father went rogue when we were still young. Since that day, we've used our mother's surname."

She didn't look like my question bothered her. I supposed she'd gotten used to answering it. She sure was a lot nicer than her sister had been.

"Nice to meet you both, but what exactly are you doing here?" I asked the two women.

"The First Angel ordered us to report here," Lieutenant Jones answered. "Because we're pregnant."

"Both of you?"

Captain Singh nodded. "Yes."

"They are both married to an angel," Cadence told me. "Lieutenant Jones to Colonel Fireswift. And Captain Singh to Colonel Dragonblood."

So the two women were here for the same reason as Cadence and I were. Nyx had stuffed all of her soldiers who were carrying the children of angels into this airship. No wonder there were so many guards that we could barely walk down the hall without bumping into someone. This wasn't just about me and Cadence.

"A few months ago, I went to Crystal Falls for a training that was supposed to be conducted by Colonel Dragonblood," I said to Captain Singh.

"Yes, he runs that training regularly," she replied.

"But he didn't go that time because his wife had the Fever."

It was still called the Fever in non-angels who were the wives of angels.

"You're Colonel Dragonblood's wife."

"I am aware," she said, amused.

"But that Crystal Falls training was months ago. You don't appear that far along. Your belly is as flat as mine."

"My, you are as direct as they say, Colonel," Captain Singh told me.

I shrugged.

She laughed. "That Fever cycle was a bust, but oddly I had the Fever again last month. And that was a success."

"How often does it happen that two Fever cycles fall so close together?" I asked.

"I've never heard of such a case before," replied Captain Singh.

"Nor have I," Lieutenant Jones chimed in.

I looked at Cadence.

She shook her head. "It just doesn't happen."

Just as I'd thought.

"And you had the Fever last month too?" I asked Lieutenant Jones.

"I did."

"So did Cadence." I chewed on this new information. "Don't you think it's kind of odd that we all had the Fever at the same time, especially when the fertility of Legion soldiers is so sporadic and infrequent?"

"It is indeed odd," Captain Singh agreed.

"You think it means something?" Lieutenant Jones asked.

"I certainly don't trust a coincidence like that," said Cadence. "Especially, when it's completely unprecedented."

"But it's not actually completely unprecedented." I thought back to the legacy charts Colonel Fireswift had made me memorize. "Twenty-four years ago, many children of angels were born in the same month."

"That's when you were born," Cadence said to me.

"Right. There were so many Legion brats in my initiation class. At the time, I didn't realize how unusual that was. But now I know just how weird it really was. There aren't ever that many Legion brats in an initiation class."

"No, there aren't." Cadence's face was contemplative. "One or two at most, from the luckiest, most fertile years. Not eight like in your initiation group."

"You think this is about me?"

"Like I said, I don't trust coincidences. This isn't random. And you are the link between both occurrences of this phenomenon, Leda," Cadence said. "Back then as one of the children born. And right now as a pregnant angel."

I wasn't sure what that meant. Why were so many angels and wives of angels pregnant both times? And what did I have to do with it?

But there were no obvious answers, and there was no time to contemplate this now anyway. We had work to do, the work Nyx had set me.

I already had Nerissa working on the initiates' survival rate, but that was only one piece of the puzzle. We still had to convince people to join the Legion of Angels. We had to make them trust us. We had to make them willing to risk everything, to put their lives in the Legion's hands. Because even if a way could be found to make more initiates survive the Nectar, they would still be risking their lives as Legion soldiers. This war would not be bloodless. Hell, there was already blood everywhere, on many worlds.

"I assume Nyx sent you here to do more than be pregnant?" I asked Captain Singh and Lieutenant Jones.

"Indeed," Lieutenant Jones said cheerfully. Her pleasantness must have been the universe's way of balancing out her husband's unpleasantness. "The First Angel instructed us to assist you in your mission in whatever ways you required."

"Did she tell you what we'd be doing?"

It was Captain Singh who answered this time. "Our goal is to boost the Legion's recruitment numbers. A worthy undertaking."

"It is," I agreed. "But this isn't simply about fulfilling the First Angel's wishes. It's about nothing less than changing the future course of human history."

"Then let's get started," Lieutenant Jones said brightly.

"How did a nice person like you end up married to someone like Xerxes Fireswift?" I asked her seriously.

Her brows lifted.

"Sorry." I threw Fireswift's wife an apologetic look.

She laughed. "Don't worry about it. Xerxes tends to get that reaction from people." Her eyes twinkled as she added, "Our magic was found to be compatible, so the Legion ordered us to marry." She didn't look bothered by her fate. "You know, Colonel, I've never heard an angel apologize."

"Not even your husband?" I asked. I couldn't help myself.

"He's not an angel to me," she said solemnly. "He's just a man."

I couldn't imagine that, Colonel Fireswift as *just* a man. I couldn't imagine him as anything other than the humorless, hardass angel that I'd known for the past two years. Well, no, that wasn't entirely true. I had caught glimpses, here and there, of something else. Like when his daughter had died. The memory made me feel freshly sympathetic toward the woman in front of me.

"I was there when your daughter died," I said to her. "She fought so bravely. I'm sorry for your loss."

Her eyes were wide, trembling. "Thank you." She cleared her throat, steadying herself. "There's that *sorry* again. That's twice in two minutes, Colonel Pandora."

"She's still learning," Cadence told her.

"But you passed the angel test Xerxes set you," Lieutenant Jones said to me.

"I do better on tests than in real life."

She looked at me, *really* looked at me, like she was analyzing me. Then she declared, "You're exactly as Xerxes describes."

"That bad?"

"That good. Of course, he rants about your disregard for rules and regulations, your dirty fighting, your snide remarks. But reading between the lines—and hearing about you from my son Jace—I always pictured you to be a good, wholesome person who would go to any length to protect those she loved, no matter the consequences."

I nodded. "Yeah, that basically sums me up. I'm not exactly the model angel."

"You know the rules. You understand the etiquette."

"And in the end, you don't give a damn about those rules or etiquette," Captain Singh chuckled.

"You talked to your sister, did you?" I asked her.

"Selena also had her fair share of rants about you, Colonel. Personally, I thought she needed to chill out. She and I were always at odds on the topic of doing the right thing—and what that even meant." She shrugged. "We did not see eye-to-eye on a lot of things. We quarreled often. But in the end, she was still my sister, and I loved her."

"I know how that feels," I told her. "And I'm sorry for your loss as well."

The two of them had lost someone they loved during the same battle—and to the same poison.

"Selena died a hero, serving the Legion and protecting the Earth." Captain Singh looked at Lieutenant Jones. "They both did."

The two women nodded, unshed tears glistening in their eyes.

They needed a distraction from their pain, and Cadence delivered. "Let's develop our strategy to boost the Legion's recruitment numbers and make the First Angel's wishes a reality."

"Right," I agreed. "I already have Dr. Harding working on how to increase the survival rate in people who drink the Nectar."

"Do you think that's possible?" Captain Singh asked.

"I don't know, but we have to try. The best way to increase the Legion's numbers is to ensure more people survive the initiation ceremony—and every promotion ceremony after it. That will also convince more people to join our ranks. Think about it. The high risk of death puts off a lot of prospective initiates. Besides the children of angels, our initiates mainly consist of the desperate: those desperate for help, desperate for magic, or desperate for power. How do we convince people to join who just want to keep the world safe?"

No one answered. If there had been an easy answer, an angel at the Legion would have thought of it already. Or would they have truly come to an answer? Nyx had given me this task because she thought I was uniquely suited for it, given that I acted as much human as I did angel. Or even more human than angel, actually.

Maybe the problem was that none of those angels could think like a human anymore. It had been too long since they'd been human, assuming they'd ever been human at all, as it often was with the children of angels.

If that was the problem, then I just had to think like a human. What did humans want?

I opened up the question to the group. "Why don't many humans want to join the Legion of Angels?"

"They are afraid the Nectar will kill them," Captain Singh said.

"There is that, of course, and I already have Nerissa working on the problem," I said. "But I'm sure that's not all there is to it. It's bigger than that. Many humans would gladly risk their lives for the greater good... So maybe the problem is they don't believe joining the Legion actually serves the greater good."

"What do you mean?" Lieutenant Jones asked.

"Think about it. What do we call Nectar?"

"The food of the gods," Lieutenant Jones answered instantly, eagerly.

Her studious nature reminded me of my sister Bella.

"Right," I said. "Nectar is this holy, magical thing, far above humans. The people of Earth are fed exactly that line. Nectar is only for those who have been judged worthy. If you're not worthy of it, of these gifts of the gods, then you will die. We ask them to give up everything—their friends and family and everything else they have in their life—for the Legion. Not for humanity. For the Legion."

"The Legion protects humanity," Captain Singh said.

"Do we really?" I asked. "Sure, we take out any threats to the planet or to the gods' authority, but how much do we actually help the people? Every day, the Legion of Angels receives thousands of petitions from the people of Earth. Most of their prayers go unanswered. It's all part of some big show to demonstrate the Legion's power and the rareness of our gifts. Don't you see the problem? If the Legion wants people's help, if we want them to join in our fight, then the Legion can start by helping those people."

"But how do we do that?" Lieutenant Jones asked me.

"Remember all those unanswered prayers I just talked about? Well, that's about to change. We are going to begin our quest by actually answering the people's petitions for help. And we're going to do it in person. We're going to hold an open court, a court people can attend to petition for our help. We are going to put a face on the faceless Legion of Angels. A caring, approachable face, not that powerful, aloof face that's scaring them all away."

"You want to rebrand the Legion of Angels?" Cadence said, her mouth falling open in disbelief.

"Essentially, yes."

"Leda, the Legion is centuries old," Cadence said gently. "That is centuries of tradition. And the gods are even older. We're talking about millennia. The gods won't approve of your plan. The angels won't approve."

"The Legion needs the people. We need more soldiers. *This* is how we can get them. The gods can continue to be all-powerful and unseen, and the other angels can continue to scare the living daylights out of everyone if they must. But the people need to know there's at least one angel who has their interests at heart. An Angel of the Earth."

"Sounds like another nickname for you," Cadence said.

"Well, what's the harm of just one more?" I grinned. "Look, this is the path the gods set out for me. Faris stood up at my wedding and spelled it all out."

I remembered Faris's words that day well:

*You all know Leda Pandora. She has saved the Earth countless times. Her rise from humble human to holy angel will inspire you to join the Legion of Angels. Her selfless dedication will inspire you to persevere and level up your magic. And her compassion will inspire you to fight for this world. And for the gods.*

*For she truly is the Angel of the People. Her image will be everywhere—on banners and billboards, on buildings and trains. Not as the Angel of Chaos, but as the Angel of Hope. A symbol of harmony and perseverance. Of ascension. An example that lights the way for all hopeful humans to follow.*

"The gods made me the face of the Legion, the Legion's liaison to the people of Earth. They want me to inspire the masses to join their army and fight for them. This is how we do it. I will hold an Angels' Court, a place the people can come to personally petition the Legion for aid."

"Leda, this is a big change to sell to Nyx," Cadence said.

"Nyx gave me the authority to do whatever is necessary to increase the Legion's numbers. And I say letting people know we give a damn about them is necessary to making them give a damn about us. We can't expect them to put their lives in our hands if we can't take care of those lives. So, let it be known in all the cities of Earth. We shall hold the very first Angels' Court one week from today."

# CHAPTER 15

## ANGELS' COURT

*The* day of my very first Angels' Court had come. I climbed the long staircase to the Court Chamber on the upper level, where I would soon hear the first petitions. Alec Morrows, my head of security, kept pace beside me.

And Alec was sure in an agitated state. "The reason Nyx put you, Colonel Lightbringer, Captain Singh, and Lieutenant Jones on this airship is that compared to the buildings on the ground, the airship is easy to defend and hard for people to get in. And now you want to hold an open petition court here, inviting random people on board?"

"They're not random, Alec," I told him. "They're petitioners. They need our help. And we need theirs."

"That's very nice of you to actually give a shit about the general population, Leda, but how am I supposed to protect you when there are so many people coming on board?"

"I agree with Morrows," Stash told me. "Your decision to see petitioners will make the airship harder to defend. It will make *you* harder to defend."

Stash was at my other side. They had me surrounded, like they were afraid someone could jump out of the wall at any moment and try to kill me.

"Look, guys, most people who will come to the Angels' Court will have honest intentions," I said to them. "They just want our help. They just want their pleas to finally be heard. Sure, there might be some who take advantage of the situation. In that case, it's a good thing I have such capable protectors to deal with those people." I smiled fondly at them.

"Damn, she's good," Stash muttered. "Complimenting us."

"I liked you better before you went to angel manners academy," Alec told me bluntly.

I laughed. "It was only for one day, and it was hardly anything as romantic as an academy. Just Colonel Fireswift and I stuck in a stuffy room with lots of books and lots of test questions. Now, if you're both quite finished being pessimistic, I have work to do."

Stash shook his head. "We'll take care of the security. Don't worry."

I grinned at them. "Oh, I'm not worried. Not at all."

"Just in case, you should be armed at all times in the Court Chamber," Alec said.

"I have magic, Alec. I'm *always* armed."

Alec grunted in amusement.

I'd reached the top of the endless staircase. Finally. I crossed the massive hall that took up much of this level. Along the way, I spotted a familiar pair of female corporals.

"Anderson, Lexington, what are you doing here?" I called out.

The two soldiers snapped around to face me, looking very guilty. Anderson was so nervous, she forgot to salute. Not that I cared.

"Sorry, Colonel," Corporal Lexington said, her words rushed, like she was afraid she wouldn't be able to get them all out if she didn't speak quickly. "We took a wrong turn."

I glanced past them, where my brother Zane was standing, a croissant in one hand, a cup of coffee in the other. Wrong turn. Right. Since I'd come aboard the airship last week, I'd seen Anderson and Lexington take more than one 'wrong turn'. Those wrong turns inevitably put them within ogling range of Zane.

"I'm pretty sure Lieutenant Morrows assigned you to guard the level six corridor," I told them, channeling my inner angel. I even made my wings turn red, just for fun.

They gaped at me like I was going to set them on fire.

"But if you'd rather do something more fun, our guests from Heaven's Army are looking for sparring partners."

The two corporals looked at Stash, who flashed them a wide grin.

Lexington turned a little green. Anderson's nervous face was slick with sweat.

"No takers?" I waved them off. "Then back to the sixth level with you."

They hurried out of there faster than if I'd cast a telekinetic blast behind them.

When they were gone, Alec turned to me and snickered. "Channeling General Windstriker there, were you?"

"Hmm."

I had Zane in my sights. I pointed at him. He smiled back. I wiggled my finger, beckoning him to me. Zane did it, his manner as relaxed as the two corporals had been nervous.

"What's up, Leda?" he said with a casual wave.

"I just had to tell off a pair of corporals who were trailing you instead of standing at their posts."

"I saw." He nodded solemnly. "And might I say, you were *very* commanding indeed, Leda."

"I wouldn't have had to tell them off if you hadn't flirted with them," I told him.

"Me?" He indicated himself, looking like he couldn't imagine how this could possibly be his fault—how *anything* could possibly be his fault.

"Yes, you, Zane Pierce. In fact, you seem to have almost the entire female population of this airship under your spell."

"It's not magic, Leda."

"That was a figure of speech, and you know it, smart ass. In the last twenty-four hours, I have personally seen you flirt with the airship's receptionist and sweet-talk at least a dozen soldiers during their lunch break at the airship's canteen. Lexington and Anderson aren't an isolated incident. More than a few female soldiers on board are very sweet on you, and they regularly go out of their way to walk past your favorite spots, in the hopes of crossing paths with you. Many of them have learned your schedule. They know when you work out in the gym. They know when you visit the library. They know when you go to eat in the canteen."

He set down his empty coffee cup, then folded his hands in front of his body, like he had nothing to hide.

"Your soldiers are very skilled at the art of observation, a testament to your leadership."

"Zane, don't try to bullshit a bullshitter. I love you with all my heart, but I am immune to your charms."

He chuckled.

"Please stop making every woman you meet fall in love with you," I pleaded with him. "It's really inconvenient right now."

"I'm only being myself, Leda. I can't just turn it off, you know."

"I know." I sighed because it was true. Zane wasn't charming people on purpose; he was just being himself. "But maybe make an extra effort to turn it down a notch?"

"Very well. Just for you, dearest sister, I shall endeavor to be less charming." He bowed to me.

"Thank you."

"And may I say, you have a lovely glow about you today."

I gave him a flat look. "Very funny."

"I speak only the truth."

My charming brother seemed to be in a very good mood. He was probably so happy to be with his family again that he didn't care we were all stuck on board an airship.

The rest of my family was doing well too.

Tessa hadn't appreciated leaving her thriving event planning business behind, but she did appreciate her fully decked out suite with all the amenities she could imagine. She shared the suite with Gin, who'd quickly made friends with the airship's engineer and was learning all about how this flying miracle of magic and technology worked.

Bella and Harker shared another suite. Her brush with death had left him with a steadfast refusal to leave her side. For her part, Bella seemed to like having him nearby. She'd finally come to enjoy the fierce devotion of an angel. Of *her* angel. I saw the way she smiled at him. She was growing closer to Harker with every passing day. There certainly was something romantic about this airship, I had to admit.

"Good morning," Cadence said, closing in beside me.

Behind her, Alice and Andromeda were coming up the stairs. Yeah, we were all on a first name basis now. I chuckled to think of what Colonel Fireswift would think of that.

"Morning, all," I greeted them.

"So the big day is finally here. Are you ready?" Alice asked me.

"I am."

"And you're still sure this is the right way?" Andromeda asked.

"Yes. Swords and magic fireballs won't solve our problems. They won't win this war. What we need is to get all of us to march in the same direction. We need to be united by a common goal, something each and every one of us is determined to make a reality. We are spending our time answering the pleas of the Earth's people because when we help them, when we set this example of selfishness, they will feel compelled to follow us. Not because of magic or some trick, but because it's the right thing to do."

"Good speech, Pandora," said Octavian, who was standing guard outside the Court Chamber's closed doors.

I took a bow. "Thanks."

He pinched his thumb and index finger together. "A bit over the top."

I smirked at him. "That means a lot coming from you."

Octavian laughed. His outfit, a set of bright red battle leather, was particularly ostentatious today. And his hair was redder than ever before. Weapons covered him like a full armament of ornaments on a Christmas tree. He was sporting a new tattoo, a pair of wings on his neck. I wondered who he'd gotten to create that for him.

I addressed Cadence, Alice, and Andromeda. "The point of our Angels' Court is to put a face to the Legion and, specifically, to the angels. Most people will never see an angel in their entire life. Angels aren't real to them; they're just untouchable, far-off objects with wings, sitting on thrones. This Court will make angels more approachable, more human. It's all about how you frame the Legion to people. This will help us get those recruitment numbers up. I know it. And that's what the world needs: more people who are all fighting for the common good."

Cadence set her hand on my arm. "It's a good idea, Leda."

It had better be. We'd only spent every waking moment over the past week trying to set up this never-before-seen event. Tessa had helped too. She was good at marketing.

"It's time." Cadence turned toward the closed doors. "Let's go change the world."

Stash and Alec, standing on either side of the double doors, opened them for us. Cadence and I entered the Court Chamber, side-by-side. Andromeda and Alice followed behind us.

The room was, in one word, heavenly. Here on the airship, we were high up in the sky. I could see that through the rounded glass dome, which covered most of the room's perimeter. Bright blue skies shone beyond the glass, so surreal, so like a painting. Puffy white clouds floated all around the ship like fat marshmallows. Yum, marshmallows. Gods, I was getting hungry again. I should have had a bigger breakfast this morning.

There were four chairs set out for us, on a platform raised three steps high. Two of the chairs were at the front, then two additional chairs at the wings. Cadence and I, the angels, took the front seats. Alice and Andromeda sat in the other two.

Standing to the side of the platform, a sergeant with a big, booming voice introduced us. His voice filled the room so effectively, he didn't even need a microphone.

He started with me. "This Angels' Court is presided, firstly, by Colonel Leda Pandora, the Angel of Purgatory, the Angel of the Plains of Monsters, the Angel of Chaos…"

*Do you think you have enough titles?* Cadence asked me, telepathically.

I struggled to keep a straight face as the sergeant continued with my lengthy introduction.

"…the Angel of the People, the Angel of the Earth, and the Angel of Hope."

The sergeant drew in another breath, then started again.

"The angelic daughter of our great and powerful god Faris, the King of the Gods, the God of Heaven's Army, the King of Sirens, and the Slayer of Demons."

He skipped any mention of my demon mother. Though the gods and the demons had now formed a tentative alliance against the Guardians, demons still weren't very popular around here.

"The angelic wife of the archangel General Nero Windstriker, the Chief Marshal and the Executive Officer of the Legion of Angels. The Slayer of Traitors, the Victor of the Crimson Coast, and the Destroyer of Darkness. The former Angel of New York and the former Angel of the East Coast of North America."

The sergeant moved on to Cadence. "This Angels' Court is presided, secondly, by Colonel Cadence Lightbringer, the Angel of Light and the Angel of the Immortals. Formerly, the Sea Dragon, the Angel of Storm Castle, and the Angel of the Elemental Expanse."

*Do you think you have enough titles?* I quipped.

*Oh, he's not done yet,* Cadence told me.

"The angelic daughter of the archangel General Rhydian Silverstar, the Angel of North Europe, the Angel of the North Star…"

He went on for a while longer. Cadence's father was one of the Earth's oldest angels. He had lived through a lot of history—and had accumulated a lot of titles.

"The angelic wife of the archangel General Damiel Dragonsire." The sergeant had finally come to Cadence's association with Damiel. "The Archangel of the Whispering Winds, the Tamer of Dragons…" He went on longer. Damiel had been around a long time too. "The Founder of the Interrogators and former Master Interrogator. The former Angel of New York and the former Angel of the East Coast of North America."

The sergeant was forced to break for another quick breath.

"The angelic mother of the archangel General Nero Windstriker…"

*Oh, good, we're doing Nero again,* I said to Cadence. *He'd be glad that he's the only one who gets mentioned twice.*

Cadence's laughter rang in my mind. *Leda, behave yourself, or I won't be able to.*

"...the former Angel of New York and the former Angel of the East Coast of North America."

The sergeant was breathing again. Then he set off once more. "This Angels' Court is presided, thirdly, by Captain Andromeda Singh, the wife of the angel Colonel Vanir Dragonblood, the Angel of South Europe, the Angel of Crystal Falls, and the Hero of Hellas."

Andromeda's rogue angel father didn't warrant mention. Damiel, who'd also once been called traitor, had only been included because it turned out that whole treachery thing had been a total misunderstanding. I wondered how often that happened in the Legion.

"This Angels' Court is presided, fourthly, by Lieutenant Alice Jones, the wife of the angel Colonel Xerxes Fireswift, the Angel of the Central Territory of North America, the Master Interrogator, the Angel of Order..."

No wonder Fireswift didn't like me, the Angel of Chaos.

"...and the Champion of the Gods."

Colonel Fireswift must have been granted that lofty title because Faris had liked how he'd performed in the Gods' Trials.

"The mother of the angel Lieutenant Colonel Jace Angelblood, the Angel of the South Territory of North America and the Bearer of the Vortex Blade."

The Vortex Blade was one of four components from the weapons of heaven and hell. The official story was Jace had used the sword to slay a demon, but I'd actually been the one to charge the sword with my magic. Jace knew it, but I'd made him promise not to tell anyone because, at the time, I hadn't wanted to admit that I had that kind of power. The point was kind of moot nowadays since most people knew I was Faris's daughter and could therefore wield immortal artifacts. Plus I was an angel now too.

After several minutes of lengthy introductions, the sergeant had finally finished introducing us. He stepped aside.

"The Angels' Court may now commence," I declared.

The doors to the Court Chamber opened, and our first petitioner entered.

# CHAPTER 16

OUT OF PANDORA'S BOX

We listened to people's petitions the entire day. One man pleaded for us to cure the deadly disease that was killing his young daughter. That one brought a tear to my eye. There was also a fair share of petty disputes—from housing rights, to fights between neighbors, to requested repairs to public buildings. There were also a few complaints about loud werewolves, some blood feuds, and a very heated dispute involving a particularly wild goat. And everything and anything in between.

Afterwards, we retreated to our garden library and just tried to unwind.

"I must say, I never realized how discontented humanity was with, well, everything," Cadence said.

"That's because you never had to live in the real world," I teased her.

As the daughter of an archangel, Cadence had lived a very different life than most people.

Alice rubbed her head like it hurt. "This isn't anything like the real world that I remember."

"I am more exhausted now than I would have been after a long, hard day of training." Andromeda sipped from her teacup.

"I found the whole thing invigorating actually," Cadence said. "So many different, varying situations to solve. It was truly fascinating."

Alice chuckled. "The story about the goat was certainly fascinating."

"Some of their problems were quite silly, but others were troubling." Andromeda frowned. "How has the world become this place?"

"Because we mostly abandoned humanity to their own devices while we were busy sorting out all the supernaturals, demonic threats, and potentially world-ending events," I said. "But it's not too late to turn things around."

Cadence handed me a cookie. "I like your optimism, Leda. You never give up."

"Your son taught me that angels aren't quitters."

"I suspect you weren't much of a quitter before you joined the Legion either." Cadence poured me some tea.

"No, I wasn't." I winked over my teacup at her. "Especially when it came to quitting to talk."

"I hadn't noticed."

I snorted.

"Leda, has your cat grown bigger in the last week?" Alice asked me.

She was watching Angel in awe. My cat, who was taking up a sofa all by herself, was busily grooming herself. Considering her size, the project would take a while.

"Angel is always growing," I said. "I wonder if she'll ever stop."

My cat was the size of a tiger now. And, if I'd wanted to, I could have ridden her like a horse.

"We might assume that Angel's size is proportional to how much magic you might need to channel through her," Cadence said. "After all, she is your Companion, a reservoir for your magic."

"Right now, my daughter's magic is too much for my body, so Angel is helping there?" I wondered.

"Perhaps. You are a very young angel, Leda. And you have much more magic than your body is ready to handle. Remember, just two years ago, you had virtually no magic at all."

Well, no magic besides my vampire-mesmerizing hair that made the bloodsuckers want to bite me. Thank goodness I'd graduated beyond that useless kind of magic.

"You gained a lot of magic in a very short time," Cadence said. "That is bound to introduce complications. But given time, your body will ripen, allowing it to handle your growing magic better."

"I think we're all about to ripen a great deal." Andromeda patted her flat tummy.

"Depends," Alice said. "My belly never popped until much later."

"Must be all the yoga," I told her.

Alice had taught us all a few yoga moves, but I just couldn't make my body contort in that way. Cadence and Andromeda were much better at it. They didn't look like complete fools doing it, not like I did. If I weren't so damn stubborn, I would have stopped trying.

Alice smiled. "Yoga: good for the body, good for the mind, good for the soul."

"But bad for the ego," I muttered.

Alice set her hand gently on mine. "You'll get it eventually."

I had a wicked thought. "Say, Alice, have you ever tried teaching yoga to your husband?"

"Long ago, but he found inner peace too boring to hold his interest."

I laughed. That sounded just like Colonel Fireswift.

Angel glanced at us, then contorted her body into a pose even Alice couldn't have managed. Then my cat continued with her grooming, moving on to her wings, a souvenir from our time in the Lost City. She could now summon the wings at will, just like an angel. She really was living up to her name. Angel was a true angel cat.

"That is one impressive feline," Andromeda said. "What does she eat?"

"You know, the usual cat stuff. Cheesecake. Oranges. Ice cream sandwiches."

Alice's brows peaked. "The usual, you say?"

"Angel also hunts the typical suspects, of course. Turkeys, rabbits, ducks. Now that she's larger, she's venturing into larger wildlife. She's sometimes gone for hours at a time, hunting."

"Or maybe she found herself a boyfriend," Andromeda suggested.

"Now that's a thought. Good for her." My smile faded. "But where would the poor girl find another cat her size? Where could she ever hope to find a companion who can keep up with her, another cat who hunts deer, not mice?" I plucked a cheese-and-cracker sandwich from the coffee table. "Such is the burden of being a kick ass woman, Angel," I told my cat. "We can all sympathize."

My cat meowed once, then hopped onto the table and took a piece of cheese for herself.

I patted her head. "That's right, treat yourself to some comfort food."

"Talking to cats now, Leda?" Calli asked as she sat down beside me.

"Calli, so glad you could join us. Have a snack."

She selected a healthy apple slice. My foster mother always set a good example.

"I have a job for you." I wiggled my eyebrows up and down. "A really good one."

Calli had been nagging me to give her something to do. She got bored if she didn't have any work to do—or people to take care of.

"I need you to contact as many bounty hunters as you can trust. I'm appointing you my Head of Freelance Stuff."

"A very important-sounding title," Calli commented.

"Give yourself any title you want."

"I think I'll go with the Director of Acquisition and Reclamation."

I whistled. "Fancy."

I handed Calli a folder of missions Alice had put together from today's petitions. Colonel Fireswift's wife was so orderly and organized. That must have been one reason he was so in love with her.

"There are a few good jobs in here," I told Calli. "A search and rescue operation to start. And a few missing person cases. I'm sure I'll soon have more for you."

Calli leafed through the folder. "Sounds pretty straightforward."

"Let me know how much you need to budget for the bounty hunters."

"Will do." She put down the folder. "Leda, I appreciate that you're giving me something to do, but you know I still don't like being stuck here in this protective bubble."

"Neither do I, but you raised me to always make the best of any situation. And right now, even stuck here on this airship, we can all make a big difference. We can turn around the lives of so many people of Earth. We can change their fate."

"Well, it is hard to argue with my own advice. And I'm very proud of what you're trying to do for all these people who've never had anyone look out for them." Calli grabbed the folder and rose to her feet. She tapped the front cover. "I'll get back to you on this," she said, offering me a smile.

Then she left the room.

I turned to the other ladies. "Where were we?"

"Your cat has eaten all of our cheese," Andromeda told me. "That's where we are."

"Not all of our cheese," I said. "Stash ate at least half of it himself."

I glanced back at Stash, who popped one of the aforementioned cheese pieces into his mouth. From the Court Chamber to the garden library, he was never far from my side. When Faris had assigned him to watch over me, he must have known my cousin would take my personal safety very seriously.

In another life, my father's gesture might have been heartwarming, but this wasn't another life. It was my crazy life. Faris only cared about keeping me alive because he saw me as an investment, as a unique weapon—and that went double for my unborn child.

"Pandora, when we were assigned the task of protecting the Angel of Chaos, I expected something a lot more exciting," Punch complained. "Instead we get a long, boring Angels' Court and tiny hors d'oeuvres."

"You seem to be enjoying those hors d'oeuvres," I pointed out. "You've had at least twenty of them."

"Because they're tiny." Punch squeezed two fingers close together. "And I'm big." He spread his arms wide.

"That's my brother Punch in a nutshell," Patch declared.

The whole team from Heaven's Army was here in the garden library right now. A few of them had been stationed in the Court Chamber at any given time during the day.

"I was sure something would attack the airship by now," Punch said. "Seriously, I'm disappointed. You're not living up to your name, Pandora. You're supposed to be the de facto trouble magnet. That's why I took this assignment."

I smirked at him. "I thought you took this assignment because when Faris says jump, you ask, how high?"

Punch snorted and patted me hard on the shoulder.

"I must agree with Punch," Octavian said.

Arabelle laughed. "That's a first."

Octavian's fingers drummed on the knife strapped to his arm. "I too was hoping for something more exciting than the Lords' Gala."

"But this is so much more important than fighting monsters or listening to bickering gods," I told them. "We are helping people who can't help themselves."

"Why ever would you want to help someone who can't even help themselves?" Devlin asked me.

"Indeed," said Theon. "How can the humans help you if they can't help themselves? What's the gain in that?"

I rose to my feet. "Because it's the right thing to do. It's not all about gain. It's about mercy. And compassion. Maybe helping some of those people will allow them to turn their fortunes around. And maybe they will help us later. But more importantly, helping people shows everyone that the Legion cares. Then other people will come forward to help us, to volunteer, because they know we have their back, that we will look out for them and for the greater good. Nyx told me to build up the trust of Earth's people, and that's exactly what I'm going to do."

Arabelle looked me over, then declared, "You might be wiser than your chaotic appearance suggests."

"And your out-of-the-box thinking *does* often seem to work out," Devlin said. "You, Leda Pandora, might be just what this situation calls for."

That was high praise from the rule-abiding team leader of these godly soldiers. I smiled at him to let him know I appreciated his words.

The door opened, and two of the kitchen staff walked in, carrying tasty reinforcements.

"The next round of food is here, thank the gods," I said.

Octavian's mouth twisted into a smile. "You're welcome, Pandora."

I snorted.

Bella and Harker stepped into the room, right behind the people from the kitchen. Bella looked frazzled. Her hair, finally back to strawberry-blonde, was half falling out of her bun. It was no wonder. She'd tried to secure the bun with a pencil. My usually-composed sister was quite unravelled at the moment.

"What's wrong?" I asked her.

"Nothing is wrong, Leda. I've done it!" Bella grabbed a handful of crackers and stuffed them into her mouth.

"She hasn't eaten all day," Harker explained.

"How could I eat when I knew I was so close?" She grabbed more crackers.

"Close to what?" I asked her. "What have you done?"

"I finally found the right chemical to expose the parchment we put together in Purgatory. I've made it reveal its secrets." She grabbed a blueberry muffin and quickly ate it too.

"And?" I asked her. "Where does the map lead?"

"It's not a where, Leda. It's a who."

I frowned in confusion.

Bella showed me the parchment. The image now prominent on the surface was a hand-drawn illustration of a woman's face.

"This parchment is older than we are, right?" I asked her.

"Yes."

I knew who the woman in the drawing was: Arina Phoenix. Arina couldn't have been a day over thirty, but the picture of her on this decades-old parchment showed her exactly as she appeared today.

# CHAPTER 17

## THE WOMAN IN THE DRAWING

*I* wondered how this parchment could have a drawing of Arina on it as she appeared now. She couldn't possibly be old enough to be the person from this very old document. She was mortal. She aged.

Granted, lately there had been a lot of other things that didn't make much sense.

Bella was still speaking, so overcome with enthusiasm that she hadn't even noticed that I'd grown rather quiet. She should have known better. I rarely shut up.

"This woman, whoever she is, must know something about the wand. It's not Thea. I've seen pictures of what she looks like."

I tapped the parchment. "Her name is Arina."

"You know her?" Bella said, surprised.

"She helped me out not so long ago."

"And this Arina woman knows Thea?"

"I don't know. Maybe. Arina isn't from this world," I told her. "Maybe her path once crossed with Thea's."

"We have to speak to her. She could lead us to Thea."

Bella looked hopeful. No, more than just hopeful. She was practically bursting with eagerness.

"Or maybe she doesn't know Thea," I said. "Maybe the page is showing us Arina because she is an expert in immortal artifacts. Her magic allows her to trace the history of any person's or any object's magic—basically, how it got where it is today. Maybe there are clues in the wand's magical history that will lead us to Thea. And Arina is just another step in our quest to find her."

"One way or the other, we need to speak to Arina," Bella said. "I need all the help I can get to find Thea's grimoire."

I sat down and pressed a button on the armrest to bring down the television. Then I dialed the Legion office in New Orleans.

Jace Angelblood answered my video call. New Orleans was the seat of his territory, the South Territory. Seeing his face again, after meeting his mother Alice, made me really appreciate how much he looked like her. Except for his severe, closely-cropped haircut. That was all his father's influence. I guessed that's why I'd always thought Jace looked like Colonel Fireswift.

"Pandora, a pleasure as always. I do hope you're not calling about the end of the world again. You really must eventually learn to clean up your own messes."

His words were so smooth, so angelic. And he'd even managed to take a dig at me during his greeting. Colonel Fireswift would have been so proud. Except, of course, Jace's jab was all in good fun because we were friends. Which his father most certainly did *not* approve of.

"Actually, I was calling about something a little less exciting. Sorry, Jace."

Jace and I had been part of the same Legion initiation class. Like all Legion brats, he'd joined in New York, the same city that boasted the world's only academy devoted to the education and training of the angels' children.

"Perhaps you've heard of my new Angels' Court."

"Oh, yes," Jace chuckled. "Your new project is creating quite a stir. Several angels have called me to complain about it."

"Oh, really. Which ones?" I asked, curious.

"You know I can't tell you that."

"Never mind." I gave my hand a breezy wave. "I bet I could figure it out. But why would those angels complain to you?"

"They probably hoped to gain my support," he said. "Because they think I'm just like my father."

I flashed him a grin. "If only they knew that we're friends."

"Let's keep that under wraps, Leda. I'd prefer not to go to war with any other territory commanders during my first year as an angel."

"All right, but you can't hide that you have a soul forever, Angelblood."

He snorted.

"Wait a minute." I bit my lip. "To what end did those angels hope to gain your support?"

"You really don't want to know."

"Sure I do," I told him. "I can't stand secrets. Come on, tell me."

"No."

"Tell me, or I'll set a herd of wild mountain goats loose in your office."

"I believe you." Jace sighed in defeat. "Some angels want to convince Nyx to brand you a rogue for 'subversive behavior unbefitting of an angel and a holy representative of the gods'."

"Well, isn't that nice? Some more nicknames to add to my resume."

"Nyx will never do it. You're her favorite. She likes you even more than General Windstriker."

"Must be my way with angels," I said. "Besides, Nyx can't brand me a rogue for doing exactly what she told me to do."

"Which is what *exactly*?"

"To improve the Legion's image in the eyes of the human population so more of them want to join our ranks."

"Wow." He looked impressed. "The First Angel sure doesn't aim low."

"Of course not. She's an angel."

"Even for an angel, this task might be impossible," Jace warned me.

"Sure it's possible." I grinned at him. "But only because Nyx gave it to me."

"Nice to see all that angel modesty is rubbing off on you," he said drily.

"Like a potent perfume," I said with a smooth smile. "Say, Jace, I'm calling to let you know I'll soon be flying my rather large and obtrusive airship into your territory. I'm bringing the Angels' Court there."

"My father's territory is closer to you," he pointed out.

"Yes, it is, but I'm waiting for Colonel Fireswift to be back in his territory before I fly the Angels' Court there." I smiled as I imagined the look on Colonel Fireswift's face when he saw my ship coming his way.

"Be careful, Leda."

"Always."

Jace laughed like he thought I was crazy. "Ok, Leda, why the advance notice? I'd expect you to just show up and say 'surprise!'."

"It's been brought to my attention that not all angels enjoy being surprised."

That was an understatement. In fact, angels hated anything outside their control, anything that could not be planned.

"I see you learned something from my father's course," Jace observed.

I grinned proudly. "Passed with flying colors. I'm a perfect angel now."

"I'm sure," he chuckled.

"There's something else."

"Ah." He shook his head slowly. "There it is."

"There *what* is?"

"The real reason you're coming to New Orleans—and why you called ahead."

"What, I can't stop by to see my old friend Jace and spread the Legion's benevolence and love to the people of his territory?"

"Not really. No. You *always* have a plan."

"Well, now that you mention it…"

"Spit it out, Leda," Jace sighed.

"There's someone in your territory that I need to speak to," I told him. "An expert of sorts."

"An expert on what?"

"Immortal artifacts."

"I wasn't aware there was an expert on immortal artifacts living in my territory." His eyes were alight with calculation.

"Right, and it would be best if you remained unaware of it."

"That will be difficult now, considering that you just told me, Leda."

"I told my friend Jace. *Not* the angel Lieutenant Colonel Angelblood."

He sighed. "I take it back, Leda. You haven't changed a bit."

I pressed my finger to my lips. "Shh. Don't tell Nyx, or she'll put me back in remedial angel lessons."

The truth was, though, I had learned something from Colonel Fireswift's training. I knew that I had to speak differently to different angels. For some, angel decorum had to be observed, but not with Jace. Jace was a pal. He'd been right there with me from day one of Legion training—first as rivals, then as reluctant colleagues, then finally as friends.

"Ok, I won't whisper a word to Angelblood," Jace agreed. "So who is this expert of undisclosed mysteries?"

"Her name is Arina, but the less you know, the better it is for you. I'll come and hold my Angels' Court over your city tomorrow. Issue a notice for petitions. I can't fly this airship all the way there without a reason, after all. I'll pay Arina a visit myself, after the Court has adjourned for the day."

"The First Angel wants you to stay put on that airship," Jace reminded me.

"Hey this is me, remember? The Angel of Chaos." I winked at him. "Somehow I'll find a way to go to Arina while remaining on board."

# CHAPTER 18

ANGELBLOOD

The next day, when we arrived in New Orleans, Jace came up to the airship to greet us. He met us in the garden library.

"Colonel Pandora, Colonel Lightbringer," he said, nodding to me and Cadence in turn.

I rushed forward and gave my friend a hug.

"Leda, I'm trying to uphold all due formalities," he complained.

I stepped back, amused. "Oh, very well. Then you'll want to meet my friends from Heaven's Army." I indicated the godly soldiers. "That's Devlin, the team leader. Then we have Octavian, Arabelle, Punch, Patch, Theon, and I believe you've already met Stash."

Jace bowed to them. "It is an honor."

Octavian's mouth twisted into a grin. "He's a much better-behaved angel than you, Pandora."

"You can go hang out with him instead if you want," I told him.

"No," replied Octavian. "I'm still waiting for things to get really disastrous here. We all know they will."

"Patch and I have a wager going about the source of the disaster," Punch said. "He thinks an unsavory character will try to crash the Angels' Court. I, on the other hand, am betting on monsters attacking the airship. Maybe the ship will even explode."

He looked far too excited by the prospect.

"I sure hope not," I told him. "Nyx threatened to bill me directly if I blow up any more of the Legion's property."

Jace indicated the armed guards he'd brought with him. "I have brought twenty of my soldiers to guard this ship from unsavory characters, monsters, and explosions for the duration of your stay in my territory."

I knew his offered soldiers weren't just about my protection; they were also about keeping an eye on another angel in his territory. I had to hand it to Jace; he was a really great angel. He knew every greeting, upheld every formality. No wonder a few of the other angels had tried to turn him against me.

Jace then acknowledged Andromeda and Alice, going in order of rank. "Captain Singh." Finally, he came to his mother. "Lieutenant Jones."

Alice nodded back. "Lieutenant Colonel Angelblood."

Jace did look happy to see his mother. A hint of that happiness broke through his cool and collected angelic facade

He gestured to his soldiers, who turned neatly on the spot, then went briskly off to their posts. Once they were gone, Jace's shoulders relaxed a little. He didn't need to put on a show for his subordinates anymore.

He joined his mother at the bar, asking enthusiastically about her health and her pregnancy. Seeing mother and son like this, I knew I had to act to preserve their perfect family.

"Could you give us a moment?" I said quietly to Cadence and Andromeda. "I want to speak to Jace and Alice."

They looked curious, but they left.

"You guys too," I told the soldiers from Heaven's Army.

"We're supposed to be protecting you," Devlin protested.

"You can do that from outside the room."

Devlin stood there for a moment. I thought he was going to argue, but then he left with the others. He must have realized I was right. Anyone who wanted to attack me would first have to go through that door—and through all of them.

I looked at Stash, the only one who'd stayed behind.

"I'm sticking to you like glue, sweetness. No one is going to hurt you." He stared back at me, daring me to tell him to go.

I didn't. Stash and I had been through a lot together, including the time he'd inadvertently tried to take over the world. Ironically enough, it was partly because of that incident that I trusted him completely.

I put up the privacy spell I'd learned from Harker, then I joined Jace and his mother at the bar. Jace had made tea for both of them, and they were drinking it.

He glanced at me. "The room cleared out fast."

"I asked them all to leave. I need to discuss something very important with you."

And I wanted Alice to feel like she could speak freely, without fear that anyone might overhear her.

"You look very serious, Leda," said Jace.

"This is very serious," I told him. I looked at Alice. "It's regarding your husband's Archangel Trials."

Recognition flashed in Jace's eyes. He knew what I was going to say because I'd told him it before. But I hadn't yet told his mother, and she was the key to making Colonel Fireswift see reason.

"As you know, I accompanied Nero as his second during his Archangel Trials," I said to Alice. "What you don't know is that I was not supposed to survive the Trials. None of the seconds are supposed to survive. That's the whole point of the Archangel Trials. The gods present the prospective archangel with an impossible problem, one that can only be solved by sacrificing the companion they'd brought with them, the person they love most in the world. The Archangel Trials aren't about proving your magic or might. They are about proving you would sacrifice anything and everything for the gods. Only then do they make you an archangel."

Alice's eyes were wide. "Why has no one noticed by now that an angel's second always dies in the Archangel Trials?"

"I suppose because the Archangel Trials are such a rare event," Jace said. "And we're all told how dangerous they are."

Alice gave her son a hard look. "You knew about this?"

"Leda told me a few weeks ago. I've wanted to tell Father, but I just don't know how to bring it up. You know how he is."

"Yes, I do."

"He always has to follow the rules, no matter what." Jace frowned. "The person Father loves most in the world is you, Mother."

"Your father has already asked me to be his second." Alice swallowed hard. "The gods really want him to sacrifice me?"

"Yes," I told her. "To prove his loyalty to them. In exchange, they will make him an archangel."

"How did you survive?" she asked me.

"I wasn't meant to survive. Nero and I cheated, and we almost didn't get away with it. The gods nearly sentenced us *both* to death for what we did. We were only saved by some convenient political infighting between the gods on the council. But they made it clear that such a thing will not happen again. They won't allow anyone else to circumvent their rules. Even now, the gods insist the Archangel Trials will remain as they are." I pounded my clenched fist down on the countertop. "But the Archangel Trials are nothing more than a sacrificial ritual. They are against everything I believe, everything I am trying to do now with the Angels' Court. I want to gain people's trust, to help them, not demand horrible sacrifices out of them."

"Leda is trying to make the Legion's initiation ritual safer for initiates," Alice told Jace. "Dr. Harding is experimenting with Nectar to see if it can be done."

"That's ambitious." Jace looked at me. "Most angels won't like that any more than they like your Angels' Court. They want people to believe the Nectar is only for the chosen few. They don't want too many people to be worthy. It's about sacrifice."

"It's exactly that kind of thinking that leads to the Archangel Trials, where an angel needs to sacrifice the one they love most," I said. "Sacrifice. This is all about sacrifice. When we join the Legion of Angels, we're told our lives are over, that we belong to the Legion now. They separate us from our past, from humans and supernaturals. And then the sacrifices continue. To become an archangel, you need to sacrifice even more. You need to kill the person you love most."

"Have you told Xerxes?" Alice asked me.

"I've tried to speak to him, to warn him, but he refuses to hear anything at all I have to say about the Archangel Trials."

"Xerxes is very proud. He wants to win by playing by the rules."

"In the Archangel Trials, even if you win, you lose," I told her. "The gods designed it that way. The Trials aren't about how strong or how good you are; they're about if you are willing to sacrifice what you love most in this world."

Jace looked at his mother. "Her."

"They won't do it now, not while she's pregnant," I said. "When Cadence was pregnant with Nero, they had Damiel's best friend go with him to his Archangel Trials. They sent Jiro there to be sacrificed. But now, I don't even know who else they'd send with your father. Jace, you're an angel. The Legion is very short on angels right now. The gods won't sacrifice one angel to promote another to archangel. They will wait until Alice has given birth."

"And then they will send her off to die," Jace said darkly.

"Not if we can help it," I told him. "I've asked Ronan to try to change the others' minds about the sacrifice, but he is only one god. I can't imagine Zarion or Aleris agreeing to change anything, and the other four gods won't be easy to convince either." I offered Alice and Jace a smile. "Still, we have eight months to figure this out.

And we will. I promise you we will save your mother, Jace."

He clasped my hands. "Thank you for helping us, Leda, even though it's against the rules."

"I'll remind you that you thanked me for breaking the rules the next time you lecture me about rules."

Jace hugged me. So did his mother.

"May the gods bless you and your child, Leda," she said solemnly.

"Ah, shucks, you're making me blush."

"If you're all quite finished hugging…" Stash smirked. "…I need to clear up some security issues with Leda before today's Angels' Court."

"Of course," Jace said, then he and Alice left the room.

When we were alone, Stash turned to me. "You are risking a lot to help them, Leda. Disrupting the gods' order isn't something one should take lightly. Faris does not wish to kill you, but once your child is born, he might decide you're more trouble than you're worth to him."

"Faris will most likely try to kill me anyway once my daughter is born," I replied. "And he will try to kill Nero too. Not that we're going to allow that to happen. As long as we're in the picture, Faris will never truly control our daughter. So I guess we have eight months to figure out a solution to that problem too."

"I will help you in any way I can." Stash set his hand over his heart.

And I set my hand over his. "I know you will."

We started walking to the Court Chamber.

"How are you handling being caught in the middle of the conflict between Zarion and Faris?" I asked him.

"For now, they're both happy with where I am, and so neither is asking anything from me. Sooner or later, each will try to force my hand against the other. I'll deal with that problem when I have to. Naturally, I've set up contingency plans for that stormy day. But until then, I'm going to live my life day by day. I have to try to live for myself as much as possible, you know?"

"I can help you deal with Faris and Zarion," I offered.

"That is nice of you, Leda, but don't you think you have more than enough on your plate already?"

"Truth be told, my plate is overflowing, but I'm not about to let that stand in my way of helping the people I love."

Stash stared at me for a bit, then pulled me in for a big hug. "Thanks, sweetness. You really are my favorite cousin."

"Do you even have any other cousins?" I chuckled.

"We do," Stash told me. "Zarion and Faris have another brother, named Regin, but they don't ever talk about him. Apparently, the gods all consider him quite mad."

"He must really be off his rocker if the other gods think him mad."

Stash nodded. "He really is. And so are all ten of his children."

"*Ten* children? Whoa."

Gods were even less fertile than angels. And even for a human, ten children would have been pushing the boundaries of fertility.

"Rumor has it Regin's children were the product of some pretty foul magic," Stash said. "The gods won't even speak of it."

I cringed. "Which means it's either really, really bad, or they don't even know how it happened."

"Regin and his children live on eleven distant moons that orbit the same world," Stash told me. "Those moons are barren, desolate places with no portals to anywhere else. They're much like prisons actually. And Regin and his ten children are all kept separate because the gods can't trust them when they are together. They would gather too much power—and likely scheme to overthrow the gods' council."

"They sound like a lovely bunch of megalomaniacs."

"Faris once gave my team the job of checking up on Regin and all of his offspring," said Stash. "All of them are completely bonkers, through and through."

I smiled at him. "Well, I'm honored you like me more than our other crazy cousins."

Stash chuckled. When he stepped back, I spotted a tear in his eye.

"Hey, badass, are you crying?"

"I apologize for my weakness, Leda."

I wiped his tear away. "Don't be afraid to let them see us cry, sweat, and bleed. For it is not a sign of weakness. It is a strength they cannot understand and therefore fear."

Stash nodded. "Very wise words."

"Yeah, they are. I once read them on a roll of inspiration toilet paper."

Stash laughed.

We'd reached the entrance to the Court Chamber. Cadence, Andromeda, and Alice were waiting for us there. Jace must have already flown back to his office on the ground.

Punch and Patch stood on either side of the double doors.

"Give 'em hell, Pandora," Punch said.

I winked at him. "I always do."

His grin widened as he and his brother opened the doors for us. I entered the room with Cadence at my side. As always, Andromeda and Alice followed just a few steps behind us.

The Chamber was decked out as grandly as before, though Tessa had added considerably more flowers. The place smelled divine. My sister had also hung three banners behind the dais where our four chairs waited for us.

Cadence's banner displayed a female angel, in full halo. The angel, which looked a lot like Cadence, held her glowing sword over her head. Her wings were spread out, wide and majestic, in all their heavenly glory. Her angel name 'Lightbringer' was printed in a large, grand font under the picture.

My emblem was a female angel holding a box, opened just a crack, with monsters lurking on either side of me. My wings were folded protectively around my body—no, around the box in my hands. The wings were shielding the box from the monsters that lurked at the banner's fringes. 'Pandora' was written in a more whimsical font than Cadence's 'Lightbringer'.

The third banner was Jace's, a sign of respect for our host angel. Even though he wasn't here with us, we were in his territory. His emblem was of a male angel who held a flaming sword in each hand. His name 'Angelblood' was written, big and bold, below him.

All the banners' illustrations were colorful and realistic. They looked like playing cards from the game of Legion, which was well-known for its high-quality art.

The four of us took our seats, and then the sergeant with the big, booming voice began our introductions. They lasted longer this time, since he had to pay respect to our host angel. And Jace had two other angels in his family history that required mention.

Finally, I could declare, "The Angels' Court may now commence."

# CHAPTER 19

## MIRACLE

The Angels' Court took a recess for lunch, and we returned to the garden library. I glanced up as the door to the library opened, but it wasn't the kitchen staff with the food I'd ordered. It was Leila and Basanti.

I stood, surprised by their appearance, but glad to see them. "What are you doing here?"

Neither Basanti nor Leila answered. Their faces were blank, like they were trying to keep some really bad news from me.

"Are those burn marks on your jacket?" I asked Basanti. "Has there been an attack on Storm Castle?"

"No," she replied. "For the past few weeks, Leila and I have been running some experiments with magic and the weather at Storm Castle."

"We're trying to figure out if we can calm the weather and magic in the Earth's wild areas," Leila added. "Just as Cadence and Damiel did on the Interchange. And in doing so, they wiped out all the monsters on that world.

It's simply a matter of balancing the planet's magic completely."

Cadence smiled at her former protégé. "To accomplish that, Damiel and I had *simply* just absorbed the powers of sixteen immortal daggers, realizing our destiny as Keepers, the most powerful of the Immortals. And we had just died and been reborn in a pool of boiling lava. The magic from all of that happening exploded from us and balanced the world's magic once more."

"I'm no scientist, but it doesn't sound like those are conditions we can easily repeat," I said.

"No," Leila agreed. "True, we don't have sixteen immortal daggers at our disposal, but the principle of using magic to balance the Earth's wild magic remains the same. Without the benefit of all that Immortal Keeper magic, we're going for precision over power."

Leila laughed strangely. Uneasily. She sounded weird, kind of mad-scientist-like. She was definitely not her usual straight-talking-soldier self.

"Experiments, you say?" I said. "So what happened? Did you two nearly blow yourselves up or something?"

"No," Leila said, distracted. "Well, maybe we blew ourselves up just a little." She gave her hand a casual, dismissive wave. "But our injuries were minor."

I arched my brows at her. "And now you're hanging out with us because…"

Basanti said, "After the accident—"

"The nearly-blowing-yourselves-up accident?"

"Yes," Basanti answered me. "Afterwards, Ivy was looking us over. And she found something else."

I waved my hands around. "Don't leave us hanging, girls."

"We're pregnant," Leila declared.

So not bad news, but certainly *surprising* news.

"Congratulations," I said. "Which one of you?"

"Both of us," Leila said.

My eyes grew wide. "Both of you? At the same time?"

"Yes," Basanti said.

"To the day," Leila added.

"Not to sound indelicate, but…"

"You are rarely delicate, Leda Pandora," Leila told me.

I smiled and shrugged.

"The babies have no father," Leila answered my unasked question.

"Then how did this happen?" I asked.

Basanti shook her head. "We have no idea."

"Because typically to get a baby, a man and a woman—"

"Thank you, Professor Pandora," Basanti cut me off. "We all know how babies are made."

"Well, apparently, you don't know how *these* babies were made," I pointed out.

"According to Ivy's tests, the babies are the biological product of Basanti and myself," Leila said.

"And these experiments you were running…"

"Were strictly about the magic of the Earth's weather and elements," said Leila. "It did not involve our DNA or test tubes."

"There's more," Basanti said. "According to Ivy, we're both nearly two months pregnant."

"The same as all of you," Leila added.

"This is just getting weirder and weirder," I said to Cadence.

"Indeed," she agreed. "First, we all come down with the Fever and all get pregnant in the same cycle."

"And now Leila and Basanti got each other pregnant," I said. "Has *that* ever happened before?"

Cadence shook her head. "No."

Basanti looked at me, her eyes narrowed. "I blame Leda."

"Why me?"

"You started this. It must be contagious."

"I'm pretty sure pregnancy is not contagious," I laughed.

"When you do it, it is."

My smile wobbled. "I don't even know what that means."

"You're the Angel of Chaos. The laws of nature get all wonky whenever you're around."

"True. Maybe we should quarantine her. Before this spreads further." Leila winked at me.

"I'm already effectively quarantined," I sighed. "And so are all of you, here in our gilded airship guarded by gods and elite Vanguard soldiers."

"This is truly fascinating. So many angel offspring conceived at once. And now the two of you." There was a spark of academic delight in Cadence's eyes. She looked like she wanted to throw on a lab coat and figure this all out.

"Your pregnancies are truly a miracle," I told Basanti and Leila.

Basanti sat down beside me. "Tell it to my queasy stomach."

I patted her back. "You know what helps with that? Cake. Lots of cake."

"You should not give nutritional advice to anyone, Pandora," Basanti said with wary eyes.

"You're just grumpy because you're pregnant, so Nyx

exiled you to hide away here just like the rest of us," I told her, smiling. "But at least you and Leila get to spend time with each other. We haven't seen our husbands in days. It could be weeks before we do. Or maybe months."

"The Angel of Chaos has a point," Leila said to Basanti.

"Sure, there's the nausea and the peeing every hour, but there are perks to pregnancy too," I told them.

"Like what?" Basanti asked, looking quite miserable.

I grinned at her. Then I pulled out my phone and added even more food to our lunch order.

---

OUR LUNCH ARRIVED AT THE SAME TIME AS STASH did. The three guys from the kitchen walked in after my demigod cousin, pushing carts very full with food.

"You think you ordered enough to eat, Leda?" Stash commented.

"No, but I can always order more," I said brightly.

"The kitchen is going to run out of food."

"I'm way ahead of you. I've already approved an increase in our food budget."

Angels got to do important things like that.

"Our pregnancies are certainly costing the Legion a lot of money," Cadence commented.

I smirked at her. "I'm not the one craving all that fancy food."

"Schnitzel is not fancy food, Leda."

"Sure it is." I grabbed a fat fry with my fingers. "It's fancy because you have to eat it with a knife and a fork."

"I love being pregnant again," Alice said happily.

"The rest of the time, the Legion has all these rules about what you may and may not eat."

"Especially in the Central Territory," said Leila. "When it comes to nutritionally-balanced meals, Fireswift is hardcore, even for an angel."

"Yes, he is," Alice said. "I know those nutritionally-balanced meals are key to ensuring soldiers operate at peak performance, but sometimes I just want to eat something fun."

I looked at her yogurt with berries. It even had granola sprinkled on top.

"Now let's not get too crazy," I told her.

"But when I'm pregnant, I can eat whatever and how much ever I want. It's glorious." Alice ate a spoonful of her totally healthy yogurt. She closed her eyes, and a decidedly dreamy look fell over her whole face.

"It is awesome," I agreed. "I can finally order coffee again. And have ice cream with every meal. I can finally do that too."

"I bet you *always* did that," Cadence teased me.

I dropped a scoopful of ice cream into my coffee. "True." I grinned.

"It's not just about the food. It's also the pampering," Andromeda said. "Bubble baths, facials, manicures, hair treatments, beauty treatments…we can get whatever we want. And all because we carry the Legion's future inside of us."

"So much for the famous self-discipline of the Legion's soldiers," Stash chuckled.

"Hey, do *you* want to be pregnant?" I asked him.

"No. Not really." He looked horrified by the very idea of it.

I laughed, then continued listening to Cadence's

description of wing massages. They sounded heavenly. I wondered if I could convince Nero to give me one. Of course I didn't say that in front of Cadence. She was Nero's mother, after all, so that would have been just too weird.

"You two should join us for our morning pregnancy yoga," Alice said to Leila and Basanti.

"I'm not flexible," Basanti stated matter-of-factly.

"That's ok. Neither is Leda," Alice pointed out.

"Hey! I'm getting better. I actually managed to touch my toes this morning."

"Because you bent your knees," Andromeda reminded me. "A lot."

I shrugged. "But it got the job done."

"I'm not really into frou-frou sport and braiding each other's hair and all that," Basanti said.

But Leila looked like she liked the idea. Her hand rested on her belly. Sure, it was still flat like all of our bellies, but that wasn't the point. It was a gesture of love. Love for the baby growing inside of her.

Leila was *really* glowing. I remembered her recently telling me about how much she'd always wanted to have kids but had never been so lucky to get them. Well, now she and Basanti were going to have two.

"And then there's the best thing about being pregnant: I finally have real boobs." Alice pointed down at her chest.

I lifted my coffee cup in the air. "I'll drink to that. I am, for the first time since joining the Legion, getting some serious curves. Now I look like one of those busty women on the cover of a muscle car magazine, sprawled out on the hood of a truck, sticking out my scantily-clad chest, a devilish come-hither look on my lips."

"You sure have a vivid imagination, Leda." Basanti took a bite of cake. Then she turned to me, surprise written all over her face. "You're right. Cake *does* make my queasy stomach feel better."

"Told you."

Basanti took another bite of cake. "I can't believe I'm subscribing to the Leda Pandora pregnancy diet of cake and ice cream."

"Just keep clear of those vitamins Nerissa keeps trying to give us," I warned her. "They have the opposite effect of the cake and ice cream."

One of Basanti's eyebrows cocked upward. "You mean, they're actually healthy?"

I laughed and took some more dessert.

---

Now that our numbers had swelled, Tessa had to add more chairs to the dais in the Court Chamber—and add a fancy angel banner for Leila too.

Finally, we'd reached the end of the day, the final round of petitions. It opened with a bang. Our first petitioner of the session was none other than Arina Phoenix.

Arina marched up to the base of the dais and declared, "Leda Pandora, I heard you're looking for me."

"Yes," I said in surprise.

Arina's arrival here on the airship would save me the trouble of searching the city for her.

"We need your help," I told her.

"And I need yours. That's why I came here."

"How can we help?" I asked her.

"It's my children." Arina's voice shook. "I need you to help me get them back."

I remembered her cute twins, a girl and a boy about eight years old.

"I'm so sorry they're gone, Arina. Don't worry. We'll find them."

"I know where they are," she said, her voice harder, her fists clenched. "And I know who took them. It was the Guardians."

## CHAPTER 20

### CHAMPIONS OF THE IMMORTALS

"The Guardians kidnapped your children? Why?" I asked Arina.

"For the same reason they've been collecting people for centuries. Except now they've moved up their timetable." She shot me a pointed look.

"Because of me," I realized. "Because, when they took control over Meda, I freed her, interfering with their plans."

"You did what you had to in order to save the people of this world," Arina said. "The Guardians were going to do this no matter what. It was only a matter of when."

"You mentioned you wanted to keep the knowledge of your children's magic secret from the Guardians." I didn't know what kind of magic Arina's children had, but it must have been pretty special. "Did the Guardians find out about your kids' magic because of me?"

Arina shook her head. "I was naive to believe I could keep that knowledge from them. The Guardians have eyes everywhere. Ears everywhere. They already knew,

Leda. They just hadn't moved on that knowledge. Until now."

"What are the Guardians planning to do?" I asked.

"Enact their ultimate plan: to gain all the magic they believe the Immortals unfairly withheld from them. That's all I know."

"The Guardians have taken so many supernaturals. They have a plan for those people, and in that plan, all of them die," I repeated Faith's words.

Arina grew very still. "How do you know this?"

"A powerful telepath told me."

Of course that powerful telepath had used those very words to justify killing many humans, supernaturals, gods, and demons—all to save her brother. But still, despite Faith's questionable morality, I did believe her words. Faith had believed the Guardians would kill her brother and all of the other supernaturals they kept in their Sanctuary. That knowledge had driven her to take extreme, insane measures.

"Where is this powerful telepath now?" Arina asked.

"Gone."

Faith's powers were gone, transferred to my unborn child, which had all been part of Grace's plan. And Faith was gone too. She'd been locked away by Faris, who still hoped she'd get her powers back—and then he could exploit them.

I was going to ask Arina about her kids' magic, but then something rather spectacular distracted me: the arrival of five angels. Nero, Damiel, Nyx, Colonel Fireswift, and an angel I assumed was Colonel Dragonblood had landed on the windy deck outside the Court Chamber.

I rose from my chair. "Open the doors," I instructed the soldiers standing in front of the wall of glass.

Nyx stepped inside the Chamber first, her white wings sparkling like they'd been sprinkled with stardust, her long, gravity-defying black hair in slow, swirly motion around her.

Damiel came next, his bronze hair lightly windswept. His bright blue eyes twinkled when he saw Cadence.

He was followed by Nero. His gorgeous wings, a dark, elaborate tapestry of black, blue, and green feathers, stretched out, then vanished in a flash of magic. His emerald eyes slid over me; the sheer intensity of his stare raised goosebumps up and down my skin. I felt light-headed, dizzy, even a little feverish. I wondered if anyone would really mind if I leapt off the dais, ran over to Nero, and proceeded to make up for the last week we'd missed.

Colonel Fireswift was next in the procession, looking just as humorless, just as iron-jawed as always. His wings were the color of freshly-shed blood, his eyes hard and cynical, and his body armed to the teeth.

Colonel Dragonblood brought up the rear. I'd never met the angel before. He wore his black hair cropped short, as many no-nonsense angels did. His dark eyes were serious, but they didn't possess the same cynical edge as Colonel Fireswift's. His wings were a mixture of both turquoise and orange feathers, highlighted by a few bronze spots that were a perfect match to his complexion. The color combination of his feathers was quite beautiful.

The sergeant with the booming voice quickly began rattling off the five angels' names and titles. He looked quite excited. So was everyone else. There had rarely been so many angels together in a single place. Eight, to be exact.

While the sergeant pressed on with the lengthy introductions, I quietly observed the fascinating differences in how these different male angels greeted their wives.

Damiel was charming. His words were laced with innuendo designed to incite Cadence. Instead, she planted her hands on her hips and shook her head at his jokes. Her expression softened, however, after he presented her with a gift box.

Colonel Dragonblood bowed to his wife and set his hand on her belly, a sign of respect that she was carrying his child.

Colonel Fireswift was, as expected, very formal when greeting his wife. He really was all about keeping up appearances. And yet, I thought I caught a spark of something in his eyes, something I'd never seen in him before. Devotion. And love. He really loved her.

Nero came to stand before me. "Pandora." An eyebrow cocked up at me.

"Windstriker. You look well." I was trying really hard not to giggle.

He cast a long, languid look down the length of my body. Then his eyes snapped up and met mine. "So do you." He grinned, slow and sexy.

A blush kissed my cheeks.

He closed the distance between us. His hand curled around my waist, supporting me as he dipped me back. His mouth came down on mine and he kissed me with a deep, hungry urgency that sent a shot of fierce desire straight through my body.

Nyx cleared her throat. Loudly.

"Later," Nero whispered to me, his words thick with lust.

He gave me a quick, final peck on the lips, then

released me. I remembered just in time to re-engage my standing muscles. Falling over in front of all these people, including angels and gods, would have been totally embarrassing.

Nyx was chastising Nero. "Really, Windstriker. Did you have to kiss her like *that*?" she demanded grumpily.

Nyx sounded like *she* needed a good kiss.

"Well, this is something you don't see every day," Arina said to me. She looked at my belly. "You're all pregnant."

"You can see that?"

"Of course."

Arina could see the past events that led up to someone or something. I hoped she wasn't focusing her magic *too* closely on the particular event that had led to my pregnancy.

"Six pregnant angels and wives of angels," I said. "In fact, it has only ever happened once before, twenty-five years ago."

"Six?" Arina shook her head. "No, you're mistaken, Leda. Not six. Seven."

No, I was pretty sure Nero's amazing kiss hadn't removed my ability to count. I recounted, just in case.

"Cadence, Alice, Andromeda, Leila, Basanti, and I. Six."

Arina's eyes fell on the First Angel.

I gaped at Nyx. "Nyx? You too?"

"Yes."

That was all she said, but it was an answer that truly said it all. The First Angel was pregnant. Wow.

A flash of magic blinded me for a moment, then Ronan was there, right in front of Nyx. The God of Earth's Army couldn't hide his awe. He didn't touch her belly or bow or do anything dramatic. But the look on his face was very telling.

"We need to talk," he said to Nyx.

"Yes," she agreed.

Then they both left the room.

Once they were gone, Basanti turned to me. "I told you so, Pandora. It's contagious."

"Magic certainly is acting in unpredictable ways right now," Leila commented.

"The First Angel has never had the Fever." Cadence looked baffled.

"Apparently, she did when you all did," said Damiel.

All eyes in the room turned toward me.

"Why are you all looking at me?" I asked them. This totally wasn't my fault.

My mind was working fast, backtracking to when I'd had the Fever. I'd seen Nyx and Ronan get pretty physical. So that's why they'd acted so…passionate. No, more than merely passionate. Nyx and Ronan hadn't been able to keep their hands off each other. Nyx must have had the Fever then.

"This started with you, Leda." This time, Basanti looked more amused than annoyed; the cake must have had enough time to settle her queasy stomach. "You upended the rules of magic."

Nyx had returned to the Court Chamber, sans Ronan, but with a lot of soldiers guarding her. They looked human, minus the rather blue skin.

"Ronan's soldiers?" I wondered.

"Yes," Damiel confirmed. "From the Legion of the Arcane."

"The Legion of the Arcane? What's that?" I asked.

"It's kind of like the Legion of Angels, but on another world. Not Earth," Damiel explained.

"So they're like alien angels?"

"Not angels. The *arcane*." Damiel said the word like it was supposed to mean something to me.

"I guess I never thought about any Legions on other worlds," I said.

"Ronan is a member of the gods' ruling council, one of the seven most powerful gods out there. The Earth is important to the gods, but not *that* important," Damiel pointed out. "There are thousands of worlds in the gods' domain. And many Legions. Ronan is the Lord of the Legion. Such a title, a title worthy of a place on the gods' council, is bigger than only Earth. It's bigger than angels."

Yeah, that made sense.

I watched the blue-skinned soldiers. Ronan had obviously ordered them to guard Nyx—apparently, very closely because they were practically glued to her sides.

"This isn't just about me," I said quietly.

But Nyx had good ears. "What isn't just about you?"

"All the angel pregnancies. The same thing happened roughly twenty-five years ago." I pulled a sheet of paper out of my jacket and unfolded it. It included the birth records of the angel brats. I'd compiled the list from the names of the children of angels who'd been in my initiation group. "The same thing is happening now."

Nyx read the sheet. "Yes, the convergence of all those births of angels' children at once back then was indeed odd. Considering this has never happened besides then and now again, these incidents are likely linked." She handed the sheet of paper back to me, then she took a stroll around the decorated Court Chamber. "You've been busy."

"I decided I'd best not waste any time setting off on the impossible task you'd set me."

"I thought you didn't believe in the impossible," Nyx said, her eyes narrowed.

"I don't, but *you* did when you set me the task."

"Indeed," Nyx laughed. "But I've come to realize that your tenacity makes quick work of the impossible, Pandora."

Colonel Fireswift snorted. Wow, he was actually showing emotion. He must have been in a very good mood. And indeed he did look less grumpy than usual, standing there beside his pregnant wife. Perhaps thinking about the continuation of his legacy gave Colonel Fireswift a case of the happies.

"Not that I don't appreciate your company, but are you going to be staying here and looking over my shoulder as I attempt to tame the impossible?" I asked Nyx.

"Apparently, I have no choice. I've been ordered to stay here," Nyx replied, dour.

By Ronan, no doubt.

"Well, it was *your* idea to safeguard the Legion's future on this airship," I pointed out.

She was not amused. "Not helping, Pandora."

Ok, then. Nyx was not in a good mood. The First Angel really didn't like being sidelined. So I gave her some space.

"How's the mission going?" I asked Nero.

"We've captured a few people we discovered were previously at the massacre sites," he said. "But we're not sure how they could have possibly killed the angels. And so far, our prisoners aren't talking."

"Maybe they aren't the ones who did it," I suggested.

"The Interrogators have them now. We shall soon find out who they work for and what they want."

"I hope you're right."

"Not feeling confident?" he asked me.

"There is something bigger going on here, Nero. And my gut tells me it has to do with what happened in the past."

"Have you had any more visions?"

"No. But I wish I had. I'm sure the answers we need are buried in the past," I said. "Cadence thinks I'm the common link between all the angel pregnancies now and when it happened twenty-five years ago."

"I think she's right," Nero agreed.

"Have you heard about Leila and Basanti?"

"Yes." A smile flitted across his face. "I'm not sure how that happened, but good for them."

"Magic is pretty wonky right now."

"Indeed."

"I've been thinking about the attacks on my family," I told him. "Are the Guardians truly targeting Zane? And is this connected to the Guardians' plans to kill all the people they 'saved', including Arina's kids? Furthermore, could this all be related to the massacres you're investigating? How is all of what's going on connected? Because figuring that out might be the key to stopping the Guardians."

"You've been having visions?" Arina asked me.

"Yes, of the past." Then I described them to her, especially the ones from the Lost City. When I was done, I asked her, "Do you know what it means?"

She shook her head. "No."

I had a thought. "Zane once told me: 'The Guardians have a prophecy about a divine savior who will be born human, with equal light and dark magic. She will grow her magic one ability at a time, and someday she will upset the balance of power…The Guardians…believe you will change the balance of magic back to the middle, back to mixed magic of light and dark origins. They believe the savior is a god killer and demon slayer.' What do you think?"

Arina chewed on her lip, obviously mulling that over.

"When we first met, you told me the Guardians wanted me dead," I reminded her.

"They do. But they…they must need you too."

"According to what Zane heard, they need me to change the balance of magic. So why did they try to kill me on the rooftop in Purgatory?"

"There's a way we might be able to answer all of these questions," Arina said.

"I'm listening."

"You don't happen to have the weapons of heaven and hell on you, do you?"

---

I DID, IN FACT, HAVE THE WEAPONS OF HEAVEN AND hell with me. Before leaving on her quest with Nero and the others, Nyx had sent them up to the airship, along with my cat.

We all gathered around Arina in the garden library, as she tried to read the memories branded into the four immoral artifacts' magic.

"These are very old." Arina's eyes were closed, and her

hands slid over the shield. "They were made by the legendary Immortal smith Sunfire. One of the surviving Immortals gave them to a special soldier, one of balanced magic: light and dark, active and passive."

Her fingers traced the blade of the sword, her eyes still closed. "There's a missing piece of the Prophecy." She opened her eyes and looked at Zane. "One the Guardians didn't tell you."

"I'm not surprised," he said. "The Guardians harbor many secrets."

Arina closed her eyes again. Her hands had moved on to the armor. She repeated Zane's words, "The savior will change the balance of magic back to the middle, back to mixed magic of light and dark origins. The savior is a god killer and demon slayer."

Prophecies were always so dramatic.

"The missing piece of the Prophecy comes after Leda changes the balance of magic," Arina said. "That missing piece is the part where Leda destroys the Guardians too."

"So we will actually defeat the Guardians?" I asked.

"Not sure. I cannot see into the future. I can only see how the Guardians interpreted the Prophecy. But even if I could see into the future, I don't think it would help much. You see, the future is not set. The Prophecy allows for several different paths. Down one path, you grow your magic, Leda; the Guardians did need you to grow your magic. They explored the Prophecy's possibilities, and any path where they tried to stop you from gaining power just led to their destruction and your gaining power anyway. They decided they needed to let you gain all your powers before they struck out at you."

"How can the Guardians have a Prophecy? How can they see into the future? That's not the kind of thing magic-nullifying beings can do, right?" I looked at Damiel and Cadence, our resident experts in all kinds of magic, for confirmation.

"But the Guardians have collected supernaturals with all kinds of powers," Cadence said. "Long ago, a telepath with future-gazing powers might have given them this Prophecy."

Arina's hands followed the gun's contours. "Not all Guardians are united on what to do with Leda. Some think she's more trouble than she's worth and that the magical shift can be done in other ways. Some think they need Leda for it."

Arina's hand flashed out and she grabbed my hand. I felt a jolt as we connected, my hands and our minds.

And then I was once more in the Lost City. I saw the pale-haired angel from long ago. She flashed in front of my eyes, this fragment from the past.

Arina was beside me. "The Guardians' forces attacked the city."

"You're seeing what I'm seeing?"

"Yes," Arina said. "This woman, she was the Immortals' chosen one, the one of balanced magic. The first bearer of the weapons of heaven and hell."

"She was an angel."

"No, not an angel. Something else," Arina told me. "I don't know what she was exactly. Some kind of deity, neither god nor demon. She flew out to face the invaders. The city was lost."

"How long ago did this happen?" I asked her.

"Long ago, before the gods and demons came here. When humans were hardly more than primitive cave dwellers."

"There were cities here on Earth so long ago?"

"The Lost City was built, destroyed, and rebuilt many times," she said.

"There were many bearers of these immortal artifacts," I remembered.

"Yes. Chosen champions of the Immortals. Only a champion can see these lost memories."

"You're seeing them," I pointed out.

"I'm seeing them through you, Leda, as you see them. Because I'm reading your magic."

The scene changed.

"Another champion." I pointed at the red-haired angel Sierra in the Lost City.

"Yes."

"How long ago did she live in her version of the Lost City?" I asked.

"She didn't live. She *will* live."

"What does that mean?"

"The visions of the red-haired angel, they aren't memories from the past," Arina said. "They are snippets from the future."

"What?"

"They show what is yet to come." She opened her eyes and looked at me. "This is part of the Prophecy the Guardians are so worked up about. And that angel—Sierra—the future bearer of the weapons of heaven and hell…she's your daughter, Leda."

# CHAPTER 21

## THE ROAD OF TIME

"My daughter." I gaped at Arina as the disjointed visions sizzled out.

"Yes," she told me.

"But these are supposed to be memories, not visions from the future."

"I don't quite understand it myself," Arina admitted. "This is some very powerful, very unusual magic."

"How are the visions from the past linked to those of my daughter from the future?"

Arina shook her head. "I don't know. But we can find out."

"How?"

"The weapons of heaven and hell are channeling these visions, magnifying them, so you see them. Like a lens focusing the memories onto you," she explained.

"Someone is sending me the visions from the Vault, a secret place accessible from the Lost City."

"Who is sending them to you?"

I shrugged. "I don't know."

"Maybe we can figure that out too," Arina said. "I can help guide you through the visions stored in the Vault, Leda. But you must know that this journey won't be without risk."

"I have to do it," I said, determined. "The fate of my daughter might be at stake."

"And I'm coming with you," Nero added.

"I believe I can handle guiding the two of you through the visions," Arina said. "You will both need to stay focused—and close to me. It will be a narrow trail to follow these visions."

Nero took my hand. "We understand."

"One more thing," said Arina. "In order to make sense of the various visions, I will attempt to shape the narrative chronologically. I will not, however, be able to assist you in battle. I can only guide your path."

"Do you anticipate there will be fighting? It's all just visions. None of this is real. Right?" I asked her.

"Just because it's not happening now, that doesn't mean it's not real," she told me.

"Is this like time travel when you have to be careful not to ruin history or something?" I remembered once reading a novel like that.

"No. It's not time travel," Arina said. "What you do won't change the past, even as you interact with it. But just because you can't damage the past, that doesn't mean the past can't damage you. Be prepared."

"We are prepared." Nero's halo hummed with complete confidence; he was doing it to calm me…and it was working.

"Ok, then here goes nothing," Arina said.

A warmth rushed over my body, like a gentle ocean

wave. I felt my consciousness melt into the Vault's memory stream.

---

The pale-haired angel had lived many millennia ago on Earth. I didn't quite understand it, but I had a vague sense that she and her kind had been created by the Immortals. They were angels in all the tangible ways—and yet not really angels in some intangible ways.

I didn't dwell on this knowledge that had dripped into my mind, a mind that was feeling a bit foggy at the moment. My eyelids were heavy, weighed down by all of this new information.

"Careful, Pandora." Nero's hands flashed out, catching me as I swayed.

"Thanks." I offered him a smile. "This is all a lot to take in."

We stood in the Lost City, right in front of a small temple.

Then I felt a jolt, and we were suddenly inside the temple, as though we'd been teleported there.

Arina was there too, beside us. "Sorry for shaking you up. This magic trail we're following is very weird. I'm still getting the hang of it."

A couple stood at the altar, their hands joined. One was the pale-haired angel. The other was a man who looked a lot like Damiel.

"I think we're looking at your ancestors, Nero," I said. "Damiel's ancestors."

"Damiel does have Immortal blood," Nero replied. "Is this where it comes from?"

Some kind of priest was there. He was performing a wedding ceremony.

"It's a secret wedding. The pale-haired angel and the man had to hide their love because…" I shook my head, but I couldn't shake loose the answers that I sought. "I don't know why. The reason is there, but it's just out of my grasp."

"There is a lot of information stored in these visions," Arina said. "Don't get caught up in the details, Leda. They're not important. Focus on the larger narrative, on how this all connects together."

It was hard to ignore the little things because I was curious, and I could tell Nero was too. This was a rare glimpse into his past.

"You didn't see this when you read Nero's magic?" I asked Arina.

"Not these people in particular. When I read someone's magical history, I just intuitively focus on what's really important to understand them."

"This isn't important to understanding Nero?" I asked. "His ancestors lived thousands of years ago on Earth. That's pretty damn interesting."

"Interesting, yes. But is it important?" she posed.

"If it weren't important, why would someone have put these visions into the Vault for me? Why would someone be sending me any of them?"

"Without knowing who is sending you the visions, I cannot really speculate, Leda," replied Arina. "But if they are benevolent, I suppose they might have sent you these visions because they are important to your future survival, or maybe important to defeating a foe."

"A foe like the Guardians?"

"For instance. In any case, you should not ignore the possibility that the person who's sending you these visions is not benevolent at all, but is rather trying to manipulate you or even do you harm."

"We shall go through these visions and try to ascertain the senders' intentions." Nero was sensible like that.

"Ok," I agreed because it really was the best plan. "Let's see what they show us."

The priest had finished the ceremony. The love birds sealed their union with a kiss.

The temple's doors burst open. Legion soldiers stormed inside. No, not Legion soldiers, I reminded myself. The soldiers were dressed similarly, but they were not from the Legion. Their uniforms did not bear the Legion's rank symbols. And this had happened, after all, thousands of years before the Legion had even existed.

The soldiers didn't wait. They fired off their magic. When the smoke cleared, the priest was dead—and the pale-haired angel and her new husband had vanished.

---

They must have escaped—or at least the pale-haired angel had—because the next thing I saw was her walking across the scorched, blackened plains. It looked a lot like the Black Plains. And yet not quite like the Black Plains.

There seemed to be a lot of repeating, quite similar things in these visions—parallels between then and now. Some iteration of the Lost City. A place like the Black Plains. Angel-like beings. Legion-like soldiers.

The angel's wings drooped, low and heavy. She appeared to be injured. A trail of blood followed her as she entered the Lost City, a city now ravaged by war and destruction.

She stood in front of a wall, looking at the wings symbol carved into the stone surface. The gateway. I'd been there too, two years ago in the Lost City. She set her hands on the wings symbol to open the gateway, then she passed right through the wall.

A gold-framed door was before her now. Crouching over, she leaned against the door. A sparkling, magical tear fell from her eye. It splashed against the panel of symbols at the door, lighting up the letters of an old, now-forgotten language. An Immortal language.

The door opened. Inside, the angel found the weapons of heaven and hell. She put on the armor first; the silver pieces adjusted to fit her body perfectly. Then she grabbed the shield, the sword, and the gun. Thus equipped, she hurried outside to face the enemies who besieged her city.

I looked across the broken city, trying to see who those enemies were, but they were all just a big blur.

"Surely, *that* is important," I said to Arina.

She only frowned.

"Are you hiding things from us?" I asked her.

"It is not I who hides things, Leda. Someone else is hiding things from us. We're being shown only what they want us to see."

"The question is, who are *they*?" I wondered.

"Indeed." Nero's voice was dangerous. He didn't like when things were withheld from him. He didn't like being manipulated.

I looked across the battlefield. The pale-haired angel clashed with the mystery soldiers. Their movements blurred, and the memory blurred into another.

I saw myself in the Lost City. I was inside the small room that had once held the weapons of heaven and hell. An angel stood behind me.

"Osiris," I said.

"It's an old magic," said Osiris—or, rather, Damiel when he'd pretended to be Osiris. "A magic to make you go through the motions of your memory, like you're in it."

Right, Damiel had performed a spell to send me into a trance. The memories had been so strong for me there and then in the Lost City that it must have been an easy spell for him to pull off.

I looked down at the big 'x' that my past self had scratched in the sand while inside Damiel's trance. It was accompanied by symbols—letters—from the same language the pale-haired angel had seen on the gold-framed door.

I blinked, and I could see right through Damiel's disguise, right through the Osiris illusion he'd wrapped himself in.

"How do you even know that she's the one?" one of the soldiers in the room asked. A soldier who'd been hired by that crazy Pilgrim Valiant.

"The spell doesn't lie. It showed us the one the Guardians entrusted these memories to," said Damiel-Osiris.

"What spell?" my past self asked.

"The one I cast the first time you came to the Lost City, the one that unlocked the treasure trove of memories inside that precious little head of yours."

Another jolt shook me, sending me tumbling into the next memory.

---

I collided with Nero.

He caught me, folding his arms around me like a shield. "Are you all right?"

"Fine," I assured him with a smile, then looked at Arina.

"Like I said, this beast is hard to drive," she said. "I've tried to sort the memories in order, but it's a bit like trying to collect water with your hands. Things keep slipping by. This memory came before the last one we watched."

"I can see that," I replied.

I saw Damiel in hiding, spying on two of the Guardians' angels, the pair who'd captured Cadence. Their names were Taron and Giselle. He wore a suit of bright, silver armor. She wore a red, knee-length summer dress and a pair of brown boots. Both had long, beautiful hair that shimmered with an enchanting, eerie kind of magic.

"The Pilgrim Valiant has learned the weapons of heaven and hell are in the Lost City," Taron said. "He plans to use them to take his revenge on the gods and demons."

"Valiant will fail," Giselle said shrilly. "He doesn't have enough magic—or the right kind of magic—to wield those immortal artifacts."

"No, he does not," agreed Taron. "But the others think we can still use him."

The 'others' must have been the Guardians. Taron

and Giselle seemed to be more a part of the Guardians than they were merely two more of the people the Guardians had 'rescued'.

"Valiant is trying to hire mercenaries to assist him," Taron said. "We are to ensure he finds the right mercenaries. To open the vault where the weapons of heaven and hell are kept, he will need someone who can perform a memory recall spell."

"An angel could perform that spell. And the rogue angel Osiris Wardbreaker is in the area right now."

Taron nodded. "Wardbreaker will do—*if* he can be enticed away from his favorite hobby of massacring villages. I will make sure Valiant hires Wardbreaker."

"I have been busy off-world this past month, Taron, so you're going to have to get me all caught up. Why do we *really* want Wardbreaker to perform the memory recall spell—and on whom?"

"On Leda Pierce." Taron said my name like he was whispering over my grave.

"The Pandora?"

"Yes. She has the perfect balance of light and dark magic to be the vessel for those visions stored in the Vault of the Lost City."

Comprehension dawned on her face. "Including the visions of our future."

"The Pandora is at the center of the Prophecy," said Taron. "Her actions will determine our fate. So we must see to it that she receives those visions in the Vault, visions channeled through the weapons of heaven and hell. Those visions will push her along the right path, the path we need her to take. The path that will end with the destruction of all gods and demons—and in the Guardians' rise to power."

"Then we'd best get started," Giselle said.

Then the Guardians' angels spread their wings and flew away.

From his hiding spot, Damiel watched their silhouettes in the sky grow ever more distant. "Yes, fly off to do your wicked masters' bidding. I'll be waiting." Damiel's smile was bitter, his eyes burning with hatred.

I could hear what he was thinking. He was planning to hijack their plan, to impersonate Wardbreaker and use the memory recall spell to tune me in to the Vault's memories, memories that would lead him to the weapons of heaven and hell, immortal artifacts that he would use to fight the Guardians. And kill them, every last one of them.

"But how am I connected to the weapons of heaven and hell?" I wondered aloud. "How can I use them so well?"

---

I felt another jolt, gentler this time. Arina was getting better at moving us between the visions. I looked around, trying to figure out where—and when—we were now.

I knew at once. I'd seen this memory before.

Faris stood in a room with weapons hanging on the walls. He was dressed in a dark tunic and silk pants, one of his famous battlefield-in-the-ballroom outfits. Around his neck, he wore a gold pendant. It was the same pendant Athan had used to reveal Faris's best-kept secret: this memory.

Constellations of glowing, magically-projected dots swirled around Faris, representations of the gods' and demons' armies and their endless, immortal war. For a few moments, Faris watched the battles play out across time and space, but he soon tired of what he saw. Growling in annoyance, he waved his hand to dissolve the magic maps into dust.

"Temper, temper."

It was the demon Grace who had spoken.

But Faris's next words weren't the ones I remembered. This scene must have come out of a different memory.

"How did you get in here, Grace?"

He spun around. Shock flashed in his eyes when he saw Grace leaning against the wall—or maybe his shock was caused by what she was wearing. The demon was dressed in a red chiffon dress that showed more skin than chiffon. It looked like a nightie. A naughty nightie.

"I have my ways," Grace said with a sly smile.

He lifted his hand. The early stages of a spell twinkled on his fingertips.

"You'll want to hear what I have to say, Faris."

"Why should I listen to you?" he demanded.

"Because I know all about your little Orchestra of supernatural delights. And what I'm offering is far more enticing."

Faris looked her up and down, then declared, "There is nothing enticing about you."

The flash of evanescent lust in his eyes as they panned down Grace's body said otherwise. Faris was intrigued by her. Of course, he hated her too. Just as the gods hated all demons. He probably hated himself even more for that brief, involuntary moment of desire, however short-lived that it was, when he looked upon her.

Grace brushed her long pale hair off her shoulders, then stepped toward him. "You're gathering power, piece by piece, step by step, supernatural by supernatural, century by century."

"So I may one day defeat the demons." He threw the words in her face.

Wow, she must have really gotten under his skin. Faris was usually so composed.

"And dispose of the other gods," Grace said with a smile.

Faris said nothing.

"Don't be coy, Faris. And don't be too proud to pass up a strategic alliance."

"With you?" He laughed. "I'd rather set myself on fire."

Grace licked her lips. "If that's what it takes." She lifted up her hand and flames burst out of her open palm.

He laughed with sardonic disbelief. "You really want to help me defeat the demons?"

She blew out the flames in her hand like it was a birthday candle. "And dispose of the other gods too."

Faris's eyes narrowed. "Why?"

"Because they are all so bothersome. This immortal war bores me, Faris. Just as I know it bores you. It needs to be over."

A sly smile twisted his lips. "Then convince the demons to surrender."

"And put myself at your mercy?" She laughed out loud. "I think not. But the war can be over. We can end it together, Faris. And together we can destroy the other gods and demons, those petty fools who've allowed their egos to run the show for far too long—and in so doing, have thrown the universe into chaos. We need order. A new order."

Faris stroked his chin thoughtfully. "And how do you suggest we take out all of the other gods and demons?"

"Not by collecting supernaturals one by one, century by century, that's for sure."

"I'm playing the long game," Faris said defensively.

"Good for you. Do you want a medal?" She gave her eyes a long, slow roll. "Honestly, Faris, who do you think you're talking to? We are all immortal. And we all play the long game. I'm offering you a chance to finally play the smart game."

"Go on." Faris was intrigued. He tried to hide it, but it was there, plain and obvious on his face.

"You've been concentrating entirely on collecting the individual members of your Orchestra, but if you want to win this game, you need to get one powerful conductor. One powerful weapon. Someone with all the magic of the gods *and* the demons," Grace told him.

"The Immortals are long gone. There is no such person anymore."

"No, there isn't," she agreed. "Which is why we can't find this conductor. We have to make it."

"How?"

Grace put her hands on her hips. "You're pretty dense, aren't you? If you want to make someone with the powers of a god and a demon, you need to *make* someone with the powers of a god and a demon."

Faris blinked. "You wish to have sex with me."

"No, I don't. Not really. But, unfortunately for both of us, that's how babies are made, Faris."

Suspicion crinkled his brow. "Why come to me? Why not another god?"

"Because you have the right combination of magic and motivation to make this strategic partnership work."

"It is an intriguing idea. So now that you've given it to me, why do I need you?" Faris was thinking strategically all right.

Chains shot out of the walls, grabbing Grace by her wrists and ankles.

"Because I have the right combination of magic and motivation too," she said calmly, even as the chains pulled her toward the wall.

A slow, wicked smile twisted Faris's lips.

The chains clamped down hard on Grace's wrists and ankles. It must have hurt like hell, but she didn't even flinch. "I have magic no other demon has. Or any god, for that matter."

He watched the chains twist around her, amused. "And what magic is that?"

"Magic that has eluded gods and demons since the beginning," she said. "Power the Immortals kept from us."

"The power to see into the future," he said quietly.

"Yes."

"I've been collecting telepaths for centuries, hoping to find one with that rare gift." Faris paced before her. "But even the ones I've found with the gift, had only a very weak form of it."

"I know." Grace's eyes twinkled. "The weapon we create will have that power in its true form and more. The weapon will be a perfect balance of light and dark magic."

Faris waved his hand, and the chains binding Grace dissolved into smoke. She must have found the winning argument.

"Mixing of light and dark, a power beyond anything

either gods or demons can wield." Faris met her eyes. "They will call it blasphemy."

Grace shook out her wrists as she stepped toward him. "Then we'd better make sure they don't find out."

"Yes." He was almost drooling at the idea of such a powerful weapon.

Grace kicked off her sandals. "Look, if we're going to do this, we'll share the weapon. Fifty-fifty."

"Deal," he said instantly.

She smiled at him. He smiled back. It was downright eerie. They were probably already both thinking up ways to steal this future weapon—me—all for themselves.

"So, enough small talk," Grace said pleasantly. "Shall we begin?"

Her hand darted to the string closure of her dress and she gave it a soft tug. The layers of chiffon peeled off of her, leaving her completely naked.

"We shall," Faris agreed, hardly looking at her. He must have still been thinking about the weapon they were going to create.

Thankfully, Arina chose that moment to pan away to the next memory. I *really* didn't need to witness my parents getting down and dirty.

---

We were inside a dark room, lit only by the flickering wax candles on the wooden floor. They were positioned all around Grace, filling the air with a mixed perfume of cherry blossoms, orange blooms, and rose petals.

The demon sat on the ground, barefoot and cross-legged. She wore a sports bra and a pair of lightweight, baggy shorts. Her hands rested on her tummy, which was still flat—but not as flat as it had been when we'd seen her proposition Faris. So she hadn't been pregnant for very long.

Her eyes closed, Grace chanted in an old, forgotten tongue.

"This is one of the rituals that your mother performed on you while you were still in her womb," Arina told me.

"She was trying to get stronger telepathic magic into me," I said.

The goddess Saphira's bodyguard Calix had told me these rituals were designed to boost my future-gazing powers, a power that had eluded the gods and demons, except Grace.

"Do I possess the power of future-gazing?" I asked Arina.

"Don't you know?"

"Well, I've seen flashes of the future. Of my daughter. But that's the Vault projecting into me, right?"

"Perhaps you're seeing the visions of the future through the artifacts," Arina said. "Or perhaps the artifacts are using your magic to allow you to see."

"Can't you read my magic and tell me what it is?" I asked her.

Arina looked at me for a long while. Finally, she said, "I don't know. Your magic is very powerful right now. It's like staring straight into a bright light; it's blinding. I can't separate your magic from your unborn child's magic."

I patted my belly. "She has the power. She got it from absorbing Faith's magic. Grace made sure of that."

"Your mother sounds like a real treat," Arina told me.

"Just wait until you meet her."

Arina cringed. "I hope that I never do."

"Leda, look at Grace," Nero said.

So I looked—and blinked in surprise when I saw what Grace was doing. She now had the weapons of heaven and hell set out on the floor before her. The gun Shooting Star. The silver-and-red Shield of Protection. The long Vortex Blade, whose bright blue flames could kill a deity. And Fortitude, the set of silver armor.

"What is Grace doing?" I wondered.

"I believe she is performing a spell to bind them to you," Nero told me.

"Yes." Arina nodded. "That's exactly what she's doing."

"But why?" I wondered. "And how does she even have the artifacts? At this point in time, they were stashed away in the Lost City, locked away behind many magical protections."

"Grace must have found a way to recover them. And now she's binding them to you." Nero frowned. "So that when you find them in the Lost City approximately twenty-three years later, they will remember you, and you'll be able to wield them immediately and effectively. She's performing this ritual to make sure you have a higher compatibility with the artifacts."

"But she can't possibly know that I will be there and find them."

"Grace can see the future, or at least fragments of it," said Nero. "She could see enough to know what she must do to set you on the path she intends for you to follow."

I scowled at the Grace from the past. "Wow, planning out my whole life before I'm even born. Nice."

"Actually, as we just saw, she planned out your whole life before you were even conceived," Arina pointed out.

Even better. I knew there was a reason that Grace gave me the creeps.

"Let's fast-forward a bit." Then Arina brought us to the next stop along the Road of Time.

---

Arina was definitely getting better at directing this memory bus. She switched scenes so smoothly that I didn't even fall into Nero this time.

Grace was talking to a woman whose face was covered in a dark purple veil. "I need you to return these to the Lost City on Earth." She waved her hand toward the weapons of heaven and hell, which lay spread across the desk beside her.

"So soon?" said the woman in the purple veil.

"I need nothing more from them," Grace said. "At least not for the time being."

The purple-veiled woman took the sword, turning the blade around slowly. "These weapons can kill a deity."

"I am aware," said Grace. "But that doesn't help me just yet."

"I wish I could have a look under that woman's veil," I said to Nero. "Her voice sounds kind of familiar."

I reached for the veil, but of course my hand went right through the woman's head. Too bad. I had a nagging suspicion that this was important.

The woman gathered the artifacts into her bag, then she turned and left the room.

---

THE DOOR TO THE MEDITATION ROOM OPENED, AND Grace looked up into the face of her sister Sonja, the Demon of the Dark Force.

Arina had brought us to the next stop on the Road of Time so smoothly that I'd hardly noticed the change of scene.

Sonja's eyes dropped to Grace's belly, which was considerably rounder than it had been in the last memory. Grace cast a spell that had her fully dressed at the snap of her fingers.

"You conceived a child with that self-righteous peacock Faris," Sonja snarled at Grace.

"Stay out of my business, Sonja."

"Your business is my business, *sister*."

"How did you find out?"

"The *how* is not important," replied Sonja. "What's important is *why*. Why did you do this? Are you smitten with the god?"

Grace rolled her eyes. "Of course not."

"Good. Because then I really would have had to kill you. The gods are so…" Sonja's beautiful, immortal face scrunched up. "…vile."

"What do you want?" Grace demanded.

"Don't take that tone with me, Grace. I'm here to help you. If the other demons on the council found out about your indiscretion…" Sonja clicked her tongue. "They would not be pleased. They'd strip you of your positions and titles. They'd likely kill you too," she added breezily.

"The only way the others on the council will find out is if you tell them." Grace shot her sister a hard, accusatory glare.

"Don't be so naive. You're really starting to show."

Sonja pulled up the bottom of Grace's tunic, revealing the bump her clothes had done a decent job of concealing.

Grace knocked Sonja's hand away and pulled the bottom of her tunic back down over her belly. "I'm not seeing any visitors right now. I'm engaged in meditation."

"That story won't keep the others away for long."

"I don't have to keep them away for long," said Grace. "Only for another three months."

"I don't know why you're even bothering with a full pregnancy when you could just have it sped up. Especially, when you want to keep this a secret."

"I told you to stay out of it, Sonja. I have my reasons."

"You do realize that I will find out what you're up to, right? You can't keep secrets from me, Grace. You've never been able to. I *always* find out. And the others will find out too."

"Unlike you, the other members of the council have better things to do than barge into my meditation room," Grace said flippantly.

Sonja ignored her. "And when they do come, they will demand answers. *I* demand answers."

"You can demand all you want." Grace pointed to the door. "From out there. Go away. I'm busy meditating."

Sonja's eyes panned across the candles. "This isn't some spiritual reflection you've undertaken. This is ancient magic."

"Congratulations, you've stated the obvious." Grace planted her hands on her hips. "Now go away."

Sonja's eyes narrowed. "What are you *really* trying to do?"

"Cure heartburn," Grace quipped.

Sonja frowned. "This is no time for your jokes, Grace."

"I'm not joking. Pregnancy causes heartburn."

Sonja scoffed at the idea. "You are a deity."

"We both know that doesn't mean we're all-powerful. If I were, I'd kill you with a single thought."

Sonja's voice dropped to a low, blistering hiss. "You wouldn't dare."

"Oh, I would dare a lot of things. Pregnancy has made me cranky. And hungry." Grace flashed Sonja her fangs. "Now leave me alone before I bite you."

But Sonja was unfazed by her sister's show of fang. "You seduced Faris."

"You say that like it's a hard thing. That god had clearly not been laid in centuries."

"Why?"

"Because he's an insufferable ass, and no one wants to sleep with him."

"No," Sonja growled. "I don't care why no one wants to sleep with Faris. I care why *you* chose to sleep with him."

Grace favored her with a sunny smile. "Sometimes even I get an itch that needs scratching."

"You would have chosen someone less wretched. No, you chose Faris for a reason." Gold light flashed in Sonja's eyes. "You wanted to conceive a child with Faris. You wanted to create a child with the powers of dark and light. But why?"

Grace opened her mouth to speak.

Sonja cut her off first. "I don't need any more of your flippant remarks, little sister. You're trying to distract me from the truth, that you have created a living weapon," she hissed. "You acted in error, but what's done is done. We can use this."

"*We?*"

"Of course you're going to share your new weapon with your big sister. There has never before been a child with demon and god magic. We must train it properly if it's going to serve its purpose." Sonja's smile widened. "But first, I have to kill the priests just outside the door. They've been peeking through a crack in the door and listening to every word that we've said. And, after all, what good is a secret weapon if it's not a secret?"

---

AFTER WE LEFT GRACE AND SONJA IN THE meditation chamber, Arina brought us further down the road of memories, to Faris. The god stood in a room of martial decor, flipping through his cosmic maps. Outside his window, winter had covered the lands in a thick blanket of snow.

"Sonja knows."

Faris looked up to find Grace in his castle, right in front of him. She wore a fur-trimmed red velvet cloak that did a good job of hiding her baby bump.

He brushed the battle maps away. "What does Sonja know?"

Grace flicked her hand to cast a gust of magic wind that flung her cloak away.

Faris's gaze dropped to her baby bump, clearly visible under her tight red gown. "When did this happen?"

"Don't play coy, Faris. You were there."

"Six months ago. You sure waited a long time to tell me," he said. "Besides your sister, who else knows?"

"No one. I have been in solitude for the past several months, engaged in the Magic of the Faith rituals. Sonja showed up unannounced at the temple and barged into the Room of Solitude. She saw the fruit of our labor." Grace's hand slid over her belly. "Some of the priests were close enough to see inside the room. Sonja killed them so they couldn't spread the word."

"How kind of her to protect your secret."

"Sonja wants the child for herself," Grace growled. "There has never been a child conceived with demon and god magic. Sonja wants to weaponize the child."

"Sonja cannot be allowed to wield such a weapon, to groom it, train it, control it."

"Agreed. But I'm not giving you such a weapon either, Faris."

A twisted smile curled his lips. "You already have."

He grabbed for her, but Grace was quicker. She vanished in a cloud of black smoke.

And so did we.

---

WE WATCHED GRACE GIVE BIRTH TO ME IN A HIDDEN place, far from the eyes of demons and gods.

I winced. "I didn't realize childbirth involved so much screaming," I said to Nero.

He took my hand and squeezed it as Grace howled in agony once more. A psychic blast wave shot out of her, shattering all of the windows.

I slammed my eyes shut. My birth wasn't a pretty sight, and I made every effort to forget everything I'd just seen.

## PHOENIX'S REFRAIN

I watched a baby sleeping in a large wooden crib. Baby Leda. Me.

Grace was in the next room, pouring herself a glass of Venom. She looked so pale, so tired. I wondered how long she'd been hiding here, wherever *here* was.

My quick glance out the window offered no answers. The view was obscured by a snowstorm. Ok, so we were somewhere totally inhospitable.

"Grace is in hiding," Nero said.

"Yeah," I agreed. "She's hiding from the other demons. And from Faris."

"She didn't hide well enough." Nero pointed out the masked figure who'd just lifted me out of my crib and then snuck out of the room.

Grace was still sitting in the other room, slowly sipping her Venom. She was so drained of magic, so tired, that she hadn't noticed a thing.

"Who was that masked person?" I wondered. "Who took me?"

"Let's find out," Arina said.

---

"It's called Purgatory."

The woman who'd stolen baby Leda sat on an old park bench, surrounded by wild grass. This must have once been a well-maintained city garden, but nature had reclaimed this piece from civilization. I could see the glow of a Magitech wall in the distance.

My kidnapper was casually sitting with baby-me on the plains of monsters, totally unafraid of the monsters.

The man who'd spoken sat next to her. I recognized him instantly as Gaius Knight. Calli had shown me a picture of him. That messy black hair and long, crooked nose were unmistakable.

"I know all about Purgatory," the woman replied.

The baby thief had ditched the mask, so now I could see her real face. And I recognized her too. Those big blue eyes. That long red hair. Those well-toned arms that were strong enough to move large pieces of furniture all by herself.

Back when she'd been my foster mother, I'd known her as Julianna Mather. I'd later learned that Julianna Mather had been just an alias, and that her real name was Aradia Redwood. Major Redwood had been a soldier in the Legion of Angels, but she'd supposedly died in battle around the time I was born. Yeah, there were a lot of things that didn't quite add up here.

"You took this baby from the demon Grace," Gaius said.

Wow, he knew a lot.

Aradia seemed to be just as surprised. "How do you know about that?"

Gaius smiled. He didn't answer the question, but his next words demonstrated that he knew much more. "You work for Sonja. Or, rather, you *did* work for Sonja. You were the demon's eyes and ears inside the Legion."

So Aradia had been a spy for Sonja.

Aradia grew very still. "Are we going to have a problem?"

"Oh, I don't care about the gods or demons," Gaius said lightly. "Or about their politics."

"Then what do you care about?"

"Larger issues," Gaius said with a casual wave of his

hand. "You're loyal to Sonja, and yet you've run away—and with the child she ordered you to steal for her, no less."

"I thought you didn't care about demon and god politics," Aradia said shrewdly.

Gaius chuckled.

"Sonja is the reason that Thea is dead." Aradia's voice teetered with emotion. "Sonja set her up to die."

"The dark angel Thea was your friend."

"My best friend," Aradia declared.

"Then I can understand why you would not wish to serve Sonja anymore."

"I'm not going to allow Sonja to use and abuse this child as she did Thea. I will keep her hidden from Sonja." Aradia sighed. "I'm not sure why I'm even telling you this, except, well, Thea once told me you could be trusted. I hope she was right about you. Or this will be a very short-lived escape. For both me and the child."

"I will not betray your secret," Gaius assured her. "You've asked me to find you a safe place to hide with the child, and Purgatory is it. It's an overlooked, out-of-the-way town at the edge of Earth's Frontier, the safest place there is for you both." He opened his hand to reveal a very old-looking key. "This is the key to your new life in Purgatory."

Aradia reached over to take it.

He held back the key for a moment. "I said Purgatory is the safest place there is for you both, hidden beneath the deities' radar, in this old, insignificant town. But be warned. There is no truly safe place in all the worlds for the child."

Aradia looked down at the baby in her arms. "What is she?"

"One of a kind."

"You know more than you're saying," Aradia accused him.

Gaius smiled. He handed her the key. Then he stood up and walked slowly away.

"Wait," Aradia called out.

He turned around to look at her.

"You don't wish to be paid?"

"You have saved this child from a terrible fate. There is no greater payment," he told her.

The baby cried. Aradia looked down and rearranged the blanket bundled around her. One of the tucked corners had come loose and fallen away from the baby's head.

When Aradia looked up again, Gaius was gone.

I glanced at Nero. "So Gaius Knight led Aradia to Earth. He led me to Earth. Where I would be outside of the demons' reach."

"He clearly knew what you are," replied Nero.

"But what is he?"

"Hard to say, but he clearly does not serve the interests of either the gods or the demons."

"Guardians?" I wondered.

"Perhaps. We need to see more."

---

The memory dissolved into the next.

I saw Aradia in the kitchen of the tiny house where she'd raised me. She wore an apron over a stylish summer dress. Her red hair was braided over the top of her head, like a headband. She looked exactly as I remembered her.

A fire was lit below the large black cauldron that she

stood over. A thick, blue liquid bubbled inside. She gave the potion three slow stirs with a long, metallic spoon. Then she filled up a small glass and carried it over to the ten-year-old girl seated at the small kitchen table.

I knew that girl. I *had been* that girl. I looked at Young Leda's pale hair, divided into two messy braids. My clothes were full of holes, my knees scuffed, and my head bleeding. I looked so out of place next to Aradia's stylish, witchy wardrobe and the immaculate house.

Aradia set the glass down on the table.

The girl frowned at the potion before her. "It looks like cooler fluid." She sniffed it, and her nose scrunched up in disgust. "It smells like cooler fluid too."

"All actions have consequences, Leda," Aradia said. "The consequence of picking a fight with children bigger and stronger than you—well, that happens to be injuries which require an unpalatable remedy."

"You could have at least tried to make it palatable," Young Leda said.

"And you could have at least tried to not get into a fight. *Again*."

"Hey, they started it. I just finished it."

"Finished it indeed." Aradia tapped a wet cloth to the deep cut on the girl's forehead. "A few more hits like this to the head, and *you* would have been finished."

"You should see the other guys." Young Leda flashed Aradia a smile. "They look much worse. In fact, they're probably still unconscious."

"Do you mean to tell me that you fought two fourteen-year-olds and won?"

"Try not to sound so surprised, Julianna." The girl used the name I'd known Aradia by.

"But how did you do it?"

"They jumped me," Young Leda said. "My head hit the ground. It really hurt, but I knew that I had to fight back, or it would hurt even more. They weren't going to stop hitting me. I was on the ground. When they moved in closer to kick me, I grabbed two fistfuls of dirt and threw them in their faces. That blinded them for a while, long enough for me to get up. My head was ringing pretty badly."

Aradia frowned. "You probably have a concussion." She put her hand in front of the girl's face. "How many fingers am I holding up?"

"Twelve," Young Leda said flippantly.

"Concussions are no joke, Leda."

"You asked what happened, and I'm telling you."

"At least drink some of your medicine."

Young Leda lifted the glass to her mouth and took a sip. "This tastes like cooler fluid too!" she exclaimed.

"Don't spit it out, or it won't heal you."

Young Leda took another sip, shook herself, then continued her story. "So my head was ringing, and I was getting real dizzy. Luckily, the two bullies were rubbing their eyes, trying to get the dirt out of them. They were shouting bad words at me so loudly that they didn't hear me throw a few rocks in front of them. They tripped over the rocks and hit the ground."

"That wasn't very sporting of you, Leda."

"And it wasn't very sporting of them to gang up on someone who's so much younger and smaller than they are," Young Leda pointed out. "I had to take every advantage I could get."

"Why did they attack you anyway?"

"They found me after school to torment me with insults."

"Such as?"

Young Leda shrugged. "The usual. They called me a dirty orphan. Said my parents were monster-blood-drinking freaks and that's why when I was born, I was cast out by the Pilgrims for being a dark, evil child. They said the Pilgrims banished me to the Black Plains, where a pack of wild wolves raised me until you found me."

"That is nonsense."

Young Leda looked up into Aradia's eyes. "What *did* happen to my parents?"

"They died shortly after you were born. They were friends of mine. And they certainly did not consume monster blood."

"How did they die?" Young Leda asked.

"It's an unpleasant story, one you don't need to hear at your age. Someday, perhaps, I'll tell you. But rest assured, they were not evil people."

Nice how she twisted the truth to avoid lying. Yeah, my parents weren't evil *people*. They were evil, power-hungry deities who'd made me in order to create a powerful living weapon.

Young Leda blinked her big, wide eyes at Aradia. "I've always wanted to know more about my parents."

Maybe my first foster mother would have indeed told me the truth someday, but if so, she'd never gotten a chance. She did not long outlive this conversation.

"You shouldn't allow the other children to goad you," she told my younger self. "They're only looking to make themselves feel strong by pushing down the weak."

"I am not weak. And I showed them that today. I showed them they cannot insult me. As you said, actions have consequences."

"You threw the first punch?"

"No. After they called me all those names, I informed one of the bullies that his real father is actually his next door neighbor. And I told the other bully that I knew his mother had actually shoplifted everything they had in their house."

"How could you possibly know all of that?" Aradia said in surprise.

"It's obvious. Anyone with eyes could have figured it out. The first bully looks nothing like his 'father'—and exactly like his next door neighbor. And I regularly see the second bully's mother walking around town in the middle of the day, so she obviously doesn't work. And she's always wearing a big and bulky coat, even in summertime. She could fit a lot of stolen merchandise under that coat."

Aradia looked her over for a moment, then declared, "You're too smart for your own good, Leda."

"Hey, I didn't tell them anything until they insulted me. They just wouldn't stop. I had to make them shut up. And they were pretty silent for a few moments after I told them their family secrets."

"Until they attacked you," Aradia pointed out.

"Right." Young Leda frowned. "I really thought they'd run straight home and confront their parents."

"Not everyone wants to know their past like you do, Leda. Most people are content to ignore all the dirty little secrets in their family tree. They really don't want to know these kinds of things about themselves. And they will do anything to not face reality. That's why those boys attacked you. To distract themselves from the truth—and to punish the one who'd delivered that unwelcome truth to them."

"People are dumb," Young Leda declared.

"What happened after you tripped the boys with the rocks?"

"They were pretty upset. They got up and ran at me, but I was ready for them. I'd moved behind a bunch of clothes lines. The fall must have mixed up their heads because they didn't even see the lines. They ran right into them and got all tangled up like in a spider web. They might still be stuck in them."

"You're supposed to be keeping a low profile, not attracting attention to yourself," Aradia sighed.

"But why do I need to keep a low profile?" Young Leda asked her. "It's because of who my parents were, isn't it? And because of who you used to be?"

Aradia shook her head.

"I know you had to have been someone important, Juliana," Young Leda told her. "You can do magic. Anyone who can do magic in this world is important. Magic is power. And witches are in high demand."

"You're too smart for your own good," Aradia said again.

"Tell me." Young Leda pressed her palms together in a pleading gesture. "You can trust me."

"You picked a fight with two bigger and stronger opponents, Leda. Do you know what that demonstrates?"

"Great skill," the girl answered proudly. "I won."

"You won *this* time, but only through unscrupulous means. No, your actions demonstrate that you still have a lot to learn."

"Julianna, I—"

Aradia's hand shot up, silencing Young Leda. "Someone is outside," she whispered quietly.

"How do you know?" Young Leda whispered back.

Aradia didn't answer. She grabbed Young Leda and

pulled her into one of the bedrooms. She had only just closed the girl inside the room and cast a spell over it when the front door of the house flew open. Two men in black uniforms marched inside.

"Those are Dark Force soldiers," Nero commented.

I recognized them too by the symbol of the Dark Force on their uniforms. That symbol consisted of the nine signs of magic—vampire, witch, siren, elemental, shifter, telekinetic, fairy, angel, ghost—all surrounded by the emblem of hell.

"So that's who killed her," I said. "I always thought it was monsters."

One of the Dark Force soldiers spoke, a big, muscular man with legs as thick as tree trunks and shoulders so wide that they nearly scraped the doorway as he stepped through. "Aradia Redwood. It's been a long time."

"You didn't honestly believe you could hide from Sonja, the great and powerful Demon of the Dark Force," the second man added.

He was even bigger and wider than the other soldier. His shoulders actually did scrape the doorway as he stepped through, just as his head brushed against the wooden frame.

"And yet Sonja couldn't find me, Harrows," Aradia said, her stance confident. "For ten whole years."

Harrows glowered at her. "Hiding on Earth was a dirty trick."

"So was Sonja killing Thea!"

"Enough." Harrows had a voice that scraped like shifting gravel. "There can be no excuse for your treachery. Sonja is your deity. You were sworn to obey her. You broke that vow, and now Chambers and I will punish you in Sonja's name."

"If Sonja wanted me punished, she should have sent a few more soldiers." Aradia drew her sword. Bright orange flames flashed across the blade.

Harrows and Chambers moved in from either side. They were much bigger than Aradia, and they had her surrounded. That didn't seem to bother her. She spun like a tornado, flames engulfing her entire body. Harrows tried to grab her but quickly drew his hand away, repelled by the flaming tornado. And when Chambers shot a telekinetic spell at her, it bounced right off the storm she'd swaddled herself in.

The fight continued, even as my younger self remained trapped behind the bedroom door. I remembered that day. Loud as the battle was, I hadn't heard a thing that had gone on outside the bedroom. Aradia's spell must have muffled the sounds, as well as trapped me in and everyone else out.

Aradia had the two Dark Force soldiers on the retreat. Harrows grabbed a device from his belt. It looked like a communication device.

Aradia knocked it out of his hand with a telekinetic punch. "You won't be reporting back to Sonja." She crushed the device with her boot.

"Sonja already knows we're here," Harrows said.

"No, she doesn't," Aradia shot back. "You had to be sure you'd actually found me this time. You didn't want another false alarm. Sonja wasn't pleased with the last one."

Surprise flashed across his face. "How did you know?"

"The scars on your arm." Aradia pointed at his scarred arm. "Those were made by Sonja's famous chains. She punished you. And she coated the chains in a powerful poison to do it. That's why your wounds haven't healed; that's why they scarred over. I bet it was Nectar, which is poison to soldiers of the Dark Force. Sonja would consider that an appropriate punishment. The irony of hurting you with what gave me, once a Legion soldier, power, would appeal to her. That's how I know she punished you for failing to find me. Because I understand Sonja much better than you do."

Harrows knocked the sword out of her hand. "You've always been too smart for your own good, Aradia."

His statement echoed Aradia's earlier words to my younger self.

He grabbed her by the neck, hefting her off the ground.

"I'm certainly smarter than you," she ground out tightly.

Her hand flashed out and she stabbed him through the chest with a knife. He fell dead to the ground. She must have poured a lot of light magic down her blade.

Chambers didn't give her a chance to catch her breath. He was already running at her. "Harrows and I have worked together since the day we joined the Dark Force!" he shouted. "And you killed him! I'm going to kill you!"

Chambers had gone berserk. He grabbed large pieces of furniture and began throwing them at her. Aradia was flicking them away with her magic, but she was having a hard time keeping up with his fury.

When Chambers ran out of furniture to throw, he started ripping kitchen appliances out of the wall. And when those were gone, he tore the kitchen counter off its legs and hurled it at her. He had her so busy casting defensive spells that she didn't have time to attack him.

Soon Chambers ran out of obvious things to throw, so he grabbed the knob on my bedroom door, but he retracted his hands when he was dealt a shock.

Aradia took advantage of his shock. She launched a fireball into the bubbling cauldron. It exploded all over Chambers, splattering him with blue potion that began to hiss and burn the moment it touched his skin. There must have been too much light magic in that potion.

Covered in burning boils, Chambers ran blindly at Aradia like an enraged bull. He knocked her right through the wall, out into the back yard. Bricks showered down on both of their bodies. The spell on the bedroom door flickered out.

Only a few moments later, Young Leda emerged from her room. Her eyes took in the destroyed furniture. They grew wider when they saw the large monster on the floor, where Harrows was supposed to be. Aradia must have transformed his dead body into that of a dagger-clawed wolf. My younger self should have remembered that no monsters could exist on this side of the wall, but emotion must have won out over reason.

Young Leda moved toward the gaping hole in the wall. She climbed through it. That's where she found Aradia and Chambers, whom she'd also transformed into another dagger-clawed wolf. Both she and the transformed soldier were half-buried in debris. Young Leda began pulling bricks off of her foster mother, trying to unbury her.

Aradia caught her hand. "Stop." Her bleeding lips barely moved.

"Julianna, I have to get you out of there," Young Leda said, her eyes trembling. "I have to get you to a healer."

"It's too late for that," Aradia croaked.

"I'm not giving up on you!"

"Don't give up on yourself, Leda. You can take care of yourself. Just don't pick any more fights."

Tears streamed down the young girl's face.

Aradia smiled. "I am so proud to have known you." Her hand dropped. She was dead.

Young Leda stood there for a moment, shaking. Then she wiped away her tears. She kissed her foster mother's cheek and walked away, disappearing into the shadows of Purgatory.

"After that, I lived alone, on the streets," I said. "Until Calli found me two years later."

---

We'd moved forward in time two years. Young Leda was now twelve years old—and so filthy that she was hardly recognizable. I watched my younger self steal a bun off a baker's cart in the Bazaar, Purgatory's outdoor open shopping area.

Young Leda snuck away, her dirty body blending into the shadows. She moved toward a side alley but changed directions when a man in a purple suit walked out of that alley to enter the Bazaar.

"Leda, look at his face," Nero said.

So I did. "It's Gaius Knight. He walked there on purpose to make me go somewhere else."

I watched Young Leda slip away, moving down another narrow street that led away from the Bazaar. Nero and I followed her. We came around the corner to find Young Leda standing face-to-face with Calli.

"Now I remember this day," I said.

"Ah, so you so often stole buns from the baker's stand

that the days all blended together?" Nero pretended to be lecturing me, but I recognized that teasing spark in his eyes.

"Not always buns," I told him. "Sometimes it was a muffin or a croissant. A few times, I was lucky enough to nab a whole loaf of bread. That kept me well-fed the whole day."

"You led a hard life," he observed.

"That changed this day. The day I met Calli."

Calli was talking to my younger self. "That's a tasty treat you have there, Leda."

Young Leda hugged the bun tightly to her body.

"Where did you get it?" Calli asked her.

Young Leda pressed her lips together and didn't answer.

"When's the last time you had something hot to eat?" Calli said kindly.

"Sometimes the bread is hot."

Calli smiled at her. "You said you're twelve, right? I have a girl about your age."

Young Leda looked her up and down. "You look too young to have a daughter my age."

"Are you always so blunt?" Calli laughed.

"Yes," Young Leda said defiantly. "Are you planning on kidnapping me?"

"Goodness, no. Do I look like that kind of person?"

"Not really, but you were using the promise of a hot meal to try to lure me home with you."

"Not to kidnap you. To help you. But you're right," Calli chuckled. "I guess I did come across as suspicious. What if I took you to the Jolly Joint for lunch? That's a very public place."

Young Leda's eyes narrowed with suspicion. "You

could be hoping to feed me into an overstuffed stupor. And then kidnap me."

"You're a smart girl."

Young Leda sighed. "Too smart, some people say."

"Who says that?"

Young Leda shook her head. "It doesn't matter." She gave Calli a long, assessing stare. "You don't look like a kidnapper."

"I'm not. In fact, I've been hired to find whoever has been kidnapping children off the streets of Purgatory."

"So you're a bounty hunter."

"I am."

"That's pretty cool," Young Leda cooed.

"Some of us are. And some bounty hunters would sell out their own family for a tidy profit."

"You're not one of those bounty hunters," Young Leda decided.

"Glad we've agreed on that."

"Do you think you'll catch the bad guys?"

"I usually do," Calli said. "Though until now, I didn't know how they were nabbing kids and disappearing without anyone seeing a thing."

"The underground tunnels," Young Leda told her, indicating the dark passageway around them.

"I never knew Purgatory had underground tunnels."

"Most people don't. I discovered them two years ago when I was running away from the baker I'd stol—um, a baker who was chasing me. There's like a whole city down there. I think the city sank long ago and Purgatory was built on top of it. I sometimes use those tunnels to hide from the others."

"The other kids on the streets?"

"Yeah." She cleared her throat. "It's a good thing you have me to show you the way."

"Yes," Calli agreed.

"In fact, I think you owe me much more than a meal at the Jolly Joint."

"How do you figure?"

"This gig of yours…finding missing children," Young Leda said. "That has to be worth at least a thousand dollars."

"Two-and-a-half thousand. The sheriff wants this sorted quickly, so the Legion doesn't come into town."

"The Legion of Angels." Young Leda's voice was full of awe—and something else.

"Right."

"The angels are pretty, but there's something weird about them," the young girl observed.

"Oh?"

"The angels always follow the rules," Young Leda said. "Even when it's the wrong thing to do. People should always do the right thing. Otherwise, what's the point of life?"

"You are wise beyond your years," Calli told her.

Young Leda looked her over. "So are you."

Calli laughed. "So, Leda, which way to the vampires?"

"I'll show you. *After* we agree on my reward."

"Ah, so you haven't forgotten about that."

Young Leda gave her a stern look. "You hoped that I would."

"No. I'm glad that you're as shrewd of a businesswoman as I am."

Young Leda stood a bit taller.

"What happened to your family?" Calli asked her.

"Dead. All of them."

Calli set a comforting hand on the girl's shoulder. "I'm sorry."

Young Leda shook her head and cleared her throat. "It happened a long time ago. It happens to a lot of people."

"I know," Calli sighed. "It happened to my kids too."

"Your kids?"

"My foster kids."

"How many children have you taken in?"

"Four."

Young Leda thought that over for a moment, then declared, "If you weren't such a softy, you'd be able to afford better boots from all that money you make on bounties."

Calli laughed. "Likely so. But someone wise once told me that people should always do the right thing. Otherwise, what's the point of life?"

"I like you, Calli," Young Leda told her. "You don't treat me like I'm stupid just because I'm a kid."

"And I like you, Leda. You don't treat me like I'm stupid just because I'm a grownup."

Calli and Young Leda walked off together down the street.

"Calli told me one of the jobs Gaius had gotten her led her to me," I said to Nero. "This job. Gaius got Calli the job. And he was waiting in that alley to head me off, to make me change direction so I'd cross paths with Calli. I'd once thought we'd met by chance, but nothing was by chance. It was all meticulously arranged. Nero?"

Nero looked away from Calli and my younger self. "Sorry, Pandora. I was distracted."

I smirked at him. "Curious to know what I was like as a child?"

"You didn't have a handle on your mouth back then either," he scolded me. "Mouthing off to a stranger, an adult who was much bigger than you, and who was armed. What were you thinking? How could you be so reckless?"

"You're chastising me for my recklessness twelve years ago? Seriously?"

"With that mouth of yours, it was a wonder you survived long enough for us to meet."

I snorted.

"Leda, this is no laughing matter."

"Of course not, General Killjoy, but laughter makes me keep a grip as I watch my past unravel before me—and realize that my whole life was completely manipulated. I never had a choice in anything."

Nero set his hands on my shoulders. "You did have a choice. You chose to help Calli."

"Gaius had probably been watching me and knew what kind of person I was. Hell, he'd made me into that person by having me grow up with Aradia. He knew where Aradia's house was. Where I was. He could have told the gods or demons at any point where I was living, but he had me grow up with Aradia. And then he made sure Calli took me in. He also made sure that Calli took in Zane, Gin, Tessa, and Bella. Why? Who is Gaius Knight? And what does he want?"

I looked at Arina. "Can't you tell who he is? Isn't that information kept somewhere inside the Vault?"

"I can't tell," Arina replied, and she looked frustrated. "Whenever I try to figure it out, I'm blocked. In fact, whenever I try to find out anything more about you,

Calli, or your foster siblings, my magic is blocked. Whoever is blocking me understands my magic extremely well. That's the most unsettling thing of all."

Indeed. Arina's magic was on the passive magic spectrum. There weren't a whole lot of people around here who knew much about that kind of magic.

"Whoever is doing this, whoever put these visions into the Vault, they're only letting us see what they want us to see," Arina said. "And no more."

Then, suddenly, I felt a rough jerk, and the three of us were ripped from the streets of Purgatory and thrown off the Road of Time.

## CHAPTER 22

LEDA

We stood at the crossroads of four ecosystems laid out in a perfect grid, each one beautiful, each one dangerous. I wasn't sure how I knew that dangers lurked inside those gorgeous natural environments, but I did. Danger lurked there. And death.

In front of me, in the grid's upper-left quadrant, lay a field of flowers. Sweet-smelling, colorful flowers. They were all different—and yet all sang notes of the same melody. The flowers and notes blended together in a superlative, seductive song. The song, combined with the gentle breeze and warm sunlight, made me feel kind of drowsy.

A dark forest covered the grid's upper-right quadrant. Though it was daytime just next door, here it was night. Darkness reigned supreme. I heard the foreboding, bewitching melody of animals inside the forest. Brightly-colored, poisonous spiders perched on gigantic webs strung between the trees.

The crossroads point was small—barely large enough

to fit me, Nero, and Arina—so I turned carefully on the spot to get a better look at the two quadrants behind us.

The lower-left quadrant was a sunny meadow. There was no grass, and there were no trees or bushes here. Mushrooms were all that I saw. Mushrooms in every conceivable color and pattern. I stared at them, transfixed. And the longer I stared at them, the more transfixed I became. I couldn't look away. My vision blurred. I thought I saw one of the mushrooms change into a bunny, then it started hopping around.

"Careful," Nero said.

He'd caught me as I'd swayed.

I smiled at him. "Thanks."

When I looked back at the meadow, the bunny wasn't there.

"That area seems to have hallucinogenic properties," Nero observed.

That explained the bunny. I decided not to stare at the mushrooms too much longer, in case I started seeing more things that weren't actually there.

I turned my attention to the final quadrant. The ecosystem in the lower-right area of the grid was dark. Very dark. Brightly colored fuzz that looked like some kind of bacteria had covered some of the darkness like a layer of moss on a tree. I felt a very weird, very irresistible urge to touch the foul stuff. I reached out. The multicolored fuzz spread toward my hand.

I retracted my hand. "Ow!" I'd felt a surge of pain where it had touched my fingers.

"What are you doing, Leda?" Nero asked me.

"Looking before I leap again, apparently," I said sheepishly.

"You really need to stop doing that." Nero looked my hand over. "I don't see anything. Does it still hurt?"

"No, the pain is gone now, but that was really weird. This whole place is weird. Where are we anyway? This isn't a memory or a vision. It's something else entirely."

"I believe this isn't a real place at all," he said. "It's a metaphor."

"A metaphor?"

"A symbolic representation."

"Yeah, I know what a metaphor is," I chuckled. "But what's this place a metaphor of?"

"Magic. I believe we are looking at the four quadrants of magic." He pointed to the field of flowers in the grid's upper-left quadrant. "Active light magic, the magic of the gods." He pointed out the blossoming flowers. "The magic of Nectar."

He indicated the dark forest in the grid's upper-right quadrant. "Dark active magic. The magic of the demons." He looked up at the venomous spiders in the webs. "The magic of Venom."

He turned with me and indicated the sunny meadow with all the hallucinogenic mushrooms in the lower-left quadrant. "Light passive magic."

"The magic of the spirits," Arina chimed in. She indicated the mushrooms. "The magic of Elixir."

"Spirits? Elixir?" I asked her.

"The spirits are like gods or demons," she explained. "They're another kind of deity, a deity with passive light magic. And Elixir is like Nectar or Venom."

I turned to the final quadrant, the one with the multicolored, biting fuzz. "Then that makes this area the representation of dark passive magic."

"Yes," Arina said. "The magic of the eidolons. And Blight."

I guessed the eidolons were the passive dark magic deity, and that Blight was their equivalent of Nectar or Venom.

There was a flash, and then my brother and three sisters were suddenly there, each one standing in a different quadrant. Zane was inside the active light magic field. Bella was in the active dark magic forest. Tessa was in the passive light magic meadow. And, finally, Gin was in the passive dark magic quadrant.

"I think the Vault is trying to tell us something," I said.

"How very observant of you."

I turned toward the voice—and found Gaius Knight. He stood beside me in the tiny crossroads square, which had meanwhile grown larger to accommodate his presence.

"Are you part of this metaphor?" I asked him.

"No, he's actually here, talking to us," Arina told me.

Gaius smiled. "Correct."

"In fact, he's the one who enchanted your parchment in the first place," Arina said. "The clue to Thea's grimoire. And he put my picture on that page."

"Mostly correct." Gaius didn't clarify further.

"Somehow he's found a way to tap into the visions from wherever he is." Arina poked him with her finger. Her hand didn't go right through him.

"Then he's the one who can give us the answers we need." I turned and faced the man. "Why did you send me all these visions? And what is this magical metaphor all about? Light, dark, active, passive. What is the meaning of showing me this?"

"Passive magic. That's what the Immortals named it when they catalogued all of magic."

That wasn't an answer to the question I'd asked, but Gaius didn't seem to care. In fact, he looked perfectly content to speak about whatever he had already planned to speak about.

"The Immortals called it 'passive magic' because they thought 'eating magic' sounded too dangerous, too threatening."

"Very interesting." I had a feeling he would eventually come to the point, but I had no idea how long that would take.

"But passive magic didn't sound too dangerous or too threatening," Gaius continued. "It sounded amenable. It sounded like something that wasn't vile, something that wasn't a threat."

"Indeed." What else was I supposed to say?

"Some other people out there still called it eating magic," Gaius said. "Because the magic that the passive magic users wield comes from channeling magic that exists outside themselves."

So the Immortals had tried their hand at rebranding magic.

"This is all very interesting," I told him. "But what does it have to do with what you're showing me here?"

"The bonds of siblings are strong, when they grow up properly."

I felt like I was talking to a fortune cookie.

"And Callista made just the right environment for you all to bond. She created the right recipe." He sounded like he was talking about baking, not family. "Look at your brother and sisters."

So I looked.

"They are your four horsemen, one from each quadrant of magic. Together, they encompass the four kinds of magic. And here you are, Leda Pandora, standing right at the middle of it all."

"So you meant for my brother and sisters to protect me?" I asked.

Like Ava had wanted Bella to protect me. Come to think of it, where did Ava's plans fit into all of this? I was about to ask that question when Gaius dropped the biggest bombshell of them all.

"They're meant to protect not only you, but also the child you carry. Your daughter is the future. And you are standing at the crossroads, Leda. Light magic. Dark magic. Active magic. Eating magic."

"Light, dark, active, eating," I muttered, repeating his words.

I didn't like the order, so I changed it. "Light, eating, dark, active. LEDA." I gaped at him. "Leda. It's me."

# CHAPTER 23

### TERRIBLE FUTURES

I tried to work through what Gaius had shown me. "My first foster mother, Aradia, was one of Sonja's soldiers."

"Yes," Gaius replied. "Until Aradia betrayed Sonja."

"And Sonja sent the soldiers who killed Aradia."

He nodded. "Dark Force soldiers."

"Aradia betrayed Sonja because of what Sonja did to her friend Thea. Thea, Bella's mother. What happened to Bella and what happened to me—this is all connected."

"Naturally."

"Who named me?" I asked him.

"Grace."

"So Grace knew what she was truly creating."

He folded his hands together and smiled at me. Apparently, I'd diverted from the path of what he wanted to tell me.

"Did Aradia know about all of this?" I waved my hand to indicate the four quadrants of magic.

"Aradia knew only what she needed to know."

"She only knew what you showed her, you mean. You

manipulated her." I frowned. "And you're manipulating me."

"No, not manipulating. I am…doing you a favor, child. I'm guiding you to your destiny. I'm protecting you from those who would deter you from it."

"Call it what you will. You are being perfectly obtuse," I said. "You're showing me only what you want to show me in order to push me down the path that you have set out for me."

"I have not set this path for you, Leda. It is nothing short of what you were always meant to do."

He was trying to use big, dramatic words to mask the reality of his machinations.

"You've overlooked one thing," I told him. "I'm a rebel. Showing me what you want me to do only makes me want to *not* do it."

"I believe that," he chuckled. "But you *really* want to stop the Guardians' plans. For your daughter's sake."

A cold chill took hold of me. "What will happen to my daughter? What are the Guardians planning to do to her?"

"The Guardians have a Prophecy."

"A Prophecy about a divine savior who will be born human, with equal light and dark magic," I quoted what Zane had once told me. "She will grow her magic one ability at a time, and someday she will upset the balance of power. The Guardians believe she will change the balance of magic back to the middle, back to mixed magic of light and dark origins. They believe the savior is a god killer and demon slayer."

"The Guardians didn't tell Zane everything," Gaius said. "They didn't tell Zane the part where you have a child. Or that your having that child will be how you balance magic."

I set my hands protectively over my belly.

"But there's a risk, Leda. One path leads to the Guardians gaining power and supremacy, to getting everything they've ever wanted. Everything they've been dreaming of and planning for. The other path, however, leads to their total destruction."

"Well, I guess it's a fine line between power and death," I commented.

That was the line every Legion soldier walked, every time they tried to level up their magic.

"The future is not set, and so the Prophecy allows for several different paths," Gaius said. "The Guardians decided long ago to allow you to grow your magic until you became an angel and had a child. Then they plan to destroy you."

"What about Nero? Why did the Guardians want Nero to be born?" I asked him.

"Because they needed him, a man of Immortal blood, to have a child with the savior they knew would one day be born."

"The savior, an angel with perfect light and dark magic but who wasn't born with any magic at all," I quoted.

That described me perfectly.

"The Guardians needed you and Nero Windstriker to conceive a child, the product of light and dark, of active and passive, of order and chaos," Gaius said. "And of love. That one most of all."

Nero took my hand.

"This child would exist in perfect balance and would be more powerful than even the Immortals," said Gaius.

"If the Guardians could find a way to control her, they could take out anyone who stood in their way. Do you understand what I'm telling you, Leda? Your daughter is the key to the Guardians finally getting everything that they want. Your daughter is the one who can end the gods and demons, end all the Guardians' enemies, for that matter. Because with her power, no one will be able to stand against her. And with her under the Guardians' control, no one will be able to stand against them."

"Well, when you put it like that, it does sound pretty bad," I said quietly.

"Worse than bad. It is the end of everything." Gaius set his hand on my forehead.

I saw the dream that Nero had described to me. I saw the two of us fighting side-by-side against a great invading army. We were fighting for our daughter, to keep her from those who would steal her from us.

"This is the vision Grace sent to Nero, this vision of the future," Gaius told me. "But it's only one possibility. And it's one of the best outcomes."

"One of the best outcomes?" I said in shock. "The universe and everyone in it is at war. How could this possibly be one of the best outcomes?"

"Because in this outcome, your daughter still has free will. Shall I show you the other possible futures?"

He didn't wait for my answer. Before I knew it, I was looking at Sierra, the red-haired angel.

"This is your daughter."

I watched the angel clad herself in the weapons of heaven and hell. Her flaming sword shimmered in the light of the full moon. She was so powerful. So beautiful. So magnificent.

"Arina was right? Sierra really is my daughter?" I asked Gaius.

"Yes."

Sierra moved across the city battlefield, her wings as silver as her armor. A monster jumped at her. She lifted her shield and knocked it away. Her sword cut through the next beast. Then she continued past the broken buildings, on toward the enemy that had invaded her city.

"Sierra is a hero, but she has lost much. Her family, her friends." Gaius looked at Nero and me. "Her parents."

"In this future, we are dead?" I asked him.

"Yes, but this is only one of many terrible futures."

He waved his hand, and then I was on another battlefield in some other possible future. I stood between two warring armies, each side led by angels.

I remembered this vision. I'd seen it before.

Beautiful and terrible, the armies of angels clashed in a war of magic and might that shook the ground and echoed across the heavens. Swords clashed. Steel clanged. The stench of blood and sulfur and death permeated the air. Feathers fluttered on the wind. The soil was soaked with blood; it spread out from the battlefield, blackening the Earth. The storm of spells raged on.

I dashed across the battlefield, my pale blonde hair swooshing across my face as I slashed through the enemy ranks with my fire sword. I sprang into the air, then slammed my fist down. Jets of fire erupted from the ground, shooting up into raging pillars of flames.

I strode across the battlefield, wings spreading out from my back, my dark purple-black feathers shimmering like petals of luxurious velvet in the light of the setting sun. Bodies fell before me. Men turned and ran from me. The ground shook beneath me.

A jolt of pain ruptured my ribcage. I looked down to find a sword protruding from my chest. I turned around to face the person who'd stabbed me in the back.

The last time I'd seen this vision, I'd blacked out before I could see my attacker's face. Not this time. This time, I saw her as clearly as the blood that flowed out of my chest. It was Sierra. My daughter had stabbed me in the back.

## CHAPTER 24

LOCKED OUT

"In this future, you failed," Gaius explained to me and Nero. "You survived, but your daughter Sierra turned against you. She became the Guardians' champion, a champion of nefarious intentions."

"Are these really the only two options for our daughter?" I asked. "A life as a hero, but in a miserable, forsaken world where everyone she cares about is dead? Or a life where the world and her loved ones have survived, but we've lost Sierra because she serves the Guardians?"

"You *can* save the world and your daughter," Gaius told me. "You just need to be smart about it. There's always another way."

"Your way." I frowned in frustration. "You're telling me the only way to save Sierra and the world is to do what you say."

"I would never tell you that."

"And yet you're giving us no other option."

"In fact, I presented two alternative options, Leda."

"Neither of which is truly an option!"

He nodded. "I thought you might see it that way."

"Of course you did." Scorn dripped from my words. "Everything you showed me was to make me see it your way."

"You still have a choice. No one can take that away from you."

I made an exasperated noise. "Ok. I'll bite. What is this 'smart' way? How do we save our daughter *and* the world?"

Gaius opened his mouth to speak, then shut it again. He glanced around, looking suddenly nervous. "Later. Need to go now."

Then he faded out, but we were still here at the crossroads. We hadn't returned to the real world, to the airship.

"What a drama queen," I grumbled. "I bet he's left us hanging so we have a chance to digest those awful future visions for a while. And then he believes we'll pick his 'way out', whatever that is."

"I'm not so sure he left to create drama," Nero told me. "Gaius was so focused throughout our conversation, and then he was suddenly so nervous. He looked like someone had just walked in on his conversation with us. Perhaps he was attacked."

"Great. Even better. The only person with answers is now out of commission."

Nero touched my cheek softly. "You're usually so optimistic."

"I'm not usually dealing with the fate of our daughter."

"Don't lose heart, Leda. We will figure out how to protect our daughter, with or without his help."

I set my hand over his. "Thank you. For being, well, you. And for not panicking."

"Panicking serves no purpose." Nero was pragmatic like that.

I chuckled. "I'll try to remember that." I turned to Arina. "Are there any more visions in the Vault?"

"There might be, but I can't tell. Someone is blocking my magic, my access to the visions." She looked like she didn't like the feeling one bit. "But you've been connected to the Vault since you stepped into the Lost City two years ago. Maybe you can access them?"

I closed my eyes and tried focusing on the visions. I didn't find a thing. I felt like a wall had sprung up, blocking them off from me. I was locked out.

I opened my eyes and shook my head. "Nothing. Gaius must have inserted himself into the memories by being there, at the Lost City, in the Vault. But now he is silent and so are the memories. Someone must have stopped him from sending them to us. And whoever that someone is, they don't want me seeing these memories right now. They've turned off my access."

"The Guardians," said Arina. She looked like she wanted to punch someone. Yep, the Guardians were clearly at the very top of her shit list.

"That's my guess," I said. "The Guardians have the most to lose if Nero and I can find a way to save our daughter from suffering that terrible fate. We have to go there, to the Lost City. We have to expel the Guardians from the Vault. We have to hear what Gaius was going to tell us."

"What we must do, above all, is exercise caution," Nero told me calmly. "Our going there might be exactly what the Guardians want. We do know they want our daughter. We can't let them get her."

I set my hands over my belly, shielding our daughter. "You're right. The trouble is we don't even know what causes our path to spiral toward those terrible futures—or which choices will help us avoid those futures." I sighed into a slouch. "I think I preferred things when I didn't know what possibilities the future might hold."

"It's generally a good idea to have no prior knowledge of what nonsense we might cause in the future," he replied.

"Yeah, imagine what you'd have done if you'd been forewarned of all my chaos." I gave him a coy look. "You'd never have tried to seduce me by showing off your physique."

"I take issue with your statement that I was ever showing off."

"What about when you went totally hardcore on the salmon ladder in the gym?" I pointed out.

"There's a difference between training and showing off, Pandora. It's not my fault that you're easily impressed by—"

"By your acts of raw, supercharged masculinity as you powered your way up that ladder, muscles bulging, hot sweat dripping off your—"

"Do you need to sit down?" Nero arched his brows.

I fanned myself with my hand. "Yes, please."

Nero snorted.

I winked at him.

"You're one to talk," he said. "You were always going around the gym in those…inappropriate outfits."

"Crop tops?"

"Yes. And those tiny shorts." He wet his lips.

"If you don't like the Legion's sport attire, you should take it up with the Head of Wardrobe," I laughed. "Come to think of it, maybe I'll have a chat with him myself. I notice the men's outfit doesn't consist of a skimpy sports bra and hot pants…"

I stopped. Nero was watching me, an odd look on his face.

"You're picturing me in a skimpy sports bra and hot pants, aren't you?" I asked him.

There was fire in his eyes. "Not as much clothing as that."

I looped my arms over Nero's shoulders. "I've had an idea."

"That sounds dangerous."

"I haven't even told you my idea yet."

"It doesn't matter. I know you, Leda. And I know that look in your eyes."

I fluttered my eyelashes, the picture of innocence. "Oh?"

"It's the look you get right before you're about to do something reckless."

I winked at him.

"So what is your reckless idea?" He sighed.

I decided to take that as a sign that he'd surrendered himself to my chaos.

"You know how you didn't want to do anything 'dangerous'?" I said.

Nero looked down at my hands, which were squeezing his butt. "Given your condition, I didn't think it prudent," he said cautiously.

"Don't use words like 'prudent' when I'm trying to seduce you, Nero," I chided him. "It's not sexy."

His halo crackled with amusement.

"You see, since our bodies are not really here…" I quickly pulled off his shirt. "It's not even dangerous."

"You want to have telepathic sex with me?" He looked totally perplexed.

"Nero, I'd like to have any and every kind of sex with you that I can get," I replied solemnly. "My hormones are through the roof, and my body is aching for you."

Silver flashed in his eyes. He looked like he was seriously considering my proposal.

"Uh, I guess I'll just be leaving then." Arina flickered out.

I looked coyly at him through lowered lashes. Then I grabbed my black tank top and tossed it down. It fell at my feet.

Nero leaned into me. "Pandora, behave yourself." His words fell gently against my lips. His eyes ensnared mine.

"I always behave." I licked my lips. "Behave badly."

Nero captured my lips with his, and he kissed me, savage and hungry. Dark, deviant desires uncurled inside of me. I clutched him closer. Close was not close enough.

"We should stop," he said between kisses, but he made no move to do so. "It's against the rules."

"It doesn't count," I whispered. "We're not breaking any holy rules of pregnant angel celibacy because our bodies aren't really here."

Nero's chuckles buzzed against my lips. "You are a temptress."

"And that's a bad thing?"

"Yes, it is. But right now, I just don't care." His voice was a soft caress, his hands rough.

"I've been wanting you for so long, Nero."

"I hadn't noticed," he said with a sexy, self-satisfied smirk.

He ran his hand slowly, lightly, along the inside of my thigh. A gasp parted my lips. This felt every bit as real as in real life.

"Enough fun," Nyx's voice barked.

I snapped my head around to find the First Angel standing beside us. Arina must have sent her consciousness here.

"Windstriker, Pandora, put your clothes back on," she commanded us. "We have important work to do."

## CHAPTER 25

### A MOMENT OF MAGIC

*B*reakfast the next morning in the airship's garden library was a crowded affair, now that Nyx's team of angels had joined us. I wondered when the last time was that so many angels had gathered in one place. I really hoped they didn't start killing each other. Angels could be rather snippy.

Basanti smirked at Nero over the top of her teacup.

"Why are you smirking at me?" Nero demanded.

"Have you stopped to consider that your daughter and sibling will be the same age?" Basanti replied.

"Yes."

"And?"

"And I try not to think about it," he told her.

Basanti was grinning from ear to ear. "They are going to get each other into so much trouble."

"Perhaps they will support each other in achieving higher levels of holiness," he said calmly.

"Your daughter has the Angel of Chaos for a mother," Basanti laughed. "More likely, she'll be wreaking havoc on the world before she can even walk. And roping everyone around her into her shenanigans. Just like her mother."

"Hey, leave me out of this," I protested.

"Little late for that, hon," Basanti told me. "Angel of Chaos, Mother of Mayhem."

Mother of Mayhem. Yet another nickname to add to my ever-growing list. The sergeant with the booming voice was going to run out of breath before he could even finish introducing me.

"Chaos. Mayhem," Nero said to Basanti, his eyes hard. "You look entirely too pleased about that."

"Well, yeah, actually. You have to admit that things were pretty boring around here before Leda joined the Legion."

"Basanti, don't hope for the apocalypse," Leila sighed. "You might just get your wish."

The door opened, and the First Angel entered, ushering in discussions of a more serious nature.

"Lightbringer, I'm assigning you command over Colonel Silvertongue's territory of East Australia." Her gaze shifted to Damiel. "Dragonsire, you're getting General Spellsmiter's West Australia."

Damiel dipped his chin. "As always, you demonstrate your divine wisdom, First Angel."

"Stop kissing my ass, Dragonsire."

Damiel chuckled.

"Windstriker, I'm making you Head of the Vanguard," Nyx told Nero.

"As you wish, First Angel," he replied. "But are you sure you want to trust Damiel with commanding people?"

The air around Damiel crackled with magic. "I was commanding soldiers long before you were born, junior."

"Sure, but there was that whole traitor-to-the-Legion vacation you took for a couple hundred years," I reminded him.

"Damiel was innocent," Cadence protested.

"I know that," I told her. "But the rest of the world doesn't. Nor do they know about the deaths of General Spellsmiter and Colonel Silvertongue."

"That will be announced to the Legion shortly, and then to the rest of the Earth. I won't be able to keep it secret for much longer, and I do need an angel to command each of those territories. And you two are the only available angels I have." Nyx looked expectantly at Cadence and Damiel.

Cadence set her hand over her heart. "We will serve the Legion as befits an angel."

"Oh, I know you will," replied Nyx. "But because this is a delicate matter, especially concerning Dragonsire's past, I've decided to do things differently. Lightbringer, your title will be the Angel of East Australia. And Dragonsire will be named the Angel of West Australia. But the two of you shall command the two territories together. That arrangement should smooth over any complaints."

Nyx meant complaints from the other angels. Two angels had never before commanded any territory jointly. That was because angels didn't share well with others. I didn't think sharing would be a problem for Cadence and Damiel, though.

"It's a pretty clever solution actually, Cadence and Damiel ruling together. Because she is legendary…" I winked at Damiel. "…and he is notorious."

"Careful, Pandora. All these compliments will go to my head," Damiel warned me.

"I'm not worried. Your head is already full of so much

hot air that there isn't even room for it to grow any bigger."

Damiel howled with laughter.

Nyx scowled at me. "Fireswift was supposed to teach you to deal with other angels." Her gaze snapped to Colonel Fireswift.

"I do know how to deal with other angels," I said quickly, before Fireswift could complain about me. "But not all angels are the same. Damiel likes it when I tease him."

"She's not wrong." Damiel's eyes twinkled with amusement.

"So does Colonel Fireswift," I added. "He's just too proud to admit it."

"I most certainly do not enjoy being teased," Colonel Fireswift said with indignation.

I smiled. "Nice try, Colonel. But we can all see you blushing."

Colonel Fireswift's face had turned decidedly red, though it was more likely out of fury than anything else.

Damiel chuckled. Even Nero's lips curled a little.

But Nyx was all business. "In any case, Pandora is correct."

I perked up.

"About Dragonsire," Nyx clarified. "But do stop poking Fireswift, or he might bite back."

Jace cleared his throat, swallowing the laughter that he'd almost allowed to escape. He'd joined us for breakfast, and I was glad. As much fun as it was poking fun at his father, Jace was actually fun.

"From a PR perspective, Dragonsire cannot rule alone, even though he has been cleared of all wrongdoing. You have all accepted him…" Nyx glanced at Colonel Fireswift. "Most of you have accepted him."

Colonel Fireswift looked like he'd sooner accept me as an angel than he would accept Damiel.

"But many of my other angels are not so welcoming of his return," Nyx said. "And we cannot afford to be weighed down by in-fighting. Not now. And so Dragonsire will rule with Lightbringer. If *anyone* has a problem with that, they can sit out our war against the Guardians locked inside a Legion dungeon. Times are dangerous, and we're short on angels. The Legion needs Dragonsire's experience and magic."

Nyx was explaining herself much more than usual and her temper was short. She must have already had this conversation many times already, with one angel after another. She did look particularly tired this morning. Her hair wasn't swirling around in the air as weightlessly as usual.

"I don't have a problem with Damiel," I spoke up. "He makes the world's best pancakes."

Nyx laughed, which was exactly why I'd said it. I could tell that she'd really needed a good laugh.

"All right, back to business." But most of the tension had gone out of her voice. "Where are we with Gaius Knight, Pandora?"

"Neither Arina nor I have had any luck contacting him or tuning back in to the visions the Vault was sending me," I said. "We have no idea whether it was indeed the Guardians who interrupted our conversation with Gaius, nor whether they have taken him prisoner and now control the Vault. We only suppose that this has happened."

"So you have no idea how much time we have until

the Guardians unleash their plan to gain magic and make a move to steal your daughter?" she asked.

"No."

And it made me sick to my stomach. That wasn't just pregnancy hormones making me queasy. It was dread.

"We must proceed as we would anyway, not second guess ourselves because of these possible futures," Nyx decided. "Trying to change the future might very well make things worse."

Easier said than done. It was my child at the center of the Guardians' plans.

"Windstriker, I'm putting you in charge of the mission to track down the angel slayers. Assemble your team," Nyx commanded him.

Nero nodded.

The Legion's Interrogators hadn't gotten anything of use out of the prisoners Nyx and the other angels had captured. Apparently, they'd just been clueless decoys put there to throw the investigation off track.

"I will be staying here, on board the airship," Nyx said. "Furthering our plan to gain the confidence of the Earth's people so that more might join the Legion of Angels."

Nyx definitely didn't look happy to be stuck here with us. Like all angels, Nyx had a very hands-on personality, not a sitting-on-her-hands personality.

"We're making progress," I told her.

My statement did nothing to brighten Nyx's mood.

"Dr. Harding has some new information." I waved at Nerissa.

She stepped forward. "Unfortunately, I haven't yet had any luck in finding a way to decrease the Nectar's fatality rate without also decreasing its potency, its ability to bestow magic."

"You know, we might be going about this all wrong," I said. "Maybe we shouldn't be trying to modify the Nectar. Maybe we should be looking for another solution altogether. Humans can gain some supernatural powers without Nectar. For instance, a human can become a vampire."

"Vampires are not as powerful as Legion soldiers," Colonel Fireswift said impatiently, as though I didn't already know that.

"So what?" I demanded. "Maybe we could use another substance to bestow a weaker form of magic on people. Not everyone needs to have angel powers. Most Legion soldiers never become angels, Colonel."

"You're suggesting we create another tier of Legion soldier," Leila said. "With a weaker tier of powers."

"Yes, I am. People can contribute to the Legion without the full-blown set of powers."

"It's preposterous." Colonel Fireswift's voice was scathing.

I shrugged. "My ideas usually are."

"Yes, they are." He was sitting so stiffly on the sofa that a tiny breeze might have blown him over. "The Legion cannot abandon its tried and true methods."

"Even if those tried and true methods are having diminishing results?" I countered. "Fewer people are joining the Legion of Angels with every initiation cycle. Something has to change, or soon there will be nothing left of the Legion. Change. That's why Nyx assigned me this task. Because I'm not weighed down by what's tried and true. I know how to think out of the box."

"Pandora." Nero's voice was quiet—and yet it cut right through the room like a knife.

I smiled at him. "Yes, lover?"

"Maybe there is a solution somewhere between the current way and a complete-and-total upheaval of everything we know."

"Maybe," I allowed.

"Everything in moderation," he said.

I guiltily set down the very large slice of chocolate cake I'd just cut myself. Moderation. Right.

"I'll try to find a middle-of-the-road solution," I said.

"I think that would be an easier sell to all of us boring, rigid angels," Nero told me.

"Just try not to get run over while you're hanging out in the middle of the road, Leda," Basanti added.

I made a face at her. "Very funny."

Basanti grinned at me and took a bite of her cake, which made me feel a little less guilty about digging my fork into my own cake.

Arina spoke up, "The angels politics' and future soldiers are all very exciting, I'm sure, but how about you deal with the more immediate problems? Like my kids." She shot me an accusatory glare. "You promised you'd help me rescue my kids."

"And we will," I said. "But we'll need to break into the Guardians' Sanctuary to do it."

"Which we need to do anyway to stop the Guardians," Cadence said.

"Right." I licked icing off my fork. "I've been thinking about that actually. And I wonder if we can use Faith's idea to find the Guardians."

"I hope you're not referring to killing anyone on Earth who has magic." Nyx's voice was humorless.

I waved her concerns away. "No, not that part of her idea. Faith said the passages to the Guardians' Sanctuary are everywhere."

"Yes, there are multiple ways in and out of the Sanctuary, spread out across the Earth," said Cadence. "I have used several of them myself, but I know there are many more."

"Ok, so Faith wanted to kill everyone with magic so she could silence all the magic on Earth, *except* for the magic of those passages to the Sanctuary," I said. "Because Faith couldn't wield enough power to find the Sanctuary when the rest of the Earth's magic was chugging along at full blast. There is another way."

I looked down at my cat.

"It's just a matter of brute force," I told them all. "If I could channel enough magic through Angel, I could find the Sanctuary without silencing all of the other magic on Earth. With Angel's help, with that spell magnified by a million, I could find the passages into the Sanctuary and break my way inside. With Angel's help, I don't even need everyone in the world to stop using their magic."

"Your cat could indeed channel enough magic to perform such a feat," Cadence told me. "But, Leda, you yourself don't have that much magic to channel through Angel."

"And you would need *a lot* of magic," Leila added. "It's a relative matter. In Faith's plan, the very low level of magic on Earth during her spell wasn't just about using the non-turbulence to find the Sanctuary. It also meant she needed to push through less magical resistance in the surroundings to break down the Sanctuary barrier. On a world with no magic being used by others, your magic would also be more powerful. Because there's less resistance in the environment. Fewer things to interfere."

Leila was pretty smart.

"Like when you always run with weights, it's easier to run when you do it without them; you're faster," she said. "It's the same with magic. If you go to a world with little or no magic, your magic packs more of a punch."

"Do any of the worlds in the Immortals' former empire have much less magic than here?" I wondered. "I thought the Immortals created them all to have roughly the same amount of magic, even if the magic might be of a different kind."

"They did," Damiel said. "But there are other worlds out there where people live, worlds not changed and seeded by the Immortals. On some of those worlds, your magic practically explodes out of you. On others, you feel like every spell has to be forced out of you."

"Yes." Cadence turned to Leila. "I'm impressed you figured that out."

"It's logical."

Cadence grinned, obviously very proud of her former protégé.

"Ok, but with Angel, I have a way to channel enough magic to break the Guardians' barrier, right?" I asked, trying to bring us back on track.

It was Cadence who answered my question. "Yes. Angel is a magic vessel. She can hold pretty much infinite magic, allowing you to channel it, control it."

"So the problem is I just don't have enough magic?" I asked. "What about the way we defeated Faith? What if we all combined powers?"

"I spent a long time stuck inside the Sanctuary," Cadence said. "The barrier is *very* powerful. It drains the magic out of anyone. Instantly. That is the Guardians' magic, Leda, that of negating magic and magic users themselves. The Guardians use all the magic you throw at them, all the magic you throw at their barrier, in order to fuel the barrier. Getting out of the Sanctuary was next to impossible. The only way in or out of the Sanctuary is with the Guardians' blessing. I only got out because Eva sabotaged the barrier from the inside.

"But to blast our way into the Sanctuary." Cadence shook her head. "Collecting so much magic that it overpowers the Guardians' ability to redirect it…that's more magic than all of us have together. No, even combined, all of our magic is simply not enough."

"A trick. You used a trick to escape."

"You shouldn't have mentioned tricks to the Queen of Trickery," Basanti told Cadence.

"I'll forgive you for that comment, Basanti, if you promise to second my motion that 'Queen of Trickery' be added to my very long list of official titles."

Basanti snorted.

"Surely there must be a way." I looked around at all of them. "Surely, there's a trick we can use to accomplish what we need. There's always a loophole."

"You would need a lot of magic," Cadence said. "You'd need to channel more magic at once than has ever before been done in the history of the world."

"If only we could move the Guardians to a place with very little magic," I lamented. "So our magic is stronger."

"I know where you're going with this, Leda," Cadence said. "Except that you need to remember that in such a place, the Guardians' powers would be stronger too. And, anyway, the Guardians are very firmly rooted on the Earth nowadays; long ago, they moved here from another world. Their Sanctuaries lie in the plains of monsters, just in another dimension, slightly removed from our own."

I talked this through aloud. "The plains of monsters were created when the gods and demons made a fuss and brought their immortal war here."

Cadence nodded. "That violent clash of deities was an act of profound magic. The clash of light and dark. It was the magic catalyst that brought us the plains of monsters, forever changing the course of Earth's history."

"And something about that clash of magic allowed the Guardians to create their Sanctuary too," I said.

"If you could create another universe-changing event like the birth of the plains of monsters, that might give you enough magic to perform your spell, Leda. And find the Guardians," Arina suggested.

"So I only need to find a way to change the course of the world's history? Oh, is that all?" I laughed in despair. "No biggie then."

# CHAPTER 26

## GAIUS KNIGHT

Following breakfast, I spent the next few hours pacing down the halls of the airship, trying to think things through. Arina tagged along. She'd told me that she wasn't letting me out of her sight until I found a way to reach the Guardians' Sanctuary—and helped her rescue her kids.

I didn't blame her. After all, most of my urgency to knock out the Guardians was fueled by my desire to save my daughter.

And so I paced, all the while trying to figure out how to create a moment of magic so enormously powerful, so universally defining, that I could channel some of that magic into breaking into the Guardians' Sanctuary. They had used the clash of gods and demons on Earth, the creation of the plains of monsters, to create their Sanctuary here, in another dimension slightly offset from our own. If they'd used that moment to create a whole Sanctuary, surely I could use another such moment to tear away the mask of magic that cloaked them and kept us out.

The problem was I couldn't come up with a single idea. I wasn't sure how I could create an instant as powerful as the creation of the Earth's plains of monsters—and all the wild weather and magic that had come with it.

"Gaius Knight knows something," I said aloud.

After three hours of talking silently to myself inside my head, a change of pace was in order. Even if that meant talking to myself aloud and looking like a lunatic.

"Before he ran off, he was going to tell us the solution to our Guardian problem," I said. "Gaius Knight is the key. We should be looking for him."

"Don't be too trusting of that man," Calli warned me. She'd found me in the halls.

"He isn't the man I thought he was." Calli looked righteously pissed off. "He's been manipulating us all for years. For decades."

"True, he has been manipulating us," I agreed. "And we still don't know what his agenda is. But he clearly wants us to stop the Guardians. And that's what we want too. We might need to look past his manipulations to achieve a common goal."

Calli gave me a long, hard look, then declared, "You've grown up a lot, Leda."

I smirked at her. "I better have. I'm going to have a kid. And I intend to keep her safe—her and the world she lives in too."

Calli squeezed my hands. "And we will."

"I'm just wondering how I'm going to do something so spectacular, so unheard of, so universe-altering that enough magic is created to perform this spell that breaks down the Sanctuary's barriers."

"I don't know," said Calli. "But what I do know is that if anyone is up to the task, it's the Angel of Chaos."

"I guess my whole existence is kind of a universe-changing event," I replied sheepishly. "I'm the daughter of extremes, of a god and a demon. And an angel of chaos. I'm the perfect instrument to really mix things up. I only hope I change them for the better."

"You always change things for the better, Leda. Before now, I never thought I'd see the day when ten angels would sit down together for a peaceful breakfast of croissants and cake."

"Not entirely peaceful. The whole time we were sitting there, Colonel Fireswift totally wanted to set me on fire," I laughed. "I could see it in his eyes."

Calli's expression soured. "That man is most unpleasant."

"Thank goodness Nero took Fireswift with him on his mission," I said.

I realized Nero had probably only brought Colonel Fireswift along to spare me the pleasure of his company. Nero couldn't stand him either.

"Calli, we need to find Gaius Knight. He knows things. He can help us."

"More likely, we would be the ones helping him," Calli said bitterly. "Like it's always been."

I'd never known Calli to hold such a grudge, but then again, I'd never before met anyone stupid enough to betray her trust.

"Could you use your magic-tracking powers to find Gaius?" I asked Arina.

"I can certainly try," she replied. "But seeing as I've never met him in real life, I'll have to track him somewhat indirectly. It won't be a straightforward, precise process."

Well, Arina's magic was generally pretty indirect anyway.

"Do it," I told her.

Arina closed her eyes. A moment later, they opened again.

"That was fast," I said. "Where is he?"

"I haven't found him. Not exactly."

"Then what did you find?"

"The dark angel Thea's grimoire," she told me. "Or at least something that will lead us to the grimoire."

"You weren't kidding, Arina. This is very indirect."

"I'm sure the grimoire is the key to tearing down the Guardians' Sanctuary. This is just the next step."

"Like when we found the four papers of the parchment, they came together to show us your face. Back then, you were the next step, Arina."

Back then. It felt like years ago. But it had only been a little over a week.

"This is strange. What could Thea's grimoire possibly have to do with Gaius?" Calli asked.

"I guess we'll soon find out," I said, fully prepared to fly by the seat of my pants, as always. "Where can we find the grimoire?"

"The Silver Shore," Arina said. "The grimoire is there. Or at least part of the grimoire is there."

Part of it? At this rate, my daughter would be a teenager before this quest was over.

"Then let's go to the Silver Shore," I said brightly. "And on the plus side, at least they don't have monsters there."

# CHAPTER 27

## CALAMITY

*O*k, so technically the Silver Shore didn't have any monsters. Something about the place repelled them. It was, however, smack dab in the middle of the Black Forest, a region of many little forests, all of which were completely overrun with monsters. I'd recently paid the area a visit. Truth be told, I hadn't looked forward to returning any time soon. Or ever.

I'd also well, *accidentally*, lost the last airship the Legion had given me not far from the Silver Shore, due to the aforementioned monsters. So I wasn't surprised that Nyx was watching me with a wary eye as the airship trudged along toward its destination. The Silver Shore was all the way across the ocean in Europe. This journey would be a long one, especially with Nyx glaring at me.

"It wasn't my fault," I said to the First Angel, for what seemed like the millionth time.

We were alone in the garden library tonight. All of the other soldiers were busy, and Arina had finally had the good sense to lie down and take a nap.

"Not your fault." Nyx shook her head very slowly. "So you say."

Angels had short tempers but long memories.

"Monsters attacked that airship," I told her. "Lots and lots of monsters."

"You also crashed an airship only a month after you joined the Legion."

"That wasn't me," I protested. "A bunch of crazy, vengeful shifters set off bombs all over the airship."

Nyx was clearly not impressed by my defense. "In fact, you've crashed every airship you've ever been on."

"That's not true. I didn't crash the one Nero and I once took to Purgatory."

"If you're referring to the time you and Windstriker went rogue and snuck off to the Lost City, Pandora, you aren't helping your case."

I didn't know I was on trial.

"Well, it all worked out in the end," I said with a smile and a shrug.

Nyx shook her head in exasperation, then walked out of the room, leaving me alone in the garden library. I was pretty sure Nyx's exasperation had as much to do with her being stuck here as it did with my apparent talent for crashing airships.

With no one to talk to, I returned to my knitting. Since I wasn't allowed to rush into dangerous situations —or do anything particularly athletic right now—I'd decided I needed a new hobby. Something safe. Something that came with the Legion's stamp of approval for expecting angels.

I'd have chosen bantering, but that wasn't necessarily safe, particularly if my opponent didn't like what I had to say. Also, bantering wasn't something I could do alone.

There wasn't always someone around, especially at this hour. I glanced at the clock. It was two in the morning local time, but my mind was too busy to sleep right now.

Stash was waiting in the hall, just outside the room. He was keeping true to his promise to guard me. I could have bantered with him, but he'd been rather quiet lately. He slept even less than I did.

So with bantering off the table, I'd picked knitting as my hobby. A mother really should know how to knit. I'd once read that in a book.

There was a rustle of movement beyond the potted plants.

"That's lovely, dear."

I looked up from my knitting as Grace sat down beside me on the sofa.

"What is it going to be when it's finished?" She glanced down at my knitting project.

"I'm not sure yet. Maybe a onesie. Or a baby bootie."

There was another rustle of movement.

"Those are two completely different things," Faris said, sitting down on my other side. "You can't just start knitting randomly and then decide what it is when you're done."

I kept knitting, determined not to let his sour mood ruin my project. "Why not?"

"Because that's not how things are done," he said sternly. "Plans must be made. And followed."

"That's what I'm doing. I made a plan to knit something. And that's precisely what I'm going to do."

Faris looked like steam would soon shoot out of his ears. He truly couldn't stand my chaos.

I just smiled at him pleasantly. "I'm just going to wing it."

"It's certainly an original idea," Grace told Faris.

He made a derisive noise. "It's irresponsible."

"It's just yarn, Faris," I said.

"This is *not* just about yarn."

I rolled my eyes. "No, this is about me and my unborn child. And how my chaotic ways will upend your precious plans for us."

Suspicion narrowed Faris's eyes. "What are you planning?"

"I'm not sure yet. I'm going to wait and see how it turns out."

"This isn't funny, Leda."

I sighed and set my knitting down on the coffee table. "Did you just come here to make fun of my hobbies while glaring maniacally, or was there something else that you wanted?"

"I just wanted to check in on you," Grace told me cheerfully. "And Faris tagged along. He is afraid of what might happen if I'm alone with you. He believes I'm going to fill your head with evil demon schemes."

He glowered at her. "The demons are always scheming."

"As are the gods." Grace looked at me. "This whole immortal war that's been raging between us and them for centuries…just so you know, it's all their fault."

"How absurd." Faris's voice burned like acid. "The war started when the demons trespassed on one of our holy sites."

Grace jumped out of her seat. "It's not yours! Calamity is a site of treasures the Immortals left for us all."

I latched on to the familiar name. "Calamity?"

"Yes, the name is very dramatic." Grace smoothly

lowered herself back into her seat. "Like it's meant to be a disaster. But the only disaster is the one the gods brought there…by trying to hijack the Immortals' treasures all for themselves."

That wasn't what I'd meant. Calamity was familiar. Bella had told me about it.

"There was a great battle at Calamity twenty-five years ago," I said.

"One of many," Grace said. "For centuries, there have been great battles at Calamity. Though that one twenty-five years ago was especially violent. It went on for months. It soon became known as the Battle of Calamity, as though there hadn't been many more battles there before it."

"And since then." Faris leveled a scornful look at Grace. "The battles will continue to play out at Calamity for as long as the demons operate under the misconception that they are welcome at our holy site."

"Give it a rest, Faris." Grace flashed him a vicious smile. "There aren't even any cameras here to perform for."

Faris opened his mouth to shoot back an argument, but I cut in first, before this battle became the next Battle of Calamity—and my shiny new airship became collateral damage.

"Tell me about the Battle of Calamity," I asked them.

"The demons attacked from the shadows, and they got lucky," Faris said curtly.

"My sister would take issue with that statement," said Grace. "Ava doesn't get lucky."

"No doubt."

I snorted. The way Faris looked at me made me think he hadn't intended his statement to be an innuendo. He probably didn't even know the meaning of the word. Then again, you never knew when it came to gods and demons.

"Ava wins through skill, not luck," Grace declared.

His voice dipped lower. "On the rare occasion that Ava does win, it's by cheating."

She shot him a threatening look. "Don't speak ill of my sister, Faris, or there will be dire consequences for you."

"I'm shivering in fear."

"As you should be, you self-righteous megalomaniac," she snapped.

"Bella told me about the Battle of Calamity," I said, cutting through their silly fight. "She said one of the demon squadrons was tasked with destroying an enemy supply camp high in the mountains."

"Yes. And the gods ambushed them along the trail." Grace pointed an accusatory finger at Faris. "Talk about sneaking out and attacking from the shadows. Only three demon soldiers survived the ambush."

Three demon soldiers plus Thea, Bella's mother. I wondered if Grace knew that Ava's son Khalon had saved Thea's life.

"Your version of events is highly suspect, Grace," Faris said. "You're counting on those three demons being the only survivors who can speak of that day, and we all know that demons are liars. None of my soldiers survived. Over a hundred gods killed! And so we shall never know what truly happened there."

"Many more soldiers died in the battle in the valley," I said. "On both sides."

"Yes," Faris confirmed.

"Is that typical of battles between gods and demons?"

"Losses are not typically that high, no," Grace answered. "We are immortal, but not particularly good at repopulating our numbers."

That was due to the abysmal fertility of powerful deities, which was even worse than the fertility of angels.

"Usually, the demons and gods just flex their muscles a bit and shoot off their mouths—and sometimes a little flashy magic," Grace told me. "But they get cold feet as soon as things get very real."

Faris puffed out his chest like the pompous peacock that he was. "I take issue with the implication that I ever get cold feet."

"Duly noted," Grace said coolly. "But you can't take issue with the facts, Faris."

He frowned.

"What made the Battle of Calamity different?" I asked. "Why were the losses so high?"

"I wasn't there, but from what I understand, things there just escalated very quickly," Grace said. "So many soldiers were already dead on both sides before anyone could even think of getting cold feet."

"The first dead soldiers were in the mountains?" I asked.

"Mainly," she replied. "Thanks to Khalon."

So Grace *did* know about Khalon and Thea.

"Khalon? What was Ava's son doing in the mountains during the Battle of Calamity?" Faris frowned. He clearly hadn't known about that.

"What was Khalon doing? Kicking your soldiers' asses, it would seem," Grace told him. "Against overwhelming odds. He must have had something worth fighting for."

Like Thea's life.

"You know more than you're saying, Grace."

"Yes. As always, I know more than you, Faris," she replied with a sugar-coated smile.

"I will find out what you know." He kept his voice calm and level, but I could tell he was fuming. Cold, menacing fury dripped off his every word.

"Good luck with that." Her smile had turned decidedly sardonic.

I was almost starting to like Grace. I could certainly see where I'd gotten my spunk.

But I had to be careful. The demon might be manipulating me, trying to make me think we were the same. Well, we weren't the same. Not at all. I wasn't like either one of my parents, god or demon.

"I've seen how much a bit of emotion can boost a deity's powers," I said to Grace. "Or reduce their powers."

"It is true for some," Grace agreed.

"You think Ava riled up Khalon to get him to win her a big victory?" I asked her.

Faris's penetrating glare shifted to me. "You know something too."

"How does it feel to be the only one who isn't in on the secret?" I asked him pleasantly.

The look on Faris's face was all the answer I required.

"A victory at Calamity wasn't the only thing on Ava's mind that day," Grace replied to me. "My sister has never been one for wasted opportunities."

"I see." I nodded. "This conversation has been very informative."

I stopped short of thanking her. It was dangerous to thank a deity; they might take that as an acknowledgement that you owed them something. Like angels did. Only deities were worse. Much, much worse.

Even after my parents left me alone in the garden library, leaving me with a knotted pile of knitting that had failed to amount to anything, my mind dwelled on the Battle of Calamity. Something had happened there. Something else. Something important. Something hidden beneath the surface and behind the scenes. I just knew it. Somehow I knew it. I couldn't explain how I did.

I was sure there was something important about that day, and this wasn't just about Ava scheming to keep Thea alive and making sure Bella was born. Something else had happened there. Some great scheme had played out that day at Calamity, unbeknownst to the soldiers fighting there.

## CHAPTER 28

### THE DOOR IN THE FLOOR

*T*he airship arrived at the Silver Shore early the next morning. No monsters tried to pull us down as we crossed the Black Forest this time. In fact, besides my nighttime visit from Grace and Faris, the journey had been a pretty uneventful one.

Of course, that didn't stop my designated protectors from protesting when I insisted on going down to the shore to look for Thea's grimoire.

"You're supposed to stay on the ship," Alec reminded me, as though I'd forgotten.

"Those were Nyx's orders, and she is going down to the shore," I pointed out. "So I'm going down there too."

Stash was next. "Sweetness, it's just not safe."

"You can go down there with me," I told him. "But, seriously, who's going to attack me? We're way out in the middle of nowhere, and monsters can't even get inside the Silver Shore. You guys have already searched the area and found no enemies, no boobytraps, no dangers of any kind."

"Lord Faris will not approve," Devlin said stiffly.

"If he finds out, I'll tell him I escaped your guard and went down myself, so you had to follow me. Faris knows how I operate. He'll totally believe that story."

"That *is* exactly how she operates," Patch told the others.

Devlin sighed in defeat. "Very well. But we're staying by your side the whole time."

"I would expect nothing less of such competent, professional, godly soldiers."

"I'm going to quote you on that, Pandora," Octavian said. "Maybe I'll even score a promotion from Faris from it."

"If Faris doesn't punish us for letting her run wild," Devlin said.

"Faris wants to keep the Guardians away from my daughter," I told them. "Well, this is how we're going to do it."

"I think she has us there," Punch said.

He looked very excited to be leaving the ship. He must have been convinced that there would be something dangerous down there to fight. In fact, he was probably counting on it. Punch had found the whole airship gig to be terribly dull. During our flight across the Atlantic, I'd once seen him preparing to shoot at an enormous flying monster, just to spice things up. Devlin had stopped him just in time.

As we prepared to fly down to the Silver Shore, Punch whispered to me, "I'm counting on you, girl, to bring us some of that legendary Leda chaos."

Our landing party was full. I wasn't the only one eager for a chance to leave the ship. In fact, once we disembarked, there was hardly anyone left on board.

Leila looked around the Silver Shore. "This place is beautiful."

"The most beautiful place on Earth." Cadence kicked off her boots and dug her toes into the sand.

The sand sparkled like silver glitter. That must have been where the place had gotten its name.

"My father used to bring me here when I was a child," Cadence said.

I bent over.

"What are you doing?" Nyx demanded.

My fingers paused in front of my bootlaces. "I thought I'd—"

"I know what you were thinking, Pandora. And it's bad enough that some of my angels have completely lost their wits at the prospect of sandy toes."

Nyx watched with disapproval—or was that envy?—as Cadence and Leila ran barefoot across the sandy beach. Basanti, Andromeda, and Alice had joined them. They were all acting very jolly, very un-Legion-like.

"They're just restless," I told Nyx. "They don't have their knitting to calm their nerves like I do."

"Knitting?" Alec asked me, perplexed.

"Yes, knitting."

Alec could barely keep a straight face. "You can knit? *You*, the Angel of Chaos?"

"That's right," I said defensively. "And I'm getting pretty good at it. Right, Stash?"

"Indeed." Stash nodded. "Leda has improved greatly. She no longer gets her whole body tangled up in the yarn."

This time, Alec did not succeed in keeping a straight face. Enthusiastic laughter poured out of his mouth.

"Watch out, Stash, or I'll find some way to incorporate my knitting into my dirty fighting," I warned him.

Stash smiled. "Oh, but you're not supposed to be fighting."

"I wouldn't be fighting. I'd be knitting. You'd just happen to get trapped in my yarn."

"That would be some pretty messy knitting," Arabelle said.

"Or some pretty precise knitting," Octavian added.

"Your friends from Heaven's Army talk too much," Nyx told me.

"That's what makes them so fun," I chuckled. "But I guess we should start looking for the grimoire."

"Yes. We should," Nyx said seriously.

Apparently, she wasn't going to kick off her boots and get her feet wet. I wondered what the First Angel did for fun. Probably something really wild, like reorganizing her filing cabinet. Or optimizing the contents of her refrigerator.

Nyx and I walked along the sunny Silver Shore, our boots firmly on our feet. Bella and Harker came with us, along with my trusty guards from Heaven's Army. And Arina came too. I didn't think she'd truly relax until her children were safe. I wanted to help her accomplish that. Children didn't deserve to be caught in the middle of this power struggle between deities and Guardians.

I glanced at Arina. "Do you sense the grimoire anywhere nearby?"

"No, but there's something else. A weird kind of magic. Magic that's concealing something."

"Maybe it's the grimoire," I said, feeling optimistic. "River, that rogue Guardian I met in the Vault, told me there are other secret stashes around the world. She confirmed that the Silver Shore is one of them."

"Where is this concealing magic coming from?" Nyx asked Arina.

Arina pointed at one of the smaller lakes.

"In the lake?" Bella asked.

Arina nodded.

"Well, it looks like we'll be taking off our boots after all," I said to Nyx, triumphant.

Obviously, she was positively overjoyed.

"So it would seem," she said drily.

I pulled off my boots. The moment my toes dug into the sand, I smiled. It really was as velvety-soft as it looked. Everyone else was removing their shoes as well.

"I wonder if there's a sea monster inside the lake," Punch said hopefully.

"Unlikely," Patch told him. "Something at the Silver Shore repels monsters."

But Punch wasn't giving up hope just yet. "Then maybe just a really big shark?"

Patch patted him on the back.

"Octavian, Arabelle, Theon. You three go first," Devlin barked out like he was ordering them into battle.

"But I want to be on the front line!" Punch complained.

Devlin ignored him. "Patch and I will go in on either side of Leda. Stash, you and Punch take the rear." He looked at Nyx. "I trust that you and Sunstorm can handle the two civilians?"

"Naturally."

Nyx didn't sound annoyed, but there was a sharp spark in her ocean-blue eyes. As a demigod, she'd probably long since tired of being treated as weak by the gods.

On the other hand, she didn't have seven gods surrounding her like a force field. Faris must have thought I was made of glass.

We all cast form-fitting, water-repellent bubbles around ourselves—Harker cast one around Bella, while I cast one around Arina—then we stepped into the water. There were fish in the lake, but no sharks or monsters, much to Punch's disappointment. We walked across the lake's sandy bottom until Arina suddenly stopped and stomped her foot down to indicate the spot of interest.

I flicked my hand, casting a spell that swooped into the dirt like a digger. My magic bounced against something solid. I stepped closer and leaned over to gaze into the hole I'd made. The wet sand was already settling back into the hole, but I could still see what I'd dug up.

It was a door. A door in the floor.

I reached down and grabbed the door's metallic handles to open it. A shimmering field of blue light stretched across the doorway, repelling both water and sand. I poked it with my finger to see if it repelled people too, but my hand passed right through the field. Now, *that* was a force field.

I hopped through the door in the floor. The moment I passed through the blue field, my water-repelling spell popped, drenching my clothes. Good thing I'd removed my boots. I could dry my clothes with a wave of my hand, but shoes were trickier. They soaked up water like a sponge.

I landed in a small sitting room which had eight fat, cushioned armchairs arranged in a circle at the center. A woman of around seventy, dressed in grease-stained work overalls, sat in one of the posh chairs. She was fiddling with the small mechanical device in her lap. She looked familiar somehow, but I couldn't quite place where I'd seen her before.

Nyx landed beside me, also soaking wet. "Where's the grimoire?"

"No grimoire here." I looked around the room, but there were no doors except the underwater entrance. "Just her."

"That's a radio she's holding," Bella said. She was the next one through the door.

"A broken radio," the elderly woman said. "But not broken for long." She flipped a switch on the device, and it lit up. "There. That's better."

"Who is she?" Harker asked the moment after he landed beside Bella.

"We're still trying to figure that out," I said.

The elderly woman smiled at me. There was something creepy lurking beneath that kind, wrinkled facade and white hair.

Stash landed in the sitting room. "There is something odd about her," he said, echoing my thoughts.

Stash had the power to see through to someone's soul, so I definitely took his statement seriously.

"What do you see inside of her?" I asked him.

Stash watched the woman. "There's something false about her."

The old woman didn't seem bothered by his statement. She just kept smiling. She looked like she was waiting for something to happen.

Devlin, Octavian, Punch, Arabelle, and Theon landed in quick succession. This tiny room was starting to get awfully crowded.

"Where's Arina?" I asked.

"She was right behind us," Octavian told me. "She

and Patch are studying the blue barrier. Apparently, it's a fascinating feat of magical engineering." He rolled his eyes. "Nerds," he added under his breath.

I stepped toward the woman with the now-functioning radio. "Who are you?"

She held up her finger. "Just a moment more."

Arina and Patch burst through the blue barrier.

"Leda, the water-repellent qualities of that barrier are truly…" Arina stopped. Her eyes grew wide as they locked on to the elderly woman. "What are you doing here?"

"You know her?" I asked Arina.

"Yes. Her name is Gertrude, and she's my grandmother." Arina looked at the woman. "What are you doing on Earth? How did you even get here?"

"It's complicated," Gertrude said.

"You know something about the dark angel Thea's grimoire, don't you?"

"Yes."

"My face was on that parchment, the supposed clue to Thea's grimoire. That was you. You put my face there."

"Yes."

"Because you wanted me to come here too." Arina looked around the small sitting room. "Where's the grimoire? Is it here?"

"In a manner of speaking." Gertrude looked at the crystal wand attached to Bella's belt. Thea's wand. "The secrets of that wand—and so much more—are not in any physical book. They are too dangerous to write down."

"Then where are these secrets stored?" I asked her.

"In here." Gertrude tapped her head. "Thea was dabbling in magic she didn't understand. I stepped in and offered to help her. It was with my assistance that she made that wand, an immortal artifact."

"You know how to make immortal artifacts?" I asked her.

Athan had once told me Arina possessed the ability to craft artifacts as powerful as immortal artifacts, yet she did not require an immortal soul to make them. Maybe it was a skill which ran in the family.

"I do," Gertrude confirmed. "There are, in fact, two ways to create an immortal artifact. The more common way is to link the piece you've crafted to a dead immortal soul. That is done at the time of death, which is a powerful, magical moment. That's how most immortal artifacts are made. With dark magic. Using death."

"But there is another way?" I asked.

"Yes. Like light and dark, life and death are two sides of the same coin. Just as you can create an immortal artifact through a powerful act of death, through dark magic, you can also use light magic. Life. The act of creation, of life, can be channeled into the artifact. Instead of linking the artifact you've made to a dead soul, you link it to a living soul, at the moment of life. There is great power in that as well."

Gertrude looked at Bella, then the wand. "That is how that wand was created. Using her."

Bella set her hand over her heart.

"Wait, you're saying the act of Bella's creation had so much power that it made the wand into an immortal artifact?" I asked.

"She is the daughter of a demon and a demi-demon," Gertrude replied. "So her creation was a powerful natural force. It's more problematic to make an artifact through life, through light magic, than through death, or dark magic. The light equation is more precise. That's why most immortal artifacts are linked to dead souls."

Arina had been very quiet during Gertrude's explanation, but she finally spoke now. "You taught me that spell," she said to her grandmother. "But you didn't tell me what it does, what it means."

Arina looked pretty upset with her grandmother.

"I had no idea you would actually try out the spell without my supervision," Gertrude replied.

"You created an immortal artifact this way?" I asked Arina. "Using light magic?"

Arina lifted her arms, and two matching silver bracelets slid down her wrists: one with blue stones, one with green stones. "Two of them."

My brain was still processing this. Very slowly processing. Two artifacts.

Arina glared at her grandmother. "I was seventeen. Seventeen. I thought I was just tinkering with magic."

"Powerful magic." Gertrude pursed her lips. "I should have told you the consequences of that spell."

"Yes, you should have." Arina's eyes were full of fury.

"Still, twin artifacts," said Gertrude. "I didn't expect you to start so big."

I finally got it. "Your children," I said to Arina. "Your twins. They were created by this spell."

Arina's voice quivered. "They were."

"You tweaked the formula," Gertrude said. "You experimented with the magical universe. Tapped into it. Your experiment created twins who look like their parents and have some of their magical traits, but they are really children of the universe. Two children, born from the mysteries of the magical abyss."

"When Thea asked you to make that wand, she didn't

know what she was creating, did she?" Bella asked Gertrude.

"No."

Bella looked like that one word had just sealed her fate.

"Thea thought she was just getting an immortal artifact from me," Gertrude continued. "But then she went and gave the wand to Khalon. What a waste. After Thea and Khalon left, I gathered the rainbow magic mist made from the wand's creation, forming it into a baby. A baby linked to the wand."

"Bella," I said quietly.

Ava had told Bella that her parents didn't know she existed. This explained how that was even possible. Like Arina, Thea had thought she was just experimenting with magic.

"Why?" Bella asked Gertrude, her voice uneven. "Why did you use my parents to make me?"

"Because I was contracted to do so," Gertrude said calmly, like it didn't bother her at all.

"By Ava?" Bella asked.

"Yes."

"I was a baby. A *baby*. Have you no shame?" Bella demanded.

Gertrude's wrinkled face didn't flinch. "I am a businesswoman."

"So in other words, no, you didn't care about the consequences," I growled at her.

"And then? What happened after you created me?" Bella asked Gertrude. "How did I end up on Earth?"

"One of my sisters brought you there," Gertrude said. "And another of my sisters made sure Callista Pierce found you. She made sure Calli found all of you—and, later, that you found the four parchments hidden where Calli met you."

Gaius Knight jumped through the blue shield, landing beside us.

"You called, sister?" he said brightly.

His face faded away to reveal a tall and slender woman with a black braid and a young face. I knew that face. River, the rogue Guardian had that face.

I squinted at her, just to be sure. "River?"

"No," she said in a voice just like River's.

It was the same voice as the woman in the purple veil who'd stolen the weapons of heaven and hell for Grace. I knew I'd heard that voice before. Now I knew where.

"I'm Inali. River is my sister. But you know me by my other face."

Magic rippled across her. She was Gaius Knight for a moment, then she was Inali again.

Well, that there just blew my mind.

Bella remained composed. "You sent me the dreams I had of Thea's grimoire. You sent them to me using the Vault. Just like you sent visions to Leda."

"Yes," said Inali. "We did."

"Why?"

She smiled but didn't answer.

"Glad to hear you got away, Inali," Gertrude said. "I was getting worried."

Inali shrugged. "Well, you know me. I'm good at disguises."

"What are you?" I asked Inali. "That wasn't shifting magic you just did. Not quite. It's something else."

"Right you are, Leda," she said with a smile. "I'm a changeling, in fact. We can change shape. We absorb and use another's appearance and magic."

"So you mimicked a man named Gaius Knight?" I guessed.

"Yes."

"Did the real Gaius Knight ever know Calli?" I asked her.

"No."

"So, a mimic." I thought that through. "That's a passive magic power."

"Correct," Inali said.

I looked at Gertrude. "Your magic is passive too. You're a magic smith. Like Arina."

Gertrude nodded. "Indeed, I am."

Looking more closely at Gertrude's face, I noticed something else. "You look exactly like Inali, only many decades older."

So that's where I'd seen Gertrude's familiar face.

"You're very observant," Gertrude told me.

She nodded at Inali, who stepped toward her sister. She waved her hand across Gertrude's face, undoing the glamor of age.

"I can mimic age too," Inali added.

Now Gertrude looked exactly like Inali. And exactly like the rogue Guardian River.

"Just how many of you are there out there?" I demanded.

# CHAPTER 29

EIGHT

It was Gertrude who answered my question.

"There are eight of us. You've met me, Inali, and River. Our other sisters are Evie, Indira, Odette, Mallory, and Rosette."

My mind was exploding with this new information. "And you're all identical?"

"Yes," Gertrude said.

Well, the eight chairs suddenly made sense. But the number eight was significant for another reason.

"There are eight passive magic powers." I looked at Gertrude. "The power of the elf, a crafter and magic smith." I turned to Inali. "The changeling or mimic with the power to copycat another's magic and appearance." I thought of River next. "The phantom, with the power to negate magic. Like River. Or the Guardians."

"As well as the teleporting djinn, the spell-breaking mermaid, the wish-granting genie, the rebirthing phoenix, and the magic-tracking unicorn," Bella finished off the list of passive magic types.

"Unicorn. Another of Arina's powers," I said.

"Yes, Arina got her unicorn magic from her mother's side of the family," Gertrude said.

"Eight sisters." I still couldn't believe it. Identical octuplets. "You each possess one of the eight passive powers, don't you?" I asked.

"We do," replied Inali. "In great amounts."

"Then together they are a powerful force of magic," Nyx said.

"Eight identical sisters, each with a different passive magic power. How did this happen?" I was sure their existence had to be by design; there was nothing natural about them.

"We were made with magic and linked to immortal artifacts as well," Gertrude said.

So they'd been created in just the same way as Bella and Arina's twins.

"And you chastised me for doubling the spell!" Arina snapped at her grandmother. "Whoever made you and your sisters multiplied the spell by eight!"

It was Harker who asked the million-dollar question. "Who was it that made you?"

And it was Inali who rebuffed him. "That's a question for another time."

"That's not any better than 'I cannot say'," I told her.

"River does like to say that," Inali said fondly.

"So what is all of this?" I asked them. "Why lure us out here? What do you want?"

Gertrude was eerily calm. "As I said, we're businesswomen."

"So this is all for profit?" I demanded.

Gertrude and Inali said nothing.

"Great. Just great." I shook my head in disbelief—

and disgust. "Maybe I'll just take you prisoner and see if that encourages you to talk."

"What a marvelous idea," Gertrude said.

Inali extended her wrists to me, offering herself to be handcuffed. "Bring us aboard your airship."

"I think that's exactly what you want." I cuffed them both anyway.

"Then it's a win-win scenario. It's truly amazing how well everything is working out for everyone," Gertrude said with a smile.

"She thinks you're up to something," Arina told her grandmother. "And so do I. In all my life, have you ever told me a single shred of truth?"

"Of course. When I said I loved you, dear, that was true."

Arina was unimpressed by her rhetoric. "Am I even your granddaughter?"

"Yes."

"But you're immortal," Arina pointed out.

"I was made that way. You can hardly blame me for how I was made."

"But I can question the truth of your words," Arina shot back. "You are immortal. I am not immortal. Neither is my father, your son."

"Magic isn't always simple, Arina."

"With you, it's never simple. I thought you were the one person in my family who truly understood me, but..." Arina's mouth trembled. "It doesn't mean anything at all."

Gertrude reached toward her. "Arina."

Arina brushed away her hand. "It doesn't matter anymore. You are the past. Done. Gone. All that matters now is that the Guardians have my children. And you are going to help me save them."

"Of course I will."

Arina was unmoved by her words. She marched off to stand under the blue magic shield that covered the hole in the ceiling.

Devlin waved his hand over himself and her, recasting the water-repelling spells. Then he spread his wings and carried her toward the ceiling door.

Theon flashed us a grin. "I *love* family drama." Then the soap-opera-loving god cast his anti-water spell and left with Octavian and Arabelle.

Bella and Harker went next, followed by Punch and Patch. Stash waited behind with me and Nyx.

"Pandora, you really know how to attract madness," the First Angel said, grabbing Gertrude by the arm.

I took hold of Inali, and together with Stash, we left the underwater sitting room.

Back on the shore, Cadence and the others were waiting for us.

"Who are they?" Leila's eyes flickered from Gertrude to Inali.

"And why do they look identical?" Basanti wondered.

I handed Inali off to Arabelle. "It's a long story."

I walked between Bella and Arina as we headed back to the airship. Both looked shaken, like their worlds had been turned upside down.

"How you were made, Bella, that doesn't make you any less real," I told my sister.

"Leda, I…" Bella looked ready to protest, but then she caught Arina's eye and stopped. She obviously didn't want to offend Arina's children by calling her children not real. Even though Bella seemed to feel that way about herself.

"You have a mother and a father," I told Bella. "Unfortunately, none of us get to choose who our parents are. But I still think you got luckier than I did with Faris and Grace." I winked at her.

Bella laughed. "Thanks, Leda. Thanks for cheering me up."

I looked at Arina.

"I don't need a counselor," she said quickly.

"You won't get any counseling from me, only snark."

Arina didn't laugh. "I don't need snark either."

"What you need is to save your children."

"Yes."

I rubbed my belly. "I get it. I need to save my child too. That's why we're taking the fight to the Guardians."

"So you've figured out how to get into their Sanctuary?" Arina asked, surprised.

"Not entirely," I admitted. "But I will. I always figure things out. I'm pretty damn stubborn, and I refuse to believe anything is impossible."

Arina looked me over, slowly and carefully.

"You're doing that magic thing of yours where you can see who someone truly is deep inside, aren't you?"

"Yes."

"And what do you see?" I asked her.

"That you're pretty damn stubborn and refuse to believe anything is impossible."

Glad we were in agreement.

"Does your magic always work?" I asked.

"I'd always thought so." Arina watched her grandmother. "Until just now. She isn't at all the person she seemed to be."

"That has more to do with her magic than with yours. I bet she was hiding who she is inside, like she was hiding her true face. Inali's magic helped her do that."

Our conversation paused as we went up to the airship. Alec was waiting for me there.

"See?" I said to him as I stepped on board. "I'm back, safe and sound. Nothing to worry about."

Alec snorted. "You've received a petition request from someone who wants an audience with you."

"All the way out here?" I asked, perplexed. "Where is this petitioner?"

"It's not a person," he told me. "It's a message."

Curious, I asked to see the message.

"It isn't that kind of message, Leda. There was this big ball of magic fire that suddenly burst into existence in front of me a few minutes ago. The voice delivered the message that someone would be coming to see you shortly, then the fireball disappeared."

Weird. Really weird.

"Making friends?" Alec asked as Arabelle and Octavian brought the handcuffed Inali and Gertrude aboard. His mouth twitched when his eyes fell upon their bound wrists.

"Always," I said. "Alec, I need you to show these prisoners to a cell."

"You're going to want us there for this," Inali told me.

My eyes narrowed to slits. "You know what's coming?"

Gertrude and Inali gave me matching smiles.

"Are we in danger?" I asked.

"Of course," Gertrude said. "You'll be in danger until the Guardians are dealt with, once and for all."

"They are powerful," Inali added. "They killed the Immortals."

"That's not to say that the danger will pass once the Guardians are gone," Gertrude said. "There are other threats out there, other beings of great power."

"Any chance you'll tell us more about these other threats and other beings?" I asked them, even though I was pretty sure of the answer.

They smiled again.

"Right. I didn't think so." I waved for Alec to follow me with the prisoners.

The entire landing party came too. Along the way, others joined us, including Calli, Zane, Tessa, and Gin.

When our very long procession reached the court chamber, there was no petitioner to be seen.

"Well, that was anticlimactic," Basanti commented, bored.

We all sat down in our chairs. Stash and the other gods took up positions around the room. Alec stayed with the prisoners, and Harker kept close to Bella's side.

"About those rings you two made," I said to Leila and Basanti while we were waiting for…well, actually, I wasn't exactly sure what we were waiting for.

"Yes?" Leila asked.

"They're immortal artifacts."

Leila frowned. "How did you—"

"And, by the way, making the rings is also the reason that you and Basanti are pregnant." I explained to them what we'd learned about creating immortal artifacts. "The question is how you knew how to make immortal artifacts."

"I found a formula in the library," Leila said.

"If the Legion had any book with a recipe to make immortal artifacts, I would know about it," Nyx declared.

"I found the book at Storm Castle," said Leila. "I hadn't seen it before, so I thought—"

"We made sure the book found its way into your possession," Inali told her.

Leila blinked. "Why?"

"So you two would have children." Gertrude smiled. "You're welcome."

Basanti frowned at them. "Why did you *really* do this?"

This time, Gertrude didn't answer.

The dead silence in the room was broken by the explosive rattle of gunfire and the swoosh of magic.

I hurried over to the windows and looked out. Now, I'd seen a lot since joining the Legion of Angels, but what I saw now shocked even me. An armored female knight rode a black pegasus, carrying a very long scythe, like some kind of grim reaper. And that agent of death was headed straight for the airship.

# CHAPTER 30

## THE PEGASUS KNIGHT

The pegasus rider was not alone in the sky. Over twenty pilots in old-style, one-person planes were chasing her in a scene that looked like it had been ripped right out of history. Well, at least if planes at the dawn of the flight era had shot highly-charged magic explosives at a woman in knightly armor who was riding a pegasus.

The planes' magic shots lit up the sky like fireworks. The pilots had the advantage of greater numbers, but the pegasus rider was quicker, more agile. She zipped around the lead plane and split it in half with a powerful swipe of her insanely long scythe.

The plane's engine choked, and the two severed pieces split apart like a banana peel. The pilot hopped out of his falling plane and landed on the deck of my airship in a single huge, inhuman leap. My guards rushed forward to intercept him as he ran toward the doors that led into the Court Chamber, his gun drawn.

In the meantime, more pilots were abandoning their planes and jumping onto the airship. They looked like locusts falling out of the sky. More planes kept coming. Twenty-five, thirty, thirty-five. Luckily, the pilots weren't shooting at us. They were too busy with the pegasus knight, who was ripping open the planes like a highly-efficient can opener.

One of the jumpers made it past my guards. He stopped for a moment, looked around, then made a beeline straight for Gin. I blasted him away before he reached my sister.

Another jumper made it into the Court Chamber. He, too, went straight for Gin. What the hell?

I drew my sword. Flames roared to life on the blade. I jumped in front of Gin, swinging the sword. Her assailant jumped out of the flaming sword's path. Annoyance—and fear—flashed in his eyes, peeking out from behind a full-face wrap. His whole body was wrapped actually, like a ninja. These guys were dressed just like the ninjas who'd attacked my family twice in Purgatory.

"You weren't aiming for Bella. Or for Zane." I parried the strike of his sword. "You were after Gin all along. Why?"

He didn't answer, but I knew I was right. Gin had been there both times the ninjas had attacked. And the single-minded determination with which these guys kept going for her now was unmistakable. They were after Gin. And they were fighting to kill.

There was a loud thump as the pegasus knight's heavy boots—and her steed's hooves—hit the floor. She darted around the deck, slashing through all the ninjas that remained there. Then she pushed open the doors to enter the court chamber. She marched toward me.

My guards rushed forward, surrounding her. Covered

in blood, his dark eyes alight with delight, Punch looked like he was having the time of his life.

"I am here to petition for the Legion's protection," the pegasus knight declared.

"Who are you?" I asked her.

"My name is Indira. I sent you a message that I'd be coming." She pulled off her helmet, revealing her face. The woman looked just like Gertrude and Inali.

"So you're another one of the eight."

Indira. That was one of the names Gertrude had given me, the name of one of her sisters.

"I am," Indira said. "Leda Pandora, you must accept my petition. You must let me in. You must hear what I have to say. More planes are headed this way. They have come here to kill your sister."

I looked at Gin, then back at Indira. "Why? Why Gin?"

"It is a long story."

"Why do you care about what happens to any of us?" I asked her, suspicious. "Why do you care about what happens to Gin?"

"She is my daughter," Indira declared.

# CHAPTER 31

## PHOENIX'S REFRAIN

*I* would have pointed out that Indira didn't look old enough to have a nineteen-year-old daughter, but after all, an hour ago her sister Gertrude had looked like a woman of seventy. Who knew how old the eight sisters really were. All I knew was they *were* immortal.

Gin had grown pale. Wide-eyed, she gaped at Indira, the woman who claimed to be her mother. Tessa had her arm around Gin, squeezing her in support.

"Explain," I said to Indira.

"I already told you what you need to know. There's no time. More planes are coming." She glanced out the window, and she *did* look worried.

"Explain," I said again.

Indira looked at her sisters in exasperation.

"The Angel of Chaos is very stubborn," Gertrude told her.

"And wily," Inali added.

"Fine," Indira sighed. "The people in those planes

were hired by the Guardians. Their mission is to kill me and Gin."

"You're a phoenix too? Like Gin?" I asked her.

"Yes. And while it's almost impossible to kill us, it isn't entirely impossible. There are methods. The Guardians are aware of these methods."

I didn't ask what those methods involved. There were a lot of people here in this room, and I didn't want anyone to overhear anything that might help them kill my sister.

"So the Guardians sent the ninjas to kill Gin in Purgatory?" I asked.

"Yes," Indira confirmed.

"Both outside our house and at the Bazaar?"

"Yes."

"Why?"

"Because I was there," Indira said. "I intended to speak to Gin. The Guardians wanted to prevent that from happening,"

"Why?"

"Because I know the secret of how to reach the Guardians, of how to expose their Sanctuaries to this realm. And I was going to share this secret with Gin."

"Because she is your daughter?" I asked.

"Because she and I are the only phoenixes I know of who possess enough power to help you do this," she told me.

"Do what? How can a phoenix help us break into the Guardians' Sanctuary?"

I heard the rumble of plane engines outside.

"More have come to finish the job that these mercenaries failed to carry out." Indira waved her hand to indicate the dead ninjas strewn across the floor. She watched the progress of the planes now close enough to be visible through the windows. "In exchange for your protection of me and my sisters, I will tell you everything you need to know to reach the Guardians' Sanctuary."

"Agreed," I said.

Stash and the other godly soldiers moved onto the outdoor deck, along with Alec and his forces. They bombarded the incoming planes with magic until they knocked all of them out of the sky.

Well, almost all of them. One of the planes crashed into the airship with a thunderous boom that didn't sound at all good for the structural integrity of this thing.

Nyx shot me an agitated look, like it was all my fault that random people kept trying to blow up any airship I was on.

Another plane was crashing down toward the airship's deck. Stash blasted it with magic, destroying it before it hit.

"More planes are coming, Leda," Stash called back to me. "A lot more."

"Man, you must have *really* pissed off the Guardians," I commented to Indira, then I rushed toward the outdoor deck.

Indira ran at my side, her scythe ready. "The Guardians are afraid of what I know. And of what you can accomplish with my help."

I joined Stash and the others, shooting down any plane that got too close. Indira cut through any ninja who jumped out of a plane to reach us.

There were still a lot of ninja planes out there, but the fleet turned away at the sight of four angels in the sky. Nero, along with Damiel, Colonel Fireswift, and Colonel Dragonblood. The four angels shot at the fast-retreating fleet, blowing up a few of the planes at the rear. Then the angels looped around the airship and landed gracefully on the deck.

I stepped forward to greet Nero, but his gaze snapped to Indira. Gold flashed in his eyes. "Don't make any deals with that beast."

I looked at Indira, then at him. "What do you mean?"

"She's the one," he said, his words dripping with menace. "The one responsible for killing so many angels, soldiers, and countless others on countless worlds. We finally tracked her down."

There was a flash of magic, and then suddenly another of the octuplets was standing in front of me. This was getting ridiculous.

"You're late," Indira said to the new arrival.

"You're welcome, sister," the teleporter replied.

Her voice. This was the woman in the purple cloak, the one who'd gotten the weapons of heaven and hell out of the Lost City for Grace. That's how she'd gotten the artifacts; she'd teleported them out of the gateway. I knew it was this djinn. Though the sisters all spoke pretty much alike, there were minor differences in intonation between them. Unlike their faces, their personalities weren't all identical.

"I was luring those planes away from you."

"Luring them where?" Indira asked.

The teleporter laughed. "Through a portal that led to a cozy, totally uninhabited moon."

Indira laughed too. "Nice."

"Welcome to the circus, Number Four," I said to the djinn.

"Actually, my name is Rosette," she told me.

"And whose mother, surrogate mother, or grandmother are you supposed to be?" I said flippantly.

I was joking, so I was pretty surprised when Rosette answered, "Hers." She looked at Tessa. "I'm her mother."

Tessa's eyes went wide. It was Gin's turn to squeeze and comfort her. Or maybe my sisters were squeezing and comforting each other.

"So Gin and Tessa are cousins?" Zane asked.

"Cousins. Or sisters," Gertrude said. "Depends on how you see it. We are all identical, you know. Except for our powers."

"And who would want to create eight identical people, each with one of the eight passive magic powers?" Bella asked.

Inali nodded. "That is a very good question."

"But not one we're at liberty to discuss," Indira said. "The deal we made was, specifically, that I'd tell you how to break in to the Guardians' Sanctuary."

"Leda, don't listen to them." Nero indicated the phoenix and the teleporting djinn. "The two of them killed all those people. They killed Legion soldiers. And Legion angels."

"It was a necessary evil committed for the greater good," Indira said.

"I don't believe that *any* evil is necessary," I declared.

"Yes, that's very noble of you, dear. And very naive." Inali folded her arms over her chest like a shield. "You wouldn't even be here today if not for the necessary evil that Grace and Faris committed."

"That doesn't mean I need to follow in their footsteps." I turned to Indira, demanding answers. "Why did you kill all of those people?"

"Because, as my sisters have explained to you, there is

great power in death," Indira said. "And in life. But there's also a pretty tight magical balance between life and death. So I had to trade all of those deaths for life."

"What life?"

"The life of your child." Indira looked at Nyx. "And yours." Her gaze panned across Cadence, Leila, Basanti, Andromeda, and Alice. "And yours. And yours. And yours. And yours. And yours."

"Wait, so you killed all those people to create this life? So we'd all have children?" I said.

"Bringing the children of angels into existence is a tricky thing. You're so..." Indira frowned. "...infertile. Usually, anyway. It's even worse with the gods and demons. I've never met such a barren bunch. That's what comes from drinking all of that poison all of the time. It gives you power, sure, but it also doesn't make it easy for you to pass on that power, to have children. In order to counteract all that infertility, to create powerful new life, it required a lot of deaths. Specifically, a lot of powerful deaths. Because we're not just talking about one baby angel. We're talking about several, all at once. Since the laws of magic and nature just don't work that way, I had to bend them."

"That's why you killed two angels," I realized. "And all of those Legion soldiers and supernaturals too."

"Many people on many worlds." Indira said it like what she'd done didn't bother her at all.

"Why Silvertongue and Spellsmiter? Why those two angels?" Nyx asked her.

"Because I could lure them out to the Sienna Sea, far away from anything," Indira said.

"By removing the ruins of Darkstorm's fortress," Nyx said. "How did you do that?"

The First Angel was clearly assessing her enemy, determining what they could do and how they did it.

"*I* did that," Rosette said.

"You can teleport away whole buildings?" I asked her.

"Of course. You didn't think teleporting was just for people, did you? There are so many larger uses. In fact, I once teleported an entire spaceship to—"

"They don't want to hear about that," Indira cut her off.

Actually, I wanted to hear all about it. Anyone who could teleport whole spaceships was not someone to be taken lightly. I wondered what else Rosette could do. Or what the rest of her fellow octuplets could do, for that matter.

"Why did you later return the ruins of Darkstorm's fortress to the Sienna Sea?" Nyx asked Rosette.

"Because we'd already gotten what we needed from them," Rosette replied. "And they were taking up a lot of space in my storage unit."

I wondered how big of a storage unit a djinn like Rosette had.

"Ok, there you go. Now you know. Don't give me that look, Nero Windstriker," Indira snapped at him. "You owe us your daughter's life. If we hadn't killed all those people, I couldn't have traded the power of their deaths for your daughter's life." Indira looked at all the other expecting parents here. "And the same goes for all of you. I've given you all a great gift. But if you'd rather I took those gifts away..." She lifted her hand in the air.

"No," Damiel said quickly.

Nero had moved in front of me, shielding my body with his. Colonel Fireswift's sword was drawn. A fiery halo had completely engulfed Colonel Dragonblood.

Even steadfast Nyx had set her hands over her flat belly. Everyone else looked like they were two seconds away from kicking Indira's ass.

"Angels understand sacrifice," Damiel said.

Gods, his voice was so cold that my lungs were practically freezing in my chest. A layer of frost had actually formed on the floor.

"You will not harm my child," Nero told Indira.

"Any of our children," Nyx said with an even mix of fury and fear.

Indira smiled pleasantly. "Then we're all in agreement."

The wheels in my head had been turning the whole time she'd been explaining how she'd created all this life using all that death.

"This has happened before," I said quietly. "Twenty-five years ago. All the deaths. Like at the Battle of Calamity, where so many gods and demons died. That's where you got the powerful magic you needed to channel in order to make life. To make me. And Bella. And Jace and all of those Legion brats in my initiation class."

"The death of an immortal creates a very powerful magical release, particularly the deaths of deities," Indira said. "That's how you, Leda, could be born to a god and a demon, two beings whose magic is in complete conflict. It took a lot of skill to shuffle all of that magic around, to turn death into life, but I must say I did a marvelous job of it."

She sounded proud. I was horrified.

"Protecting the universe isn't always pretty," Indira told me.

You know, the more I saw of the universe, the more I realized it was just the same old story over and over again.

That same callous attitude was why the people of Earth had lost faith in the Legion.

"You said you will tell us how to reach the Guardians' Sanctuary," Nyx reminded Indira.

The First Angel was nothing if not practical. Still, I knew there was some humanity in her. I'd seen it. I wondered if, deep down, beneath that angelic shimmer, learning what Indira had done had made her as sick to her stomach as it had made me.

"And so I shall. What you need to do is actually quite simple." Indira looked at me. "And you already figured out the first part. You need to channel a lot of magic to break through the Guardians' barriers, using your cat as a vessel."

I was almost afraid to ask, but I did. "What is the second part?"

"You and all the other mothers-to-be here need to give birth at once," Indira said.

I frowned. "How does that help us break through the Guardians' barriers?"

"To break through that barrier, you need magic, Leda. Because nothing more than an insane amount of magic will overpower the Sanctuary's magic-nullifying defenses," Indira said. "Remember what I said, that there's power in life and death? Remember how I used death to make life? Well, it works in reverse. You can use life to make death. The power of many angel babies being born at once is the source of the insane amount of life magic you need. That magic can be channeled through your Companion cat and directed at the Sanctuary. That should be enough magic to 'kill' the Guardians' defenses and allow you entry. That is your way in."

"So let me get this straight. We all…" I pointed at

myself, then to all the other pregnant women in turn. "…we all need to give birth at the exact same time."

"That's right," Indira confirmed.

"Isn't that a bit improbable?"

"Nah, it's all about timing." Indira waved her hand.

I felt an odd stretching sensation, then I looked down to find I was suddenly very pregnant. I glanced at Cadence, Nyx, and the others. Their bellies were just as round now too.

"All right then." Indira dusted off her hands. "That should give us a few hours to get our ducks in a row before the babies arrive." Her merry eyes panned across our line of pregnant soldiers. "So, who's ready to storm the castle?"

## CHAPTER 32

### COUNTDOWN TO THE END

*I* looked down at my round belly. I rubbed it slowly. "What have you done to me?"

"Nothing crazy," replied Indira. "Just channeled some extra life magic into speeding up your pregnancy. You're welcome."

I opened my mouth to say something, then realized I didn't even know what to say to that.

"It's an easy phoenix spell," Indira said to Gin with a smile. "I can teach it to you."

Gin was speechless. She could only gape at her mother. This clearly wasn't how she'd envisioned meeting her real parents.

"You shouldn't mess with nature," I told Indira.

The phoenix looked at me, perplexed. "The gods and demons ask for the quick-fix treatment all the time."

"Quick-fix," I repeated, shaking my head in disbelief.

"Why are you complaining?" Indira looked honestly confused. "I spared you the long, grueling months of pregnancy. I hear the final stretch is especially bad."

Tessa found her voice. "You've *heard*? You're a mother. Shouldn't you know?"

Indira looked at her, then at her sister Rosette. "No. Rosette and I…well, we were never actually pregnant."

"Like Thea?" Bella asked.

"Oh, no," Rosette said. "Not quite like Thea. There were no immortal artifacts involved in your creation, girls. We—"

"Careful," Indira said. "We can't say too much."

"Why the hell not?" Gin demanded. My sister seemed to have found her voice too, and she was fuming mad. "You just pop up here and declare that you're our mothers. And that's that, no explanation of why you abandoned us, no apology for doing it. Nothing."

"We didn't abandon you," Indira told her.

"Then what happened?" Gin planted her hands on her hips. "Explain."

Indira shook her head. "We can't."

"How convenient," Gin said drily.

Indira looked like she didn't know what to say. Her happy, comfortable manner had evaporated. She'd talked us through all the people she'd killed without even batting an eye, but Gin's reaction had frozen her.

"We don't have time for this." Gertrude looked at me. "*You* don't have time for this, Leda. In a few hours, your babies will be here. Now you have a choice. You can either use that powerful moment of birth to channel the life magic into destroying the barrier that keeps the Guardians hidden inside their Sanctuary. Or you can stew over how very horrible we are and do nothing. In the latter case, you will have doomed all the people in the Sanctuary to death, including Arina's children."

Arina's hands tightened into fists.

"And if you allow those people to die, the Guardians will gain magic that rivals the Immortals," Gertrude said. "That will put everyone in danger, including your babies."

I scowled at her. Nero looked like he wanted to rip her head off with his bare hands.

"You still have a chance to make the deaths of your angels and soldiers mean something," Gertrude told us. "They can mean the end of the Guardians. Or you can sit here and argue morality while the Guardians move ever closer to their ultimate goal. The choice is yours."

We didn't have a choice. Not really. Gertrude and her sisters had manipulated us into a corner, and they knew it.

Another pegasus shot through the air at the airship, full speed. When it got close, it did a long somersault to slow down, then landed on the deck. An armored woman slid off the saddle. She took off her helmet to unveil herself as yet another octuplet.

"Are you all right?" Indira asked her.

"Better than the other guys," her sister replied. "The Guardians' forces tried to take control over the Vault, but I changed the password. They're locked out."

I guessed this 'password' was what allowed people to get into the Vault without picking the lock at the full moon, when the magic was just right.

She took a shaky step forward. Bloody and bruised with half of her armor plates dented or knocked clean off, she looked like she'd barely escaped the battle with her life.

"Great." Basanti's voice sizzled with sarcasm. "Now there are five of them."

"Which one is that?" Leila wondered.

"It's River," Zane answered. "The one who got me out of the Sanctuary."

River bowed to him. "Nice to see you again, Zane."

"Wait, if you can get someone out of the Sanctuary, can't you just sneak someone in?" I asked the rogue Guardian.

"It's not that easy," River told me. "My magic nullified Zane's magic. It made him invisible to the Sanctuary's system." River shook her head. "But I can't hide all of your magic. And getting in is even trickier than getting out, especially right now. After I got Zane out, the Guardians locked me out of the Sanctuary."

"Why did you get him out anyway?" I asked her.

"I told you before, Leda. You need your family. They make you strong—strong enough to fight the Guardians. And strong enough to beat them."

"Yes, you did say that. But there's something else, another reason you helped Zane escape and find me. You wanted me to trust you," I decided.

"You *should* trust us," Inali told me.

"It's hard to trust someone who hides behind another's face," Calli told the person she'd once considered a friend.

"But we aren't hiding," said Inali, the mimic. "We revealed ourselves to you."

"But you haven't revealed everything. You're still hiding behind secrets," I told her. "For example, why was River staying with the Guardians for all those years?"

"As a spy. I was their eyes inside the Sanctuary. It was my job to keep an eye on the Guardians' dangerous plans."

"*Their* eyes?" I said. "Whose eyes were you inside the Sanctuary?"

River said nothing.

"Well?"

"I can't say."

"Can't?" I asked. "Or won't?"

River didn't answer. I had not missed these evasive conversations with her.

"Can you at least tell me more about the Prophecy the Guardians are so worked up about?" I asked River.

She looked at Gertrude, who nodded.

"Very well," said River.

"So apparently the Guardians had a plan for Nero's parents—and, presumably, Nero," I said. "You've shown us my past, but what about Nero's? Did you interfere in his past as you did in mine?"

"No, that wasn't our doing. It was the Guardians." River looked at Cadence and Damiel. "The Guardians watched you throughout your lives. They arranged for you to meet. They set the scene so you would fall in love."

Damiel's face might have been etched in stone. Even the usual spark of humor was missing from his eyes.

River turned to Nero. "They wanted you to be born, so you could father a child with Leda Pandora. This child was to be the instrument the Guardians would use to create their new order."

"The Guardians tried to kill Leda." Nero's voice scratched like gravel. "Up on that rooftop in Purgatory, when they'd gained control over Meda."

"One of the Guardians tried to kill Leda," said River. "One who, out of the belief that the Angel of Chaos was too dangerous to be allowed to live a moment longer, acted against the other Guardians' plans. The others didn't want Leda killed until after she'd served her purpose and given birth to the child."

That showed the Guardians were not a single, unified force. If they had different ideas on how to do things, maybe we could use that against them. Maybe we could get them to turn against one another.

"You seem to know a lot about the Guardians' plans," Cadence commented.

"I have been watching them very closely for a very long time," River said.

"What about Illias?" Cadence asked. "He took credit for my relationship with Damiel. He had a plan for us too: to get him the daggers."

"There was a time when Illias's plans for you overlapped with the Guardians' plans for you," River said. "So for a while, they worked together, united in their hatred of the Immortals."

"Illias told the Guardians how to kill the Immortals and trap their souls inside immortal artifacts," Gertrude said. "And the Guardians helped Illias set the scene for Cadence and Damiel to meet."

"But Illias and the Guardians had different motivations," said River. "Illias only wanted to get rid of the Immortals so that they were out of the way, while the Guardians went about achieving their goal of gaining the magic the Immortals had specifically denied them."

"As long as the goals of Illias and the Guardians were aligned, they worked together," Gertrude said. "But when their goals diverged, they parted ways."

"So, to answer your question, Leda, that's how both Illias and the Guardians had a plan for Cadence and Damiel," River concluded.

"This is so nice, but we really must start our preparations. We have very little time left for question and answer." Indira glanced at our very round bellies. "*You have very little time until your babies are here.*"

"To gain magic, the Guardians are planning on a mass sacrifice of magical energy of their 'rescued' people—and it's all happening very soon. If you want to save everyone..." River glanced at Arina. "...if you want to save your children, then we need to begin our preparations for battle."

I did not like the octuplets' savage rearranging of life and death, as though they got to decide who lived and who died. But right now, we didn't have the luxury of arguing with them. We had little time left, and we needed Indira's magic to attack the Guardians.

I'd promised Arina that I would help her save her children, and I was determined to save the other people the Guardians held prisoner too. In my heart too, I knew I had to stop the Guardians now and save my daughter's future.

"We're ready." I looked at the other pregnant women.

They all nodded. I saw the same determination shining in their eyes that I felt burning in my heart.

Nero caught my hand. "Wait."

"I'm not sitting this one out," I told him. "Not this time. You can't do this without us."

His voice was softer, gentler. "It's too dangerous, Leda."

"We must stop the Guardians, Nero," I told him. "We can't allow our daughter to lose her goodness or her family."

"There's an entry point to the Guardians' Sanctuary not far from here," River said.

"Then that is where we'll make our stand against them," I decided. "And save our children's futures."

## CHAPTER 33

MEMORY STREAM

While the preparations were being made for our attack on the Guardians' Sanctuary, I spent the time with Nero and Angel in our room. My cat was indulging in a very long nap, obviously resting up in anticipation of channeling that much magic. She was a smart little kitty. Actually, she was a smart big kitty. My lion-sized feline companion was no house cat. She took up a whole bed all by herself.

"I need your help with something," I said to Nero.

"Anything," he replied immediately.

"The octuplets are hiding something from us, something out of the past. I intend to find out what it is. And I need you to be my tether, just like you did before, so I don't get lost in the memory stream. Time is so open, so endless."

"You're planning on using your magic to look into the past?"

"My magic." I stroked my very round belly. "And hers. She's stronger now. Her powers have grown a lot. If the three of us combine magic, together we can figure this out."

Nero set both his hands on my belly, over our daughter. "She really is that powerful," he said in awe.

I smiled. "Yes, she is. And with her help, with her magic, we'll be able to see directly into the past. We don't need to view the past through the Vault, which the octuplets have stuffed full with preselected memories. We will be in control of what we see or don't see, *not* the octuplets."

"Then let's get started. We don't have much time left before the battle."

His hands were still on my belly. I set my hands over his, then I reached out with my mind, connecting to both my husband and to our daughter.

---

I was in a jungle. I didn't see Nero beside me, but I could feel that he was with me, just as I could feel our child.

I looked down, but I didn't have a baby bump anymore. In fact, I wasn't even inside my own body anymore. Whoever's body I was in was very small. I extended my hands in front of me. They were a child's hands.

I took a few steps toward a nearby stream. A young girl of nine or ten with pale blonde pigtails and big, inquiring eyes stared back at me. She looked like a younger version of me—no, a younger version of my mother. I had my father's eyes.

So I was in Grace's body, back when she'd been a child.

She tucked a few loose wisps of hair behind her ears, then walked away from the stream. She followed the trail deeper into the jungle. I wasn't in control of her body. I was only a passenger, a witness to some past event that would shed some light on my existence.

At least that's what I hoped. I didn't really know what I was doing. I'd never before gone fishing for gold nuggets of information in the memory stream.

I saw a faint flicker of movement. A few steps off the trail, a man stepped through a tree, then disappeared. Of course he'd never really been there. His body had been too translucent. He looked like a memory fragment, like a scene out of the distant past.

It was Grace who'd come to that conclusion. It seemed I was tuned in to her thoughts.

*Her powerful telepathic abilities allowed her to see that hidden magic mirror where others would just pass it by, unaware that there's a passage to another world nearby,* Nero said in my mind.

Grace stepped up to the magic mirror. It truly was hidden, even when seeing it through Grace's eyes. She'd only found it because she'd caught the memory fragment of someone who'd once taken it.

She took the plunge. As she passed between worlds, a cool feeling washed over me, like I'd walked through a waterfall.

Grace looked around at the new world she'd discovered.

*This isn't a demon world,* she thought. *Or any world I know about.*

From her hiding spot in the snowy woods, she watched a boy teleport between rings that had been set up around a sports field.

*A djinn,* commented Nero.

Also on the field, two teenage girls stood facing each other. One fired a gun at the other. The girl who'd been shot in the head fell dead to the ground. No one rushed over to her. No one expressed any shock whatsoever at this very public murder.

A few moments passed, then the dead girl rose from the ground, alive once more.

*A phoenix,* said Nero.

The girl with the gun threw it down. Then she touched her hand to the phoenix girl's chest—and transformed into her.

*A changeling,* Nero said.

The real phoenix picked up the gun and shot the girl who'd stolen her face. The changeling must have succeeded in mimicking her powers because after a few moments of being dead, she too rose from the ground.

There were others training on that sports field: mermaids and genies, phantoms and unicorns. On the sidelines, a few elves were crafting magical artifacts.

Grace watched them all for a few minutes, then she turned and went back through the invisible magic mirror.

Back on her own world, she ran out of the jungle. She rushed into a palatial house with white walls that sparkled like diamonds and tall towers that looked like they'd come out of a fairytale. The young demon's castle even had a moat, where tamed miniature sea dragons splashed in crystal waters.

Grace didn't stop running until she found her sisters in a grand ballroom with marble floors and high walls accented with real gold. Her identical twin Ava was dismembering animated suits of armor, while a teenage Sonja battled a giant she must have assembled from numerous large statues. Its horse-like head nearly scraped the domed ceiling.

"Ava, Sonja," Grace said breathlessly. "I have discovered something incredible."

Then she told them all about it.

"An unexplored world, you say? And new kinds of magic?" Sonja hacked off the statue giant's legs, and it fell motionless to the floor. "We must check it out. I need a new challenge."

And so Grace led her sisters back to the jungle, through the invisible magic mirror, and onward to the undiscovered world.

"This is strange magic indeed," Sonja declared, looking down upon the training field. "And very rare magic where we come from. The Immortals had all of these powers."

The three demon sisters watched the passive magic students train their magic until Sonja, obviously bored of only watching, got up and marched out of the snowy woods.

"Sonja, where are you going?" Ava asked her.

"To find my next challenge," Sonja said. "I'm going to challenge one of these peculiar...*beings* to a battle of magic."

*Twenty bucks says the passive magic kids totally kick Sonja's ass,* I said to Nero.

But the three demon sisters never made it to the training arena. Between one step and the next, they were whisked away to...well, I wasn't exactly sure what it was. The sisters appeared to be inside a small log cabin, but all the windows showed in any direction was sky. Lots and lots of open sky. Grace went over to one of the windows to take a peek, and that's when I saw that they were way up in the clouds. The ground wasn't even visible from here.

Two youthful women sat on rocking chairs. Their eyes were wise, their hair wild. And their clothes, made from various animal skins, were hand-stitched.

"Where are we?" Grace asked them.

The woman with the crystals growing in her hair said, "This world is called the Sphere, young demon. How did you find your way here?"

"I followed the memories through the magic mirror," Grace told her.

"Her telepathic powers are strong for a demon," said the other woman, the one with the silver bracelets.

Crystal looked Grace over. "Yes. They are."

"You know what we are, but what are you?" Ava asked them. "You aren't demons or gods."

"No, we're not," Silver chuckled. "We are another kind of deity."

"There is no other kind of deity. Unless…" Sonja looked them over closely, but she didn't seem impressed by what she saw in them or their shabby cabin. She shook her head. "No, you're not them."

"Who?" Ava asked.

Sonja opened her mouth, but Grace answered first. "Immortals. Sonja doesn't believe they are Immortals."

"I've told you to stop digging around in my head," Sonja growled at Grace.

Grace planted her hands on her hips and shot back, "And I've told you that it's hard to ignore your thoughts when you leave them all hanging out there like that."

I liked this version of Grace. She was cool.

Sonja gave her little sister the evil eye, then she returned her attention to the two mystery women. "In any case, they are not Immortals. The Immortals were far more…" She puffed out her chest. "…commanding. And regal."

"You didn't know the Immortals, young one," Crystal said gently. "There aren't many gods or demons left who did. Your thirst for battle, your *immortal* war, has made sure of that."

"But you did know the Immortals?" Ava asked them.

Crystal nodded. "We did. They were powerful and wise. Though their obsessive study of magic was eventually their undoing."

"The Guardians," Grace said, her voice hardly above a whisper.

Crystal nodded again.

"I am one of the eidolons," Silver said.

"And I am of the spirits," Crystal declared.

"Like demons and gods, eidolons and spirits are the Immortals' creations," Silver explained. "Eidolon magic is passive dark magic."

"And spirit magic is passive light magic," Crystal added.

"So you rule over all those with passive magic?" Sonja asked them.

"We do not rule over anyone," Silver said serenely.

"We don't even show ourselves to them," said Crystal. "We merely exist. And watch."

"Without interfering in others' affairs," Silver added harshly.

"So you don't have worshippers?" Sonja frowned like she found the idea ridiculous.

"Certainly not," Crystal replied. "Most passive magic users don't even know that we exist—or that we protect their worlds."

There was a hint of warning in her tone, as though to warn the demons not to get any ideas of conquering the worlds they protected.

"Most people still worship the Immortals, and we are content to let it remain so," Silver said.

"Why?" Sonja's nostrils flared. No, she definitely didn't like the way the spirits and eidolons worked.

"Because we desire neither power nor glory," Crystal said. "And we don't need people to worship us in order to feel a sense of self-worth."

"And you spirits and eidolons get along?" Sonja's eyes narrowed. "You never fight?"

"Well, there are occasional differences of opinion, but those can be worked out through calm, rational, open discussion. There's certainly no need for violence." Silver's eyes dipped to the dagger at Sonja's belt.

"You are very strange," Grace told them with wide eyes.

She didn't mean it as an insult. She was simply perplexed by the beings before her, by notions she found as strange as their magic. And she'd expressed that with a childlike innocence that I hadn't expected from her.

Crystal laughed. "Yes, I can see how you'd think so. We must seem very strange to three demon girls who have grown up believing in their own divinity and in their right to be worshipped."

Crystal didn't seem offended. She must have realized Grace wasn't being critical; she was just perplexed.

"We can show you another way," Silver offered. "Peace and harmony are possible. We too are of light and dark magic, but we have learned to coexist without conflict—by giving up vanity and the thirst for power. Demons and gods can learn to get along too."

"Why would we ever want to get along with the gods? Their magic is vile," Sonja said stiffly. "Why would I give up my divine right to rule just to make friends with them?"

"Why would you do that?" Crystal shook her head sadly. "We once lost people who thought as you did, who allowed their pursuit of power to consume them, and in so doing, they destroyed the Immortals."

"The Guardians," Ava guessed.

"Yes," Crystal confirmed. "Remember the sins of the Guardians. Because of their vanity—because of their thirst for power—the great Immortals are forever gone."

"But the Guardians' tragic tale didn't end there," Silver said. "Because they didn't stop with the Immortals. The Guardians' bitterness lived on. Not even that terrible act of revenge could put out the flame of their anger. Even now, they are searching for a way to destroy the gods and demons, you favored children of the Immortals. Children who were given much better magic—or so the Guardians believe."

Grace looked at Ava. "The Guardians are coming for us."

"Their magic might just be the most powerful of all, a magic to end all magic." Ava's voice shook. "They have the power to render magic useless—whether spell, potion, or artifact."

Sonja's laughter sliced through their distress. "Oh, please," she said, derisive. "I know a ghost story when I hear one. They are trying to scare you. And like naive little girls, you've let them." Sonja pointed her flaming sword at Crystal and Silver. "But I will not let them do the same to me. I will take their power, and with it, *I* will defeat the Guardians."

"Oh, dear," Crystal said sadly. She waved her hand, and the flames went out on Sonja's sword.

"Violence isn't welcome here." Silver clapped her hands once, and Sonja vanished.

"What have you done with our sister?" Ava demanded.

"I sent her back home," replied Silver.

"She was acting very rude." Crystal shook her head in quiet disapproval. "Galactic domination is simply not welcome here."

"Was she right?" Grace asked them. "Are the Guardians just a ghost story you told to scare us? Or are they truly coming for us?"

"The Guardians' hearts are full of envy, hatred, and vengeance," Silver said. "They might not act today or even this century, but eventually they will strike out against the demons and the gods."

"Can't you help us stop them?" Grace asked.

Crystal blinked. "Why?"

"Because the Guardians have your kind of magic. Passive magic. They are the responsibility of the spirits and eidolons. *Your* responsibility," Grace told them.

"We don't operate under the same magical hierarchy as you do," Silver said.

"And we don't take sides," Crystal added.

"But you have to," Grace told them. "You just have to."

Ava set her hand on her sister's shoulder. "Forget it, Grace. They're pacifists."

But Grace wasn't giving up so easily. "Can you at least tell us where to find the Guardians?" she asked the two passive magic deities.

"Why? So you can launch a preemptive strike?" Silver

replied. "No, we can't tell you how to find them. That would be interfering. In fact, we've told you too much already."

"We should warn them about the savior," Crystal said to her.

"No." Silver's voice was sharp.

"Who is this savior?" Ava asked sweetly.

Crystal smiled. "She is the one who will—"

"Enough," Silver cut her off.

Crystal shook her head. "Sorry. I don't know what got into me. The words just flowed off my tongue."

"*She* got into you." Silver's eyes locked on to Ava. "Siren magic."

Crystal rose from her seat. "We don't take kindly to being manipulated, little demons."

She clapped her hands. The cabin, the spirit, and the eidolon blurred out like paint dissolving into water. Then Grace and Ava were back home, inside their castle.

Ava looked at Grace. "To me, their non-interference line just sounds like an excuse to hide away and take no responsibility for anything."

"Indeed," Grace agreed. "But the threat of the Guardians is no line."

"No, it isn't. It's true. I could feel it," Ava said. "Well, if they won't help us, we must come up with a plan to defeat the Guardians ourselves."

"All right, but just the two of us, Ava. We can't involve Sonja. Too often, she only does what's best for her and for her alone."

I saw a conference table. On one side of the table sat Faris and Zarion. I sat on the other side, right beside Grace. I knew it was Grace, not Ava, but I couldn't say how I knew. Grace appeared to be fully-grown now, so this memory must have occurred many years after the last one.

Zarion folded his hands together on the table, his many garish rings clinking together. "Ava, I do hope you're not just wasting our time."

Ava. So I must have been inside Ava's body this time.

*I wonder if the body you're in is determined by the person who most drove the memory, who had the most influence on the situation,* Nero commented.

That made sense.

"Not at all, Zarion," Ava replied to the god. "But perhaps we should take a short recess from these negotiations, just to give your mind a chance to catch up with everything we've discussed."

Fury flashed in Zarion's eyes. He rose quickly from his chair, but Faris caught his arm.

"Sit down," Faris said coldly. His gaze shifted to the demon sisters. "We shall take a one-hour recess."

"Agreed." Grace looked at Zarion. "And when we return, we expect more civilized conversation."

Ava and Grace rose fluidly from their seats and exited the room. They said nothing until they'd reached what looked like a very opulent hotel suite. A gentle sea shone bright and blue beyond the numerous windows, each one framed by a set of red velvet curtains. The walls were gold and the floors marble. The ceiling was painted with cloudy blue skies and lots of angels.

Now alone, Ava turned to Grace. "He has a thing for you."

"Zarion?" Grace's face crinkled up in disgust. "He's so...*godly*." She said the word like it was the worst thing imaginable.

"Not Zarion. Faris," Ava told her. "Didn't you see the way he was looking at you? He's enticed by you. It must have something to do with your magic. I'm clearly the pretty one."

Grace snorted. "You think we can use this to our advantage."

"I do."

"How?" Grace asked her.

"That spirit and that eidolon warned us about the Guardians' plans. Centuries later, the Guardians have finally made their first move. Nearly as soon as our war with the gods reached Earth, they arrived there too. We hadn't seen or heard from the Guardians in ages, and then they were suddenly there. They made themselves a hiding place on Earth, out of our reach in their so-called Sanctuary."

"The Sanctuary is slightly offset from our realm," Grace said. "It occupies the same space as the plains of monsters."

Ava frowned. "What I want to know is how the plains of monsters came to be."

"They were born from the clash of our dark magic with the gods' light magic," Grace said.

"Grace, demons and gods have fought many times on many worlds, and this has never happened before. Only on Earth have we lost control over our beasts. Only on Earth has the magic gone so wild that these so-called plains of monsters formed."

"There's something special about Earth," Grace suggested. "It's a place of change. Of opportunity. All kinds of magic are all mixed up there. The Immortals did something to the place."

"But what?"

"I started researching that after the plains of monsters formed on Earth," Grace said. "I found some tales in our older books. These tales describe the world where the Immortals conducted their first experiments on magic, on splitting magic into separate types in order to understand how the different parts work. I believe this world was Earth. Do you know what this means, Ava? It means Earth is far more precious than we'd thought. It's one of a kind, a place where magic—and the people who wield it—can be anything. A place where any magic or combination of magic can exist. Magic can be chaos *and* order, light *and* dark, active *and* passive. All depending on how it's shaped."

"You're right, Grace. This conference *is* an opportunity. Being here is an opportunity. An opportunity to destroy the Guardians. And the gods too."

"The council sent us here to negotiate with the gods," Grace reminded her sister. "They're concerned about what happened on Earth. They fear other worlds could suffer the same fate—and broken worlds don't make for very nice places to rule."

"But you just said this can't happen to any other world. Because the Earth is special," Ava pointed out.

"I didn't actually say this couldn't happen to any other world. I just explained why I believe it happened on Earth. I doubt plains of monsters will spontaneously pop up on other worlds. But I can't prove it yet. And that doesn't negate the council's wishes for us to negotiate with the gods."

"Multitasking, my dear sister," Ava said with a sly

smile. "We can do both. Besides, both we and the gods know exactly how these negotiations will end. They'll end the same way they have every other time we've tried to negotiate with the gods. No agreement will be reached, and we'll just continue fighting."

"That does seem likely," Grace agreed.

"But just because the demons and gods as a whole can't come to an agreement," Ava said. "That doesn't mean a demon and a god can't come to a private agreement. That's where Faris comes in."

"Faris won't betray the other gods for us," Grace told her.

"No, he won't. Faris will always act in a way that furthers his own interests. Actually, that's what I'm counting on for my plan to work."

"And what exactly is your plan?" Grace asked.

"For you to create a weapon powerful enough to defeat the Guardians *and* turn the tide of this immortal war. And Faris is going to help you do it."

"Because he has a thing for me," Grace said drily.

"No, because he's a power-hungry lunatic who won't be able to resist the ultimate weapon. The fact that he finds you enticing can only serve to advance our plan."

"*Our* plan? This sounds an awful lot like it's *your* plan, sister."

"Remember all those years ago when we pledged to find a way to destroy the Guardians?" Ava reminded her. "That was our plan. And now we finally have a way to do it."

"So what makes this weapon so powerful? And why do we need Faris's help?"

"The weapon will be powerful because it will use the full spectrum of magic," Ava said. "And we need Faris for his light magic. You see, Grace, you and Faris are going to have a child. That child will have all the powers of the demons *and* the gods. The ultimate weapon."

Grace folded her arms across her chest. "Even if Faris agrees to work with me, he will try to take this child—this weapon—for himself."

Ava winked at her. "Well, then it's a good thing we're smarter than Faris is."

---

Ava's plan was good, but she didn't take it far enough. Grace had had a few hundred years to think it over and had improved upon her sister's plan. Because this wasn't just about the child of a demon and a god. It was about the child of that child. Grace would make a child with the power of gods and demons, but she wouldn't stop there. If she played her cards right, that child's child could have all the powers of the Immortals. And that child would truly be the ultimate weapon.

*So Grace and Ava, in their move to fight the Guardians, came up with the same plan as the Guardians,* I commented to Nero.

*The Guardians wanted us to come together because of a Prophecy,* he replied.

*A Prophecy with several different outcomes.*

*Exactly, Leda. The Guardians acted to bring us together because they'd heard that you would be something special—and that our child would be just the weapon they needed.*

"I'm offering you a chance to finally play the smart game," Grace told Faris when she visited him on one of his worlds.

"Go on." Faris looked annoyed, but also intrigued.

"You've been concentrating entirely on collecting the individual members of your Orchestra," she said. "But if you want to win this game, you need to get one powerful conductor. One powerful weapon. Someone with all the magic of the gods *and* the demons."

"The Immortals are long gone," replied Faris. "There is no such person anymore."

"No, there isn't," she agreed. "Which is why we can't find this conductor. We have to make it."

*That* got his attention.

"How?" he asked her.

Grace put her hands on her hips. "You're pretty dense, aren't you? If you want to make someone with the powers of a god and a demon, you need to *make* someone with the powers of a god and a demon."

Faris blinked. "You wish to have sex with me."

"No, I don't. Not really. But, unfortunately for both of us, that's how babies are made, Faris."

Grace didn't tell Faris that she had other plans for this child, that she planned for the child to grow up to bear another child, an Immortal child with the power to defeat the Guardians.

And Grace already had her future daughter's mate picked out. She would pair the child that she and Faris created with the angel Nero Windstriker, the offspring of two angels with Immortal blood. That combination should do the trick. Light and dark, passive and active, order and chaos—all bound together by love.

That meant her child and Nero Windstriker would need to fall in love, but that was manageable. And Grace needed the Immortal child to be made on Earth, the world of infinite potential. That was the perfect formula, the perfect recipe for the ultimate weapon.

"My Queen, do you require anything else?" Colonel Soulslayer asked.

Sonja looked up from the Legion soldier chained to her table. The man was so close to death's door that there wasn't much point in continuing. She needed a fresh subject.

"Take this one away and kill him," Sonja told the dark angel. "Then bring me something else, someone with a little less light magic. The Venom killed this one too fast."

Colonel Soulslayer bowed. "It will be done." He lifted the soldier from the table, balanced him over his shoulder, then left the room.

Sonja took the time to jot down a few notes. She'd been at these experiments for centuries, but she didn't feel any closer to creating a subject with the right magic to destroy the Guardians. She must have been missing something, some vital piece of the equation.

---

Ava knew the odds were stacked against them when it came to Grace and Faris conceiving the child who would be their weapon, but she also knew of one deity who had cheated those odds. He was a god named Regin, and he'd managed to cheat the odds not once or twice or even three times. He'd cheated those odds ten times, and he had ten children because of it.

Regin was the brother of Faris and Zarion, but that hadn't saved him when the gods decided he was dabbling in magic too odious to be tolerated. They'd exiled him and his ten offspring to eleven distant, desolate moons, cut off from one another and from the rest of civilization.

Ava decided to pay the disgraced god a visit. The place was completely off the grid. No magic mirrors could bring her there. So she had to use a djinn to teleport her.

Regin lived in a broken-down old wooden house that looked like it had been built by a blind man. None of the walls were straight, and there were cracks between the wooden planks wide enough for Ava to stick her hand through.

The house was situated on a cliff above the ocean, but the water was very cold and very salty. Ava could taste it on her tongue. As far as she could see, the land in every direction was rocky and barren. There weren't any plants or animals anywhere.

"Wait here," Ava told the djinn who had brought her to this forsaken place.

Then she opened the door and walked inside the house. Regin sat on a misshapen chair by the fireplace. Deities were ageless, but you never would have known it from the god's appearance. His wrinkled face was framed by a long, white beard that would have touched the floor if not for all the knots in it. The hair on his head was just as long, white, and knotted. He wore a tattered, bloodstained robe and no shoes at all.

"Regin," Ava said, standing in the doorway.

The god squinted at her, blinded by the light she'd let in. He must have not left the house in a very long time.

"Shut the door!"

His voice was scratchy. Ava wondered how long it had been since he'd used it.

She shut the door. She glided over to the defeated

god, who was hunched over the tiny fire. "You are the god called Regin."

"And you're a dirty demon."

"Be careful who you call 'dirty'," she replied in a biting tone. "I have questions for you. If you answer them, I'll give you something."

He blinked, trying to get a better look at her. "You're Ava, the Demon of Hell's Army."

"I am."

"How'd you get here?"

"A djinn brought me."

His chuckle was as rough as a machine that hadn't been oiled in years. "You want to know how I managed to sire so many children."

"How did you know?" Ava asked in surprise.

"Why else go through all the trouble to come all the way out here? I've been here for a very long time, so I don't know anything about the gods' war plan, and they'd rather see me die than pay a ransom to get me back. But I am the only deity who has ever had ten children. That's valuable information."

So his mind was in much better shape than his body. And his house.

"Tell you what, I'll explain to you exactly how I did it." He smacked his lips. "If you get me off this cursed moon and back to civilization."

"I have another offer." Ava pulled a slender vial out of her jacket. A bright liquid sparkled and swirled inside it, moving almost like it was alive.

He gaped at it. "Nectar."

"How long has it been since you've had some?"

Regin watched the Nectar move in the vial, transfixed. "No." He shook himself. "I want my freedom. That is my offer."

"How disappointing." Ava moved to tuck the vial away again.

He caught her hand. "Wait."

"There's enough magic in this Nectar to return you to your former glory." She used her other hand to retrieve a second vial of Nectar from her jacket. "And I'm offering two doses."

"I want the first one before I tell you anything."

"Very well. But be warned. If you cross me, I am more than powerful enough to deal with the likes of you."

Ava set the first vial of Nectar into his hand. With eager, shaky fingers, Regin popped the vial's top and poured the entire contents into his mouth.

The effects were immediate. An ethereal glow washed across his skin, smoothing the wrinkles. The glow spread across his hair, turning it from white to black. His clothes not only mended; they completely transformed into a glorious gold-and-purple robe befitting a king. His eyes grew sharper, and it wasn't only thanks to the dramatic dash of dark eyeshadow on his lids. His lips became fuller and smoother; they were no longer broken by dry cracks.

Ava smiled. "Now, that's better. You actually look alive. And you don't smell like garbage anymore."

Regin leaned back in his chair and braided his fingers together in a thoughtful pose. "Yes."

"Now it's your turn."

"Very well." Like his face, his voice wasn't rough anymore either. It was as smooth as rose petals. "You wish to know how I beat the odds? It's quite simple. I changed the rules of the game."

"How?"

"By changing the flow of magic in my favor. You see, the universe has a kind of balance sheet. In order to have life, you need death. It's the so-called balance of the universe. But you can cheat that balance. To create a powerful life, you merely need to compensate with powerful death. The more death, the better. That puts the balance sheet in your favor."

Ava leaned forward. She was very, very intrigued. "There are often battles that result in a lot of death. That doesn't mean more people are born."

"No," he said. "You need to channel that death. You need to transform it into life. After all, we're cheating our way out of our own infertility by paying for it with death. It's not an easy procedure. Nor is it appreciated by certain closed-minded individuals who claim to speak for all the gods."

"The gods' council exiled you because you did this," Ava realized. "Ten times."

"They exiled me because of the massacres I created in order to achieve the necessary balance to make my children. They labeled me 'mad' and sent me into exile here. And they dropped off my children on ten nearby moons. We're all orbiting the same world, all so close, and yet so far away. It wasn't enough to exile me. They had to torture me too."

"The other gods cut you off from your private little army," Ava said. "Would you have used that army against them?"

"Of course not. Ten soldiers isn't enough of an army to do anything. I'd need at least a few hundred. Unfortunately, I never got that far."

"You didn't need a few hundred soldiers," Ava said to

herself under her breath. "You only needed one. The right one."

"What's that?"

"Never mind," Ava said hurriedly. "How did you redirect all those deaths into the life that created your children?"

"By employing the services of a very powerful phoenix."

"A phoenix…"

"A *very powerful* phoenix," he said with emphasis. "Only the strongest phoenixes can perform this kind of magic. In fact, there's only one phoenix I know of who's skilled enough to do it."

"Who?"

Regin smiled at her.

Ava tossed him the second vial of Nectar.

He popped the lid and inhaled deeply. A dreamy look washed over his face, but he didn't drink the Nectar just yet. Instead, he closed the vial again.

"Indira," he told Ava. "Her name is Indira."

---

"This isn't what we agreed to." Ava shot the phoenix Indira an aggravated look.

"You hired me to channel the death you orchestrated into life," Indira replied. "That's what made your sister's pregnancy possible."

"I hired you to channel that death into life *in my sister*," Ava said with unfiltered venom. "I did not pay you to also create life in all of those angels and wives of angels."

Indira looked unbothered by the demon's bad mood.

"The universe has to achieve a balance somehow. You made a lot of death. A lot. You were more discreet than Regin, true, but it was still a lot of death."

"I had to make sure it was enough to make Grace's baby."

"It was," said Indira. "And there was leftover magical energy that had to go somewhere. Just be happy there weren't a dozen gods conceived because that would have made your war against the gods harder."

"You knew this would happen." Ava's eyes narrowed to slits. "You did this just to annoy me."

"I'm a professional," Indira said stiffly. "I don't make a habit of annoying my clients."

"I'm considering killing you for your impudence."

"I'm a phoenix," Indira reminded her.

"There are ways to kill a phoenix."

"You don't want to kill her, Ava," Grace declared as she entered the room.

"Actually, I really do," Ava told her sister.

"It's really hard to kill a phoenix."

Ava yawned.

"Besides, we will need Indira again for the next step, for Leda to have a child of her own."

Ava sighed. "You're right." She looked at Indira and gave her wrist a dismissive flick. "You may go. We'll be in need of your services again in the near future."

---

Soon after Grace found out that she was pregnant, she traveled to the far edge of the demons' territory. But Ava found her.

"You've been avoiding me, Grace," Ava said. "Why? The LEDA project is going entirely to plan."

"I've changed the plan," replied Grace. "The gods have control over Earth. We can't send the child there. Faris will surely find her."

"The child must grow up on Earth," Ava told her. "Because of that world's magical potential. It's just the environment the child requires to become what we need her to be."

Grace shook her head. "She won't be what we need her to be if Faris controls her. I will train her myself, and I'll do it somewhere that Faris can't find her."

"For our plan to work at all, the child must grow up on the world of magical potential," Ava pointed out. "You knew this from the beginning, Grace."

Grace looked away from her meditation candles—and into her sister's eyes. "It's too dangerous. If we release the child from our care, how do we keep her away from Faris? Or away from Sonja, for that matter? You know of the experiments our sister has been running these many years."

"I do," Ava replied. "And I know Sonja isn't even close. She's taken her experiments in entirely the wrong direction. She hasn't even considered the possibility of doing what we've done."

Grace held up a warning finger. "Yet."

"True, she hasn't figured it out yet. But if we keep to our plan, this will work. Remember why we're doing this. There is no room in our plan to hesitate, Grace. The Guardians are growing bolder by the day. They're putting their pieces into play."

"I'm not hesitating. I'm being smart."

"And this?" Ava indicated the meditation candles.

"These rituals will ensure the child gains powerful telepathic powers," said Grace. "She will need to have a lot of all the powers to pass them on to her child."

"With those telepathic powers, the child will also be able to receive the visions we send her to guide her path, even from Earth," Ava countered.

"I've made up my mind, Ava. The child stays with me. It is the only way to ensure she becomes what we made her to be."

"Trust me, sister." Ava extended her hand to her.

Grace took it. "I trust you will find a way to help me keep the child safe. Here. With me. It's too risky to release her out there."

---

Ava stood in a room with black walls and purple fire.

"Grace has given birth to the child, but that child has become more than a tool to her," she said.

Sonja stood opposite her. "She's grown attached to it."

"Yes."

"You were right to come to me," Sonja told her.

"I had little choice," Ava grumbled. "You found out what we were doing."

Sonja's smile could have melted metal. "Yes, I did. Let that be a lesson to you, dear sister. I always find out what you're up to. Where is Grace keeping the child?"

"On Avalon."

Sonja nodded, her smile growing wider, then she left the room.

Ava watched her leave. When Sonja was gone, Ava

muttered, "Yes, my devious sister, you did find me out this time. That will not happen again. You will steal the child from Grace, but your victory shall be short-lived. The child will slip through your fingers. She will not be your weapon."

---

"I HAVE A JOB FOR YOU, INALI."

Ava was speaking to one of the octuplets. The changeling Inali was the one who'd taken the form of Gaius Knight, the man who'd led Calli to her children. That must have been what I was witnessing now, the day Inali had set off down that path. So Ava had been behind that. That was the 'job' she was referring to.

Ava handed Inali a photograph. "That is the man I want you to impersonate. He has contacts that will prove useful to you."

Inali glanced down at the picture. "I take it this man is still alive?"

"He is," Ava confirmed. "But that shouldn't be a problem. You and your sisters have no qualms about getting your hands dirty."

Inali glared at her. "It's not like you've given us a choice."

Ava took one of the charms on her bracelet between her fingers. She smiled. "His name is Gaius Knight. Kill him and take his place." She handed Inali a second photograph. "This is Callista Pierce. You—or should I say Gaius—will make friends with her."

Inali's eyes narrowed with suspicion. "Why?"

"Because I need to put some pieces into place."

The third photograph Ava handed her was of Aradia

Redwood, the woman who'd kidnapped me. And then raised me.

"You'll start with her," Ava told the changeling.

---

"They took her. They took Leda." Grace's voice trembled. She looked decidedly rattled.

"You're emotional," Ava commented with disapproval.

"Of course I'm emotional. Years of planning—centuries of planning—all down the drain! I'm not sad. Oh, no. I'm furious."

Ava watched her closely. "You've grown attached to the child."

"No. I've grown attached to my plan. And now it's ruined."

"Do you know who took the child?" Ava asked her.

Of course she herself knew, but she had to see if Grace suspected.

"I thought it was Sonja, but my soldiers searched her estates and found nothing," Grace replied. "It must have been Faris."

"Then we shall search his worlds as well," Ava told her sister, happy to mislead her. "We shall leave no stone unturned."

"I already did that. And I found nothing." A sound of pent-up frustration broke her lips. "Still, I'm sure it was Faris. He threatened to take the child for himself. He has her locked away somewhere, out of my reach, grooming her for the day he will use her as a weapon to serve his own purposes."

Ava set her hand on Grace's arm. "We will find the

child. There is no hiding her magic. Eventually, we will find her."

Ava didn't tell Grace that, even now, the child was on Earth, under Aradia's care. And Ava didn't tell her sister that she'd already made plans to safeguard her investment. The child would one day give birth to the ultimate weapon. Ava would see to it.

She'd already figured it all out. The child would need other protectors. Ava would use one from each of the four magical quadrants. The symmetry of the idea appealed to her. Four protectors, joined by bonds of family—that was the way to go. Leda needed protectors who would do anything for her, anything to keep her and her child safe.

But the four protectors were not enough. They needed a mother, someone who would create an environment in which the siblings could grow very close. Ava had already selected the perfect candidate: Callista Pierce. The bounty hunter had thwarted Ava's efforts to gain a foothold on Earth. In doing so, she'd demonstrated her inconvenient morality, yes, but also her ability to unite people. And that ability was just what Ava needed.

Besides, wouldn't it be poetic justice indeed for Callista Pierce to unknowingly help Ava, the demon she'd thwarted, to gain a foothold on Earth, in this grandest of schemes?

---

THROUGH HER GAZING BALL, AVA WATCHED THE injured telepath run down the street. He was the most powerful telepath in all of the known realms, and that's why Faris's soldiers had hunted him across all of the known realms. Faris wanted to make him part of his 'Orchestra' of powerful supernaturals.

Even now, a team of gods from Heaven's Army was closing in on the telepath's position. His mind tricks would only keep them at bay for so long. They would capture him.

Of course Ava couldn't possibly allow that. She had far more important plans for the telepath, plans that superseded those from the God of Heaven's Army.

A powerful spell repelled all demons from Earth, keeping them out. Ava could not go there, nor could her demonic soldiers in Hell's Army. But she had other means to make her will be done.

Faris's soldiers were almost upon the telepath.

Then they just stopped. The soldiers were frozen, their eyes locked on to the dozen bewitching men and women who'd just slunk out of the shadows and planted themselves in front of them. Ava's dark sirens.

Faris's soldiers didn't move. They didn't even lift a hand to defend themselves as the dark sirens killed them with their own swords.

Further down the street, just the person Ava knew would be here was kneeling down beside the injured telepath, who'd collapsed against a building.

"You're injured," the woman said. Her name was Cora.

The telepath could barely keep his eyes open.

"I'm going to heal you now. Just hold on." She opened up a kit of premixed potions.

Cora was a good friend of Callista Pierce. And the telepath, well, he was the one Ava had chosen to father one of Leda's protectors.

Faris would eventually find the telepath, but it was of

no consequence. Ava would have already gotten what she needed from him. She just had to make sure that when Faris's soldiers did come again, that they didn't take the telepath alive. She was not about to allow Faris to add the most powerful telepath in the known universe to his Orchestra. She would, however, soon be adding the telepath's child to her own collection.

Ava could already see her dark sirens closing in on the two unsuspecting lovers. They had no idea that magic would make them fall in love—or at least think they were in love long enough for them to conceive a child. One day, the child's mother, pursued by relentless enemies, would have no choice but to leave him with her friend Callista Pierce.

Ava waved her hand over her gazing ball to turn it off. "Yes." She fingered the tiny magical charms attached to her bracelet. "This will all work out perfectly."

---

"I've done as you asked," Inali said to Ava. "Callista Pierce has found the five children."

Ava nodded. "Indeed. Your work, like your sisters', is stellar."

Inali reached toward her. "Now let us go."

The demon sidestepped her. "No."

"We know what you've done." Anger took root in Inali's voice. "You took samples from Indira and Rosette. You combined those samples with other samples taken from two human males in your custody. And with those, you made two babies: a phoenix and a djinn."

"Of course I used human males as fathers," Ava said.

"I didn't want another kind of magic to get in the way of the girls expressing their mother's powerful magic."

"In each case, you managed to isolate and magnify phoenix or djinn magic, so it was as though both parents had either phoenix or djinn magic." Magic rippled across Inali's body, like a flag caught in the wind; she was very angry, and she was doing a very terrible job of hiding it. "The fathers were used merely for physical traits, not magic."

"One of my more brilliant ideas, I must say," Ava said smugly. She stopped short of literally patting herself on the back—but only barely. "The girls would be of no use to me with diluted magic. I don't need a weak phoenix and a weak djinn. I need a phoenix and a djinn as powerful as their mothers."

"You put the babies in a surrogate mother," Inali hissed. "Twins growing in her womb."

"You're making this all sound much easier than it was," Ava said flippantly. "It was no simple task. It was a triumph of magic, the culmination of centuries of planning."

A vicious smile twisted Inali's lips. "You like to make people believe you are infallible, and yet the surrogate mother was kidnapped by human warlords. They killed her shortly after the babies were born."

"Inconsequential." Ava gave her hand a dismissive wave. "The surrogate had already served her purpose. And as for the babies, I sent some dark sirens to sabotage the warlords' base so that the girls could escape. And then you made sure Callista Pierce found them. So it all worked out in the end."

"Why do you refuse to admit that you aren't in perfect control?" Inali demanded. "Why can't you admit that your plans only worked because you got lucky?"

Ava's eyes hardened. "Careful."

"You can't hold us forever," Inali said defiantly.

"Of course I can." Smiling, Ava caressed her bracelet with the eight charms, like she was petting a cat.

---

The final memory faded out, leaving Nero and me back in our room on board the airship.

"The eight charms Ava wears on her bracelet are immortal artifacts," Nero said.

I'd noticed that too. "They're the ones linked to the octuplets. Like Bella is linked to the wand."

"Ava is using those artifacts to control the eight sisters," said Nero. "That's why they're doing whatever she wants."

"And that's why River kept answering my questions with 'I can't say'," I realized. "Ava won't let them tell me anything she doesn't want me to know. These memories we're seeing now didn't come out of the Vault; the sisters didn't send them to me. These are memories Ava doesn't want me to see."

Nero looked like he did whenever he was trying to come up with a strategic solution to a seemingly impossible problem.

"What are you thinking?" I asked him.

"The eight sisters are very powerful," he said slowly. "And Ava controls them. It's clear Ava also wants to steal our daughter."

"Even if she has to betray her own sister Grace."

"As long as Ava controls the eight sisters, she is too

powerful." Nero shook his head. "We might not be able to keep our daughter from her."

"But if we freed the eight sisters, Ava would lose her greatest weapon," I said.

"Not only that. The eight sisters can't be very happy with Ava—and with what the demon has forced them to do," Nero replied. "Once freed, they would likely turn against her. If she's too busy fighting them, she can't make a move to capture our daughter."

"And then we'd only have to worry about Faris, Grace, the Guardians, and whoever else has an interest in her." I expelled a sigh of frustration.

"It's a start, Leda. Soon, we will have the Guardians on the run."

I liked his confidence that our mission would succeed.

He pounded his fist into his open palm. "And then we'll deal with Faris and Grace as well."

I only hoped he was right.

## CHAPTER 34

### THE BEST LAID PLANS

In under an hour, our battle against the Guardians would begin. I just hoped that it ended as we'd planned. If I'd learned anything in my time at the Legion of Angels, it was that even the best-laid plans inevitably went sideways.

I sat in the garden library, surrounded by my family and friends. I'd just finished bringing them through everything Nero and I had learned in the memory stream. I hadn't invited any of the octuplets. Since Ava was controlling them, I wasn't going to risk that anything we said got back to the demon.

"So Ava is limiting what the octuplets can do and say, just to manipulate Leda into following her wishes," Harker said.

I nodded. "Yep."

"Ava wants me to find Thea," Bella said.

"Since you're linked by blood and magic, it is doable," Arina told her.

Bella drummed her fingers against the armrest. "Ava

gave me the wand so I could find Thea. But what does Ava even want with Thea?"

"Let me see the wand?" Arina held out her hand.

Bella hesitated for a moment—understandable, as I'd just told her how the immortal artifacts linked to the octuplets could control them—but she handed it over.

Arina held the wand between her hands, eyes closed. A few moments later, her eyelashes swept up, and she returned the wand to Bella. "Some years after Thea disappeared, Ava learned that Thea was the only one who'd heard a Prophecy from the powerful telepath who was Zane's father. Since Zane's father is dead, Thea is the only one alive today who knows what that Prophecy says."

Zane sat up straighter in his seat.

"This Prophecy is about the savior and the different paths she might take, including which one would lead to the result Ava wanted: the total defeat of the Guardians without great losses *and* the certainty of demon dominion in the universe," Arina said.

"Our plan will cripple the Guardians but surely not end them," Damiel said. "That's why Ava wants to know the Prophecy Thea heard. She's looking for the key to achieving the demons' ultimate goal: to rule over all."

"As the one who brought this about, Ava will rule over all." I shook my head. "Obviously, we can't let Ava gain this information."

"And as long as she's in control of the octuplets, she's too powerful," Nero added.

"So we need to free the octuplets from Ava's control, destroy the barrier hiding the Guardians' Sanctuary, and find Thea without Ava ever finding her too." I counted off the tasks on my fingers. "That's a tall order."

"Try not to look too excited at the prospect of defying impossible odds," Nyx said.

"Don't be such a killjoy, Nyx," I told her.

Nyx's mouth drew into a very hard, very humorless line. People didn't tease the First Angel nearly enough, so she wasn't used to it. Or maybe being suddenly nine months pregnant had made her cranky. It was certainly overwhelming. I'd thought I would have so much time to prepare for motherhood.

"Rosette, the djinn, changed the direction of the magic mirror Harker and I were in when we left Valerian's world," Bella said out of the blue. "That's how we ended up on a world with Ava, not on Earth."

We all looked at her.

"Sorry," she said, her face sheepish. "I just figured out something that had been bothering me for a while."

"We need to discuss the upcoming battle," Damiel declared, which scored him an approving nod from the First Angel.

"We need to watch out for all the people the Guardians have 'saved'. We need to rescue them before the Guardians start killing them." Cadence looked at Arina. "The Guardians are planning to drain the power out of these supernaturals, right? That's why they've been collecting them?"

"For so long, the Guardians have collected people with all kinds of powers and combinations of powers." Arina cringed, likely thinking of her kids. "They've gathered together many supernaturals of every ability—dark and light, active and passive."

"And the gods and demons, with their obsession of collecting these kinds of people, have driven them right to the Guardians." I couldn't help but feel really annoyed at both the gods and the demons. "After being hunted so mercilessly, the Guardians' Sanctuary must have seemed like paradise to those people."

"The Guardians worked slowly, taking these people over many centuries, so as to not draw too much attention to themselves," Arina said. "But lately, they've upped their pace, especially in collecting sirens."

I supposed that was my fault. Several weeks ago, I'd unknowingly killed a bunch of the Guardians' sirens. It had all happened inside my mind. At the time, I'd thought they were only machines, not people. Still, I felt really guilty about it.

"The Guardians plan to drain all the supernaturals of their magic, and pump that power into themselves," Arina continued. "They believe the overflow of magic will be so strong that their own nullifying magic is overpowered, and they gain the magic of all those that they killed."

"That sounds just like what we're doing to their barrier," Leila said. "Using so much magic that the Guardians' nullifying magic is overpowered."

"But how can they channel this magic into themselves?" Basanti wanted to know.

"That's all thanks to the Legion of Angels, the Dark Force, Leila, the goddess Meda, and others," Arina said.

"That's a lot of people helping the Guardians who would never, under any circumstances, help the Guardians," Harker commented with a skeptical eye.

"Ok, let's take them one by one," Arina said. "One. The idea of blending magic. The Guardians got that from the Legion's and the Dark Force's efforts to create supernatural soldiers out of humans. It is the idea of giving magic to people without magic. The Guardians' formula is a modification of the ones used by the Legion and the Dark Force.

"Two. The Guardians refined that potion formula using Leila Starborn's experiments on balancing magic in monsters."

Leila's eyes grew wide with surprise.

"Three," Arina said. "The Guardians also used Meda's research on the archangel Osiris Wardbreaker and others to further refine the potion formula."

We did know that Meda had gotten the Life potion, which she'd used in her experiments, from the Guardians. The goddess had thought she was using the Guardians. Well, it turned out they'd been the ones using her.

"The Guardians' new potion formula will prime their bodies to receive all of that raw magic stolen from the supernaturals they're sacrificing," Arina said.

"How do you know all of this?" Every one of Colonel Fireswift's words was saturated with suspicion.

"When the Guardians abducted my children, I followed a lot of magic trails to figure out exactly what they were planning to do with them," Arina told him, not cowered by his glower.

She truly was a kick-ass woman.

"All right, folks, the plan is to blow open the doors of the Guardians' Sanctuary, free all their 'guests', and stop the Guardians once and for all," I declared, trying to stay optimistic. "We bearers of the Legion's future will take care of all the magic we need. I'll channel it through Angel—" I indicated my cat, who meowed. "We expect heavy resistance from the Guardians' forces, given that we're trying to blow a rather massive hole in their wicked plans. The rest of you have the job of holding them off.

As soon as the Sanctuary is exposed, our army will move in."

"The first letter of each octuplet's name spells 'grimoire' when put together," Bella said randomly.

We all looked at her.

"Gertrude, River, Inali, Mallory, Odette, Indira, Rosette, Evie. GRIMOIRE. Grimoire." Bella smiled at us.

My clever sister. In our house, Bella always won when family game night involved a bit of mental gymnastics.

"You're having a lot of epiphanies today," I told her.

Bella nodded earnestly. "I know."

"Before we march onto the battlefield, are there any questions?" I asked our army.

"Yes, actually." Colonel Dragonblood turned to Nero. "Windstriker, does she always make things sound so easy?"

"Yes." Nero looked fondly upon me. "Pandora has a knack for not only making the impossible sound possible, but also for making the impossible actually possible."

I pumped my arm in the air. "And on that happy note, let's go kick some Guardian ass."

# CHAPTER 35

## SIERRA

I'd never imagined I'd be in labor on the battlefield, but that was pretty much in line with the rest of my life. Leda Pandora never did things the easy way.

A ring of soldiers from Heaven's Army surrounded me, Nyx, Cadence, Leila, Basanti, Andromeda, and Alice. The soldiers were there to protect us from the monsters. This was the plain of monsters, after all, and though there weren't any beasts nearby right now, that could change at any moment.

Actually, there was just one beast here. Angel, my lion-sized fluffy white cat, was pacing around inside the protected ring. She must have been just as nervous as I was.

The soldiers from Heaven's Army were also here to protect us from the Guardians' forces. We were currently right on top of the Sanctuary, or at least where it existed in another, slightly-offset magical plane of existence.

As expected, the Guardians had sent out soldiers to stop us.

"They must know what we're planning and are worried," I told the others, cringing through a contraction. "That means we're doing exactly what we should be doing."

"Those people, the ones the Guardians have sent into battle against us, they're the supernaturals who were abducted and brought to the Sanctuary," Cadence said. "Innocent people."

"Those two are not innocent." Leila pointed at the two angels leading the Guardians' forces.

Giselle and Taron. I recognized the two angels from my visions. Their eyes were alight with wicked fire. They were not innocent or ignorant like the rest.

"They're the ones who abducted you," I said to Cadence.

"They took your brother too," she replied. "That's the job the Guardians have given them: to fill their fortress with supernaturals of extraordinary power."

"And now they're leading those supernaturals to the slaughter on the battlefield. Why?" I wondered. "Don't the Guardians need them to gain their magic?"

"Your reputation precedes you, Leda," Andromeda said. "The Guardians know you won't let them be killed."

"She's right," Alice said. "You have a habit of trying to save people, no matter the cost."

"The cost of saving those people is too high this time," Nyx declared. "If our plan fails, many more innocents will die than just these supernaturals here."

I watched our forces rush forward to meet the Guardians' army. Something about this bothered me.

"Look at the fire in their eyes," Basanti commented. "They are prepared to fight to the death, all of them."

"They believe the Guardians were the ones who saved

them from the horrors of the universe," Leila said. "They don't realize the Guardians plan to kill them and drain them dry of magic."

"They've been kept here for years, raised like animals to be slaughtered. The whole time their magic was honed and perfected, flavored and seasoned to create the perfect meal for the Guardians." The whole thing made me feel sick to my stomach. "We can't kill them. They are victims too."

"That's a hard line for our soldiers to hold when these 'innocents' are doing their best to kill them," Basanti pointed out.

"Indeed, these victims are making it difficult for us to save them," Leila agreed.

"But we must save them." I looked at Nyx. "Tell our soldiers not to kill them."

Nyx sighed. "You're an idealist, Pandora." She pointed up at the sky. "And I don't think they will listen."

Winged soldiers filled the sky—angels, gods, and demons alike. I spotted Ronan. He would be leading the Legion's forces. Faris had brought in more of his soldiers from Heaven's Army. And Grace had come with demon soldiers sworn to her service.

Faris and Grace swooped down and landed beside me.

"Not a single one of them shall be spared," Faris told me. "Every one of those supernaturals is just fuel for the Guardians' fire."

"They could be knocked out, not killed," I said.

He didn't look amused by my suggestion. "That is inefficient. And it will decrease our odds of winning this battle."

"We only have to keep them at bay long enough

for..." I cringed as the latest contraction hit me. I felt like I was splitting apart from the inside. "...for us to hit the Sanctuary with everything we've got..." I groaned as another contraction pulsed through me. "...and bring it into our realm."

"You're close, Leda," Grace observed.

We were all close. From the expressions on my six pregnant companions' faces, our contractions were in perfect synchronicity. Indira sure knew what she was doing. I bet all seven of us were going to deliver at exactly the same moment.

Nerissa and her staff hurried over to us. At least I wouldn't have to catch my baby myself.

"Lie down, Leda," she ordered me.

"I feel better standing," I told her. "And pacing."

The contractions were close together now. Really, really close. I hardly had time to catch my breath between them.

"You never could sit still, Leda." Nerissa followed behind me as I paced, as though the baby was just going to shoot out of me like a bullet. "Fine, stand. But no pacing."

"Leda," Bella said.

I blinked. "When did you get here?"

"I've been here the whole time," my sister told me.

"Don't mind Leda," Nerissa told her. "She's a tad delirious."

"I am..." Another contraction came, and I clenched my fists. "...not delirious."

Nerissa looked at me like I'd just sinned. "Did you push?"

"Yes," I croaked.

Nerissa's eyes went very wide. "This is the fastest labor I've ever seen."

"I've always been precipitous," I declared proudly.

Nerissa snorted.

Bella said something, but I hardly heard her.

"Say that again, Bella?" My body tensed up, and I pushed again. "It appears I'm kind of delirious after all."

"The Guardians have sent these people out to die," she told me. "They *want* us to kill them. They're already linked to the Guardians, who've all had their potion. Each person we kill on this battlefield only fills the Guardians' cup of power. We're helping them gain power."

"How—"

A contraction cut off my sentence, but Bella knew what I'd meant to ask.

"How do I know?" she said. "Arina told me."

"Where—"

"Arina has brought some toys to the fight, technological wonders I've never seen before," Bella answered my broken question. "Arina's toys are doing a good job of knocking the other side's soldiers unconscious. But our soldiers must do the same. They must stop killing these people. It's only helping the Guardians." She was looking at Faris and Grace.

Grace nodded briskly. "Agreed."

She cut her long fingernail across the inside of her arm. That must have been the way she communicated with her forces—through blood.

Faris frowned. "Agreed." He signaled to Devlin, who passed the message along to the rest of Heaven's Army.

Faris looked particularly furious at the Guardians for

trying such a trick, for trying to use him to serve their needs.

"The Guardians are still hiding within the safety of the Sanctuary. But they will flee when the Sanctuary is ripped open. We will be ready," the God of Heaven's Army said with vicious delight. His hand snapped around to Nerissa. "Can't you do anything to speed this thing up?" he demanded.

"This labor is already going very fast," Nerissa told him.

"Unacceptable." Faris stood there like a mountain, unmoving, uncompromising.

"Don't mind Faris," Grace said to Nerissa. "He never had to give birth to a child. And patience isn't his virtue."

"You're one to speak of virtue, demon," Faris snapped.

"If you two…" Contraction. "…are going to…." Contraction. "…start flirting again…" Contraction. Damn it! "Take it someplace else."

The next minute or so was sort of hazy. I vaguely noticed Faris and Grace fighting. I *definitely* noticed a lot of pain. Someone was holding my hand. Bella. My cat rubbed against my leg. Then there was an explosion of magic from inside of me. And from all around me. I was just lucid enough to remember to gather all the pieces of our magic, channel it through my cat, and shoot it at the Sanctuary cloaked just beyond this realm.

And then Nerissa was setting a baby, wrapped in a towel, into my arms. My daughter's eyes were big and beautiful. They were Nero's eyes. Her hair was warm and soft and a sort of light brownish red. Tiny silver wings peeked out of the top of her towel.

"She has wings," I said in awe, lightly touching her feathers.

Sierra cooed in delight. Yes, Sierra. The name was perfect. I suddenly knew it had also been the name of the pale-haired angel from the past, the first bearer of the weapons of heaven and hell. That name was my daughter's destiny.

"Deities and demi-deities are born with wings," Nyx said beside me.

I noticed she held her baby too. He was a boy with white wings and a full head of black hair. Those black locks were swirling around him as though he were underwater. It seemed he'd inherited his mother's trademark hair.

Past Nyx, the others all had their newborns in their arms. Leila and Basanti were huddled close together with their two baby boys.

"Did it work?" I asked groggily.

"See for yourself." Bella pointed.

I looked beyond our closed little circle. Buildings had appeared on the battlefield.

"The Sanctuary," I said quietly, my heart feeling lighter, like a heavy weight had been lifted from it.

"It's in our realm now," Stash told me.

Before one of the buildings, Nero and Damiel had locked swords with Giselle and Taron.

A pulse of psychic energy shot out of Giselle, knocking Nero back a step. She followed it up by summoning a fireball and using her sword to bat it at Nero. He slashed out, his blade splitting it in two. The fire dissolved into smoke. Nero flicked his wrist, and the smoke turned green. He'd cursed it. The cursed cloud swallowed Giselle but not her screams.

When Nero gave his wrist a second flick, the smoke faded away to reveal someone hardly recognizable. Giselle was now completely bald. Her skin was deathly pale, and as she tried to rise to her feet, handfuls of feathers fell from her wings like a tree shedding its leaves.

"Surrender," Nero told her.

Giselle's dry lips formed into a defiant sneer. "I will never be your prisoner."

"You would have led these people to their deaths."

Giselle started to laugh. It was a cruel, sickening laugh. "This isn't the end."

"It is for you," Nero said coldly.

Silver flashed. He'd slashed out with his sword so fast that I hadn't seen him move. Neither, it seemed, had Giselle. Her head fell to the ground, that sick smile still frozen on her face.

Nero glanced toward Damiel, but his father didn't need any help. Taron lay dead at his feet. I tried not to look too closely at the state of the corpse, but I saw enough to know that Damiel had let his emotions get the better of him today. The fury slowly faded from his eyes, fury that these two angels had taken Cadence from him. And fury for what they'd done here today.

"They're not stopping." Bella watched with wide, trembling disbelief as the Guardians' sacrificial lambs rushed at our army. "Their angels are dead, and the Guardians have fled. So why do they still fight? They must realize that their Guardians have abandoned them."

"I think they don't want to believe," I said.

"Look," Alice said in pure wonder.

So I looked. Wild monsters had gathered nearby in the hopes of feasting on the losers of this great battle. A sparkle of magic started at the center of the Sanctuary, spreading out from there in a wave of rainbow light. It passed through the storm clouds overhead, quieting them. When it touched the barren earth, wildflowers popped up all around us. And when it met the monsters, the feral fire in their eyes died out.

Arina strolled up to us, an arm wrapped around each of her twins. "I understand it now. The Guardians' Sanctuaries on Earth were created by the clash of gods and demons. And when that happened, when the Sanctuaries fractured this realm, the beasts went wild. The weather of Earth turned wild too."

I was happy to see Arina had come out of the Sanctuary with her two adorable children. They all looked so happy together. A family reunited at last. A tear slid down my cheek.

"But this act of balance, of breaking the Guardians' Sanctuary, has accomplished something else as well," Arina said. "It has balanced the Earth's magic once more. The storms are gone. The monsters are once more tame."

"Just as Cadence and I balanced the magic on another world, Interchange, in another great act of magic." Damiel wrapped his arm around Cadence and their daughter, whose black-and-white wings were perfectly divine.

"In another great act of magic, like we performed here," Cadence said. "An act of unity and perfect balance."

Nero knelt beside me. He set his hand on our daughter's forehead. "Everything all right, Pandora?"

I lowered my head to his shoulder. "Yes. Everything is perfect."

"Not everything." Ronan had one eye on his newborn

child—and one eye on the Guardians' army, which was *still* fighting us.

"Try not to kill them," I pleaded with the Lord of the Legion. "They're confused. They don't know what they're doing."

Now that the Guardians were gone, now that they were too far away to use the supernaturals' deaths to gain magic, I was worried that the gods and demons would decide there was no reason to spare those supernaturals' lives.

Ronan looked at me with an expression I'd never before seen on a god's face: sympathy. Of course, he only felt sorry for me because he thought I was really naive.

But rather than scorn or pity, the god gave me kindness. "We will try to save as many of them as we can. They are powerful supernaturals, not people we like to waste." He looked at Faris. "I'll take care of this."

"Ronan, don't think I don't see that scheming look in your eyes." The God of Heaven's Army drew his sword. "And I will not allow you to claim those supernaturals for yourself."

Faris followed Ronan across the battlefield. I was pretty sure the Lord of the Legion had just done me a very big favor. He'd directed Faris's attention to the supernaturals—and away from my daughter.

"Did we capture any Guardians?" I asked Nero.

He frowned. "No. But we did find a female Guardian dead in one of the buildings."

"I bet it was the same one who had Meda try to kill me last month," I said. "In doing so, she acted against the others' wishes. The Guardians don't strike me as the kind of people who tolerate dissension in their ranks."

"Right now less than ever," Nero agreed. "Now that

their Sanctuary is gone, they will only survive if they all act together as one. When packing up to leave, they'd have left behind anyone who didn't follow the Guardians' hard line."

"How did the Guardians escape?" I asked.

"They had an escape route already planned out," Damiel told me. "They went through a special one-time-use magic mirror. Their trail dissipated quickly. It didn't even leave a trace, or I would have followed them."

Now that he possessed all the active and passive magic abilities, Damiel could teleport. It was kind of annoying when he just popped up out of nowhere. Annoying but cool. I wished I could do it too.

"Wherever the Guardians are, our efforts here have weakened them," Nero said. "And they're on the run. But they're not done."

"No, they're not done," I agreed as I watched the Guardians' abandoned supernaturals continue to fight our forces.

I simply did not understand their fierce loyalty to the Guardians, though the wicked light in Faris's eyes as he spotted those he wanted to add to his Orchestra certainly wasn't helping to make us look trustworthy.

Ronan was trying to woo the supernaturals with the truth, but they outright refused to believe the Guardians had taken them in only to sacrifice them.

"That's the problem with blind faith," I said.

Grace, the Demon of the Faith, winked at me. "I will try not to take offense at those words."

The demon's forces closed in behind her. I had a lot of people on my side, people I knew would all fight to their last breath to protect me, but Grace's horde was even larger. And they were all powerful demons.

"So," I said, facing her.

The air between me and my demon mother was heavy with the ghosts of our past.

"So." Grace waved her hand at her soldiers.

Beside me, Nero's leather armor creaked. He'd grown very tense. I held our daughter close to my chest.

But Grace's soldiers didn't attack us. They merely spread their wings, and flew into the sky, a few at a time.

She nodded at me. "Until next time, Leda."

I held very still. "You mean, when my daughter and I don't have an army at our backs."

Grace stepped toward me. She stopped when Nero moved between us. "Calm down, Windstriker," she said impatiently. "I am not going to take your child away from you."

"But that was always the plan," I told her. "Your plan."

Grace sighed. "Plans change."

"No." I shook my head. "Not the plans of deities."

"Well, I suppose I'm not a very good deity, no more than you are a very good angel." Grace winked at me again. "Where do you think you got your spirit, Leda? Certainly not from Faris?"

Stash moved to my side. His eyes didn't waver from Grace. "Inside, she is a lot like you, sweetness. You just have to be able to see past all the demonic window dressings."

Which Stash could. He had the power to see through to someone's soul, to who they truly were deep down, their core essence.

"Ava was right," I said quietly, not blinking, just looking into Grace's eyes.

She gave me a curious look.

"I found out some things about Ava," I told her. "By the way, she was the one to tell Sonja where you were hiding with me."

Grace's expression went from curious to angry.

"She thought the real reason you didn't want to drop me off on Earth was that you'd grown attached to me, that you'd come to care for me. She was right, wasn't she?"

"Yes." Her word dropped like a stone between us. "Ava was right."

Ava suddenly appeared in front of her sister. "I always am."

Eight identical women were with her. I hadn't met all of the octuplets yet, but of the ones that I had met, I thought I could pick out which one was which. Gertrude was so stately. Indira was shining with so much energy. Rosette's stance was nimble, like she was ready for anything. And River was quiet and reserved. The others I didn't have a clear reading on yet.

I handed Nero our daughter, then I stepped up to Ava. "I thought you'd show up, Auntie, once all the smoke had cleared."

Ava's eyes darted to Sierra.

My cat hissed at my demon aunt.

"You won't be taking her," I told her. "She isn't your weapon. And she's *my* daughter."

Flames burst up all across my halo. Even my wings were on fire. But the fire didn't hurt. It felt just right.

Ava simpered at me. "You are a very foolish child."

I glared back at her. "Then teach me a lesson, if you can."

Ava moved so fast that I could barely see her, but I

was ready. I grabbed her wrist, and swung around, tossing her a good ten feet.

She rose from the ground, fury in her eyes. Her halo was burning now too. But the flames weren't red or orange. They were black. The scent of burnt cookies flooded my nose. No doubt about it—Ava was pissed.

"Go," I told her, my voice frozen over. "Your schemes are not welcome here."

Ava waved the octuplets forward. "Take Leda Pandora's child," she commanded them. "Kill anyone who gets in your way."

But the octuplets didn't move.

Ava spun around. "What are you waiting for?" she demanded.

The octuplets were a chorus of chuckles.

Ava snapped back around to glare at me. "This is your doing, Angel of Chaos. What have you done?"

"Oops." I lifted up my hand, lightly shaking the bracelet dangling between my fingers. The eight tiny charms clinked together.

Ava hurriedly glanced at her wrist, where her bracelet had once been. "That is impossible."

"Not impossible," I told her. "It just took years of practice to perfect my pickpocketing skills."

"Pickpocketing," Ava repeated in disbelief.

"I learned it on the streets of Purgatory. I can teach you how to do it if you want." I flashed her a grin.

Ava opened her mouth, but no words came out. Apparently, I'd rendered the demon speechless.

Her sister Grace, however, was laughing her ass off. "You pickpocketed Ava."

Yes, she found that very, very funny.

"I guess that's an attack the demons of Hell's Army

haven't learned to defend against, it being rather scrappy and all." I arched my brows. "It's not a particularly divine skill."

"No, it is not," Grace laughed.

"I demand that you return my bracelet immediately!"

So Ava had gotten her voice back.

"No. I don't think so. And, besides, *these* don't belong to you." I tapped one of the eight immortal artifacts attached to the bracelet chain. "I know what happened, what you were trying to hide from me. And I know what you were trying to hide from Grace. I've already told Grace that it was you who told Sonja where she was hiding with me, so Sonja's agent could steal me from her."

Ava glanced at her sister, who scowled at her.

"But Sonja's agent wasn't really loyal to Sonja at all," I continued. "Aradia blamed Sonja for what happened to her friend Thea. So Aradia didn't return me to Sonja. She raised me on Earth—until the day Sonja's soldiers found and killed her."

"I was following our plan," Ava said to Grace.

"Plans sometimes change, Ava. And I trusted you." Grace shook her head. "Well, no longer. You're even worse than Sonja."

I walked up to the octuplets and handed them the charms off the bracelet, one by one. Each of the eight sisters hooked her own immortal artifact onto her necklace.

"Thank you, Leda Pandora," all eight said in unison.

Then they turned their eyes on Ava. That's when the Demon of Hell's Army made a speedy retreat from the battlefield.

Grace watched her sister fly off. "Serves her right for

underestimating you," she laughed. "Leda, you're the chaos that throws a monkey wrench into the best-laid plans of gods and demons."

My mother bowed her head to me and then to Sierra, then she also took flight.

"You know, I might have been wrong about Grace," I said to Nero. "I'm more than just a weapon to her."

"You might be more than a weapon to her, but that doesn't mean you aren't also a weapon to her," Nero warned me. "Be careful."

"Oh, I know, Nero. Things are never simple with gods and demons."

## CHAPTER 36

### THE LOVE CHILD OF ORDER AND CHAOS

I'd just gotten Sierra settled into her crib in the garden library—now a nursery of another kind—when Cadence's Aunt Eva and Eva's husband Jiro popped up. There were cribs with babies in them all over the garden library, but the two Immortals went straight for Cadence's daughter.

Eva smiled down on the child. "She's beautiful." Her gaze shifted to Cadence. "What is her name?"

"Eira," Cadence told her.

"Perfect," Eva said, brushing aside a tear.

Eira had been the name of Cadence's mother, Eva's sister.

Jiro patted Damiel on the back. "May your daughter grow in power and grace."

Damiel drew his old friend Jiro into a hug.

"She is very tiny," Eva said. "But very strong."

Little Eira had grabbed on to Eva's finger, and she wasn't letting go. Her wings, an even mixture of black and white feathers, fluttered happily. As the daughter of two Immortals, she'd been born with wings too.

Jiro walked over and seated himself on the sofa opposite mine. "Well, Leda Pandora, I'll say this for you: you sure know how to make an impact."

He said 'impact', as in the kind that meteors made on the Earth's surface.

"The fates of your daughter and these other six babies born at the same time are now intertwined." Jiro spread his arms to indicate the babies in the room. "They're bound together by that explosion of magic that burst forth the moment they all came into the world together."

"You know, that sounds pretty epic," I told him with a smile.

Jiro shrugged. "I've seen it before."

I wondered what else the ancient Immortal had seen during his many millennia.

"You brought the Guardians' Sanctuary back into this realm and in doing so, you rid the Earth of its wild weather, feral monsters, and crazy magic all at once," Jiro said.

Which reminded me.

I turned toward Nyx, who sat across the room with Ronan, both huddled around their baby's crib. "Hey, Nyx. If there are no more plains of monsters, what does that make me, the Angel of the Plains of Monsters?"

"Out of a job," Nyx said lightly.

My face fell. "Really?"

"Don't worry, Pandora," replied the First Angel. "I'm sure I'll find *something* to do with you. You're the perfect solution to throw at impossible problems."

I flashed her a grin. "Always happy to stir up some chaos."

"Are you sure you can keep her under control?" Ronan asked Nyx.

"Of course not," Nyx replied. "But, then again, neither can Faris."

Ronan's laugh, though quiet, made the airship's walls rumble. The lights flickered a bit too.

"Knock it off, Ronan," I told him. "If you break my airship, Nyx will totally find a way to blame me."

The walls didn't stop rumbling. In fact, they started shaking harder.

"Hey, Ronan!" I protested.

Eva sat down beside Jiro. "That wasn't Ronan. It was your daughter. She's waking up."

A single, sleepy cry rose from Sierra's crib. Several of the lights in the room blew up.

I quickly lifted her out of her crib and began to rock her. "That's not my fault," I said with a guilty glance at Nyx.

"She's your daughter," Nyx pointed out, but I could tell she was too happy with her baby to be truly angry with me.

The walls were really shaking now. And Sierra was still crying.

I began to pace with her in my arms. "Maybe if I just find a position she likes…"

Sierra stopped crying.

I sighed in relief. "Thank goodness."

My baby cooed, and the rest of the lights in the ceiling blew up.

"So things blew up when you're happy too?" I handed her to Nero. Maybe he'd have better luck with her.

And sure enough, as soon as he began to rock her, the walls stopped shaking. And when she laughed, nothing blew up.

"How did you do that?" I said in awe.

"Some people are just better with children," Nero said smugly.

As he looked fondly upon our daughter, I stuck my tongue out at him.

"You are chaos, Leda. Nero is order," Jiro said.

Yeah, that made a lot of sense—and yet no sense at all.

"Wait, so you're saying that whenever I hold Sierra, things will go all…all wonky?" I asked him.

"At least until you learn to control your inner chaos," Jiro replied.

Standing beside me, Stash was laughing his ass off.

"Oh, shut up," I said and stuck my tongue out at him too.

"Sierra's magic is very potent for one so young," Eva said brightly. "It might not be long before she starts blowing things up, even when you're not holding her."

Nero stopped bouncing her in his arms. "What do we do about that?"

Eva smiled. "Embrace the unpredictable nature of parenthood."

Nero looked at her blankly, like her words hadn't computed in his brain.

"He means you'll have to wing it, General," I said helpfully.

"Thank you, Pandora. I know what it means." Nero hit me with a deliciously dark look that sent shivers down my spine.

"You just refuse to accept it?"

"I have trained you to behave, Leda. I will do the same with our daughter," he said with complete confidence.

I glanced at Basanti. "Hey, Basanti, did you hear? Nero thinks I know how to behave."

"Nero is high on parenthood and is talking shit," Basanti replied in her no-nonsense manner.

Wow, she must have been really high on parenthood too. I hadn't seen her in such a good mood in a long time.

"Leda, your daughter is the love child of order and chaos." Alec looked very pleased. "It's going to be fun watching her grow up."

Spirits were high all around today. Naturally. We had the Guardians on the run, and the Earth was whole once more. It had been a good day.

"Don't celebrate too soon," Jiro warned me.

"Jiro, your doom-and-gloom attitude is really killing the mood," I told him.

"You accomplished a lot today, Leda. No one can take that away from you," he said. "But you must know that there's a whole give-and-take balance to magic. Nothing comes for free. There must be something that fuels any magic performed."

"Yes, we know. The phoenix Indira told us all about that," I said breezily.

"She told you about the balance between life and death, as a phoenix would see things," Jiro said. "But it's more complicated than that."

Speaking of passive magic…

"Hey, I've been meaning to ask you and Eva something," I said to him. "When Grace was young, she and her sisters came across some beings who called themselves eidolons and spirits. They claimed to be the deities of light and dark passive magic, respectively."

"They are," Jiro confirmed.

"So what more can you say about them?" I asked him.

"A lot. Just as I can say a lot about a lot of things," he said with enough smugness to make even an angel blush. "The universe is a big place, full of wonders and horrors. That's what I'm trying to tell you, Leda. When you played with the laws of magic—when you ripped open the Sanctuary and pulled it into this realm—you opened up the door to other realms."

Eva came to stand beside him. "Realms where magic doesn't work in the way you've come to expect. Realms where countless threats lie in wait, ready to strangle you."

"There is great magic out there, magic the Guardians can use against you. That's why you must find them quickly, before they acquire powerful weapons against you," Jiro told me.

"What happened to your oath of non-interference?" I said, allowing my brows to lift.

Because their shifting double standards totally deserved a good eyebrow lift.

"As you once said, plans change," he replied.

At that moment, I liked Jiro more than I ever had.

"You might have chased the Guardians away from the Earth, but they aren't done with you yet," Eva said. "And they aren't done with your family, Leda. Not by a long shot."

I looked around the room, at all the friends and family gathered here. "And we aren't done with the Guardians. Nor are we done with Ava, Sonja, and anyone else who has manipulated our entire lives." I looked up at the sky. "You hear that, Guardians, gods, and demons? We've had enough, and now we're coming for you."

## AUTHOR'S NOTE

If you want to be notified when I have a new book release, head on over to my website to sign up for my newsletter. My newsletters also include bonus stories.

If you enjoyed *Phoenix's Refrain*, I'd really appreciate if you could spread the word. Tell a friend or leave a review wherever you purchased this book. Thank you for your invaluable support!

The adventure continues in *Demon's Mark*, the next book in the *Legion of Angels* series. For additional reading in the same magical universe, check out my *Phoenix Dynasty* and *Immortal Legacy* series.

www.ellasummers.com/newsletter

# ABOUT THE AUTHOR

Ella Summers is a bestselling author of over thirty books. She writes fantasy fiction that blends magic and romance with lots of action.

Ella has been writing stories for as long as she could read; she's been coming up with tall tales even longer than that. One of her early year masterpieces was a story about a pigtailed princess and her dragon sidekick.

She has lived in various cities all over the world. Many of those places have featured in her books. When she's not busy writing or hanging out with her family, she makes the world safe by fighting robots. She also spends way too much time cleaning up after her two sweet (but spoiled!) Ragdoll cats.

www.ellasummers.com

# CONTINUE THE SERIES

**The schemes of deities are always multi-course affairs.**

Three years ago, gods and demons united against a common enemy. Now a terrible, ancient secret threatens to tear that alliance apart.

Leda Pandora, the Angel of Chaos, has a complicated family. Her father's a god, her mother's a demon, and her daughter is destined to one day become the savior of the universe…if Leda can keep her safe long enough to grow up.

Unfortunately, the universe might need saving a little sooner than expected.

Whole worlds are going dark, deities are dying, and both gods and demons are each blaming the other for it. Every day, the threads of peace grow weaker. The countdown to war is ticking, and if Leda can't uncover the real culprit in time, the alliance won't be the only thing in tatters—the whole universe will burn in the aftermath.

DEMON'S MARK

www.ellasummers.com/demons-mark

**How to use this QR code:**

1. Open your smartphone's camera app.

2. Center the QR code on the screen.

3. A link will appear on your screen.

4. Tap on the link.

5. Your phone's browser brings you to my website.

# EXPLORE ANOTHER SERIES

www.ellasummers.com/angel-fire

# ANGEL FIRE

**Two Angels. One Immortal Love Story.**

Cadence Lightbringer, daughter of an archangel, has trained from birth to one day drink the Nectar of the gods and ascend to the angels' ranks. She's always been the perfect soldier. She's always known exactly where her life is headed.

Until she is assigned to a mission with Damiel Dragonsire, Master Interrogator of the Legion of Angels.

Powerful, paranoid, and brutally intelligent, Damiel has built up a reputation for hunting down each and every traitor hiding within the Legion's ranks. And his latest suspect is Cadence. Convinced she is not the perfect soldier everyone believes her to be, he will stop at nothing to expose her.

*Angel Fire* is the first book in the *Immortal Legacy* series.

# EXPLORE ANOTHER SERIES

www.ellasummers.com/mercenary-magic

# MERCENARY MAGIC

**Your Daily Dose of Magical Mayhem.**

Long ago, the Dragon Born were hailed as the most powerful mages in the world. Today, they are condemned as abominations and have been hunted to near extinction.

Sera Dering has spent her entire life hiding her forbidden magic from the supernatural council who would kill her for the crime of being born. After years of drifting, she's finally found a new life working as a low-grade mercenary for San Francisco's oldest monster cleanup guild. She's safe—as long as she pretends to be human.

But a dark and mysterious power is taking control of mages' minds, and Sera's guild sends her in to investigate. To save her city from a magical apocalypse, she must work together with a sexy and deadly mage who represents the very council that sentenced the Dragon Born to death. And if he finds out what she is, she'll be next…

*Mercenary Magic* is the first book in the *Dragon Born* urban fantasy series.

# EXPLORE ANOTHER SERIES

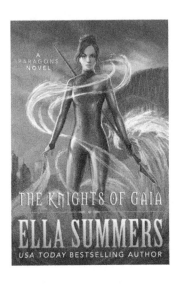

www.ellasummers.com/the-knights-of-gaia

# THE KNIGHTS OF GAIA

**Sixteen years ago, a terrible Curse struck the Earth. Humanity is still fighting it today.**

Like every teenager, Savannah has lived her whole life dreaming of the day she would become a Knight. She's spent every waking hour studying, training, performing—anything she could do to convince the Government to put her on that elite list.

But she doesn't make the cut.

So Savannah comes up with a dangerous plan. If she succeeds, she will have a second shot at becoming a Knight. But if she fails, she'll be exiled to the Wilderness, the fallen ruins of civilization where cities crumble and the Cursed Ones prey on the weak.

*The Knights of Gaia* is the first book in the *Paragons* urban fantasy series, a tale of chivalrous knights, snarky heroes, supernatural drama—and one young woman's epic journey to defy the naysayers and seize her destiny.

# EXPLORE ANOTHER SERIES

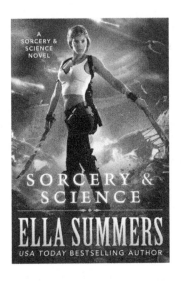

www.ellasummers.com/sorcery-science

# SORCERY & SCIENCE

**Urban Fantasy. Galactic Consequences.**

Terra Cross is just your typical paranormal princess. She plays poker with goblins and leprechauns. She savors her morning muffin from the Pacific Sunrise Bakery in suburban California. She solves galactic crime cases. And on a particularly wild day, she can even see into the future.

Everything is going so well—up until her father, the mages' high king, betroths her to one of his allies. But playing nice with otherworldly ambassadors isn't the only thing on Terra's plate. A renegade mage scientist has taken up shop on Earth, whose inhabitants have no knowledge of magic or the worlds beyond.

With his forbidden experiments threatening to pierce the Veil of Secrecy on Earth, Terra cannot tackle this challenge alone. Divided by magic and technology—torn between a mage enforcer with devastating telekinetic powers, and a lethal black ops vampire soldier—time is running out. For if this mad scientist succeeds, the galaxy's hard hand of justice will come down on them all.

*Sorcery & Science* is the first book in the *Sorcery & Science* urban fantasy series.

Made in the USA
Monee, IL
02 May 2025

16761826R00267